Praise for *New York Times* bestselling author Diana Palmer

"Diana Palmer is one of those authors whose books are always enjoyable. She throws in romance, suspense and a good story line."
—*The Romance Reader*

"[Palmer]…is the queen of desperado quests for justice and true love."
—*Publishers Weekly* on *Dangerous*

"Diana Palmer is a mesmerizing storyteller who captures the essence of what a romance should be."
—*Affaire de Coeur*

Praise for *New York Times* bestselling author Brenda Jackson

"Brenda Jackson writes romance that sizzles and characters you fall in love with."
—*New York Times* bestselling author Lori Foster

"[Brenda] Jackson is a master at writing."
—*Publishers Weekly*

Author of more than one hundred books, **Diana Palmer** is a multiple *New York Times* bestselling author and one of the top ten romance writers in America. She has a gift for telling even the most sensual tales with charm and humor. Diana lives with her family in Cornelia, Georgia. www.DianaPalmer.com.

Brenda Jackson is a *New York Times* bestselling author of more than one hundred romance titles. Brenda lives in Jacksonville, Florida, and divides her time between family, writing and traveling. Email Brenda at authorbrendajackson@gmail.com or visit her on her website at www.brendajackson.net.

New York Times **Bestselling Author**

DIANA PALMER

MYSTERY MAN

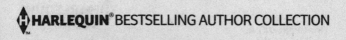

ISBN-13: 978-1-335-14683-0

Mystery Man

Copyright © 2019 by Harlequin Books S.A.

The publisher acknowledges the copyright holders of the individual works as follows:

Mystery Man
Copyright © 1997 by Diana Palmer

Cole's Red-Hot Pursuit
Copyright © 2008 by Brenda Streater Jackson

Recycling programs for this product may not exist in your area.

This edition published by arrangement with Harlequin Books S.A.

For questions and comments about the quality of this book, please contact us at CustomerService@Harlequin.com.

® and TM are trademarks of Harlequin Enterprises Limited or its corporate affiliates. Trademarks indicated with ® are registered in the United States Patent and Trademark Office, the Canadian Intellectual Property Office and in other countries.

www.Harlequin.com

Printed in U.S.A.

CONTENTS

MYSTERY MAN

Diana Palmer

CHAPTER ONE

"It was a dark and stormy night..."

A pair of green eyes glared at the twelve-year-old boy by the window who intoned the trite words in a ghostly voice.

He shrugged. "Well, everybody starts a murder mystery that way, Janie," Kurt Curtis told his older sister with a grin.

Janine ran restless fingers through her short black hair, muttering at the few words on her computer screen. "I don't," she murmured absently. "That's why I sell so many of them."

"Diane Woody," he intoned, "bestselling authoress of the famous Diane Woody Mystery series." He scowled. "Why do you use your pen name for your main character's name? Isn't that redundant?"

"It was the publisher's idea. Could you ask questions later?" she mumbled. "I'm stuck for a line."

"I just gave you one," he reminded her, grinning wider. He was redheaded and blue-eyed, so different from her in coloring that most people thought he was someone else's brother. He was, however, the image of their maternal grandfather. Recessive genes will out, their archaeologist parents were fond of saying.

Their parents were on a new dig, which was why Janine was in Cancún working, with Kurt driving her nuts. Dan and Joan Curtis, both professors at Indiana University, were in the Yucatán on a dig. There had been several other archaeologists on the team, most of whom had to return to take classes. Since this was a newly discovered, and apparently untouched, Mayan site, the Curtises had taken a temporary leave of absence from their teaching positions to pursue it. It wasn't feasible to take Kurt, who was just getting over a bad case of tonsillitis, into the jungles. Neither could they leave him in the exclusive boarding school he attended.

So they'd taken him out of his boarding school for two months—with the proviso that Janine tutor him at home. They'd rented this nice beach house for Janine, where she could meet her publisher's deadline and take care of her little brother. He was well now, but she had him for the duration, which could easily mean another month, and she had to juggle his homebound school assignments with her obligations. The dig was going extremely well, Professor Curtis had said in his last email message through the computer satellite hookup at their camp, and promised to be a site of international importance.

Janine supposed it would be. The benefit of it all was that they had this gorgeous little villa in Cancún overlooking the beach. Janine could write and hear the roar of the ocean outside. It gave her inspiration, usually. When Kurt wasn't trying to "help" her, that was.

She was just slightly nervous, though, because it was September and the tail end of hurricane season, and this had been a year for hurricanes. One prognosticator called it the year of the killer winds. Poetic. And frightening. So far there hadn't been too much to worry them here. She prayed there wouldn't be any more hurricanes. After all, it was almost October.

"Did you notice the new people next door?" Kurt asked. "There's a tall, sour-looking man and a girl about my age. He's never home and she sits on their deck just staring at the ocean."

"You know I don't have time for neighbors," she murmured as she stared at the screen.

"Don't you ever stop and smell the flowers?" he asked with disgust. "You'll be an old maid if you keep this up."

"I'll be a *rich* old maid," she replied absently as she scrolled the pages up the screen. "Besides, there's Quentin."

"Quentin Hobard," he muttered, throwing up his hands. "Good Lord, Janie, he teaches ancient history!"

She glared at him. "He teaches *medieval* history, primarily the Renaissance period. If you'd listen to him once in a while, you might discover that he knows a lot about it."

"Like I can't wait to revisit the Spanish Inquisition," he scoffed.

"It wasn't as horrible as those old movies suggest," she said, sitting up to give him her undivided attention.

"I was thinking more along the lines of 'Monty Python,'" he drawled, naming his favorite classic television show. He got up and struck a pose. "Nobody escapes the Spanish Inquisition!"

She threw up her hands. "You can't learn history from a British comedy show!"

"Sure you can." He leaned forward, grinning. "Want to know the *real* story of the knights? They used coconut shells for horses—"

"I don't want to hear it," she said, and covered her ears. "Let me work or we're both going to starve."

"Not hardly," he said with confidence. "There's always royalties."

"Twelve, and you're an investment counselor."

"I learned all I know from you. I'm precocious on account of the fact that I'm the youngest child of scientists."

"You'd be precocious if you were the youngest child of Neanderthals."

"Did you know that the *h* in Neanderthals is silent and unpronounced? It was written wrong. It's a German word," he continued.

She held up a hand and her glare grew. "I don't need lessons in pronunciation. *I need peace and quiet!*"

"Okay, I get the message! I'll go out and fish for sea serpents."

She didn't even glance his way. "Great. If you catch one, yell. I'll take photos."

"It would serve you right if I did."

"Yes. With your luck, if you caught one, it would

eat you, and I'd spend the rest of my life on this beach with a lantern like Heathcliff roaming the moors."

"Wrong storyline. I'm your brother, not your girlfriend."

"Picky, picky."

He made a face and opened the sliding glass door.

"Close it!" she yelled. "You're letting the cold air out!"

"God forbid!" he gasped. He turned back toward her with bright eyes. "Hey, I just had an idea. Want to know how we could start global cooling? We could have everybody turn on their air conditioners and open all their doors and windows..."

She threw a legal pad in his general direction. Not being slow on the uptake, he quickly closed the sliding door and walked down the steps of the deck onto the sugar-white sand on the beach.

He stuck his hands into his pockets and walked toward the house next door, where a skinny young girl sat on the deck, wearing cutoffs with a tank top and an Atlanta Braves hat turned backward. Her bare feet were propped on the rail and she looked out of sorts.

"Hey!" he called.

She glared at him.

"Want to go fishing for sea serpents?" he asked.

Her eyebrows lifted. She smiled, and her whole face changed. She jumped up and bounced down the steps toward him. She was blond and blue-eyed with a fair complexion.

"You're kidding, right?" she asked.

He shrugged. "Ever seen anyone catch a sea serpent around here?"

"Not since we got off the plane," she said.

"Great!" He grinned at her, making his freckles stand out.

"Great?"

"If nobody's caught it, it's still out there!" he whispered, gesturing toward the ocean. "Just think of the residuals from it. We could sell it to one of the grocery store tabloids and clean up!"

Her eyes brightened. "What a neat idea."

"Sure it is." He sighed. "If only I knew how to make one."

"A mop," she ventured. "A dead fish. Parts of some organ meat. A few feathers. A garden hose, some shears and some gray paint."

A kindred soul. He was in heaven. "You're a genius!"

She grinned back. "My dad really is a genius. He taught me everything I know." She sighed. "But if we create a hoax, I'll be grounded for the rest of my life. So I guess I'll pass, but…"

He made a face. "I know what you mean. I'd never live it down. My parents would send me to military school."

"Would they, really?"

"They threaten me with it every time I get into trouble. I don't mind boarding school, but I hate uniforms!"

"Me, too, unless they're baseball uniforms. This year is it, this is the third time, this is the charm.

This time," she assured him, "the Braves are going to go all the way!"

He gave her a long, thoughtful look. "Well, we'll see."

"You a Braves fan?" she asked.

He hadn't ever cared much for baseball, but it seemed important to her. "Sure," he said.

She chuckled. "My name is Karie."

"I'm Kurt."

"Nice to meet you."

"Same here."

They walked along the beach for a minute or two. He stopped and looked back up the deserted stretch of land. "Know where to find a mop?" he asked after a minute.

Blissfully unaware that her young brother had just doubled his potential for disaster, Janine filled her computer screen with what she hoped was going to be the bare bones of a new mystery. Some books almost wrote themselves. Others were on a par with pulling teeth. This looked like one of those. Her mind was tired. It wanted to shape clouds into white horses and ocean waves into pirate ships.

"What I need," she said with a sigh, "is a good dose of fantasy."

Sadly there wasn't anything on television that she wanted to watch. Most of it, she couldn't understand, because it was in Spanish.

She turned the set off. The one misery of this trip was missing her favorite weekly science fiction series. Not that she didn't like all the characters on

it; she did. But her favorite was an arrogant, sometimes very devious alien commander. The bad guy.
She seemed to be spending all her productive time
lately sighing over him instead of doing the work that
she got paid to do. That was one reason she'd agreed
to come to Cancún with her parents and Kurt, to get
away from the make-believe man who was ruining
her writing career.

"Enough of this!" she muttered to herself. "Good
heavens, you'd think I was back in grammar school,
idolizing teachers!"

She got up and paced the room. She ate some
cookies. She typed a little into the computer. Eventually the sun started going down and she noticed
that she was short one twelve-year-old boy.

She looked at her watch. Surely he hadn't gotten the time confused? It was earlier here than in
Bloomington, Indiana, where Kurt lived with their
parents. Had he mistaken the time, perhaps forgotten to reset his watch? Janine frowned, hoping that
she hadn't forgotten to set her own. It would be an
hour behind Kurt's, because her apartment in Chicago was in a different time zone from Kurt and her
parents' in Indiana.

He was in a foreign country and he didn't speak
any more Spanish than she did. Their parents' fa-
cility for languages had escaped them, for the most
part. Janine spoke German with some fluency, but
not much Spanish. And while English was widely
spoken here in the hotels and tourist spots, on the
street it was a different story. Many of the local

people in Cancún still spoke Mayan and considered Spanish, not English, a second language.

She turned off her computer—it was useless trying to work when she was worried, anyway—and went out to the beach. She found the distinctive tread of Kurt's sneakers and followed them in the damp sand where the tide hadn't yet reached. The sun was low on the horizon and the wind was up. There were dark clouds all around. She never forgot the danger of hurricanes here, and even if it was late September, that didn't mean a hurricane was no longer a possibility.

She shaded her eyes against the glare of the sun, because she was walking west across the beach, stopping when Kurt's sneakers were joined by another, smaller pair, with no discernible tread. She knelt down, scowling as she studied the track. She'd worked as a private eye for a couple of years, but any novice would figure out that these were the footprints of a girl, she thought. The girl Kurt had mentioned, perhaps, the one who lived next door. In fact, she was almost in front of that beach house now.

The roar of the waves had muffled the sound of approaching footsteps. One minute, she was staring down at the tracks. The next, she was looking at a large and highly polished pair of black dress shoes. Tapered neatly around them were the hem of expensive slacks. The legs seemed to go up forever. Far above them, glaring down at her, were pale blue eyes under a jutting brow in a long, lean face. The lips were thin. The top one was long and narrow, the lower one had only a hint of fullness. The cheekbones were high and the nose was long and straight. The hairline was just slightly receding around straight brown hair.

Two enormous lean hands were balled into fists, resting on the hips of the newcomer.

"May I ask what you're doing on my beach?" he asked in a voice like raspy velvet.

She stood up, a little clumsy. How odd, that a total stranger should make her knees weak.

"I'm tracking my…" she began.

"Tracking?" he scoffed, as if he thought she were lying. His blue eyes narrowed. He looked oddly dangerous, as if he never smiled, as if he could move like lightning and would at the least provocation.

Her heart was racing. "His name is Kurt and he's only twelve," she said. "He's redheaded and so high." She made a mark in the air with her flat hand.

"That one," he murmured coolly. "Yes, I've seen him prowling around. Where's my daughter?"

Her eyebrows rose. "You have a daughter? Imagine that! Is she carved out of stone, too?"

His firm, square chin lifted and he looked even more threatening. "She's missing. I told her not to leave the house."

"If she's with Kurt, she's perfectly safe," she began, about to mention that he'd been stranded once in the middle of Paris by their forgetful parents, and had found his way home to their hotel on the west bank. Not only had he maneuvered around a foreign city, but he'd also sold some of the science fiction cards he always carried with him to earn cab fare, and he'd arrived with twenty dollars in his pocket. Kurt was resourceful.

But long before she could manage any of that, the man moved a step closer and cocked his head. "Do you know where they are?"

"No, but I'm sure…"

"You may let your son run loose like a delinquent, but my daughter knows better," he said contemptuously. His eyes ran over her working attire with something less than admiration. She had on torn, raveled cutoffs that came almost to her knee. With them she was wearing old, worn-out sandals and a torn shirt that didn't even hint at the lovely curves beneath it. Her short hair was windblown. She wasn't even wearing makeup. She could imagine how she looked. What had he said—her *son*?

"Now, just wait a minute here," she began.

"Where's your husband?" he demanded.

Her eyes blazed. "I'm not married!"

Those eyebrows were really expressive now.

She flushed. "My private life is none of your business," she said haughtily. His assumptions, added to his obvious contempt, made her furious. An idea flashed into her mind and, inwardly, she chuckled. She struck a pose, prepared to live right down to his image of her. "But just for the record," she added in purring tones, "my *son* was born in a commune. I'm not really sure who his father is, of course…"

The expression on his face was unforgettable. She

wished with all her heart for a camera, so that she could relive the moment again and again.

"A commune? Is that where you learned to track?" he asked pointedly.

"Oh, no." She searched for other outlandish things to tell him. He was obviously anxious to learn any dreadful aspect of her past. "I learned that from a Frenchman that I lived with up in the northern stretches of Canada. He taught me how to track and make coats from the fur of animals." She smiled helpfully. "I can shoot, too."

"Wonderful news for the ammunition industry, no doubt," he said with a mocking smile.

She put her own hands on her hips and glared back. It was a long way up, although she was medium height. "It's getting dark."

"Better track fast, hadn't you?" he added. He lifted a hand and motioned to a man coming down toward the beach. *"¿Sabe donde están?"* he shot at the man in fluent Spanish.

"No, lo siento, señor. ¡Nadie los han visto!" the smaller man called back.

"Llame a la policía."

"Sí, señor!"

Police sounded the same in any language and her pulse jumped. "You said *police*. You're going to call the police?" she groaned. That was all she needed, to have to explain to a police officer that she'd forgotten the time and let her little brother get lost.

"You speak Spanish?" he asked with some disbelief.

"No, but police sounds the same in most languages, I guess."

"Have you got a better idea?"

She sighed. "No, I guess not. It's just that…"

"Dad!"

They both whirled as Karie and Kurt came running along the beach with an armload of souvenirs between them, wearing sombreros.

"Gosh, Dad, I'm sorry, we forgot the time!" Karie warbled to her father. "We went to the *mercado* in town and bought all this neat stuff. Look at my hat! It's called a sombrero, and I got it for a dollar!"

"Yeah, and look what I got, S—*mmmmffg.*" Kurt's "Sis" was cut off in midstream by Janine's hand across his mouth.

She grinned at him. "That's fine, *son*," she emphasized, her eyes daring him to contradict her. "You know, you shouldn't really scare your poor old *mother* this way," she added, in case he hadn't gotten the point.

Kurt was intrigued. Obviously his big sister wanted this rather formidable-looking man to think he was her son. Okay. He could go along with a gag. Just in case, he stared at Karie until she got the idea, too, and nodded to let him know that she understood.

"I'm sorry…*Mom*," Kurt added with an apologetic smile. "But Karie and I were having so much fun, we just forgot the time. And then when we tried to get back, neither of us knew any Spanish, so we couldn't call a cab. We had to find someone who spoke English to get us a cab."

"All the cabdrivers speak enough English to get by," Karie's father said coldly.

"We didn't know that, Dad," Karie defended. "This is my friend Kurt. He lives next door."

Karie's dad didn't seem very impressed with Kurt, either. He stared at his daughter. "I have to stop José before he gets the police out here on a wild-goose chase. And then we have to leave," he told her. "We're having dinner with the Elligers and their daughter."

"Oh, gosh, not them again," she groaned. "Missy wants to marry you."

"Karie," he said warningly.

She sighed. "Oh, all right. Kurt, I guess I'll see you tomorrow."

"Sure thing, Karie."

"Maybe we can find that garden hose," she added in a conspiratorial tone.

He brightened. "Great idea!"

"What the hell do you want with a hose?" Karie's father asked as they walked back up the beach, totally ignoring the two people he'd just left.

"Whew!" Kurt huffed. "Gosh, he's scary!"

"No, he isn't," Janine said irritably. "He's just pompous and irritating! And he thinks he's an emperor or something. I told him we lived in a commune and you're my son and I don't know who your father is. Don't you tell him any differently," she added when he tried to speak. "I want to live down to his image of me!"

He chuckled. "Boy, are you mad," he said. "You don't have fights with anybody."

"Wait," she promised, glaring after the man.

"He reminds me of somebody," he said.

"Probably the devil," she muttered. "I hear he's got blue eyes. Somebody wrote a song about it a few years ago."

"No," he mumbled, still thinking. "Didn't he seem familiar to you?"

"Yes, he did," she admitted. "I don't know why. I've never seen him before."

"Are you kidding? You don't know who he is? Haven't you recognized him? He's famous enough as he is. But just think, Janie, think if he had gray makeup on."

"He could pass for a sand crab," she muttered absently.

"That's not what I meant," he muttered. "Listen, they call this guy Mr. Software. Good grief, don't you ever read the newspapers or watch the news?"

"No. It depresses me," she said, glowering.

He sighed. "Mr. Software just lost everything. For the past year, he's been involved in a lawsuit to prevent a merger that would have saved his empire. He just lost the suit, and a fortune with it. Now he can't merge his software company with a major computer chain. He's down here avoiding the media so he can get himself back together before he starts over again. He's already promised his stockholders that he'll recoup every penny he lost. I bet he will, too. He's a tiger."

She scowled. "He, who?"

"Him. Canton Rourke," he emphasized. "Third

generation American, grandson of Irish immigrants. His mother was Spanish, can't you tell it in his bearing? He made billions designing and selling computer programs, and now he's moving into computer production. The company he was trying to acquire made the computer you use. And the software word processing program you use was one he designed himself."

"That's Canton Rourke?" she asked, turning to stare at the already dim figure in the distance. "I thought he was much older than that."

"He's old enough, I guess. He's divorced. Karie said her mother ran for the hills when it looked like he was going to risk everything in that merger attempt. She likes jewelry and real estate and high living. She found herself another rich man and remarried within a month of the divorce becoming final. She moved to Greece. Just as well, probably. Her parents were never together, anyway. He was always working on a program and her mother was at some party, living it up. What a mismatch!"

"I guess so." She shook her head. "He didn't look like a billionaire."

"He isn't, now. All he has is his savings, from what they say on TV, and that's not a whole lot."

"That sort of man will make it all back," she said thoughtfully. "Workaholics make money because they love to work. Most of them don't care much about the money, though. That's just how they keep score."

His eyes narrowed. "You still haven't guessed why he looks familiar."

She turned and scowled at him. "You said something about gray makeup?"

"Sure. Think," he added impatiently. "Those eyes. That deep, smooth voice. Where do you hear them every fourth or fifth week?"

"On the news?"

He chuckled. "Only if they had aliens doing it."

His rambling was beginning to make sense. Every fourth or fifth week, there was a guest star on her favorite science fiction show. Her heartbeat increased alarmingly. Her breath caught in her throat. She put a hand there, to make sure she was still breathing.

"Oh, no." She shook her head. She smiled nervously. "No, he doesn't look like *him*!"

"He most certainly does," Kurt said confidently. "Same height, build, eyes, bone structure, even the same deep sort of voice." He nodded contemplatively. "What a coincidence, huh? We came here to Mexico to get you away from the television so you could write without being distracted by your favorite villain. And his doppelgänger turns up here on the beach!"

CHAPTER TWO

"I DON'T LIKE having you around that boy," Canton told his daughter when they were back in their beach house. "His mother is a flake."

Karie had to bite her tongue to keep from blurting out the truth. Obviously the Curtis duo didn't want it known that they were little brother and big sister, not son and mother. Karie would keep her new friend's secret, but it wasn't going to be easy.

Her eyes went to the new hardcover murder mystery on the coffee table. There was a neat brown leather bookmark holding Canton's place in it. On the cover in huge red block letters were the title, *"CATACOMB,"* and the author's name—Diane Woody.

There was a photo in the back of the book, on the slick jacket, but it was of a woman with long hair and dark glasses wearing a hat with a big brim. It didn't even look like their neighbor. But it was. Karie knew because Kurt had told her, with some pride, who his sister was. She was thrilled to know, even second-hand, a big-time mystery writer like Diane Woody. Her father was one of the biggest fans of the bestselling mystery author, but he wouldn't recognize her from that book jacket. Maybe it was a good thing. Apparently she didn't want to be recognized.

"Kurt's nice," she told her father. "He's twelve. He likes people. He's honest and kind. And Janine's nice, too."

His eyebrows lifted as he glanced at her over his shoulder. "Janine?" he murmured, involuntarily liking the sound of the name on his lips.

"His...mother."

"You learned all that about him in one day?"

She shrugged. "Actions speak louder than words, isn't that what you always say?"

His face softened, just a little. He loved his daughter. "Just don't go wandering off with him again, okay?"

"Okay."

"And don't go to his home," he added through his teeth. "Because even if he can't help what he's got for a mother, I don't want you associating with her. Is that clear?"

"Oh, yes, sir!"

"Good. Get dressed. We don't have much time."

IN THE DAYS that followed, Kurt and Karie were inseparable. Karie, as usual, agreed with whatever her father told her to do and then did what she pleased. He was so busy trying to regroup that he usually forgot his orders five minutes after he gave them, anyway.

So Karie and Kurt concocted their "sea serpent," piece by painstaking piece, concealing it under the Rourke beach house for safety. Meanwhile, they watched World War III develop between their respective relatives.

The first salvo came suddenly and without warning. Kurt had gone out to play baseball with Karie. This was something new for him. His parents were studious and bookwormish, not athletic. And even though Janine was more than willing to share the occasional game of ball toss, she wasn't a baseball fanatic. Kurt had grown to his present age without much tutoring in sports, except what he played at the private school where his parents sent him. And that was precious little, because the owners were too wary of lawsuits to let the children do much rough-and-tumble stuff.

Karie had no hang-ups at all about playing tackle football on the beach or smacking a hardball with her regulation bat. She gave the bat to Kurt and told him to do his best. Unfortunately, he did, on the very first try.

CANTON ROURKE CAME storming up onto the porch of the beach house and right onto the open patio without a knock. Janine, lost in the fifth chapter of her new book, was so foggy that she saw him without really seeing him. She was in the middle of a chase scene, locked into character and time and place, totally mindless and floating in the computer screen. She stared at him blankly.

He looked furious. The blue eyes under that jutting brow were blazing from his lean face. He had a hardball in one hand. He stuck it under her nose.

"It's a baseball," she said helpfully.

"I know what the damned thing is," he said in a tone that would have affected her if she hadn't been deep in concentration. "I just picked it up off my living-room floor. It went through the bay window."

"You shouldn't let the kids play baseball in the house," she instructed.

"They weren't playing in the damned house! Your son slammed it through the window!"

Her eyebrows rose. Things were beginning to focus in the real world. Her mind lost the last thread of connection with her plot. Before she lost her bearings too far, she saved the file before she swung her chair back to face her angry neighbor.

"Nonsense," she said. "Kurt doesn't have a baseball. Come to think of it, I don't think he knows how to use a bat, either."

He threw the ball up and caught it, deliberately.

"All right, what do you want me to do about it?" she asked wearily.

"I want you to teach him not to hit balls through people's windows," he said shortly. "It's a damned nuisance trying to find a glass company down here, especially one that can get a repair done quickly."

"Put some plastic over the hole with tape," she suggested.

"Your son did the damage," he continued with a mocking smile. "The repair is going to be up to you, not me."

"Me?"

"You." He put the ball down firmly on her desk,

noticing the computer and printer for the first time. His eyes narrowed. "What are you doing?"

"I'm writing a bestselling novel," she said honestly.

He laughed without humor. "Sure."

"It's going to be great," she continued with building anger. "It's all about a—"

He held up a big, lean hand. "Spare me," he said. "I don't really want to hear the sordid details. No doubt you can draw plenty of material from your years in the commune."

"Why, yes, I can," she agreed with a vacant smile. "But I was going to say that this book is about a pompous businessman with delusions of grandeur."

His eyebrows lifted. "How interesting." He stuck his hands into his pockets and she fought a growing attraction to him. He really did have an extraordinary build for a man his age, which looked to be late thirties. He was lean and muscular and sensuous. He didn't have a male-model sort of look, but there was something in the very set of his head, in the way he looked at her, that made her knees go weak.

His eye had been caught by an autographed photo peering out from under her mousepad. She'd hidden it there so that Kurt wouldn't see it and tease her about her infatuation with her television hero. Sadly when she'd moved the mouse to save her file, she'd shifted the pad and revealed the photo.

His lean hand reached out and tugged at the corner. He didn't wear jewelry of any kind, she noticed, and his fingernails were neatly trimmed and immaculate. He had beautiful hands, lightly tanned and strong.

"I like to watch the television series he's in," she said defensively, because he was staring intently at the photo.

His gaze lifted and he laughed softly. "Do you?" He handed it back and in the process, leaned close to her. "It's one of my favorite shows, too," he said, his voice dropping an octave, soft and deep and sensuous. "But this is the villain, you know, not the hero."

She cleared her throat. He was close enough to make her uncomfortable. "So what?"

"He looks familiar, doesn't he?" he murmured dryly.

She glared up at him. He really was far too close. Her heart skipped. "Does he?" she asked. Her voice sounded absolutely squeaky.

He stood up again, his hands back in his pockets, his smile so damned arrogant and knowing that she could have kicked him.

"Don't you have a business empire to save or something?" she asked irritably.

"I suppose so. You can't get that show down here, at least not in English," he added.

"Yes. I know. That was the whole purpose of coming here," she murmured absently.

"Ah, I see. Drying out, are we?"

She stood up. "You listen here…!"

He chuckled. "I have things to do. You'll see to the window, of course."

She took a steadying breath. "Of course."

His eyes slid up and down her slender body with more than a little interest. "Odd."

"What?"

"Do you mind if I test a theory?"

Her eyes were wary. "What sort of theory?"

He took his hands out of his pockets and moved close, very deliberately, his eyes staring straight into hers the whole while. When he was right up against her, almost touching her, he stopped. His hands remained at his side. He never touched her. But his eyes, his beautiful blue eyes, stared right down into hers and suddenly slipped to her mouth, tracing it with such sensuality that her lips parted on a shaky breath.

He moved again. His chest was touching her breasts now. She could smell the clean, sexy scent he wore. She could feel his warm, coffee-scented breath on her mouth as he breathed.

"How old are you?" he asked in a deep, sultry tone.

"Twenty-four," she said in a strangled voice.

"Twenty-four." He bent his head, so that his mouth was poised just above hers, tantalizing but not invasive, not aggressive at all. His breath made little patterns on her parted lips. "And you've had more than a handful of lovers?"

She wasn't listening. Her eyes were on his mouth. It looked firm and hard and very capable. She wondered how it tasted. She wondered. She wished. She…wanted!

"Janine."

The sound of her voice on his lips brought her wide, curious eyes up to meet his. They looked stunned, mesmerized.

His own eyes crinkled, as if he were smiling. All she saw was the warmth in them.

"If you're the mother of a twelve-year-old," he whispered deeply, "I'm a cactus plant."

He lifted his head, gave her an amused, indulgent smile, turned and walked away without a single word or a backward glance, leaving her holding the ball. In more ways than one.

SHE GOT THE glass fixed. It wasn't easy, but she managed. However, she did dare Kurt to pick up a bat again.

"You don't like him, do you?" he queried the day after the glass was repaired. "Why not? He seems to be good to Karie, and he isn't exactly Mr. Nasty to me, either."

She moved restlessly. "I'm trying to work," she said evasively. She didn't like to remember her last encounter with their neighbor. Weakness was dangerous around that tiger.

"He's gone to California," Kurt added.

Her fingers jumped on the keyboard, scattering letters across the screen. "Oh. Has he?"

"He's going to talk to some people in Silicon Valley. I'll bet he'll make it right back to where he was before he's through. His wife is going to be real sorry that she ran out on him when he lost it all."

"No foresight," she agreed. She saved the file. There was no sense working while Kurt was chattering away. She got up and stretched, moving to the patio window. She paused there, staring curiously. Karie was sitting on the beach on a towel. Nearby, a man stood watching her; a man with sunglasses on and a suspicious look about him.

"Who's that? Have you seen him before?" she asked Kurt.

He glanced out. "Yes. He was out there yesterday."

"Who's watching Karie while her father's gone?"

"I think there's a housekeeper who cooks for them," he said. "He's only away for the day, though."

"That's long enough for a kidnapper," she said quietly. "He was very wealthy. Maybe someone wouldn't know that, would make a try for Karie."

"You mystery writers," Kurt scoffed, "always looking on the dark side."

"Dark side or not, he isn't hurting Karie while I'm around!" She went right out the patio door and down the steps.

She walked toward the man. He saw her coming, and stepped back, looking as if he wasn't sure what to do.

She went right up to him, aware that her two years of martial arts training might not be enough if he turned nasty. Well, she could always scream, and the beach was fairly crowded today.

"You're on my property. What do you want?" she asked the man, who was tall and well-built.

His eyebrows rose above his sunglasses. *"No hablo inglés,"* he said, and grinned broadly.

She knew very little Spanish, but that phrase was one she'd had to learn. "And I don't speak Spanish," she returned with a sigh. "Well, you have to go. Go away. Away! Away!" She made a flapping gesture with her hand.

"Ah. *¡Vaya!*" he said obligingly.

"That's right. *Vaya.* Right now."

He nodded, grinned again and went back down the beach in the opposite direction.

Janine watched him walk away. She had a nagging suspicion that he wasn't hanging around here for his health.

She went down the beach to where Karie was sitting, spellbound at the scene she'd just witnessed. "Karie, I want you to come and stay with Kurt and me today while your dad's gone," she said. "I don't like the way that man was watching you."

"Neither do I," Karie had to admit. She smiled ruefully. "Dad had a bodyguard back in Chicago. I never really got used to him. Down here it's been quieter."

"You do have a bodyguard. Me."

Karie chuckled as she got up and shook out her towel. "I noticed. You weren't scared of him at all, were you?"

"Kurt and I studied martial arts for two years. I'm pretty good at it." She'd didn't add that she'd also worked as a private investigator.

"Would you teach me?"

"That might not be a bad idea," she considered. "Tell you what, Kurt and I will give you lessons on the sly. You may not want to share that with your dad right now. He's mad enough about the window at the moment."

"Dad isn't mean," Karie replied. "He's pretty cool, most of the time. He has a terrible temper, of course."

"I noticed."

Karie smiled. "You have one, too. That man started backing up the minute you went toward him. You scared him."

"Why, so I did," Janine mused. She grinned with pride. "How about that?"

"I'm starved," Karie said. "Maria went to the grocery store and she won't be back for hours."

"We'll make sandwiches. I've got cake, too, for dessert. Coconut."

"Wow! Great!"

Janine smiled. She led the way back to the beach house, where an amused Kurt was waiting.

"Diane Woody to the rescue!" he chuckled.

She made a face at him. "I'm reading too much of my own publicity," she conceded. "But the man left, didn't he?"

"Left a jet trail behind him," her brother agreed.

"What are you working on…oh! It's *him*!" Karie gasped, picking up the photo of the television star in makeup that Janine had left on the desk. "Isn't he cool? It's my favorite show. I like the captain best, but this guy isn't so bad. He sort of looks like Dad, you know?"

Janine didn't say a word. But inside, she groaned.

SHE WAS FEEDING the kids coconut cake from a local store, and milk when a familiar threatening presence came through the patio doors without knocking. She gave him a glare that he simply ignored.

"Don't you live at home anymore?" he asked his daughter irritably.

"There's no cake at our place," Karie said matter-of-factly.

"Where's the housekeeper? I told her to stay with you."

"She went shopping and never came back," Janine said shortly. "Your daughter was on the beach being watched by a very suspicious-looking man."

"Janine scared him off," Karie offered, with a toothy grin. "She knows karate!"

The arrogant look that Canton Rourke gave her was unsettling. "Karate, hmmm?"

"I know a little," she confessed.

"She went right up to that man and told him to go away," Karie continued, unabashed. "Then she took me home with her." She glowered at him. "I could have been kidnapped!"

He looked strange for a space of seconds, as if he couldn't quite get his bearings.

"You shouldn't have been out there alone," he said finally.

"I was just lying on my beach towel."

"Well, from now on, lie on the deck," he replied curtly. "No more adventures."

"Okay," she said easily, and ate another chunk of cake.

"It's coconut cake," Kurt volunteered. "That little grocery store has them. Janie gets them all the time for us. They're great."

"I'd offer you a slice of cake, Mr. Rourke, but I'm sure you're in a terrible hurry."

"I suppose I must be. Come on, Karie."

His daughter took a big swallow of milk and got up from the table. "Thanks, Janie!"

"You're very welcome." She glanced at Canton. "Housekeepers don't make very good bodyguards."

"I never meant her to be a watchdog, only a cook and housecleaner. Apparently I'd better look elsewhere."

"It might be wise."

His eyes slid down her long legs in worn jeans, down to her bare, pretty feet. He smiled in spite of himself. "Don't like shoes, hmmm?"

"Shoes wear out. Skin doesn't."

He chuckled. "You sound like Einstein. I recall reading that he never wore socks, for the same reason."

Her eyes lifted to his face and slid over it with that same sense of stomach-rapping excitement that she experienced the first time she saw it. He did so closely resemble her favorite series TV character. It was uncanny, really.

"Are you sure you don't act?" she asked without meaning to.

He gave her a wry look. "I'm sure. And I'm not about to start, at my age."

"There go your hopes, dashed for good," Kurt murmured dryly. "He's not an illegal alien trying to fit in with humans, Janie. Tough luck."

She flushed. "Will you shut up!"

"What did you do with that autographed photo?" he asked as he passed the desk.

"Oh, she never has it out when she's working," Kurt volunteered. "If she can see it, she just sits and sighs over it and never gets a word on the screen."

He scowled, interested. "What sort of work do you do?"

"She's a secretary," Kurt said for her, gleefully improvising. "Her boss is a real slave driver, so even on vacation, she has to take the computer with her so that she can send her work to the office."

He made an irritated sound. "Some boss."

"He pays well," she said, warming to Kurt's improvisation. She sighed. "You know how it is, living in a commune, you get so out of touch with reality." She contrived to look dreamy-eyed. "But eventually, one has to return to the real world and earn a living. It really is so hard to get used to material things again."

His face closed up. He gave her a glare that could have stopped traffic and motioned to Karie to follow him. He stuck his hands into his pockets and walked out the door. He never looked back. It seemed to be a deep-seated characteristic.

Karie grinned and waved, following obediently.

When they were out of sight along the beach, Kurt joined her on the patio deck.

"What if that man wasn't watching Karie at all?" she wondered aloud, having had time to formulate a different theory. "What if he's a lookout for the pothunters?"

Kurt scowled. "You mean those people who steal artifacts from archaeological sites and sell them on the black market?"

"The very same." She folded her arms over her T-shirt. "This is a brand-new site, unexplored and uncharted until now. Mom and Dad even noted that it seemed to be totally undisturbed. The Maya did some exquisite work with gold and precious jewels. What if there's a king's ransom located at the dig and someone knows about it?"

Kurt leaned against the railing. "They know it can happen. It did last time they found a site deep in the jungle, over near Chichén Itzá. But they had militia guarding them and the pothunters were caught."

"Yes, but Mexico is hurting for money, and it's hard to keep militia on a site all the time to guard a few archaeologists."

"Dad has a gun."

"And he can shoot it. Sure he can. But they can't stay awake twenty-four hours a day, and even militia can be bribed."

"You're a whale of a comfort," Kurt groaned.

"I'm sorry. I just think we should be on our guard. It could have been someone trying to kidnap Karie, but they've just as much incentive to kidnap us or at least keep a careful eye on us."

"In other words, we'd better watch our backs."

Janine smiled. "Exactly."

"Suits me." He sighed. "What a shame your alien hero can't beam down here and help us out. I'll bet he'd have the bad guys for breakfast."

"Oh, they don't eat humans," she assured him.

"They might make an exception for pothunters."

"You do have a point there. Come on. You can help me do the dishes."

"Tell you what," he said irrepressibly. "You do the dishes, and I'll write your next chapter for you!"

"Be my guest."

He gave her a wary look. "You're kidding, right?"

"Wrong. Go for it."

He was excited, elated. He took her at her word and went straight to the computer. He loaded her word processing program, pulled up the file where she'd left off, scanned the plot.

He sat and he sat and he sat. By the time she finished cleaning up the kitchen, he was still sitting.

"Nothing yet?" she asked.

He gave her a plaintive stare. "How do you *do* this?" he groaned. "I can't even think of a single word to put on paper!"

"Thinking is the one thing I don't do," she told him. "Move."

He got up and she sat down. She stared at the screen for just a minute, checked her place in the plot, put her fingers on the keyboard and just started typing. She was two pages into the new scene when Kurt let out a long sigh and walked away.

"Writers," he said, "are strange."

She chuckled to herself. "You don't know the half of it," she assured him, and kept right on typing.

CHAPTER THREE

JANINE WAS WELL into the book two days later when Karie came flying up the steps and in through the sliding glass doors.

"We're having a party!" she announced breathlessly. "And you're both invited."

Janine's mind was still in limbo, in the middle of a scene. She gave Karie a vacant stare.

"Oops! Sorry!" Karie said, having already learned in a space of days that writers can't withdraw immediately when they're deep into a scene. She backed out and went to find Kurt.

"What sort of party?" he asked when she joined him at the bottom of the steps at the beach.

"Just for a few of Dad's friends, but I persuaded him to invite you and Janie, too. He feels guilty since he's had to leave me alone so much for the past few years. So he lets me have my way a lot, to try and make it up to me." She grinned at Kurt. "It's sort of like having my own genie."

"You're blackmailing him."

She laughed. "Exactly!"

His thin shoulders rose and fell. "I wouldn't mind coming to the party, if you're having something nice to eat. But Janie won't," he added with certainty. "She hates parties and socializing. And she doesn't like your dad at all, can't you tell?"

"He doesn't like her much, either, but that's no reason why they can't be civil to each other at a party."

"I don't know about that."

"I do. He'll be on his best behavior. Did you know that he reads her books? He doesn't know who she really is, of course, because I haven't told him. But he's got every book she's ever written."

"Good grief, didn't he look at her picture on the book jacket?" Kurt burst out.

"I didn't recognize her from it. Neither will he. It doesn't really look like her, does it?"

He had to admit it didn't. "She doesn't like being recognized," he confided. "It embarrasses her. She likes to write books, but she's not much on publicity."

"Why?"

"She's shy, can you believe it?" he chuckled. "She runs the other way from interviews and conventions and publicity. It drove the publishing house nuts at first, but they finally found a way to capitalize on her eccentricity. They've made her into the original mystery woman. Nobody knows much about her, so she fascinates her reading public."

"I love her books."

"So do I," Kurt said, "but don't ever tell her I said so. We wouldn't want her to get conceited."

She folded her arms on her knees and stared out to sea. "Does she have a, like, boyfriend?"

He groaned. "Yes, if you could call him that. He's a college professor. He teaches ancient history." He made a gagging gesture.

"Is he nice?"

"He's indescribable," he said after thinking about it for a minute.

"Are they going to get married?"

He shrugged. "I hope not. He's really nice, but he thinks Janie should be less flaky. I don't. I like her just the way she is, without any changes. He thinks she's not dignified enough."

"Why?"

"He's very conservative. Nice, but conservative. I don't think he really approves of our parents, either. They're eccentric, too."

She turned to look at him. "What do they do?"

"They're archaeologists," he said. "Both of them teach at Indiana University, where they got their doctorates. We live in Bloomington, Indiana, but Janie lives in Chicago."

"They're both doctors?"

He nodded and made a face. "Yes. Even Janie has a degree, although hers is in history and it's a bachelor of arts. I guess I'll be gang-pressed into going to college. I don't want to."

"What do you want to do?"

He sighed. "I want to fly," he said, looking skyward as a bird, probably a tern, dipped and swept in the wind currents, paying no attention to the odd creatures sitting on the steps below him.

"We could glue some feathers together," she suggested.

"No! I want to fly," he emphasized. "Airplanes, helicopters, anything, with or without wings. It's in my blood. I can't get enough of airplane movies. Even space shows. Now, that's really flying, when you do it in space!"

"So that's why you like that science fiction show Janie's so crazy about."

"Sort of. But I like the action, too."

She smiled. "I like it because the bad guy looks like my dad."

He burst out laughing. "He's not the bad guy. He's the other side."

"Right. The enemy."

"He's not so bad. He saved the hero, once."

"Well, so he did. I guess maybe he isn't all bad."

"He's just misunderstood," he agreed.

She chuckled. They were quiet for a minute or two. "Will you try to get Janie to come to our party?"

He smiled. "I'll give it my best shot. Just don't expect miracles, okay?"

She smiled back. "Okay!"

As it turned out, Janine had to go to the Rourke party, because for once her little brother dug in his heels and insisted on going somewhere. He would, he told her firmly, go alone if she didn't care to go with him.

The thought of her little brother in the sort of company the Rourkes would keep made her very nervous.

She didn't socialize enough to know much about people who lived in the fast lane, and she'd never known any millionaires. She was aware that some drank and used drugs. Her sheltered life hadn't prepared her for that kind of company. Now she was going to be thrust into the very thick of it, or so she imagined. Actually she had no idea what Canton's friends were like. Maybe they were down-to-earth and nice.

She hadn't anything appropriate for a cocktail party, but she scrounged up a crinkly black sundress that, when paired with high heels, pearl earrings and a pearl necklace that her parents had given her, didn't look too bad. She brushed her flyaway hair, sprayed it down and went to get her black leather purse.

"I didn't even have enough warning to go and buy a new dress. I hate you," she told Kurt with a sweet smile.

"You'll forgive me. I'll bet when he's dressed up, he's really something to look at," he replied.

"I've seen him dressed up."

"Oh. Well, he's supposed to be the stuff dreams are made of. Karie says half the women in Chicago have thrown themselves at him over the years, especially since his wife remarried."

"They live in Chicago?" She tried to sound disinterested.

"Part of the time," he affirmed. "They have an apartment in New York, too, in downtown Manhattan."

"He may not ever be super rich again," she reminded him.

"That doesn't seem to discourage them," he assured her. "They're all sure that any man who could make it in the first place will be able to get it back."

There was a sort of logic to the assumption, she had to admit. Most men who made that sort of money were workaholics who didn't spare themselves or any of their employees. Given a stake, there was every reason to believe Canton Rourke could rebuild his empire. But she felt sorry for him. He wouldn't ever know who liked him for himself and who liked him for what he had.

"I'm glad I'm not rich," she said aloud.

"What?"

"Oh, I just meant that I know people like me for myself and not for what I've got."

He folded his arms across his neat shirt. "Do go on," he invited. "Tell me about it. What was that invitation you got back home to come to a cocktail party and explain how to get published to the hostess's guest of honor, who just happened to have written a book…?"

She sighed.

"Or the rich lady with the stretch limo who wanted you to get her best friend's book published. Or the mystery writer wannabe who asked for the name of your agent and a recommendation?"

"I quit," she said. "You're right. Everybody has problems."

"So does Mr. Rourke. If you get to know him, you might like him. And there's a fringe benefit."

"There is?"

"Sure. If you nab him, you can buy him a plastic appliance like the one your favorite alien wears and make him over to suit you!"

The thought of Canton Rourke sitting still for that doubled her over with laughter. He'd more than likely give her the appliance face first and tell her where she could go with it.

"I don't really think that would be a good idea," she replied. "Think how his board of directors might react!"

"I suppose so. We should go," he prompted, nodding toward the clock on the side table.

She grimaced. "All right. But I don't want to," she said firmly.

"You'll enjoy yourself," he promised her. "Nobody knows who you are."

She brightened. "I didn't think of that."

"Now you can."

He opened the door for her with a flourish and they walked down the beach through the sand to the Rourke's house. It was ablaze with light and soft music came wafting out the open door of the patio. Several people holding glasses were talking. They all looked exquisitely dressed and Janine already felt self-conscious about her own appearance.

Kurt, oblivious, darted up the steps to his friend Karie, wearing a cute little dress with a dropped waistline and a short skirt that probably had cost more than Janine's summer wardrobe put together. As she went up the steps, she paused to shake the sand out of her high heels, holding on to the banister for support.

"Need a hand?" a familiar velvety voice asked. A long, lean arm went around her and supported her while she fumbled nervously with her shoe, almost dropping it in the process.

"Here." He knelt and emptied the sand out of the shoe before he eased it back onto her small foot with a sensuality that made her heart race.

He stood up slowly, his eyes meeting hers when they were on the same level, and holding as he rose to his towering height. He didn't smile. For endless seconds, they simply looked at each other.

"This was Kurt's idea," she blurted breathlessly. "I didn't even have time to buy a new dress…"

"What's wrong with this one?" he asked. His lean hand traced the rounded neckline, barely touching her skin, but she shivered at the contact.

"You, uh, seem to have quite a crowd," she faltered, moving a breath away from him.

"Right now, I wish they were all five hundred miles away," he said deeply, and with an inflection that made her tingle.

She laughed nervously. "Is that a line? If it is, it's probably very effective, but I'm immune. I've got a son and I've lived in a com…"

He held up a hand and chuckled. "Give it up," he advised. "Kurt is twelve and you're twenty-four. I really doubt that you conceived at the age of eleven. As for the commune bit," he added, moving close enough to threaten, "not in your wildest dreams, honey."

Honey. She recalled dumping a glass of milk on a pushy acquaintance who'd used that term in a demeaning way to her. This man made it sound like a verbal caress. Her toes curled.

"Please." Was that her voice, that thin tremulous tone?

His fingers touched her cheek gently. "I'm a new experience, is that it?"

She shivered. "You're a multimillionaire. I'm working for wages." Not quite the truth, but a good enough comparison, she thought frantically.

He leaned closer with a smile that was fascinating. "I gave up seducing girls years ago. You're safe."

Her wide eyes met his. "Could I have that in writing, notarized, please?"

"If you like. But my word is usually considered equally binding," he replied. His hand fell and caught hers. "As for the multimillionaire bit, that's past history. I'm just an ordinary guy working his way up the corporate ladder right now. Come in and meet my guests."

His fingers were warm and strong and she felt a rush of emotion that burst like tangible joy inside her. What was happening to her? As if he sensed her confusion and uncertainty, his fingers linked into hers and pressed reassuringly. Involuntarily her own returned the pressure.

As they gained the top of the steps, a vivacious brunette about Janine's age came up to them with a champagne glass in her hand. She beamed at Canton until she saw him holding hands with the other woman. Her smile became catty.

"There you are, Canton. I don't believe I know

your friend, do I?" she asked pointedly, glancing at Janine.

"Probably not. Janine Curtis, this is Missy Elliger. She's the daughter of one of my oldest friends."

"You're not that old, darling," she drawled, moving closer to him. She glared at Janine. "Do you live here?"

"Oh, no," Janine said pleasantly. "I live in a commune in California with several men."

The other woman gaped at her.

"Behave," Canton said shortly, increasing the pressure of his fingers. "This is Janine Curtis. She's here on vacation with her little brother. That's him, over there with Karie. His name's Kurt."

"Oh." Missy cleared her throat. "What a very odd thing to say, Miss...Curtsy?"

"Curtis." Janine corrected her easily. "Why do you say it's odd?"

"Well, living in a commune. Really!"

Janine shrugged. "Actually it wasn't so much a commune as it was a sort of, well, labor camp. You know, where they send political prisoners? I voiced unpopular thoughts about the government..."

"In America?!" Missy burst out.

"Heavens, no! In one of the Balkan countries. I seem to forget which one. Anyway, there I was, with my trusty rifle, shooting snipers with my platoon when the lights went out..."

"Platoon?"

"Not in this life, of course," Janine went on, unabashed. "I believe it was when I was a private in the Czech army."

Missy swallowed her champagne in one gulp. "I must speak to Harvey Winthrop over there. Do excuse me." She gave Canton a speaking look and escaped.

Canton was trying not to laugh.

Janine wiggled her eyebrows at him. "Not bad for a spur-of-the-moment story, huh?"

"You idiot!"

She smiled. He wasn't bad at all. His eyes twinkled even when he didn't smile back.

"I'm sorry," she said belatedly. "She's really got a case on you, you know."

"Yes, I do," he replied. He brought up their linked hands. "That's why I'm doing this."

All her illusions fell, shattered, at her feet. "Oh."

"Surely you didn't think there was any other reason?" he mused. "After all, we're almost a generation apart. In fact, you're only a year older than Missy is."

"So I'm a visual aid."

He chuckled, pressing her fingers. "In a sense. I didn't think you'd mind. Enemies do help one another on occasion. I'll do the same for you, one day."

"I'm not that much in demand," she said, feeling stiff and uncomfortable now that she understood his odd behavior. "But you can have anyone you like. I read it in a magazine article."

"Was that the story they ran next to the one about space aliens attending the latest White House dinner?" he asked politely.

She glowered up at him. "You know what I mean."

He shrugged. "I'm off women temporarily. My wife wrote me off as a failure and found someone richer," he added, with a lack of inflection that was more revealing than the cold emptiness in his eyes.

"More fool, her," she said with genuine feeling. "You'll make it all back and she'll be sorry."

He smiled, surprised. "No, she won't. The magic left during the second year of our marriage. We stayed together for Karie, but eventually we didn't even see each other for months at a time. It was a marriage on paper. She's happier with her new husband, and I'm happier alone." He stared out to sea. "The sticking point is Karie. We ended up with joint custody, and that doesn't suit her. She thinks Karie belongs with her."

"How does Karie feel?"

"Oh, she likes tagging along with me and going on business trips," he said. "She's learning things that she wouldn't in the exclusive girls' school Marie wants her in. I pulled her out of school and brought her here with me for a couple of weeks, mainly to get her out of reach of Marie. She's made some veiled threats lately about wanting more alimony or full custody."

"Education is important."

He glared at her. "And Karie will get the necessary education. She's only missing a few weeks of school and she's so intelligent that she'll catch up in no time. But I want her to have more than a degree and a swelled head when she grows up."

She felt insulted. "You don't like academics?"

He shrugged. "I've been put down by too damned many of them, while they tried to copy my software," he countered. "I like to design it. But in the past, I spent too much time at a computer and too little with my daughter. Even if I hadn't lost everything, taking a break was long overdue."

"You went to Silicon Valley, Karie said."

"Yes. Among other reasons, I was looking for guinea pigs." He glanced down at her with a faint scowl. "Come to think of it, there's you."

"Me?"

"I need someone to test a new program for me," he continued surprisingly. "It's a variation on one of my first word processors, but this one has a new configuration that's more efficient. It's still in the development stages, but it's usable. What do you think?"

She wasn't sure. She'd lost whole chapters before to new software and she was working on a deadline.

"Don't worry about it right now," he said. "Think it over and let me know."

"Okay. It's just that… Well, my boss wants this project sent up within a month. I can't really afford to change software in the middle of it."

"No, you can't. And I didn't mean I wanted you to download the program within the next ten minutes," he added dryly.

"Oh. Well, in that case, yes, I'll think about it."

His hand tightened over hers. "Good."

He led her through his guests, making introductions. Surprisingly his friends came from all walks of life and most of them were ordinary people. A few were very wealthy, but they didn't act superior or out of order at all. However, Missy Elliger watched Janine with narrow, angry eyes and faint contempt.

"Your guest over there looks as if she'd like to plant that glass she's holding in the middle of my forehead," she commented as they were briefly alone.

"Missy likes a challenge. She's too young for me."

She glanced at him. "So you said."

His eyes searched hers. "And I'm not in the market for a second Mrs. Rourke."

"Point taken," she said.

His eyebrow jerked. "No argument?"

Her eyes sparkled. "I wasn't aware that I'd proposed to you," she replied with a grin. "We're temporary neighbors and frequent sparring partners. That's all."

"What if I'd like to be more than your neighbor?" he asked with deliberate sensuality.

Her grin didn't waver. That was amusement in his face, not real interest. He was mocking her, and he wasn't going to get away with it. "Quentin might get upset about that."

"Quentin? Is there a real husband somewhere in the background?" he probed.

She hesitated. He hadn't bought the commune story, so there was no way he was going to buy a secret husband. This man was a little too savvy for her usual ways of dissuading pursuers.

"A male friend," she countered with a totally straight face.

The hand holding hers let go, gently and unobtrusively, but definitely. "You didn't mention him before."

"There wasn't really an opportunity to," she countered. She smiled up at him. "He's a college professor. He teaches medieval history at the University of Indiana on the Chicago campus, where my parents teach anthropology."

His stance seemed to change imperceptibly. "Your parents are college professors?"

"Yes. They're on a dig in some Mayan ruins in Quintana Roo. Kurt's been ill with tonsillitis and complications. They took him out of school to get completely well and I'm tutoring him with his lessons until he goes back. We're near our parents, here in this villa, and I can get some work done and take care of Kurt as well."

He was wary, now, and not at all amused. "I suppose you have a degree, too?" he continued.

She wondered about the way he was looking at her, at the antagonistic set of his head, but she let it go by and took the question at face value. "Well, yes. I have an honors baccalaureate degree in history with a minor in German."

He seemed to withdraw without even moving. He set his glass on an empty tray and his lean hands slid into his pockets. His eyes moved restlessly around the room.

"What sort of degree do you have?" she asked.

It was the wrong question. He closed up com-

pletely. "Let me introduce you to the Moores," he
said, taking her elbow. "They're interesting people."

She felt the new coolness in his manner with a
sense of loss. She'd either offended him or alienated
him. Perhaps he had some deep-seated prejudices
about archaeology, which was the branch of anthropology in which both her parents specialized. She
was about to tell him that they were both active in
helping to enact legislation to help protect burial sites
and insure that human skeletal remains were treated
with dignity and respect.

But he was already making the introductions, to
a nice young couple in real estate. A minute later,
he excused himself and went pointedly to join his
friend Missy Elliger, whom he'd said was too young
for him. Judging by the way he latched on to her
hand, and held it, he'd already forgotten that she was
too young for him. Or, she mused humorously, he'd
decided that Missy was less dangerous than Janine.
How very flattering!

But the rest of the evening was a dead loss as far as
Janine was concerned. She felt ill at ease and somewhat contagious, because he made a point of keeping
out of her way. He was very polite, and courteous,
but he might as well have been on another planet. It
was such a radical and abrupt shift that it puzzled her.

Even Karie and Kurt noticed, from their vantage
point beside a large potted palm near the patio.

"They looked pretty good together for a few minutes," Kurt said.

"Yes," she agreed, balancing a plate of cake on

her knee. "Then they seemed to explode apart, didn't they?"

"Janie doesn't like men to get too close," Kurt told her with a grimace. "The only reason her boyfriend, Quentin, has lasted so long is because he forgets her for weeks at a time when he's translating old manuscripts."

"He what?" Karie asked, her fork poised in mid-air.

"He forgets her," he replied patiently. "And since he isn't pushy and doesn't try to get her to marry him, they get along just fine. Janine likes her independence," he added. "She doesn't want to get married."

"I guess my dad feels that way right now, too," Karie had to admit. "But he and my mom were never together much. Mom hates him now because she couldn't get exclusive custody of me. She swore she'd get me away from him eventually, but we haven't heard from her in several weeks. I suppose she's forgotten. He's forgetful, too, sometimes, when he's working on some new program. I guess that's hard on moms."

"He and Janie would make the perfect couple," Kurt ventured. "They'd both be working on something new all the time."

"But it doesn't look like they'll be thinking about it now," Karie said sadly. "See how he's holding Missy's hand?"

"He was holding Janie's earlier," Kurt reminded her.

"Yes, but now they're all dignified and avoiding

each other." She sighed. "Grown-ups! Why do they have to make everything so complicated?"

"Beats me. Here. Have some more cake."

"Thanks!" She took a big bite. "Maybe they could use a helping hand. You know. About getting comfortable with each other."

"I was just thinking that myself," Kurt said. He grinned at his partner in crime. "Got any ideas?"

"I'm working on some."

Meanwhile, oblivious to the fact that she was soon going to become a guinea pig in quite another way than software testing, Janine sat in a corner with a couple whose passion was deep-sea fishing and spent the next hour being bored out of her mind.

CHAPTER FOUR

"NEVER, NEVER GET me roped into another party at the Rourkes'," Janine told her brother the next morning. "I'd rather be shot than go back there."

"Karie said she went home with her parents, after the party," Kurt said cautiously.

She pretended oblivion. "She, who?"

"Missy Elliger," he prompted. "You know, the lady who had Mr. Rourke by the hand all night?"

"She could have had him by the nose, for all I care," she said haughtily, and without meaning a word of it.

He glanced at her, and smiled secretively, but he didn't say anything.

"I think I'll invite Quentin down for the weekend," she said after a minute.

His eyebrows were vocal. "Why?"

She didn't want to admit why. "Why not?" she countered belligerently.

He shrugged. "Suit yourself."

"I know you don't like him, but he's really very nice when you get to know him."

"He's okay. I just hate ancient history. We have to study that stuff in school."

"What they're required to teach you usually is boring," she said. "And notice that I said 'required to.' Teachers have to abide by rules and use the textbooks they're assigned. In college, it's different. You get to hear about the *real* people. That includes all the naughty bits." She grinned. "You'll love it."

He sighed irritably. "No, I won't."

"Give Quentin a chance," she pleaded.

"If you like him, I guess he's okay. It just seems like he's always trying to change you into somebody else." He studied her through narrowed eyes. "Are you sure you don't like Karie's dad?"

She cringed inside, remembering how receptive she'd been last night to his pretended advances, before she knew they were pretend. She'd tingled at the touch of his hand, and he probably knew it, too. She felt like an idiot for letting her emotions go like that, for letting them show, when he was only using her to keep Missy at bay. And why had he bothered, when he spent the rest of the night holding the awful woman's hand?

"Yes, I'm sure," she lied glibly. "Now let me get to work."

"Will Quentin stay here?" he asked before he left her.

"Why not?" she asked. "You can be our chaperon."

He sighed. "Mom and Dad won't like it."

"I'm old enough, and Quentin probably wants to marry me," she said. "He just doesn't know it yet."

"You wouldn't marry him!" he exclaimed.

She shifted. "Why not? I'm going on twenty-five. I should get married. I want to get married. Quentin is steady and loyal and intelligent."

Also the wrong sort of man for Janine to get serious about, Kurt thought, but he held his tongue. This wasn't a good idea to get his sister more upset than she already was. Besides, he was thinking, having Quentin here just might make Karie's dad a little jealous. There were all sorts of possibilities that became more exciting by the minute. He smiled secretively and waved as he left her to her computer.

"Janie's boyfriend is coming to stay," he told Karie later, making sure he spoke loudly enough that her father, who was sitting just down the beach, heard him.

"Her boyfriend?" Karie asked, shocked. "You mean, she has a boyfriend?"

"Oh, yes, she does," he said irritably, plopping down beside her in the sand. "He teaches ancient history. He's brainy and sophisticated and crazy about her."

Karie made a face. "I thought you said she wasn't interested in getting married."

"She said this morning that she was," he replied. "It would be just my luck to end up with him as my brother-in-law."

Karie giggled at the concept. "Is he old?"

"Sure," he said gloomily. "At least thirty-five."

"That's old," she agreed.

Down the beach, a young-thinking man of thirty-eight glared in their general direction. Thirty-five wasn't old. And what the hell was Janine thinking to saddle herself with an academic? He wanted to throw something. She had a degree, he reminded himself. Her parents were academics; even her boyfriend was.

But Canton Rourke was a high-school dropout with a certificate that said he'd passed a course giving him the equivalent of a high-school diploma. He'd been far too busy making money to go to college. Now it was too late. He couldn't compete with an educated woman on her level.

But he was attracted to her. That was the hell of it. He didn't want to be. Freshly divorced, awash in a sea of financial troubles, he had no room in his life for a new woman. Especially a young and pretty and very intelligent woman like Janine. He'd been smitten before, but never this fast or this furiously. He didn't know what he was going to do.

Except that he was sure he didn't want the college professor to walk away with his neighbor.

JANINE CALLED QUENTIN later that day. "Why don't you fly down here for a couple of days," she suggested.

"I can't leave in the middle of the summer semester, with classes every day," he replied. "I've got students who have makeup exams to take, too."

She sighed. "Quentin, you could leave early Friday and fly back Sunday."

"That's a rather large expense for two days' holiday," he replied thoughtfully.

She felt her temper oozing over its dam. "Well, you're right about that," she agreed hotly, "my company is hardly worth the price of an airline ticket."

"Wh...what?"

"Never mind. Have a nice summer, Quentin." She hung up.

Kurt stuck his head around the door. "Is he coming?"

She glared at him and threw a sofa pillow in his general direction.

Kurt went out the patio door, whistling to himself.

JANINE SANK INTO the depths of depression for the next hour. She and Quentin were good friends, and in the past few months, they'd gone out a lot together socially. But to give him credit, he'd never mentioned marriage or even a serious relationship. A few light, careless kisses didn't add up to a proposal of marriage. She was living in pipe dreams again, and she had to stop.

But this was the worst possible time to discover that she didn't have a steady boyfriend, when she wanted to prove to Canton Rourke that he had no place at all in her life. As if she'd want a washed-up ex-millionaire, right?

Wrong. She found him so attractive that her toes curled every time she thought about him. He was the stuff of which dreams were made, and not because he'd been fabulously wealthy, either. It was the man himself, not his empire, that appealed to Janine. She wondered if he'd believe that. He was probably so used to people trying to get close to his wallet that he never knew if they liked him for himself.

But she didn't want him to know that she did. If only Quentin hadn't been so unreasonable! Why couldn't he simply walk out on his classes, risk being fired and spend his savings to rush down here to Cancún and save Janine's pride from the rejection of a man she coveted?

She burst out laughing. Putting things back into perspective did have an effect, all right.

The phone rang. She picked up the receiver.

"Janie?" Quentin murmured. "I've reconsidered. I think I'd like to come down for the weekend. I can get Professor Mills to take my Friday classes. I need a break."

She grinned into the telephone. "That would be lovely, Quentin!"

"But I'll have to leave on Sunday," he added firmly. "I've got to prepare for an exam."

"A few days will be nice. You'll like it here."

"I'll pack plenty of bottled water."

"You won't need to," she told him. "We have plenty. And at the restaurants, we've never had a problem."

"All right then. I'll phone you from the airport when I get in. I'll try to leave early in the morning, if there's a flight. I'll phone you."

"Bring your bathing trunks."

There was a pause. "Janine, I don't swim."

She sighed. "I forgot."

"Where are your parents?"

"Still out at the dig."

"You'd better book me in at a nearby hotel," he said.

"You could stay with Kurt and me…"

"Not wise, Janine," he murmured indulgently. "We aren't that sort of people, and I have a position to consider. You really must think more conventionally, if we're to have any sort of future together."

It was the first time he'd mentioned having a future with her. And suddenly, she didn't want to think about it.

"I understand that the Spaniards landed near Cancún, on Cozumel," he said. "I'd love to take the time to search through the local library, if they're open on Saturday. I read Spanish, you know."

She did know. He never missed an opportunity to remind her. Of course, he also spoke Latin, French, German and a little Russian. He was brilliant. That was what had attracted her to him at first. Now, she wondered what in the world had possessed her to ask him down here. He'd go off on an exploration of Spanish history in the New World and she wouldn't see him until he was ready to fly out. On the other hand, that might not be so bad.

"I'll meet you at the airport."

"Good! See you Friday. And Janine, this time, try not to forget to take the car keys out of the ignition before you lock the door, hmmm?"

She broke the connection and stared out the window. What in heaven's name had she done? Quentin's favorite pastime was putting her down. In the time since she'd seen him, she'd forgotten. But now she remembered with painful clarity why she'd been happy to leave Bloomington, Indiana, behind just a few months ago and move to a small apartment in Chicago. How could she have forgotten?

Later in the day, she noticed again the man who'd been watching Karie on the beach. He was downtown when she took the kids in a cab to visit one of the old cathedrals there, for research on the book she was writing.

He didn't come close or speak to them, but he watched their movements very carefully. He had a cellular phone, too, which he tried to conceal before Janine spotted it. She went toward a nearby policeman, intent on asking him to question the man. About that time, her intentions were telegraphed to the watchful man, and he immediately got into a car and left the area. It disturbed Janine, and she wondered whether or not she should tell Canton about it. She didn't mention it to Karie or Kurt. After all, it could have been perfectly innocent. There was no sense in upsetting everyone without good reason.

They arrived back at the beach house tired and sweaty. The heat was making everyone miserable. Here, at least, there was a constant wind coming off the ocean. She made lemonade for the three of them and they were sitting on the patio, drinking it, when Canton came strolling along the beach below them.

He was wearing dark glasses and an angry expression. He came up onto the deck two steps at a time. When he reached the top, he whipped off the dark glasses and glared at his daughter.

"When I got back from Tulsa, the house was empty and there was no note," he said. "Your lack of consideration is wearing a little thin. Do I have to forbid you to leave the house to get some cooperation?"

Karie groaned. "Dad, I'm sorry!" she exclaimed, jumping up out of her chair. "Kurt and Janie asked me to go to town with them on a re—"

"Recreational trip," Janine added at once, to forestall her young guest from using "research trip" and spilling the beans about her alter ego.

"Recreational trip," Karie parroted obediently. "I was so excited that I just forgot about the note. Don't be mad."

"I've lost half a day worrying where you were," he said shortly. "I've phoned everyone we know here, including the police."

"You can take away my allowance for three years. Six," she added helpfully. "I'll give up chocolate cake forever."

"You hate chocolate," he murmured irritably.

"Yes, but for you, I'll stop eating it."

He chuckled reluctantly. "Go home. And next time you don't leave me a note, you're grounded for life."

"Yes, sir! See you, Janie and Kurt. Thanks for the trip!"

"I have to wash my pet eel," Kurt said at once with a grin at Janie, and got out of the line of fire.

"Craven coward," she muttered after him.

"Strategic retreat," Canton observed with narrowed eyes. He looked down at her. "You're corrupting my daughter."

"I'm what?"

"Corrupting her. She never used to be this irresponsible." His eyes grew cold. "And if you're going to have your boyfriend living here with you, without a chaperon, she isn't coming near the place until he leaves!"

She actually gaped at him. "Exactly what century are you living in?" she exclaimed.

"That's your boyfriend's specialty, I believe, ancient history," he continued. "I've seen too many permissive lifestyles to have any respect for them. I won't have my daughter exposed to yours!"

"Permissive...exposed..." She was opening and closing her mouth like a fish. "You're one to talk, with your hot and cold running women and your... your cover girl lovers!"

"Escorts," he said shortly. "I was never unfaithful to my wife. Which is a statement she damned sure couldn't make! I'm not raising Karie to be like her."

She felt pale and wondered if she looked it. Her hands were curled painfully into the arms of her chair. She'd never been verbally attacked with such menace. "My boyfriend is a respected college professor with a sterling moral character," she said finally. "And for your information, he insists on staying in a hotel, not here!"

He stood there, towering over her, hands deep in his pockets, barely breathing as his blue eyes went over her light cotton dress down to the splayed edges of her skirt that revealed too much of her lovely, tanned long legs.

She tossed the skirt back over them and sat up, furious. "But even if he did decide to stay here, it would be none of your business!" She got to her feet, glaring up at him. "You can keep Karie at home if you're afraid of my corrupting influence. And you can stay away, too, damn you!"

The speed with which his lean hands came out of his pockets to catch her bare arms was staggering. He whipped her against the length of him and stared down into shocked, wide green eyes.

"Damn you, too," he said under his breath, searching her face with an intensity that almost hurt. "You're too young, too flighty, too emotional, too everything! I'm sorry I ever brought Karie down here!"

"So am I!" she raged. "Let me go!" She kicked out at his leg with her bare foot.

The action, far too violent to be controlled, caused her to lose her balance, and brought her into a position so intimate that she trembled helplessly at the contact.

His hands were on her back now, preventing a fall, slowly moving, sensuous. "Careful," he said, and his voice was so sensual that she lost all will to fight.

Her fingers clenched into the front of his knit shirt. She couldn't make herself look up. The feel of his body was overpowering enough, without the electric pull of those blue, blue eyes to make her even worse. She didn't move at all. She wasn't sure that she could. He smelled of spice and soap. She liked the clean scent of his body. In the opening of his shirt there was a thick mat of hair showing, and she wondered helplessly if it went all the way down to his slacks. She wondered how it would feel under her hands, her cheek, her mouth. Her thoughts shocked her.

His big hands splayed on her back, moving her closer. His breath at her temple stirred her short hair warmly.

His nose moved against her forehead, against her own nose, her cheek. His thin lips brushed her cheek and the corner of her mouth, pausing there as they had once before, teasing, taunting.

She felt her breath shaking out of her body against his lips, but she couldn't help it. His mouth was the only thing in the world. She stared at it with such hunger that nothing else existed.

His hand came up. His thumb brushed lightly against her lower lip, and then slightly harder, tugging. As her lips parted, his head bent. She felt the whispery pressure with a sense of trembling anticipation, with hungry curiosity.

"Close your eyes, for God's sake," he breathed as his mouth opened. "Not your mouth, though..."

She imagined the kiss. She could already feel it. It would be as unexpected as the sudden surge of the wind around them. She felt her body stiffen with the shock of desire it kindled in her. She'd never had such an immediate reaction to any man. He would be experienced, of course. His very demeanor told her that he knew everything there was to know about kissing. She was lost from the very first touch. Her eyes closed, as he'd told them to, and her mouth opened helplessly. She heard someone moan as she anticipated the heat and passion of his embrace…

"Do you know who I am?" he asked.

Her eyes opened. He hadn't moved. He hadn't kissed her. His mouth was still poised, waiting. She'd…imagined the kiss. Her eyes shot up, struggling to cope with steamy emotions that had her knees shaking.

His eyes held hers. "I'm not your college professor," he murmured. "Are you missing him so much that even I can stand in for him?" he added with a mocking smile.

She tore out of his arms with pure rage, her face red, her eyes and hair wild.

"Yes!" she cried at him. "I'm missing him just that much! That's why I invited him to come down to Cancún!"

His hands went back into his pockets, and he didn't even look ruffled. She was enraged.

His eyebrow jerked as he looked at her with kindling amusement, and something much darker. "You're still too young," he remarked. "But whatever effect your boyfriend has had on you is minimal at best."

"He has a wonderful effect on me!"

His eyelids dropped over twinkling eyes. "Like I just did?"

"That was…it was…"

He moved a little closer, his stance sensually

threatening. "Sensuous," he breathed, watching her mouth. "Explosive. Passionate. And I didn't even kiss you."

Her hand came up in a flash, but he caught it in his and brought the damp palm to his mouth in a gesture that made her catch her breath. His eyes were intent, dangerous.

"We come from different worlds," he said quietly. "But something inside each of us knows the other. Don't deny it," he continued when she started to protest. "It's no use. You knew me the minute we met, and I knew you."

"Oh, sure, when I was a soldier in the Czech army in some other life…!"

The back of his fingers stopped the words, gently. "I'm not a great believer in reincarnation," he continued. "But we know each other at some level. All the arguments in the world can't disguise it."

"I don't want you!" she sputtered.

His fingers caught hers and held them almost comfortingly. "Well, I want you," he said shortly. "But you're perfectly safe with me. Even if you didn't have a boyfriend, you'd be safe. I don't want involvement."

"You said that already."

"I'm saying it again, just to make the point. We're neighbors. That's all."

"I know," she snapped. She moved away, and his hand let go. "Stop touching me."

"I'm trying to," he replied with an odd smile. "It's like giving up smoking."

"I don't like you to touch me," she lied.

He didn't even bother with a reply. "I wouldn't dare kiss you," he said. "Addictions are dangerous."

She expelled a shaky breath. "Exactly."

His pale eyes searched hers for a long moment, and the world around them vanished for that space of seconds.

"When you've had a couple of serious affairs and I've remade my fortune, I'll come back around."

She glared at him. "I don't like rich people."

His eyebrows shot up. "I'm not rich and you don't like me."

"You're still rich inside," she muttered.

"And you're just a little college girl with a heartless boss," he murmured. He smiled. "You could come to work for me. I'd give you paid holidays."

"You don't have a business."

"Yet," he replied, smiling with such confidence that she believed in that instant that he could do anything he liked.

"But you will have," she added.

He nodded. "And I'll need good and loyal employees."

"How do you know I'd be one?"

"You're working on your vacation. How much more loyal could you be?"

She averted her eyes. "Maybe I'm not exactly what I seem."

"Yes, you are. You're the most refreshing female I've met in years," he confessed reluctantly. "You're honest and loyal and unassuming. God, I'm so tired of socialites and actresses and authoresses who attract attention with every move and can't live out of the limelight! It's a relief to meet a woman who's satisfied just to be a cog instead of the whole damned wheel!"

She felt a blush coming on. He had no idea what her normal life was like. She was a very famous authoress indeed, and on her way to a large bankroll. She wasn't a cog, she was a whole wheel, in her niche, and even reviewers liked her. But this man, if he knew the truth, would be very disillusioned. He'd lost so much because he'd trusted the wrong people. How would he feel if he knew that Janine had lied to him?

But that wouldn't really matter, because he didn't want an intimate relationship and neither did she.

"Well, as one neighbor to another, you're fairly refreshing yourself. I've never met a down-on-his-luck millionaire before."

He smiled faintly. "New experiences are good for us. Short of kissing you, that is. I'm not that brave."

"Good thing," she replied, tongue-in-cheek. "I don't know where you've been."

He smiled. He laughed. He chuckled. "Good God!"

"I don't," she emphasized. "You are who you kiss."

"Bull. Your mouth doesn't know one damned thing about kissing."

"Oh, yes, it does."

His chin lifted. "I might consider letting you prove that one day. Not today," he added. "I'm getting old.

It isn't safe to have my blood pressure tried too much in one afternoon."

"Is it high?" she asked with real concern.

He shrugged. "It tends to be. But not dangerously so." He searched her eyes. "Don't care about me. You're the last complication I need."

"I was about to say the same thing. Besides, I have a boyfriend."

"Good luck to him," he replied with a short laugh. "If you're pristine at twenty-four, he's lacking something."

Her mouth opened without words, but he was already leaving the deck before the right sort of words presented themselves. And of all the foul names she could think of to call him, only "scoundrel" came immediately to mind.

"Schurke!" she yelled in German.

He didn't break stride. But he turned, smiled and winked at her. His smile took the wind right out of her sails.

While she was still trying to think up a comeback, he walked on down the beach and out of earshot. The man was a mystery—and what she felt when he was around her was a puzzle she was unsure she'd ever solve.

CHAPTER FIVE

FOR THE NEXT HOUR, Janine did her best to look forward to Quentin's forthcoming visit. She and Quentin were good friends, and in the past, while she was still living at home, they'd gone out a lot together socially. But to give him credit, he'd never mentioned marriage or even a serious relationship. A few light, careless kisses didn't add up to a proposal of marriage.

On the other hand, what she experienced with Canton Rourke was so explosive that all she could think about was the fact that one day soon, she'd have to go back to Chicago and never see him again. In a very short time, she'd come to know their down-on-his-luck neighbor in ways she never should have. She wanted him just as much as he wanted her, despite the fact that he infuriated her most of the time. But she was living in dreams again, and she had to stop. Having Quentin here even for a weekend might snap her out of her growing infatuation with Canton Rourke.

Quentin came down three days later. He got off the plane in Cancún, looking sweaty and rumpled and thoroughly out of humor. He sent a dark glare at a young woman with red hair who smiled at him sweetly and then sent a kiss his way.

Quentin glared after the woman as he joined Janie, carry-on bag in hand. He wiped his sweaty light brown hair with his handkerchief, and his dark eyes weren't happy.

"English majors," he spat contemptuously. "They think they know everything!"

"Some of them do," Janine remarked. "One of my English professors spoke five languages and had a photographic memory."

"I had old Professor Blake, who couldn't remember where his car was parked from hour to hour."

"I know how he felt," she murmured absently as she scanned the airport for the rental car she was driving.

He groaned. "Janie, you didn't lock the keys in it?"

She produced them from her pocket and jangled them. "No, I didn't. I just can't remember where I put it. But it will come to me. Let's go. Did you have a nice flight?"

"No. The English professor sat beside me on the plane and contradicted every remark I made. What a boor!"

She bit her tongue trying not to remind him that he did the same thing to her, constantly.

"God, it's hot here! Is it any cooler at the hotel?"

"Not much," she said. "There's air-conditioning inside. It helps. And there's always a breeze on the beach."

"I want to find the library first thing," he said.

"And then the local historical society. I speak Spanish, so I'll be able to converse with them quite well."

"Do you speak Mayan?" she asked with a smile. "I do hope so, because quite a few people here speak Mayan instead of Spanish."

He looked so uncomfortable that she felt guilty.

"But most everyone knows some English," she added quickly. "You'll do fine."

"I hope that redheaded pit viper isn't staying at my hotel. Where is my hotel, by the way?" he demanded.

"It's about three miles from my beach house, in the hotel zone. I can drive you to and from, though. I rented the car for a month."

"Isn't it dangerous to drive here?"

"Not any more dangerous than it is to drive in Chicago," she replied. "Ah. There it is!"

"I thought your brother was with you," he remarked.

"He is. He has a playmate, and he's staying with her family today." She didn't add that he'd refused to go to meet Quentin, who wasn't one of his favorite people.

"I see. Is he still as outspoken and ill-mannered as ever?"

She hated that smug smile of his. This was going to be a fiasco of a vacation, she could see it right now.

KURT WAS POLITE to Quentin; just polite and no more. He spent the weekend tagging after Karie and avoiding the beach house where Quentin was poring over copies of old manuscripts he'd found in some archives. They were all in Spanish. Old Spanish.

"This is sixteenth century," he murmured absently, with pages spread all over the sofa and the floor while he sat cross-legged on the small rug going from one to another. "Some of these verbs I don't even recognize. They may be archaic, of course…"

He was talking to himself. Across from him, Janine was poring over a volume on forensic medicine, searching for new methods of bumping off her villains.

Into the middle of their studious afternoon, Karie and Kurt came back from a walk on the beach, with Karie's father looming menacingly behind them. Both children were flushed and guilty-looking.

Janine laid her volume aside and sighed. "What have you done, now?" she asked Kurt with resignation.

"Remember the garden hose I bought them?" Canton asked her with barely a glance for the disorderly papers and man on the floor.

"Yes," Janine said slowly.

"They were hacking it up with a very sharp machete under the porch at our place."

"A machete? Where did you get a machete?" Janine exclaimed to Kurt.

Before he could answer, Quentin got to his feet, his gold-rimmed glasses pushed down on his nose for reading. "I told you that you'd never be able to handle Kurt by yourself," Quentin said helpfully.

Janine glared at him. "I don't 'handle' Kurt. He's not an object, Quentin."

Canton had his hands deep in his pockets. He was looking at Quentin with curiosity and faint contempt.

"This is our neighbor, Mr. Rourke," Janine introduced. "And this is Quentin Hobard, a colleague of my parents' from Bloomington, Indiana. He teaches ancient history at Indiana University."

"How ancient?" Canton asked.

"Renaissance," came the reply. He held up a photocopied page of spidery Spanish script. "I'm researching—"

Midsentence, Canton took the page from him and gave it a cursory, scowling scrutiny. "It's from a diary. Much like the one Bernal Díaz kept when he first came from Spain to the New World with Cortés and began protesting the *encomienda*."

Quentin was impressed. "Why, yes!"

"But this writing deals with the Mayan, not the Aztec, people." Canton read the page aloud, effortlessly translating the words into English.

Rourke finally looked up. "Who wrote this?" he asked.

Quentin blinked. He, like the others, had been listening spellbound to the ancient words spoken so eloquently by their visitor.

"No one knows," the scholar replied. "They're recorded as anonymous, but he writes as if he were a priest, doesn't he? How did you read it?" he added. "Some of those verbs are obsolete."

"My mother was Spanish," Rourke replied. "She

came from Valladolid and spoke a dialect that passed down almost unchanged from the Reconquista."

"Yes, when Isabella and Ferdinand united their kingdoms through marriage and drove the Moors from Spain, in 1492. They were married in Valladolid," Quentin added. "Have you been there?"

"Yes," Rourke replied. "I still have cousins in Valladolid."

This was fascinating. Janine stared at him with open curiosity, met his glittery gaze and blushed.

"Well, thank you for the translation," Quentin said. "I'd be very interested to have you do some of the other pages if you have time."

"Sorry," Rourke replied, "but I have to fly to New York in the morning. I should be back by midnight. I wanted to ask Janie if she'd keep my daughter while I'm away."

It was the first time he'd abbreviated her name. She felt all thumbs, and was practically tongue-tied. "Why...of course," she stammered. "I'd be glad to."

"I'll send her over before I leave. It'll be early."

"Good luck getting a flight out," Quentin murmured.

Canton chuckled. "No problem there. I have a Learjet. See you in the morning, then." He glanced down at the book lying on the sofa and his eyebrows went up. "Forensic medicine? I thought history was your field."

"It is," Janine said.

"Oh, she does that for her books," Quentin said offhandedly.

"The ones I'm trying to sell," she added quickly, with a glare at Quentin.

He didn't understand. He started to speak, but Janine got to her feet and walked Canton to the door.

"I took the machete away from them, by the way, and hid it." He glanced past her at the kids, who were on the patio by now. "Don't let them out of your sight. Good God, I don't know what's gotten into them. Why would they hack up a perfectly good garden hose?"

"Fishing bait to catch gardeners?" she suggested.

He made a gruff sound. Behind her, Quentin was already reading again, apparently having forgotten that he wasn't alone.

"Dedicated, isn't he?" he murmured.

"He loves his subject. I love it, too, but my period is Victorian America. I don't really care much for earlier stuff."

He searched her eyes. "Do tell?"

"You're very well educated," she remarked. "You read Spanish like a native."

"I am a native, as near as not, even if I don't look it," he replied. He lifted his chin. "As for the education part, I was a little too busy in my youth to get past the tenth grade. I have a certificate that gives me the equivalent of a high-school diploma. That's all."

She went scarlet. She'd had no idea that he wasn't college educated. He'd been a millionaire, and had all the advantages. Or had he?

The blush fascinated him. He touched it. "So you

see, I'm not an academic at all. Far from it, in fact. I got my education on the streets."

Her eyes met his. "No one who could invent the software you've come up with is ignorant. You're a genius in your own right."

His intake of breath was audible. He looked odd for a moment, as if her remark had taken him off guard.

"Weren't your parents well-off?" she asked.

"You mean, did I inherit the money that got me started? No, I didn't," he replied. "I made every penny myself. Actually, Miss Enigma, my father was a laborer. I had to drop out of school to support my sister when he died of cancer. I was seventeen. My mother had already died when I was fourteen."

She did gasp, this time. "And you got that far, alone?"

"Not completely alone, but I made every penny honestly." He chuckled. "I'm a workaholic. Doesn't it show?"

She nodded. "The intelligence shows, too."

He cocked an eyebrow and there was an unpleasant smile on his firm mouth. "Buttering me up, in case I make it all back?"

She glowered. "Do I look as if money matters to me?"

"Women are devious," he replied. "You could look like an angel and still be mercenary."

Her pride was stung. "Thanks for the compliment." She turned to go back in.

He caught her arm, pulled her outside and shut

the door. "Your pet scholar in there is an academic," he said through his teeth. "That's why you keep him around, isn't it? And I don't even have a high-school diploma."

"What does that matter?" she said with equal venom. "Who cares if you've got a degree? I don't! We're just neighbors for the summer," she added mockingly. "Just good friends."

His eyes fell to her mouth. "I'd like to be more," he said quietly.

The wind was blowing off the ocean. She felt it ruffle her hair. Sand whipped around her legs. She had no sense of time as she looked at his face and wondered about the man hidden behind it, the private one that he kept secret from the world.

Suddenly, with a muffled curse, he bent and brushed his lips lightly over hers, so softly that she wasn't sure he'd really done it.

"Thanks for looking after Karie," he said. "I'll pay you back."

"It's no hardship."

"Like children, don't you?" he murmured.

She smiled. "A lot."

"I love my daughter. I'd like a son, too." His gaze lifted to meet hers and he saw the pupils dilate suddenly. His jaw tautened. "Don't sleep with him," he said harshly, jerking his head toward the door.

Her jaw fell. "Sleep…!"

"Not with him, or anyone else." He bent again. This time the kiss was hard, brief, demanding, possessive. His eyes were glittering. "God, I wish I'd never met you," he said under his breath. And without another word, he turned and left her at the door, windblown and stunned, wondering what she'd done to make him kiss her—and then suddenly get angry all over again. She could still feel the pressure of his mouth long after she went back into the living room and tried to act normally.

KARIE WAS A joy to have around, but she and Kurt seemed to find new ways to irritate Quentin all the time. From playing loud music when he was studying his manuscripts to refusing to leave Janine alone with him, they were utter pests.

And there was one more silent complication. The man was back again. He didn't come near the house, but Janine spotted his car along the highway most mornings. He just sat there, watching, the sun glinting off his binoculars. Once again, she started toward the road, and the car sped away. She was really getting nervous. And she hadn't heard from her parents.

She tried to explain her worries to Quentin, but he'd found a reference to Chichén Itzá in the manuscript and was dying to go there.

"There's a bus trip out to the ruins, but it takes all day, and you'll be very late getting back."

"That doesn't matter!" he exclaimed. "I have Saturday free. Come on, we'll both go."

"I can't take Kurt on a trip like that. He's still recovering."

He glared at her. "I can't miss this. It's the opportunity of a lifetime. There are glyphs on the temple that I really want to see."

She smiled. "Then go ahead. You'll have a good time."

He pursed his lips and nodded. "Yes, I will. You don't mind, do you?"

"Oh, of course not," she said. "Go ahead."

He smiled. "Thanks, Janine, I knew you'd be understanding about it."

When was she ever anything else, she wondered. He didn't mind leaving her behind, when they were supposed to be spending their vacation together. But, then, that was Quentin, thoughtless and determined to have his own way. She thought that she'd never forget the sound of Canton Rourke's deep voice as he translated that elegant Spanish into English. Quentin had been impressed, which was also unusual.

"Your neighbor looked very familiar, didn't he?" Quentin asked suddenly.

She had to fight down a thrill at just the mention of him. "He should. Haven't you looked at a newspaper recently? Canton Rourke? Founder of Chipgrafix software?"

"Good Lord!"

"That was him," she said.

"Imagine, a mind like that," Quentin mused. "He doesn't look all that important, does he? I would have passed him on the street without a second glance. But he still reminds me of somebody… Aha! I've got it! The alien on that science fiction series…"

"No," she said, shaking her head. "He doesn't really look much like him at all, once you've been around him for a while."

"Sounds like him, though," he countered. "Nice voice."

He wasn't supposed to like Canton Rourke. He was supposed to be jealous and icy and contemptuous of the man. She sighed. Nothing was going according to plan. Nothing at all.

KARIE SPENT THE next day with Janine while Quentin boarded a tour bus at his hotel and was gone all day and most of the night. He came over the next afternoon by cab, on his way to the airport.

"I had a great time at Chichén Itzá," he told Janine. "Of course, the English whiz was on the tour, too," he added sourly. "She's from Indianapolis and is going back on the same flight I am. I hope they seat her on the wing. She knows all about the Maya culture. Speaks Spanish fluently," he added with pure disgust. "Has a double major in English and archaeology. Show-off."

She didn't quite look at him. "Is she married?"

"Who'd have her?" he spat. "She's so smug. Read the stelae to me before the tour guide could."

She smothered a grin. "Imagine that."

"Yes." He still looked disgusted. "Well, it's been a wonderful trip, Janine. I'm glad you talked me into it. I've got some great things to take back to my classes, including several rolls of film at Chichén Itzá that I'll share with the archaeology department. Think your parents might like some shots?"

She hesitated to mention that they'd taken more slides of the site than most tourists ever would. "You might mention it to them," she said tactfully.

"I'll do that. Well, I'll see you when you come home to visit your parents, I suppose. Any word on how your parents are coming along at that new site?"

She shook her head. "I'm getting a little worried. I haven't heard anything in a couple of weeks, not even one piece of email."

"Hard to find electrical outlets in the jungle, I imagine," he said and then grinned at his joke.

She didn't smile. "They have an emergency generator and a satellite hookup for their computers."

"Well, they'll turn up," he said airily, ignoring her obvious concern. "I have to rush or I'll miss my flight. Good to have seen you. You were right, Janine. I did need a break."

He brushed a careless kiss against her cheek and went back out to his waiting cab.

And that was that.

JANINE WAS HALFHEARTEDLY reading a tome on forensics while Kurt and Karie had gone out to the beach to watch a boy go up on a parasail, which she'd forbidden them to go near. The abrupt knock at the patio wall caught her attention. Her heart jumped when she found Karie's dad standing there, dressed in lightweight white slacks and a tan knit shirt that showed anyone who cared to look just how powerful the muscles in his chest and arms were. For a man his age, he was really tremendously fit.

"I'm looking for Karie," he said without greeting.

She was still stung from his cold words while Quentin had been poring over his photocopies. "They're down the beach watching a parasail go up. Don't worry, I told them not to go near the thing."

He went to the railing, shaded his eyes and stared down the beach. "Okay, I see them. They're wading in the surf, watching."

"Oh."

He turned back to her and searched her flushed face quietly. "Where's the boyfriend?"

"Gone back to Indiana. You just missed him."

"Pity," he said languidly.

She laughed mirthlessly. "Right."

He glanced at her computer screen. A word processor had been pulled up, but no files were open. "That's obsolete," he stated. "Why aren't you using the ncw one?"

"Because it takes me forever to learn one." She smiled at him. "I guess they're all child's play to you. I couldn't write a computer program if my life depended on it!"

That was interesting. "Why not?"

"Because I can't do math," she said simply. "And I don't understand machines, either. You must have a natural gift for computer science."

He felt less inferior. "Something like that, maybe."

"You didn't go to school at all to learn how to write programs?"

He shook his head. "I worked with two men who were old NASA employees. They learned about computing in the space program. I suppose I picked up a lot from them. We started the company together. I bought them out eventually and kept going on my own."

"Then you must have known how to get the best and brightest people to work for you, and keep them."

He smiled faintly. "You aren't quite what I expected," he said unexpectedly.

"Excuse me?"

"Some academics use their education to make people who don't have one feel insignificant," he explained.

She smiled ruefully. "Oh, that would be a good trick, making a millionaire feel insignificant because I have a degree in history."

"What do you do with it?" he asked unexpectedly.

She stared at him. "Do with it?"

"Yes. Do you teach, like your parents?"

"No."

"Why not? Are you happy being a secretary and working for a slave driver?"

She remembered, belatedly, the fictional life she'd concocted. "Oh. Well, no, I don't, really. But degrees are a dime a dozen these days. I know a man with a doctorate in philosophy who's working at a fast-food joint back home. It was the only job he could get."

He leaned against the wall, with his hands in his pockets. "How fast do you type?"

"A little over a hundred words a minute."

He whistled. "Pretty good."

"Thanks."

"If I can get the refinancing I need, you can come to work for me," he suggested.

Was he trying to make up for his behavior when he'd said he was sorry he'd ever met her? She wondered. "That's a nice offer," she said.

"Think about it, then." He shouldered away from the wall. "I'll go get Karie and tell her I'm back."

"They won't have gone far. Have you found out anything about that man who was watching her?" she added, concerned.

He scowled. "No."

"I guess that's good."

"I wouldn't say that," he said absently. His eyes met hers. "Has he turned up again?"

She sighed. "He's been around. He bothers me."

"I know. I'll keep digging and see what I discover."

She was staring at the computer, sitting there like a one-eyed predator, staring at her with its word processing program open and waiting.

"Busy?" he asked.

"I should be."

He held out a hand. "Come along with me to get Karie. Your work will still be there when you get back."

She smiled, tempted. This was going to be disastrous, but why not? It was just a walk, after all.

She turned off the computer and, hesitantly, took the hand he offered. It closed, warm and firm, around hers.

"I'm safe," he said when she flushed a little.

"We'll hold hands, like two old friends, and pretend that we've known each other for twenty years."

"I'd have been four years old…"

His hand contracted. "I'm thirty-eight," he said. "You don't have to emphasize that fourteen-year jump I've got on you. I'm already aware of it."

"I was kidding."

"I'm not laughing." He didn't look at her. His eyes were on the beach as they descended the steps and walked along, above the damp sand.

Kurt gave them a curious look when he saw them holding hands. He waved, grinned and went back to chasing down sand crabs and shells, the parasail already forgotten. Karie was much further down the beach, talking to some girls who were about her age. She hadn't looked their way yet.

"When are your parents due back?" he asked.

"God knows," she replied wearily. "They get involved and forget time altogether. They're like two children sometimes. Kurt and I have to keep a close eye on them, to keep them out of trouble. This time, we're a little worried about pothunters, too."

"Pothunters? Collectors, you mean?"

"Actually I mean the go-betweens, the people who steal archaeological treasures to sell on the black market. Sometimes they already have a buyer lined up. This is a brand-new site and my parents think it's going to be a major one in the Mayan category. If it's a rich dig, you can bet that they'll be in trouble. The government can't afford the sort of protection they'll need, either. I just hope they're watching their backs."

"They should be here, watching the two of you," he murmured.

"Not them," she said on a chuckle. "It's been an interesting upbringing. When I was twelve, I sort of became the oldest person in my family. I've taken care of Kurt, and them, since then."

His fingers eased between hers sensuously. "You should marry and have children of your own."

Her heart leapt. She'd never thought of that in any real sense until right now. She felt the strength and attraction of the man beside her and thought how wonderful it would be to have a child with him.

Her thoughts shocked her. Her hand jerked in his.

He stopped walking and looked down at her. His eyes searched hers in the silence of the beach, unbroken except for the watery crash of the surf just a few feet away.

The sensations that ripped through her body were of a sort she'd never felt with anyone. It was electric, fascinating, complex and disturbing. They seemed to talk to each other in that space of seconds without saying a word.

Involuntarily she moved a step closer to him, so that she could feel the heat of his body and inhale the clean scent of it.

He let go of her hand and caught her gently by the shoulders. "Fourteen years," he reminded her gently. "And I'm a poor man right now."

She smiled gently. "I've always been on the cutting edge of poor," she said simply. "Money is how you keep score. It isn't why you do a job."

"Amazing."

"What is?"

"That's how I've always thought of it."

Her eyes traced his strong face quietly. "This isn't a good idea, is it?"

"No," he agreed honestly. "I'm vulnerable, and so are you. We're both out of our natural element, two strangers thrown together by circumstances." He sighed deeply and his lean hands tightened on her shoulders. "I find you damnable attractive, but I've got cold feet."

"You, too?" she mused.

He smiled. "Me, too."

"So, what do we do?"

He let go of her shoulders and took her hand again. "We're two old friends taking a stroll together," he said simply. "We like each other. Period. Nothing heavy. Nothing permanent. Just friends."

"Okay. That suits me."

They walked on down the beach. And if she was disturbed by his closeness, she didn't let it show.

Karie was now talking to an old woman holding four serapes, about a fourth of a mile down the beach from the house.

"Dad!" she cried, running to catch his hand and drag him to the old woman. "I'm glad you're back, did you have a good trip? Listen, you know I can't speak Spanish, and I've got to have this blanket, will you tell her?" she asked in a rush, pointing to an exquisite serape in shades of red and blue.

He chuckled and translated. He spoke the language so beautifully that Janine just drank it in, listening with pleasure.

He pulled out his wallet and paid for the serape, handing it to Karie as the old woman gave them a toothy grin and went back along the beach.

"Don't do that again!" he chided his daughter. "It isn't safe to wander off without letting anyone know where you are."

"Okay, I won't. I spotted her and this blanket was so pretty that I just had to have it. But I couldn't make her understand."

"I'll have to tutor you," he mused.

"Yes, you will, and Kurt, too. I've got to show this to him! Glad you're home, Dad!" she called over her shoulder.

She tore off back down the beach toward Kurt, the serape trailing in the wind.

"You speak Spanish beautifully," Janine said. "How did you learn it so fluently?"

"At my mother's knee," he replied. "I told you that she was from Valladolid, in Spain." He smiled. "I went there when I finally had enough money to travel, and found some cousins I'd never met."

"Were your parents happy together?"

He nodded. "I think so. But my father worked long hours and he wasn't very well. My mother was a cleaning lady for a firm of investment brokers, until she died. I'm sorry Karie had to be torn between two parents. She still loves her mother, as she should. But now there's a stepfather in the picture. And he's a little too 'affectionate' to suit me or Karie. So we find excuses to make sure she has time alone with just her mother."

She lifted her eyes to his. "What happens if he shows up while she's there?"

"Oh, I had a long talk with him," he said easily, and one corner of his mouth curved. "He knows now that I have a nasty temper, and he doesn't want to spend the rest of his life as a soprano. Consequently he'll keep his hands off my daughter. But Marie wants custody, and she's been unpleasant about it in recent months. I've told her how I felt, and she knows what I'll do if she pushes too hard. I may not have money, but I've got a hot temper and plenty of influence in the right places."

She smiled. "Is it really true?"

He pursed his thin lips and glanced at her. "If we weren't just old friends, I'd show you."

"But we are, of course. Old friends, that is."

"Of course!"

They walked on down the beach, content in each other's company. Janine thought absently that she'd never been quite so happy in her life.

They reached the beach house and she started to go up the steps.

"I have to fly to Miami in the morning on business."

"You just got back from New York!" she exclaimed.

"I'm trying to regroup. It's wearing," he explained.

"I'm meeting a group of potential investors in Miami. I'm going to take Karie along with me in the Learjet this time. Would you and Kurt like to come?"

Her heart leapt. She could refuse, but her brother would never speak to her again if she turned down a flight in a real baby jet.

"Will the plane hold us all?" she asked with honest curiosity.

"It seats more than four people," he said dryly.

"You'll have to have a pilot and a copilot..."

"I fly myself," he replied. "Don't look so perplexed, I'm instrument rated and I've been flying for many years. I won't crash."

She flushed. "I didn't mean to imply...!"

"Of course you didn't. Want to come?"

She shrugged. "Kurt loves airplanes and flying. If I say no, he'll stake me out on the beach tonight and let the sand crabs eat me."

He chuckled. "Good. I'll come by for you in the morning."

"Thanks."

"De nada," he murmured. His eyes narrowed as he studied her. He glanced down the beach, where Karie and Kurt were now oblivious to the world, building a huge sand castle near the discarded serape that Karie seemed to find uninteresting now that she owned it.

"What is it?" she asked when he hesitated.

"Nothing much," he replied, moving closer. "I just wanted to answer that question for you. You know, the one you asked earlier, about men with Latin blood?"

"What quest…!"

His mouth cut the word in half. His arm caught her close against the side of his body, so that she was riveted to him from thigh to breast. His mouth was warm and hard and so insistent that her heart tried to jump right out of her chest. The light kisses that had come before were nothing compared to this one.

Against his mouth, she breathed in the taste of him, felt his teeth nibble sensuously at her upper lip to separate it from the lower one. Then his tongue shot into her mouth, right past her teeth, in an intimacy that corded her body like stretched twine. She stiffened, shivering, frightened by the unexpected rush of pure feeling.

"Easy," he breathed. His slitted eyes looked right into hers. "Don't fight it."

His mouth moved onto hers again, and this time there was nothing preliminary at all about the way he kissed her. She felt the world spinning around her wildly. She held on for dear life, her mouth swelling, burning, aching for his as the kiss went on and on and on.

When his head finally lifted, her nails were biting into the muscles of his shoulders. Her hair was tousled, her eyes misty and wild, all at once, as they met his.

Her mouth trembled from the pressure and passion of his kiss. He looked down at it with quiet satisfaction.

"Yes," he whispered.

His head bent again, and he kissed her less passionately, tenderly this time, but with a sense of possession.

He let her go, easing her upright again.

She couldn't seem to find words. Her eyes sought reassurance in his, and found only a wall behind which he seemed hidden, remote, uninvolved. Her heart was beating her to death, and he looked unruffled.

"You're young for a woman your age," he remarked quietly.

She couldn't get words out. She was too busy trying to catch her breath.

He touched her swollen lips gently. "I won't do that again," he promised solemnly. "I didn't realize... quite how vulnerable you were." He sighed, brushing back her wild hair. "Forgive me?"

She nodded.

He smiled and dropped his hand. "I'll see you and Kurt in the morning."

"Okay."

He winked and walked back down the beach, totally unconcerned, at least on the surface. Inside he was seething with new emotions, with a turmoil that he didn't dare show to her. Innocence like that couldn't be faked. She wasn't in his league, and he'd better remember it. That sort of woman would expect marriage before intimacy, he knew it as surely as if she'd said it aloud. She wasn't modern or sophisticated. Like her academic parents, she lived in another world from the one he inhabited.

Of course, he was thinking to himself, marriage wouldn't be so bad if it was with a woman he liked and understood. He laughed at his own folly. Sure. Hadn't he made that very mistake with his first wife? He'd better concentrate on his business empire and leave love to people who could handle it.

All the same, he thought as he entered his house, Janine was heaven to kiss.

CHAPTER SIX

THE NEWS THAT he was going to get to fly in a Learjet made Kurt's head spin. He didn't even sleep that night. The next morning, he was awake at daybreak, waiting for his sister to wake up and get dressed so they could leave.

"He won't be here yet," she grumbled. "It's not even light!"

"All the more reason why we should be ready to go when he does get here," he said excitedly. "A *real* Learjet. My gosh, I still can't believe it!"

"You and airplanes," she mumbled as she made coffee. "Why don't you like bones and things?"

"Why do you like old books?"

"Beats me."

"See?"

She didn't see anything. She was wearing shorts with a white T-shirt, her usual night gear, and neither of her eyes seemed to work. A cup of coffee would fix that, she thought as she made it.

"Do I hear footsteps?" he asked suddenly, jumping up from the table in the kitchenette. "I'll go see if someone's at the door."

Unbelievably it was Canton. "Why don't you go

over and keep Karie company while your sister gets ready?" he invited. "She's got cheese danishes and doughnuts."

"Great! Hurry up, sis!" he called over his shoulder.

Janine, still drowsy, turned as Canton came into the small kitchenette area, stifling a yawn. "Sorry. I didn't expect you this early."

"Kurt did," he chuckled.

She smiled. "He barely slept. Want some coffee?"

His eyes slid down to the white T-shirt. Under it, the darkness of her nipples was visible and enticing. As he looked at them, they suddenly reacted with equal visibility.

Janine, shocked, started to cross her arms, but he was too quick for her.

As her arms started to lift, his hands slid under the T-shirt. His head bent. He kissed her as his thumbs slid gently over her soft breasts and up onto the hard tips.

She made a harsh sound. His mouth hardened. He backed her into the wall and held her there with his hips while his hands explored her soft body. All the while, his mouth played havoc with her self-control, with her inhibitions.

"The hell with this," he growled.

While her whirling mind tried to deal with the words, his hands were peeling her right out of the T-shirt. Seconds later, his shirt was unbuttoned and they were together, nude from the waist up, her soft breasts buried in the thick pelt that covered his hard muscles.

She whimpered at the heat of the embrace, at the unexpected surge of passion she'd never experienced before. Her arms locked around his neck and she lifted herself to him, feeling the muscles of his thighs tighten and swell at her soft pressure.

He lifted his mouth a breath away and looked into her eyes from so close that she could see the faint specks of green there in the ocean blue of his eyes.

"What the hell are we doing?" he whispered harshly.

Her eyes fell to his swollen mouth. "At your age, you ought to know," she chided with dry humor.

His hips ground into hers. "Feel that?" he snapped. "If you don't pull back right now, I'll show you a few more things I ought to know at my age."

She was tempted. She never had been so tempted before. Her eyes told him so.

That vulnerability surprised him. He'd expected her to jerk back, to be flustered, to demand an apology. But she wasn't doing any of those things. She was waiting. Thinking. Wondering.

"Curious?" he asked gently.

She nodded, smiling self-consciously.

"So am I," he confessed. He eased away from her, holding her arms at her sides when he moved back so that he could see the exquisite curves of her body. She was firm and her breasts had tilted tips. He smiled, loving their beauty.

"I like looking at you," he said, but after a second, he let her go.

She moved back, picking up her T-shirt. She pulled it on and brushed back her hair, her eyes still curious and disturbed when she looked at him.

He was buttoning his shirt with amused indulgence. "Now you know."

"Know...what?"

"That I'm easy," he murmured, provoking a smile on her lips. "That I can be had for a kiss. I have no self-control, no willpower. You can do whatever you like with me. I'm so ashamed."

She burst out laughing. He was impossible. "I'll just bet you are," she murmured.

He held up a hand. "Don't embarrass me."

"Ha!"

"No kidding. I'm going to start blushing any minute. You just keep that shirt on, if you please, and stop tormenting me with your perfect body."

She searched his eyes, fascinated. She'd never dreamed that intimacy could be fun.

He rested his hands on his hips. "Well, we've established one thing. I know too much and you don't know a damned thing."

"I do now," she replied.

He chuckled. "Not much."

She studied her bare feet. "Care to further my education?"

His heart seemed to stop beating. He hesitated, choosing his words. "Yes."

She lifted her gaze back to his face and searched it quietly. "So?"

"We're flying to Miami," he reminded her.

"I didn't mean right now."

"Good thing. I'm hopeless before I've had two cups of coffee."

She grinned at the obvious humor.

He moved close and took her by the waist. "Listen, we're explosive together. It feels good, but we could get in over our heads pretty quickly. You're not a party girl."

She frowned. "What do you mean?"

"If you had a modern outlook on life, you wouldn't be a virgin at your age," he said simply. "You're looking for marriage, not a good time. Right?"

"I never thought about it like that."

"You'd better start," he replied. "I want you, but all I have to offer is a holiday affair. I've been married. I didn't like it. I'm free now and I want to stay that way."

"I see."

"This isn't something I haven't said before, Janie," he reminded her. "If you want me, with no strings attached, fine. We'll make love as often as you like. But afterward, I'll go home and never look back. It will be a casual physical fling. Nothing more. Not to me."

She felt confusion all the way to the soles of her feet. She was hungry for him. But was it only physical? Was it misplaced hero worship? And did she want more than a few nights in his arms?

He made her feel uncomfortable. All her adult life she'd spent her days and nights at a computer or with her nose stuck in books. She'd never had the sort of night life that most of her friends had. Intimacy was too solemn a thing for her to consider it casually. But with this man, here, now, she could think of nothing else.

He touched her cheek gently. "Do you want the truth? You're a repressed virgin in the first throes of sexual need, and you're curious. I'm flattered. But after you've spent a night in my arms, no matter how good it is, you're going to have doubts and you're not going to be too happy with yourself for throwing control to the winds. You need to think this through before you do something you might regret. What about the man back in Indiana? Where does he fit in? And if you have an affair with me, how will he feel about you, afterward? Is he the sort of man who'd overlook it?"

"No," she said without thinking.

He nodded. "So don't jump in headfirst."

She sighed. He made it sound so complicated. Imagine, a man who wanted her that much taking time to talk her out of it. Maybe he did care a little, after all. Otherwise, wouldn't he just take what was blatantly offered and go on with his life?

"Just friends," she said with a grin, looking up at him. "Very old friends."

"That's right."

"Okay. But you have to stop kissing me, because it makes me crazy."

"That makes two of us." He stuck his hands into his pockets to keep them off her. "And you have to stop going braless."

"I didn't know you'd be here this early, or I wouldn't be."

He smiled. "Just as well," he confessed. "I wouldn't have missed that for the world."

She chuckled. "Thanks."

"Get dressed, then, would you? Before all this bravado wears off."

She gave him a wicked grin and went to get dressed for the trip.

It was a wonderful, joyful trip. Canton let Kurt sit in the cockpit with him and they talked about airplanes and jets all the way to Miami.

When they got to town, a big white stretch limousine met them at the airport. To Kurt, who was used to traveling in old taxis and beat-up cars, it was an incredible treat. He explored everything, under Canton's amused eyes.

"It's just a long car," he informed the boy. "After a while, they all look alike."

"It's my first time in a limo, and I'm going to enjoy it," he assured him, continuing the search.

Janine, who frequently went on tour and rode around in limos like this, watched her brother with equal amusement. She'd wanted to take him with her on the last trip, but he couldn't lose the time from school. Only illness had gotten him this break.

"Aren't you curious?" Canton asked her. "You seem very much at home in here."

Her eyebrows lifted. "Do I? Actually I'm very excited."

"Are you?"

She smiled sweetly, and turned her attention back to Kurt.

Later, while Canton was in his meeting, Karie and Kurt went to a big mall with Janine, where they peeked and poked through some of the most expensive shops in town. By the time they ended up at an exclusive chocolatier shop and bought truffles, they were all ready to go home.

Canton accepted a chocolate on the way back to the airport, smiling as he tasted it. "My one weakness," he explained. "I love chocolate."

"He's a chocoholic," Karie added. "Once, he went rushing out in the middle of the night for a chocolate bar."

"Sounds just like Janie," Kurt replied with a smile. "She keeps chocolate hidden all over the house."

"Hidden?" Canton probed.

"We stop her from eating it if we find any in her hiding places. She gets terrible migraines when she eats it," he explained. "Not that it ever stopped her. So we have to."

"She's just eaten two enormous truffles," Karie said worriedly.

Janine glared at the kids. "I'm perfectly all right,"

she informed them. "Anyway, it doesn't *always* give me migraines," she told her brother firmly.

THAT NIGHT, LYING in the bed and almost screaming with pain, she remembered vividly what she said to Kurt.

She lost her lunch, and then her supper. The pain was so bad that she wished for a quick and merciful death.

She didn't even realize that Kurt had gone to get Canton until she felt his hand holding hers.

"You don't have anything to take?" he prompted.

"No," she squeaked.

He let go of her hand and called a doctor. Scant minutes later, a gentleman in a suit administered a whopping injection. And only a little later, pain gave way to blessed oblivion.

SHE WOKE WITH a weight on her arm. Her eyes opened. Her whole head felt sore, but the headache was so subdued that it was almost a memory.

She looked toward the side of the bed, and there was Canton Rourke, in a burgundy robe, with his face lying on her arm. He was sound asleep, half in a chair and half against her side of the bed.

"Good heavens, what are you doing here?" she croaked.

He heard her, blinking to sudden alertness. He sat up. He needed a shave and his hair was tousled. His eyes were bloodshot. He looked tired to death, but he was smiling.

"Feel better?" he asked.

"Much." She put a hand to her head. "It's very sore and it still hurts a little."

"He left a vial of pills and a prescription for some more. I'm sorry," he added. "I had no idea that Karie would take you to the chocolate shop."

"She couldn't have stopped me," she replied with a pained smile. "They have the best, the most exquisite chocolates on earth. It's my favorite place in the world. And it was worth the headache. Where did you find a doctor in the middle of the night?"

"Karie had appendicitis when we were down here a couple of years ago," he replied. "Dr. Valdez is one of the best, and he has a kind heart."

"Yes, he does. And so do you. Thanks," she said sincerely.

He shrugged. "You'd have done it for me."

She thought about that. "Yes, I would have," she said after a minute.

He smiled.

He stretched largely, wincing as his sore muscles protested.

"Come to bed," she offered with a wan smile, patting the space beside her. "It's too late to go home now."

"I was just thinking the same thing."

He went around to the other side of the bed, but he kept his robe on when he slid under the covers.

"Prude," she accused weakly.

He chuckled drowsily. "I can't sleep normally with

Karie anywhere around. Usually I wear pajama bottoms, but they're in the wash, hence the robe."

"That's considerate of you."

"Not really," he confessed. "Actually, I *am* a prude. I don't even like undressing in front of other men." His head turned toward hers. "I was in the Marine Corps. You can't imagine how that attitude went down with my D.I."

She chuckled and then grabbed her head. "Modesty shouldn't be a cardinal sin, even in the armed services."

"That's what I told him."

She took a slow breath. Her head was still uncomfortable.

"Go back to sleep," he instructed, drawing her into his arms. "If it starts up again, wake me and I'll get the pills."

"You're a nice man," she murmured into his shoulder.

"Yes, I am," he agreed. "And don't you forget it. Now go to sleep."

She didn't think she could, with him so close. But the heavy, regular beat of his heart was comforting, as was the warmth of his long, muscular body against her. She let her eyelids fall and seconds later, she slept.

There was a lot of noise. She heard rustling and footsteps and the clanking of metal pans. It all went over her head until something fell with an awful clatter, bringing her eyes open.

"Where the hell are the frying pans? Don't you have a frying pan?" he asked belligerently.

She sat up gingerly, holding her head. "I don't think so," she told him.

"How do you scramble eggs?"

She blinked. "I don't. Nobody here eats them."

"I eat them. And you're going to, as soon as I find a—" he expressed several adjectives "—frying pan!"

"Don't you use that sort of language in my house," she said haughtily.

"I've heard all about your own vocabulary from Kurt, Miss Prim and Proper," he chided. "Don't throw stones."

"I almost never use words like that unless my computer spits out a program or loses a file."

"Computers do neither, programmers do."

"I don't want to understand how a computer works, thank you, I only want it to perform."

He chuckled. "Okay. Now what about pots and pans?"

"It won't do you any good to find one, because I don't have any eggs."

He presented her with a bowl of them. "Our housekeeper came back this morning laden with raw breakfast materials. I even have bacon and freshly baked bread."

"I hope you don't expect me to eat it, because I can't," she murmured weakly. "And I'm going to need some of those pills."

He produced them, along with a small container of bottled water. "Here. Swallow."

She took the pills and lay back down, her eyes bloodshot and swollen. "I feel terrible," she whispered.

"Is it coming back?"

"Yes. It's not so bad as it was yesterday, but it still throbs."

"Stop eating chocolate."

She sighed. "I forget how bad the headaches are when I don't actually have one."

"So Kurt says."

"There are pans in the drawer under the stove," she said helpfully.

He opened it and retrieved a tiny frying pan. He held it up with a sigh. "Well, I guess it'll hold one egg, at least. I have to have an egg. I can't live without an egg every morning, and damn the cholesterol."

"Addictions are hell," she murmured.

He glared at her. "You have to have your coffee, I notice. And we won't mention chocolate…"

"*Please* don't," she groaned.

He shook the frying pan at her. "Next time, I'll go along when you shop. You'll have to get through me to get at any chocolate."

She stared at him with blank eyes. "That sounds very possessive."

He returned her quiet scrutiny. His eyes began to warm. "Yes, it does, doesn't it?" The smile faded. "Just remember. I'm not a marrying man. Not anymore."

"Okay. I promise not to ask you to marry me," she agreed, groaning when movement set her headache off again. She rolled over and held her head with both hands.

"The pills should take effect soon," he said sympathetically. "Have you had coffee yet?"

"No," she whispered.

"That might be making it even worse. Here, I'll get you a cup."

"Excuse me?"

He poured black coffee into a cup, added a little cold water to temper the heat and sat down beside her.

"If you drink coffee all the time, you can get a headache from leaving it off. Caffeine is a drug," he reminded her.

"I know. I remember reading about withdrawal, but I was too sick when I first woke up to want even water."

"Just the same, you'd better have some of the hair of the dog."

"Chocolate has caffeine," she remarked as she sipped the strong coffee. He made it just as she did—strong enough to melt spoons.

"So it does. Want a chocolate truffle?"

She glared at him and sipped another swallow of coffee.

"Sorry," he murmured. "Low blow."

"Wasn't it?" She laid back down with a long sigh. "Why are you being so nice to me?"

"I have a soft spot for problem chocoholics," he gibed. He smiled at her as he got up. "Besides, we're old friends."

"So we are," she mused, wincing with pain.

He tossed the empty eggshells into the garbage can. He searched through drawers until he found a fork. "No wire whip," he muttered.

"I don't torture my food."

He glanced at her. "A wire whip isn't torture. It's an absolute necessity for scrambled eggs and any number of exquisite French cream sauces."

"Listen to the gourmet chef," she exclaimed.

"I can cook. I've done my share of it over the years. I wasn't born rich."

She rolled over on her side to stare at him. "How did you grow up?"

He chuckled. "On the lower east side of Manhattan," he told her. "In a lower middle class home. My father worked long hours to support us."

"Your mother?"

"She died when my younger sister was born," he explained. "I was fourteen. Dad had a boy and an infant girl to raise and provide for. He did the best he could, but he wore out when I was seventeen, and I had to take over. He died of lung cancer." He glanced at her. "And, no, he didn't smoke. He worked in a factory brimming over with carcinogens. He wasn't literate or educated, so he did the work he could get."

"I'm sorry. That must have been rough on all of you."

"It was." He stirred the eggs absently. "I took care of him myself for as long as I could. We couldn't afford nursing care. Hell, we couldn't afford a doctor, except at the free clinic." He drew in a long breath.

"I was holding down two jobs at the time, one full-time at a printing shop and the other part-time at an investment house, as a janitor." He gave her a long look. "Yes, that's where I learned the ropes. One of the older executives lost his son in a traffic accident in New Jersey about the same time my father died. He worked late and we ran into each other occasionally and talked. Eventually, when he found out how hard it was for me, he started teaching me about money. By God, he made an investment wizard out of me, long before I started designing software and linked up with the ex-NASA guys. And I never even got to thank him. He dropped dead of a heart attack before I made my first million." He shook his head. "Ironic, how things work out."

"Yes." She watched him move. He had an elegance of carriage, a sensuous arrogance that made him a pleasure to watch. Muscles rippled in his arms and chest under the close fitting knit shirt and slacks he wore. "Are you still close to your sister?"

He didn't answer for a minute. "My sister died of a drug overdose when she was sixteen. It was my fault."

CHAPTER SEVEN

"WHAT DO YOU MEAN, it was your fault?" she asked, curious.

"She got in with a bad crowd. I didn't even know," he said. "I was just too damned busy—working, trying to stay afloat with Marie, being a new dad, all those things. I tried to keep an eye on her. But I didn't know who she was dating. It turned out that she was in a relationship with our neighborhood drug dealer. He was her supplier. One night, she took too much. They called me from the emergency room. The rat took off the minute she went into cardiac arrest."

"He got clean away, I gather?"

Canton stirred eggs until they cooked, and then took them off the stove before he answered. "No, he didn't," he said deliberately, "although it took me a few years to get rich enough to go looking for him. He's doing ten years on a dealing charge. I hired private detectives to watch him. It didn't take long to catch him with enough evidence to send him up. But it didn't bring her back."

She could sense his pain. She sat up in bed, grimacing as the movement hurt her head. "I know. But there's only so much you can do to keep people out of trouble. If they really want to hurt themselves, you can't stop them, no matter how much you love them."

He glanced at her over the eggs he'd just spooned onto a plate. "You see deeper than most people. Much deeper."

She shrugged. "That can make life pretty hard sometimes."

"It can make it worth living, as well."

She smiled back. "I suppose so."

"I don't suppose you have a toaster?"

"Waste of money," she said. "The toast never comes out warm enough to butter. I make it in the oven broiler."

"That's what I was afraid of."

All the same, he accomplished cinnamon toast with a minimum of fuss, though, and then spoon-fed her delicious scrambled eggs and a bite of toast with some strong black coffee.

She smiled as he put the empty plate aside. "You're a nice man," she said.

"You needn't sound so surprised," he replied. "I'm just a man."

"A man who built an empire all alone," she elaborated.

"I had plenty of help. The problem is that when people get famous, they stop being people to the public. I'm no different than when I used to get my little sister up and ready for school. I'm just older and better dressed."

"People get lost in the glamour, I guess," she agreed.

"All too often, they do. Making money is mostly just plain hard work and sacrifice. No sane person would do anything to excess just to make money."

"Then why did you?" she asked.

"For fun," he replied. "I love creating computer software. It's a challenge to combine numbers and logic and make a new program from scratch that does exactly what you want it to. I never thought about making money."

She chuckled softly. "But you did."

"A hell of a lot of it," he said, nodding. "And it was nice, while it lasted. But you know what?" he added, leaning closer. "I'm just as happy now, with the challenge of making it all back again."

She understood that. It was the same with her, when she wrote a book. She wondered what he'd say if he knew what she did for a living, that she'd deceived him into thinking she was just a secretary on holiday. His opinion of famous women wasn't very high. Of course, she wasn't all that famous. And he wasn't in love with her, either. Perhaps she was making a problem of it.

"You look pale," he remarked. He smoothed back her hair, concern in his blue eyes as he studied her wan, drawn face. "You've had a hard night. Why don't you try and get some sleep? I'll watch Kurt for you."

"Thanks. I think it might help."

He drew the sheet over her. "I'll lock up on my way out. Has Kurt got a key?"

"Yes. But he won't remember where he put it.

It's in his windbreaker pocket that zips up. It's on the couch."

"I'll take it with me." He bent and kissed her forehead gently. "Will you be all right alone, or do you want me to stay?"

"I'll be fine now," she promised. She smiled drowsily, because the pills were starting to take effect. "Thanks."

He shrugged. "Old friends help each other out," he reminded her.

"I'll remember that if you're ever in trouble."

He looked funny for a minute. She reached up and touched his dark hair. "Doesn't anyone look after you?"

"Karie tries to, I guess."

"No one else?"

He thought about that. "Actually no," he said finally.

She traced his high cheekbone. "Then I will, when I'm better."

He gave her an inscrutable look and got to his feet, frowning. "I'll check on you later. Need anything else?"

"No. And thanks for breakfast. You're not a bad cook."

"Anyone can scramble eggs."

"Not me."

"I'll teach you one of these days. Sleep tight."

She lay back and closed her eyes. He cleaned up the kitchen quickly and efficiently, and then went out and locked the door behind him.

BY EARLY AFTERNOON, Janine was improved enough to get up and dress, which she did, in jeans and a white tank top.

"God, you're young," he remarked when she joined him in the living room.

Her eyebrows lifted. She was still pale, and wore only a little pink lipstick. "I beg your pardon?"

"You're young," he muttered, hands deep in the pockets of his loose-fitting slacks. His blue eyes had narrowed as he studied her lithe figure and her blemishless complexion.

"Twenty-four isn't exactly nursery-school age," she said pointedly. "And you aren't over the hill."

He chuckled. "I feel it, sometimes. But, thanks, anyway."

She averted her eyes. "You must know that you're devastating physically."

There was a silence that eventually made her look at him. His face had tautened, his eyes had gone glittery. Their intent stare made her pulse leap.

His chin lifted almost imperceptibly. "Come here," he said in a deep, velvety tone.

Her legs obeyed him at once, even though her mind was protesting what amounted to nothing less than an order.

But when he reached for her, it didn't matter. Nothing mattered, except the pressure of his arms around her and the insistent, devouring hunger of the hard mouth on hers.

She leaned into him with a sigh, all hope of self-protection gone. It could have led anywhere, except that young, excited voices floated in through the patio door, warning of the imminent arrival of the kids.

He let her go with obvious reluctance. "I could get addicted to your mouth," he said huskily.

"I was thinking the same thing," she agreed with a breathless laugh.

"Don't get your hopes up," he mused, glancing toward the door where footsteps grew louder. "We'd have better luck on the floor of Grand Central Station."

"I noticed."

Before she could add anything else, Kurt and Karie came running into the beach house carrying some huge feathers.

"Where did you get those?" Janine asked.

"A guy was selling them on the beach. Do you know where we can get a skeleton?"

She blinked. "A what?"

"Not a real one." Kurt cleared his throat. "Karie and I are sort of studying anatomy. We need a skull. Or something."

"They sell cow skulls at the *mercado* in town." Canton reached into his pocket and produced two twenty-dollar bills. "That ought to do it."

"Okay. Thanks, Dad!" Karie exclaimed. "How about cab fare to town?"

He produced more bills. "Come right back," he said firmly. "And if you get lost, find a policeman and have him call me."

"Will do. Thanks!"

They were off at a dead run again. Janine and Canton stood on the deck and watched them head toward the front of the house. A movement caught Janine's attention.

There he was again.

The man was standing near the front of the house, beside a sedan. The kids hailed a taxi that had just come from one of the big hotels on a nearby spit of land. They climbed in and as Janine watched in barely contained horror, the man climbed into his vehicle and proceeded to follow the cab.

"Did you see that?" she asked her companion worriedly.

"See what?" he asked.

"A man got into a car and followed the cab."

He frowned. "I didn't notice the man. What was he driving?"

"Some old beat-up sedan. I've seen it before." She grimaced. "It probably wasn't a good idea to let them go off alone. If my parents have found something major, who knows what a determined pothunter might do? What if someone's after Kurt?" she suggested.

He took in a deep breath and rammed his hands deep into his pockets. "I was just thinking the same thing, but too late. I'll go after them. Don't worry. Even a pothunter would think twice about abducting an American child right off the streets of Cancún."

"I'm not so sure."

SHE PACED THE floor until Canton returned with the children in tow. They had their skull and were content to stay on the beach and study it. Janine was worried, though, and not only about the mysterious man. She was worried because Canton seemed to deliberately downplay the incident, as if it didn't really concern him very much. She wondered why, because he looked much more preoccupied than she'd seen him before.

"I was too sick to ask before. How did it go in Miami with your investors?" she asked after she'd fixed them a pot of coffee.

"I did better than I expected to," he replied. "Apparently they think I can pull it off."

"I agree with them."

He searched her eyes and smiled. "Nice of you."

She shrugged. "You're that sort of man. I'll bet your employees are crazy about you."

"I offered you a job, I seem to recall," he mused. "Come work for me. I'll make you rich."

"I'm not sure I want to be." She glanced up. "Money isn't everything, but it must be a help when you have death-defying parents." She drew in a long breath. "And I still haven't heard from them. I phoned the university this morning. They haven't heard anything, either."

"How do they contact you?"

"There's a small satellite link they use in the field," she explained. "They can send me email anytime they like. But even the local guide service hasn't been able to contact them. I haven't told Kurt. I thought it best not to. This is a big deal, this new site. I couldn't bear it if anything's happened to them."

"Why didn't you say something before?" he muttered. "I may not have millions, but I have influence. Give me that phone."

It was impossible to follow what he was saying, but one of the names he mentioned in his conversation was very recognizable.

"You know the president of Mexico?" she exclaimed when he hung up.

"You don't speak Spanish," he reminded her, "so how did you know that?"

"I recognized his name," she returned. "Do you know him?"

"Yes, I know him. They're going to send someone right out in an aircraft to look for your parents. I'd go myself, but the Learjet isn't ideal for this sort of search."

"How will they know where to look?"

"They had to contact the appropriate government agency to get permission to excavate, didn't they?"

She smiled her relief. "Of course they did. Thank you," she added belatedly.

"Don't mention it. Now drink your coffee."

BY THE END of the day, there was a telephone call. It was brief and to the point, but welcome.

"They're fine," Canton told a nervous Janine when he put down the receiver. "Their communications equipment had a glitch, and they had to send a runner to the nearest town to fetch an electronics man. He only arrived today. No problems."

"Oh, thank God," she said fervently.

He smiled at her rakishly. "Don't I get anything?"

She moved toward him. "What would you like?" she asked, aware that the kids were close by, sitting on the darkened deck, watching some people down the beach play music and dance in the sand. "A reward?"

"That would be nice," he murmured when she reached him.

"A gift certificate?" she suggested.

His hands framed her face and lifted it. "I had something a little more…physical…in mind."

She felt as breathless as she sounded when she spoke. "How physical?" she whispered.

"Nothing dire." His mouth covered hers and he kissed her softly, sweetly, deeply. His arms enveloped her gently and the kiss grew to a shattering intensity in the soft silence of the room.

He let her go by breaths. "You're a drug," he breathed shakily.

"I know. So are you." She moved closer, only to find herself firmly put away.

"You're the marrying kind," he reminded her. "I'm not."

"It might not matter."

"It would," he said.

She sighed heavily. "Prude."

He chuckled. "Count on it. Your lipstick is smudged."

"I don't doubt it." She ran a finger around her mouth and fixed the smear. "I'll bet you make love like a pagan."

He smiled slowly, confidently. He leaned toward her slightly, and his voice lowered to a deep purr. "I do."

Her eyes lowered demurely. "Show me," she whispered.

He was barely breathing at all, now. His fists clenched by his side. "This isn't a game. Don't tease."

She looked up again, saw his eyes glitter, his jaw clenched as tightly as the lean hands in fists on his thighs.

"I'm not teasing," she said quietly. "I mean it. Every word."

"So do I," he replied. "I am not, repeat *not*, taking you to bed."

She threw up her hands. "Are you always so cautious? Is that how you made those millions?"

"I don't mind a calculated risk, with money. I mind one with human bodies. Mistakes happen in the heat of passion. I'm not taking chances with you, ever. You're going to marry some normal, steady man like your professor boyfriend and live happily ever after."

"Is that an order?"

"You bet!"

She searched his face with sad eyes. "I'd only spend the rest of my life dreaming about you."

"It's the glamour," he said flatly. "If I were a poor man, or a wage earner, you'd feel differently. Hell, I can look in a mirror! I know what women see, without the glitter. You're a working girl and I've been a multimillionaire. A little hero worship is inevitable."

"You think I'm attracted to your wallet?" she exclaimed on a hushed laugh. Only a working girl! She was world famous. He didn't know that, though.

"No, I don't think you're a gold digger," he said emphatically. "But I do think that you're attracted to an image that doesn't really exist."

"Images don't kiss like you do."

"I'm leaving. I don't like losing arguments."

"Neither do I. Stay and finish this one."

He shook his head. "Not a chance. Get some sleep. I'll see you tomorrow. Karie!" He raised his voice. "Time to go!"

"Coming, Dad!"

He walked out the front door, joined immediately by Karie. They called good-nights over their shoulders, leaving Janine and Kurt by themselves. The room seemed to close in around them.

"Mom and Dad are fine," she told her young brother, putting an affectionate arm around his shoulders as they watched the Rourkes stroll down the beach toward their own house. "Canton called the president's office and they sent out a search party."

He whistled. "Nice to have influence, huh?"

"Nice for us," she agreed. "It's a relief to know they haven't been kidnapped or something."

"You bet!" He glanced up at her. "He reads your books, did you know?"

Her heart jumped. *"Canton Rourke?"*

"Karie says he's got everything you've ever written, including *Catacomb*. Good thing he hasn't looked at the photo."

"He wouldn't recognize me if he did," she said. "I hope."

"Why don't you tell him?" he asked curiously.

She grimaced. "It's too late for me to tell him now. He'd want to know why I didn't before." She shifted. "He doesn't like famous women."

"He likes you. It won't matter."

"Think not? I wonder," she said thoughtfully.

"He's a great guy."

"So Karie says." She remembered the car following them, then, at the mention of his friend. She glanced down at him. "Have you seen that man again, the one I attacked on the beach?"

"Why, yes, I have. He was in town when we were at the *mercado*," Kurt said. "He saw us watching him and took off when I walked toward a policeman."

"I don't like it."

"Neither do I. He's after something. Reckon it's us or Mom and Dad?" he queried.

"I don't know. I'm going to pay more attention to what's going on around us, though, you can count on that."

She went to bed, but the memory of Canton's kisses kept her awake far too long. She got up, dressed in her long white embroidered gown and strolled out onto the deck.

In the moonlight, she saw a figure on the beach, turned toward the Rourke house. Something glinted in the moonlight, something like metal. Could it be a telescope? There was a light on in Canton's living room. There was a figure silhouetted against the

curtains. The glint flashed again. Her heart jumped.
What if it was a gun, trained on Canton?

She never thought of consequences. Without a
thought for her own safety, she darted up to the front
of the Rourke home and then rushed out from the
side of it toward the man, yelling as she went.

The man was surprised, as she expected, but he
reacted much too quickly. He raised an arm and motioned. Before Janine could slow her steps, before she
even realized what was coming, two men shot out of
the darkness with a sheet. It went over her head and
around her. There was a sharp blow to her head, and
after the pain came oblivion.

SHE WOKE UP with a splitting headache and nausea.
The floor rocked under her, and her bed was unusu-
ally hard. She opened her eyes and rolled over, right
onto the hard floor. As she righted herself, she saw
where she was. This wasn't her house. It was a boat,
a big cabin cruiser, and the man who'd been stalk-
ing the children was suddenly there, yelling furiously at his two shorter companions. They seemed
to be pleading with him, their hands raised in sup-
plication. He wasn't responding. He shouted at them
even more.

She groaned involuntarily and they looked toward
her menacingly. She knew then, at once, that if she
didn't keep her head, she was going to die, right here.
The tall man had a pistol tucked into his belt, and his
hand suddenly rested on it.

She closed her eyes and pretended to be unconscious. If he knew that she saw and recognized him, she had little doubt that she'd be a goner. A minute later, she was tossed onto the bunk and rolled over. Her hands were tied firmly behind her.

"No es la muchacha Rourke, ¡idiotas! Es una mujer—es la otra, la vecina," the tall man raged at them.

She didn't understand Spanish, but the words "Rourke girl" and "not" were fairly familiar after two weeks in Mexico. They thought she was Karie! They'd meant to kidnap Karie, and because she'd run out from the Rourke house, in the darkness they'd mistaken her for Karie. They'd got the wrong person. God in heaven, they were after Karie!

The child's life might depend on her now. If they were willing to go to these lengths, to kidnapping at gunpoint, to get Karie, they were deadly serious about what they meant to do. A potential witness, Janine might become expendable any minute. She had to get away, she had to warn Canton and Karie. The reason behind the kidnapping wasn't important right now, but warning them was.

She pretended to sleep. The men stood over her, talking quickly. The tall one muttered something that sounded ominous and his companions agreed with whatever he'd said and followed him up on deck.

The noise of a motor sounded, but not loudly enough to be that of the cabin cruiser itself. This was a big, expensive ship. Obviously there was a small launch used for getting to and from shore. There was money behind this attempted kidnapping. The question was, whose, and what did they stand to profit by it? Canton had no money, at least, not yet. Perhaps he had a trust or a Swiss bank account about which no one knew anything.

Her heart raced madly as she relaxed her arms and wrists. She'd deliberately tensed them while she was being bound, an old trick her karate teacher had taught her. Now the bonds were much looser than they would have been. It would take time and concentration to get them off, but she had a chance. God willing, she'd get free. Then she could worry about how to escape. If the boat was close to shore, she could probably swim it. If there was no riptide, that was. A riptide might carry her miles off course. And if it were possible to swim to shore, why was a launch needed by her captors?

She couldn't waste time worrying about that, she decided. First things first. She'd get loose. Then she'd figure out how to get off the ship.

All she needed now was luck and a little time.

CHAPTER EIGHT

THE ROPES WERE tied securely. After several minutes of twisting and turning and contorting, she couldn't manage to loosen them even enough to get a finger free, much less an entire hand.

It was like one of her books, she thought with dark humor, but by this point, her heroine would be free and giving her captors hell.

Janine hated reality.

There was the sound of the launch returning, and suddenly she knew real fear. The man had a gun. He was impatient, and angry that the kidnapping had gone awry. He might shoot her. It might be the only way for him.

She thought about her parents and Kurt. She thought about Canton. Death had never been a preoccupation of hers, but now she couldn't escape it. She might die here, in her nightgown, without ever having the chance to say goodbye to the people she loved most. And almost that bad was the realization that the sequel to *Catacomb* was barely one third of the way finished. They'd give it to another writer to finish. Oh, the horror of it!

As she gave renewed effort to her attempt to get

away, she heard voices again, and suddenly the door of the cabin opened. The tall man was back, wearing a ski mask and gloves. Obviously he didn't think she'd been conscious enough to recognize him before, so he was disguised. That was hopeful. If he meant to kill her, he wouldn't need a disguise. But there was a pistol in his hand. He moved toward her, noting that she was wide-awake and watching him.

With a rasp in his voice, he ordered her, in thickly accented English, to stand up. He marched her ahead of him to the starboard side of the big cabin cruiser, and prodded her toward the rail.

"Jump," he commanded.

There was no launch below. It looked a frightfully long way to the water, and her hands were still tied.

"I'm not going to jump like this, with my hands tied!" she raged at him.

The gun was prodded firmly into her back. She felt a pressure on her bound wrists, and they were suddenly free, a knife having parted them.

"Get off the boat or die," the voice said harshly. "This is the only chance you'll get."

She didn't wait around to argue. She was a strong swimmer and there was a moon. It wasn't that far to shore. She could see the lights of the beach houses from here. Odd, lights at this hour of the morning...

The pistol punched her spine. She said a quick prayer, stood on the rail with her arms positioned and dived into the water.

It was cooler than she expected, but not so bad once she accustomed herself to the water. She struck out for shore, her heart throbbing as she waited to see if the man would shoot her in the back once she was on her way. If he was willing to kidnap a child, what would stop him from murdering a potential witness? He was wearing a ski mask now, though; he must have thought that she hadn't had a good look at him. She'd never opened her eyes fully just after she'd regained consciousness. That might save her life.

She swam, counting each stroke, not even pausing for breath as she went steadily toward shore.

There was one bad place where she felt the surge of the waves, but she managed to get through it by relaxing her body and letting the waves sweep her on toward the beach.

She was getting tired. The blow to her head, the disorientation, the lack of sleep all combined dangerously to make her vulnerable to the effort she was expending. She rolled onto her back, floating, while above her the moon made a halo through the clouds. It looked unreal, all gossamer. She was trying to recall some lines about moons and silver apples when she heard a splashing sound close by. All at once, an arm snaked around her head, under her jaw, and she cried out.

"I've got you," Canton's deep voice rasped at her ear. "I'm going to tow you to shore. Are you all right?"

"Head hurts," she whispered. "They hit me."

"Good God!" He turned and struck out for the shore. He was a much more powerful swimmer than she was, each stroke more forceful than the last as he made his way through the waves to the shallows where he could finally stand up.

He tugged her along with him, fighting the powerful undertow. When he was through it, he bent and lifted her sopping wet form in the gown and started toward her beach house.

"The lights…are on," she managed to say weakly.

"I heard you yell," he said curtly. "You weren't in your bed or anywhere else. I've been searching for almost an hour. It only just occurred to me that the cabin cruiser was sitting out there anchored. It's gone now, but I've got the police after it. I thought you were on it. I was watching it with binoculars when I saw you come on deck with someone and jump off."

"I didn't jump. He pushed me off," she said. Every step he took jarred her poor head. She touched her temple. "Oh, dear God, I'm so tired of headaches! That animal hit me over the head!"

His arms contracted. He didn't speak, but his silence was eloquent.

"It's a miracle you didn't drown," he said through his teeth. "By God, someone's going to pay for this!"

"They're after Karie," she whispered, clutching at his soaked shirt. "I heard the tall man mention her name. It's the same man, the one who was…following the kids."

His face went even harder. "Marie," he muttered. "I couldn't meet her financial demands, so she's stooped to kidnapping to make me fork out the money she wants. Damn her!"

"She wouldn't hurt Karie," she mumbled.

"Not intentionally. But they hit you thinking you were Karie, didn't they?"

"I'm afraid so."

He muttered something else and carried her up into her darkened beach house.

"Kurt isn't awake?" she asked worriedly.

"No." He went through to her bedroom, stood her by the bed, stripped her quite forcefully and deftly and stuck her under the covers without a word. "Stay right there until I change clothes. I'm taking you in to the hospital."

"But Karie..." she moaned.

"We'll all go. I'll wake Kurt on my way out. No nausea?" he asked, hesitating in the doorway. For the first time, she saw that he had on trousers and a shirt, but no shoes. "No confusion?"

"Not yet..."

"I'll be right back."

She heard him bang on Kurt's door, heard her brother's thready reply. Her head throbbed so that she couldn't think at all. Kurt came into the room, worried and nervous when he saw her white face.

"What happened?" he exclaimed.

"Some men kidnapped me and took me out to a cabin cruiser," she rasped. "Kurt, put that wet gown in the bathtub and get me a nightgown out of my drawer, please."

"Kidnapped you?"

"They thought...I was Karie, you see," she muttered. She held her head. "Boy, am I going to have a headache now."

"How did they get you?" he persisted.

"I went out when I saw moonlight glinting on a gun barrel. I thought they were going to shoot Canton."

"And you rushed in to the rescue." He shook his head. "I wish I could convince you that you aren't Diane Woody," he groaned, "before you die trying to act like her."

"I got the point, just now," she assured him. "The gown?"

"Sure."

He carried the gown off to the bathtub and didn't come back. Canton did, dressed and impatient. "Where are your clothes?" he demanded, and started looking for them before she could answer him. "These will do."

He closed the door, tossed her underwear to her and jerked the covers off. "No time for a bath right now," he said. "You'll have to go as you are. Here." He helped her into her underthings as if he'd done it all his life. He slid a cool cotton sundress over her head, slid sandals onto her bare feet, then picked her up and strode out of the room with her. It was all too quick for her to feel embarrassment, but she was certain that she would, later.

"I want my purse and my makeup," she said weakly.

"You don't need either. I'm not flat broke and you're too sick for makeup."

"I look awful without it," she whispered weakly.

"That's a matter of perspective." He called to

Kurt. The boy had just finished wringing out her gown. He came running, and locked the door behind them before they all went to Canton's waiting rental car. Karie was already in the front seat, wide-awake and concerned when she saw Janine.

"Is she going to be all right?" she asked quickly.

"Of course she is." Canton helped her into the back seat and motioned Kurt in beside her.

He drove like a madman to the hospital, ignoring traffic signs and other motorists. His set expression kept the children from asking any more questions.

He strode right into the emergency room with Janine in his arms and started shooting orders in Spanish right and left the minute he got through the doorway.

In no time at all, Janine was tested for everything from blood loss to concussion and placed in a private room.

"Slight concussion without complications," Canton said a minute later, dropping into a chair beside her bed.

"The kids?" she murmured drowsily.

"Down the hall. They have a guest room."

"What about you?" she persisted.

He took her cool hand in his and leaned back, still holding it. "I'm not leaving you for a second," he murmured, closing his eyes.

She felt warm all over, protected and cherished. Her fingers curled trustingly into his and clung. They must have given her something in that shot, she thought as the world began to recede. She was certainly sleepy.

It was daylight when she woke. Canton was standing by the window, his back to it, staring at her in the bed. Her eyes opened and she looked across at him with slowly returning consciousness.

She felt as if she'd known him all her life. The odd feeling brought a smile to her face.

He didn't return it. His eyes were wary now, watchful. "How are you feeling?" he asked, and even the tone of his voice was different.

"Better. I think," she qualified.

His hands were in his pockets. He didn't move any closer to the bed. His face was drawn, his jaw taut.

While she pondered his sudden change of attitude, the door opened and a nurse came in.

"I'm just going off duty," she said. She had a book under her arm and she approached the bed a little shyly. "I won't bother you right now, I know you're still feeling under the weather. But I bought *Catacomb* as soon as it came out and it's just the most wonderful mystery I've ever read. I recognized you the minute I saw you, even though the photo in the back is pretty vague. I know your real name, you see, as well as your pen name. I have all your books." She moved closer, smiling shyly at Canton. "I was telling Mr. Rourke what a thrill it was to get to see you in person. I don't want to intrude or anything. I just wondered if I left my book, if you'd sign it? I put a slip of paper with my name inside the cover. If you don't mind."

"I don't mind," Janine said with a wan smile. "I'll be glad to."

"Thank you!" The young nurse laid the book on the bedside table, flushing. "It's a pleasure. I mean it. I just think you're wonderful! I hope you get better very soon. Thank you again. I really appreciate it. Gosh, you look just like I pictured you!"

She rushed out the door, going off duty, with stars in her eyes. Janine looked toward the door with painful realization.

"So you know," she said without looking at him.

"You could have told me. You knew I read your books. I had *Catacomb* on the side table at my party."

"I knew. Karie told Kurt that you read my books." She studied her hands. "You'd said that you hated famous women, authoresses and actresses." She shrugged, still not meeting his eyes. "I didn't know how to tell you after that."

He didn't speak. His eyes were stormy.

"Did the nurse tell you?"

"No," he said, surprising her into looking up. "Kurt spilled the beans. He was upset. He said that you got into the worst scrapes because you thought you were your own heroine. I asked what he meant, and Karie said you were acting like Diane Woody." He took a slow breath. "It wasn't much of a jump after that. The nurse had brought your book with her to read on her breaks. She saw you and recognized you at once when they brought you onto her ward."

"A conspiracy."

He laughed without humor. "Of a sort. Fate."

She didn't know what to say. The man who'd taken such exquisite, tender care of her now seemed to want nothing more to do with her. She was sorry that he'd had to find it out the hard way. But they had more immediate problems than her discovered identity.

"What about the men who kidnapped me?" she asked, changing the subject.

"They're being hunted" was all he had to say.

"They weren't after my parents at all," she remarked after a long silence. "But I'm sorry they're trying to take Karie."

"I've put on some extra security."

"Good idea."

He was still glaring in her direction. "Kurt told me what you did."

"I have a bad habit of rushing in headfirst," she said.

"You thought the man had a gun aimed at me," he continued relentlessly.

She cleared her throat. "It looked like it. It was probably a pair of binoculars, but I couldn't be sure."

"So instead of yelling for help, you rushed him. Brilliant!"

She blushed. "You could be dead instead of yelling at me!"

"So could you!" he raged, losing his temper. "Are you a complete loon?"

"Don't you call me names!"

He went toward her and she picked up the nearest thing to hand, a plastic jug full of ice, ready to heave.

He stopped and her hand steadied.

Into the standoff came Kurt and Karie, stopping in the doorway at once when they realized what was going on.

"He's the good guy," Kurt said pointedly.

"That's what you think!" she retorted, wide-eyed and furious.

"Put the jug down," Kurt entreated, moving to her side. "You're in no condition to fight."

He took the jug away from her.

"The voice of reason," she muttered as she gave it to him.

"The still, small voice of reason," he agreed with a grin. "Feeling better?"

"I was," she said darkly, glaring toward Canton.

His expression wasn't readable at all. "I have some things to do," he said. "I'll leave Kurt here with you for the time being."

"When can I go home?" she asked stiffly.

"Later today, if there are no complications."

"I have to have someone translate for me, about insurance and so forth."

"The nurses speak English," he stated. "So do the people in the front office."

"Fine."

He gave her one last, long look and motioned to his daughter. He didn't say goodbye, get well, so long, or anything conventional. He just left with Karie.

"It's my fault," Kurt said miserably. "I spilled the beans."

"It was inevitable that someone would," she reassured him. "No harm done. A millionaire and a writer are a poor combination at best."

"He isn't a millionaire."

"He will be, again. I don't move in those circles. I never did."

"He stayed in here all night," he said.

She shrugged. "He felt responsible for me, I suppose. That was kind of him." She squared her shoulders. "But I can take care of myself now." She glanced at him. "You didn't try to contact Mom and Dad about this?" she asked with concern.

He shook his head. "We thought we'd wait."

"Thank God!" She sat up. Her head still throbbed. She lay back down against the pillow with a rough sigh. "I wonder what he hit me with," she said. "It must have been something heavy."

"The doctor said it was a light concussion and you were lucky. From now on, let the police do hero stuff, okay?"

She chuckled. "I suppose I'd better."

She stayed one more night in the hospital, this time with Kurt for company. The next morning, she did all the necessary paperwork and checked herself out early.

They went back to the beach house in a cab, arriving just as Canton Rourke and his daughter were getting into their rental car.

She paid the cabdriver, being careful not to look at Canton. It did no good. He came storming across the sandy expanse with fierce anger in his lean face.

"Just what the hell are you doing home?" he demanded. "I was on my way to the hospital to get you."

"How was I to know that?" she asked belligerently. She was still pale and wobbly, despite her determination to come home. "You left with no apparent intention of returning. I can take care of myself."

He looked vaguely guilty. His eyes went to Karie. He motioned her back into the house. She waved and obeyed.

"I'll go talk to Karie while you two argue," Kurt said helpfully, grinning irrepressibly as he ambled toward Karie's house.

"Everybody's deserting me," she muttered, turning toward the house, purse in hand. Kurt had asked Canton to bring it to the hospital the morning after Janine had regained consciousness, and he had. The money had been a godsend, because she had to get a cab to the house.

"I wouldn't have, if you'd leveled with me from the beginning. I hate being lied to."

She turned on him. "You have no right to ask questions about me. You're not a member of my family or even a close friend. What makes you think I owe you the story of my life?"

He looked taken aback. His shoulders moved under the thin fabric of his gray jacket. "I don't know. But you do. I want to know everything about you," he said surprisingly.

"Why bother to find out?" she asked. "I'll be gone in less than a month, and we're not likely to run into each other again. I don't move in your circles. I may be slightly famous, but I'm not a millionaire, nor likely to be. I keep to myself. I'm not a social animal."

"I know." He smiled gently. "You don't like crowds, or life in the fast lane. Marie did. She felt dead without noise and parties. She liked to go out, I liked to stay home." He shrugged. "We were exact opposites." His blue eyes narrowed. "On the other hand, you and I have almost too much in common."

"I've already told you, I'm not going to propose to you," she said solemnly. "I like being independent. You need to find a nice, quiet, loving woman to cook you scrambled eggs while you're fighting your way back up the corporate ladder. Someone who likes being yelled at," she added helpfully.

"I didn't yell."

"Yes, you did," she countered.

"If I did, you deserved it," he returned shortly. "Running after armed felons, for God's sake! What were you thinking?"

"That I was going to make a citizen's arrest, for one thing." She searched his lean face. "You say you've read my books. Didn't you read the book jackets?"

"Of course," he muttered.

"Then tell me what I did for a living before I started writing novels."

He had to think for a minute. He frowned. His eyes widened and dilated. "For God's sake! I thought that was hype."

"It was not," she replied. "I was a card-carrying private detective. I'm still licensed to carry a weapon, although I don't, and I haven't forgotten one single thing I know about law enforcement."

"That's how you learned the martial arts."

She nodded. "And how to approach a felon, and how to track a suspect. I was doing just fine until the would-be kidnapper pointed a gun at you and I did something stupid. I rushed right in without thinking."

"And it almost got you killed," he added.

"A miss is as good as a mile. Thank God I have a hard head."

He nodded. He touched her hair gently. "I'm sorry I yelled."

She shrugged.

"I mean it," he stated with a smile.

She sighed. "Okay."

She was a world away from him now. He wasn't sure that he could breach the distance, but he had thought of a way to try. "Are you still a licensed private investigator?"

She nodded.

"Then why don't you come to work for me and help me crack this case?"

She pursed her lips. "I'm on a deadline," she said pointedly.

"You can't work all the time."

She considered it. It was exciting to chase a perpetrator. But more important than the thrill of the chase was to prevent someone from taking Karie away. Just thinking about that blow on the head made her furious. They'd thought she was Karie and they had no qualms about hurting her physically. They needed to be stopped, before they did something to harm the child.

"I'll do it," she said.

He grinned. "I can't pay you just yet. But I'll give you a pocketful of I.O.U.s. I promise they'll be redeemable one day."

She chuckled. "I believe it. Okay. That's a deal, then. But I'll need a couple of days to rest up." She touched the back of her head. "I've still got a huge bump."

"No wonder," he muttered, glowering at her. "You are a nut."

"Hiring me doesn't entitle you to call me names," she declared.

He held up both hands. "Okay, I'll reform."

HE DIDN'T. HE kept muttering all the while several days later while they were lying in wait for the perpetrators to try again, her deadlines forgotten in the excitement of the chase.

"This is so damned boring," he grumbled after they'd been lying behind a sand dune, watching the kids build sand castles for over two hours.

"Welcome to the real live world of detective work," she replied. "You watch too much television."

His head turned and his lips pursed as he studied her. "So do you. Particularly of the science fiction variety."

She glared at him. "That's hitting below the belt."

"Is that any way to talk to a man of my rank and station?" he asked. His lips pursed. "I could have you interrogated, you know," he said in the same mocking tone her favorite series TV character used. He cocked one eyebrow to enhance the effect. "I could do it myself. I have a yen for brunettes."

She cleared her throat. "Stop that."

"Hitting you in your weak spot, hmmm?" he taunted.

"I don't have any weak spots," she replied.

He moved closer, rolling her over onto her back. "That's what you think." He bit off the words against her shocked mouth.

CHAPTER NINE

FOR JUST AN instant she gave in to her longing for him and lay back, floating on waves of pure bliss as his mouth demanded everything she had to give. His lean body fit itself to hers and delicious thrills ran down her spine. She moaned, pulling him closer, the danger forgotten as she gave in to her hunger for him.

But her sense of self-preservation was too well developed not to assert itself eventually. When his thigh began to ease her long legs apart, she stiffened and wriggled away quickly, with a nervous laugh.

"Cut that out," she murmured. "We're on a case here."

He was breathing roughly, his eyes glittery with amusement and something deeper. "Spoilsport," he said huskily. "Besides, you were the one trying to seduce me a few days ago."

She put her hand over her wildly beating heart. "Scout's honor, I won't try it again," she promised.

His eyes narrowed. "I didn't ask for any promises," he said. "Take off that blouse and lie back down here—" he patted the sand beside him "—and let's discuss it."

She shook her head, still smiling. "We have to

catch a kidnapper," she reminded him. "So don't distract me."

"I told you, this is boring," he said. "I'm not used to inactivity."

"Neither am I, but this goes with the job description." She peered up over the dune. The kids were still working on that sand castle, making it more elaborate by the minute. But there was no one in sight, no one at all. The kids had been kept close while Janine got over her concussion and was recovering. Perhaps the kidnappers had given up.

She murmured the thought aloud. Canton lay on his back with his arm shading his eyes from the sun. "Fat chance," he said curtly. "Marie wants her cut of the money and she'll go to any lengths to get it. Karie knows how she is. Poor kid. The last time I went off on business, before the divorce, Marie had one of her lovers upstairs and she was screaming like a banshee with him. When I got home, Karie was sitting on the steps out front in the snow."

She was shocked. "What did you do?"

He sat up, glancing at her. "What would you have done?" he countered.

She shrugged. "I'd have thrown him out the front door as naked as a jaybird and left him to get home the best way he could," she said.

He chuckled. "You and I think alike."

"You didn't!" she exclaimed.

He nodded. "Yes, I did. But I have a more charitable heart than you do. I threw his clothes out after him."

"And your wife?"

"I think she knew it was all over. She packed and left with a few veiled threats, and something to the effect that she needed other men because I couldn't satisfy her in bed."

She rolled over and looked up at him. Men were vulnerable there, in their egos, she thought. His eyes were evading hers, but there was pain in the taut lines of his face.

"They say that—"

He cut her off. "Don't start spouting platitudes, for God's sake," he muttered. "I don't want any reassurances from a woman who's never had a man in the first place."

"I was only going to say that I don't think sex matters much unless people love each other. And if they do, it won't really make any difference how good or bad they are at it."

He shifted, lying on one elbow in the sand. "I wouldn't know. I married Marie because she was outgoing and beautiful, one of the sexiest women I'd ever known. I had money and she wanted it. I thought she wanted me. Life teaches hard lessons. Glitter can blind a man."

"It can blind anyone. I'm sorry it didn't work out for you."

"We had ten years together," he said. "But only the first few months counted. I had my head stuck in computer programs and she was traveling all over the world to every new fashionable resort for the next nine years. Karie had no family life at all."

She made an awkward movement and peered over

the dune. The kids were still fine, and nobody was in sight.

"Karie seems happy with you," she said.

"I think she is. I haven't been much of a father in the past. I'm trying to make up for it." He studied her face and smiled gently. "What about you and Kurt? Do your parents care about you?"

She chuckled. "In their way. They're flighty and unworldly and naive. But we take care of them."

He sighed and shook his head. "Parenting is not for the weakhearted."

"I guess not. But kids are sweet. I've always loved having Kurt around."

He pursed his lips and narrowed his eyes and watched her. "Do you want kids of your own?"

"Yes."

He didn't say anything else. He just went on watching her, looking at her with intent curiosity.

"Is my face on crooked?" she murmured, blushing.

He reached up and touched her cheek, very gently. "It's a sweet face," he said solemnly. "Full of concern and mischief and love. I've never known anyone like you. You aren't at all what I thought successful writers were. You're not conceited or condescending. You don't even act like a successful writer."

"I wouldn't have a clue," she replied. "And I'll tell you something. I know a lot of successful writers. They're all nice people."

"Not all of them."

She shrugged. "There are always one or two bad apples in every bunch. But my friends are nice."

"Do they all write mysteries?"

She shook her head. "Some are romance authors, some write science fiction, some write thrillers. We talk over the internet." She cleared her throat. "Actually a number of us talk about the villain on that science fiction series. We think he's just awesome."

He chuckled. "Lucky for me I look like him, huh?"

She laughed and pushed him. He caught her and rolled over, poised just above her with his face suddenly serious. "That isn't why you're attracted to me, is it?" he asked worriedly.

"I think maybe it was, at first," she admitted.

"And now?"

She bit her lower lip. "Now…"

His thumb moved softly over her mouth, her chin. "Now?"

Her eyes met his and the impact went right through her. Her lips parted. "Oh, glory," she whispered unsteadily.

"Oh, glory," he agreed, bending.

He kissed her in a way he never had before, his mouth barely touching hers, cherishing instead of demanding. His arms were warm but tender, the pressure of his long, powerful body not at all threatening. When he lifted his mouth, hers followed it, her dazed eyes lingering on his lips.

His breathing was as ragged as hers. He touched her face with quiet wonder. It was in his eyes, too, the newness of what he was feeling. He looked odd, hesitant, uncertain.

"I don't have a dime," he said slowly. "Maybe I'll make my fortune back, maybe I won't. You could end up with a computer programmer working for wages."

Her heart jumped. "That sounds like you're talking about something permanent."

He nodded. "Yes."

"You mean…as in living together."

"No."

She blushed. "Sorry, I guess I jumped the gun…"

His fingers pressed against her lips. He struggled for the right words. "It's too soon for big decisions," he said, "but you might start thinking about marriage."

She gasped.

Her reaction hit him right in his pride. Obviously she hadn't even considered a permanent life with him. He cursed and rolled away from her, getting to his feet. He stared out toward the kids, toward the sea, his hands stuck deep in his pockets.

She didn't understand his odd behavior. She got up, too, hesitating.

He glanced at her uneasily. "I'm thirty-eight," he said.

"Yes, I… I know."

"You're twenty-four," he continued. "I suppose your professor is closer to the right age. He's got a degree, too, and he fits in with your family." His eyes went back to the ocean.

She felt a vulnerability in him that made her move closer. "But I don't love him, Canton."

He turned slowly. "I like the way you say my name," he said softly.

She smiled hesitantly. "I like the way you say mine," she replied shyly. Her eyes fell. "Are you sorry you mentioned marriage?"

He moved a step closer. "I thought you were."

Her eyes came up.

"You gasped," he said curtly. "As if it were unthinkable."

"You'd only just said a few days ago that you never wanted to get married again," she explained.

"A man says a lot of things he doesn't mean when a woman's got him tied up in knots," he murmured. "God in heaven, can't you see how it is with me? I want you. But I'm not in your league educational-wise, and I'm flat busted. My wife left me for someone who was better in bed. I'm pushing forty... What are you doing?"

Her hands were busy on the front of his shirt, working at buttons. "Taking your clothes off," she said simply. She looked up with wide green eyes. "Do you mind?"

He didn't seem to be able to speak. His mouth was open.

She pushed the shirt aside, over the expanse of thick hair and hard muscle. He wasn't darkly tanned, but he was sexy. He smelled of spices. She smiled and buried her face in his chest, pressing her lips to it.

He shivered.

She looked up, still caressing him slowly. "You've seen me without any clothes at all, although my head was hurting too much at the time for me to enjoy it. Turnabout is fair play."

"It's a public beach," he noted, barely able to speak.

"You proposed."

"I didn't," he protested huskily. "I said I wanted you to think about it."

Her eyes went back to his chest. He was moving helplessly against the slow caress of her fingers. "I've thought about it."

"And?"

"I like kids." She looked up. "I'd like several. I make a good living writing books. I can take care of the bills until you settle on what you want to do, or while you make your fortune back. I'm good at budgeting, and Karie likes me. I like her, too."

He couldn't get his breath. "You're driving me mad," he said through his teeth.

Her eyebrows lifted. Her eyes darted to the movement of her hands on his bare chest and back up again to his stormy eyes. "With this?" she asked, fascinated.

His chest rose and fell heavily. His hands covered hers and stilled them. "I've been more concerned with a failing empire and my employees' futures lately to pay much attention to women. It's been a long dry spell," he added. "You understand?"

"Sort of."

"I suppose I'm not the only one who spends too much time at the computer," he mused.

She shifted a little. "I've never found men very attractive physically."

"Oh?"

"Well, until now," she amended. Her searching eyes met his. "I used to dream about traveling. Now I have the most embarrassing dreams about you."

He grinned. "Do tell."

"I wouldn't dare."

"If you'll marry me, we can do something about them."

"I have to marry you first?"

He smiled gently. "My mother was Spanish. She raised me very strictly, in an old-world sort of way. I never messed around with virgins. I'm much too old to start now."

"In other words, good girls get married before they get…"

"I'll wash your mouth out with soap if you say it," he promised.

She wrinkled her nose at him. "I'll bet you'd say it."

"And more," he agreed. "I have a nasty temper."

"I noticed."

"So you know the worst already. And since you aren't experienced, and you have no one to compare me with in bed," he added, tongue-in-cheek, "I'll seem worldly and wise to you." He pursed his lips. "Now, that's an encouraging thought."

She looped her arms around his neck. "I love

you," she said softly. "You'll seem like Don Juan to me."

He actually blushed.

"Shouldn't I say that I love you?" she asked.

His arms tightened. "Say it a lot," he instructed. "Karie says it sometimes, but Marie never did. Funny, I never noticed, either." He smiled. "I like the way it sounds."

"You could say it back," she pointed out.

He cleared his throat. "I don't know."

"It's easy." She looked briefly worried. "If you mean it."

"Oh, I mean it, all right," he said, and realized with a start that he did. He hadn't given much thought to the emotional side of his turbulent relationship with her, but the feeling was definitely there. He wanted her, he liked her, he enjoyed being with her. And he most certainly did…love her.

Her eyes had brightened. "You do?"

He nodded. He searched her face quietly. "It's risky, marriage."

"No, it isn't. We'll love each other and take care of Karie, and Kurt when we need to. We'll have kids and love them and I'll never leave you."

His jaw tautened. His arms closed around her bruisingly, and he held her for a long time without speaking. His tall body shuddered as he felt the full impact of commitment.

She closed her eyes and sighed, moving her soft cheek against the thick hair on his chest. "I like hairy men," she whispered. "It's like holding a teddy bear."

He chuckled, his voice deep at her ear. "Thank God. I'd hate to have to shave my chest every day."

Her arms tightened. "When?" she asked dreamily.

He made the transition without trouble. "Whenever you like," he said. "We have to get rings and arrange a ceremony. It should be easy in Mexico." He lifted his head. "I have a town house in Lincoln Park. I've divided my time between Chicago and New York, but I only have an apartment in New York. I'll try to hold on to it. You might want to go shopping in Manhattan from time to time, or visit your publishers."

She grinned. "You're a prince."

"I'm a pauper," he insisted.

She sighed. "That's okay. I like you better poor. You'll always know that I married you for what you didn't have."

He burst out laughing and lifted her high in his arms. "So I will."

The kids, hearing the commotion, came up the beach to see what all the laughter was about.

"We're going to get married," Canton told them, totally forgetting that he'd only asked Janine to think about marriage. He wasn't about to let her get away. He watched his daughter's face, and was relieved when he saw it light up.

"You're going to marry Janine? She'll be my stepmom? Cool!" She rushed up and hugged Janine with all her might. "Oh, Janine, that's just the best present I ever got for my birthday!"

"Today's your birthday?" Janine exclaimed. "I didn't know!"

"I got her a cake and a present. We were going to have you both over tonight to celebrate," Canton explained. He grimaced. "I got so wrapped up in what we were talking about, I forgot to mention it."

"I have a neat video game for you," Janine told the girl. "Set on Mars. It's a mystery."

"Cool! I love space stuff."

"Yes, I noticed," Janine chuckled. She sighed. "I'm going to love having you for a stepdaughter. But let's leave the step off of it, okay?" she added. "How about Mom and daughter?"

"That suits me," Karie said warmly.

"What about me?" Kurt wailed. "Won't I get to stay with you anymore? I'll be stuck with...*them*?" His voice trailed off as he looked past Janine. "What in the world are they doing here?"

Janine turned, and there were her parents, sweaty and stained with dirt, both wearing khakis and wide-brimmed hats, waving from the deck of the beach house.

"Something must have happened," she said. "Come on." She took Canton by the hand and they all went back down the beach, the stakeout for the would-be kidnappers forgotten for the moment.

THE INTRODUCTIONS WERE made quickly. Professors Dan and Joan Curtis were fascinated by Canton Rourke, whom they'd certainly heard of. To learn that he was marrying their daughter caused them both to be momentarily tongue-tied.

"You don't know each other very well," Joan cautioned worriedly.

"We have so much in common that discovering each other will be a lifelong pleasure," Canton said, and won her over on the spot.

She grinned at him, looking just like Janine, with her dark hair and green eyes. Dan was tall and thin with graying hair and blue eyes. He looked older than ever as he sat sprawled in a chair sipping cold bottled water.

In the middle of the living room was a huge crate. Dan nodded toward it. "That's why we're back."

Janine's eyebrows rose. "Something special?"

"A few good pieces," Dan replied. "We've tried to contact our man in the Mexican government, but our satellite link was sabotaged."

"It was what?" Janine exclaimed. "I knew there had been problems, but I hadn't realized the extent."

"We've had a pothunter on our tails," Dan replied. "A very determined one. He shot at us."

Janine sat down, with Canton right behind her, his hand on her shoulder.

"We're all right," Joan said. "But we thought it would be wise to get back to civilization as quickly as possible. We jumped into the Land Rover, with that—" he indicated the crate "—and drove back at top speed. We lost our guide on the way. He was behind us in his truck, but we didn't see him again. We phoned the police the minute we got in. They should be along momentarily."

"If there's anything I can do, I'll be glad to help," Canton volunteered.

"He got us in touch with you," Janine added helpfully. "He knows the president of the country personally."

The Curtises were impressed. They both stared at Canton with renewed interest.

"Would the pothunters try anything here in Cancún?" Janine asked worriedly.

"For what's in that box, they would," Dan said mournfully. "In a way, I'm sorry we found such a brilliant site. We've mapped everything, taken photos, documented every step of the excavation so that nothing was overlooked. That will help future expeditions in their excavations."

"Won't the government send someone to take possession of these pieces?" Janine asked.

"Certainly," Joan replied with a smile. "It's just a matter of getting them down here. And keeping the pothunters away until they can."

Dan Curtis took a pistol from his pocket and put it on the table. "This business is getting to be very dangerous."

"Archaeology always was," Janine said pointedly. "Even in the early days. But it's worthwhile."

"We always thought so, didn't we, dear?" Joan asked her husband, with a loving hand on his shoulder.

His hand went up to take hers. "We still do. But we're getting old for this."

Dan stared at the crate again. "I hope that isn't going to get any of us hurt. We almost checked into a hotel instead of coming here, but this seemed wiser."

"It is," Canton said firmly. "I've got a man watching my beach house. He can get another man to help him and watch this one, too."

Joan frowned. "Why do you have someone watching it?"

"Because my mom tried to have me kidnapped," Karie explained. "Janine got kidnapped instead and hit on the head and was in the hospital…"

"What?" Joan and Dan exclaimed together.

"I'm fine," Janine said gently, holding up a hand. "I haven't forgotten any of my training."

"You and detective work," Joan moaned. "Darling, archaeology would have been so much safer!"

"Ha! You're the ones who got shot at, remember?" Janine replied. "Anyway, we saved Karie from kidnappers, but we're not sure that they've given up. It's been sort of hectic around here for the past week."

"And here we come with more trouble," Dan groaned.

Janine patted him on the shoulder. "It's okay, Dad. There are enough of us to guard the crate and Karie. We'll be fine."

"Of course we will," Canton agreed.

Dan and Joan exchanged wan smiles, but they didn't look convinced.

"Just out of idle curiosity, what have you got in the box?" Janine asked.

"Several Mayan funerary statues, some pottery,

a few tablets with glyphs on them and some gold jewelry with precious stones inlaid. Oh, and a jeweled funeral mask."

Janine's eyes widened. "A king's ransom," she said.

"And all the property of the Mexican government, as soon as we can turn it over," Dan added. "We're hoping to keep at least one or two of the pots for our own collection at the university, but that's up to the powers-that-be."

"Considering what you've gone through to get it, I imagine they won't begrudge you a piece or two," Canton said. He moved forward. "It's been nice to meet you. I have to get Karie home and make a couple of business calls. We'll see you later."

"I'll walk out with you," Janine said after the Curtises had made their goodbyes.

Karie went ahead of them. Canton slid his arm around Janine's shoulders and held her close. "Complications," he murmured.

"More and more. Maybe the kidnappers will back off, with so many people around."

"Maybe they'll join forces with the pothunters," he murmured.

She poked him in the side with her elbow. "Stop being pessimistic. This is all going to work out. It has to, and soon. I want to get married."

"What a coincidence, so do I!" he murmured facetiously.

She laughed, turning her face up to his. "The sooner the better," she added.

He nodded. "The sooner, the better." He bent and kissed her gently. "Go home."

"Be careful."

"You, too. I'll phone you later. Lock your doors. I'm going to make a few telephone calls and see what I can do to help things along."

"Have your ex-wife arrested," she suggested.

"Nice sentiment, but not practical." He chuckled. "All the same, there may be some way to discourage her. I'll find one." He winked. "Stay out of trouble."

"You do the same."

CHAPTER TEN

"I CAN'T BELIEVE THIS," Joan Curtis said heavily. "My daughter is marrying Mr. Software. Do you have any idea how famous he is, how much money he's made in his life?"

"He's broke right now," Janine stated.

"He'll never be broke, not with a mind like his," Dan said with a grin. "He's one smart guy. He'll make it all back, with interest."

"Even if he doesn't, it won't matter. I'm crazy about him," Janine confessed.

"It seems to be mutual. And here I thought you were going to wait around forever for Quentin to propose," Joan teased. "I'm glad that never happened, Janine," she added. "Quentin was never the man for you."

"I know that, now. I just drifted along until I met Canton."

"Listen," Joan called suddenly, her eyes on the television. "They're tracking a hurricane. They say it's coming this way!"

"A hurricane?" Dan groaned. "Just what we need!" He glanced at his daughter. "You didn't mention this."

"I didn't know," she said. "I don't speak Spanish!"

"It's in English now," Joan observed.

Janine looked sheepish. "Well, I've been rather out of things for several days, and I haven't been watching television."

"No wonder," Dan mused.

"You must have noticed the wind picking up, and the clouds," Joan said, sighing. "They've just said that they may have to evacuate the coast if it comes any closer. And it looks as if it's going to."

"I had hoped to get a plane back to the States," Dan said, glancing worriedly at the crate. "Now what do we do?"

"We go further inland," Janine said at once. "Canton has a rental car. We need a van, so that we can take your cargo with us."

"With pothunters and potential kidnappers two steps behind." Dan Curtis sighed. "Remember the old days in graduate school, when the most dangerous thing we did was set off a cherry bomb in the dean's car?"

"You what?" Janine exclaimed, grinning.

Dan grinned and exchanged a look with his wife. "We weren't always old," he murmured.

"No time for reminiscing," Joan said, and she was picking up things as she went. "Get cracking. We have to pack up and get out of here, quick."

Before she had a case packed, Canton and the kids were back.

"Hurricane Opal is headed our way," he began, noticing the disorder in the living room.

"We know," Janine said. "We're packing up to go inland. We need to rent a van."

"Leave that to me. There's safety in numbers. We'll go together. I have a friend who owns an estate halfway between here and Chichén Itzá. He'll be able to have us stay. And he has armed security," he added with a chuckle.

"Armed security?" Janine was intrigued.

"He was a mercenary in his younger days. Now he's a married man with two kids. They moved down here from Chicago because of the tough winters. Not much snow in Quintana Roo," he added merrily.

"What interesting people you know, Mr. Rourke," Dan remarked.

"Call me Canton. Yes, I do have some unique acquaintances. I'll see about that van. Karie, you stay here with Kurt and Janine."

"Oh, Dad, does he have a TV?" she asked worriedly. "I have to watch the Braves game. It's the playoffs!"

"They're never going to win the series," he began.

She stuck out her lower lip. "Yes, they are! I believe in them!"

He just shook his head.

TWO HOURS LATER, they were fighting headwinds and rain as they plowed down the long narrow paved road toward the estate of Canton's friends.

The jungle was on either side of them. They saw small *pueblos* nestled among the trees, many with satellite dishes and electricity. Advertising signs were nailed to trees and even the sides of small wooden buildings here and there. There were huge speedbreakers at the beginning and end of each little town they passed.

Down the dusty streets, children played in the rain and dogs barked playfully. As they went past the small, neat houses, they could see hammocks nestled against the walls, ready to be slung again each night. The floors of the whitewashed houses, though earthen, were unlittered and smooth. Tiny stores sat among unfamiliar trees, and in several places, religious shrines were placed just off the road.

Two tour buses went by them. The buses were probably bound for ancient Mayan cities like Chichén Itzá. Janine and Kurt had been on one during their first week in Cancún. The large vehicles were surprisingly comfortable, and the tour guides were walking encyclopedias of facts about present and past in the Yucatán.

"You're very quiet," Joan remarked from the front seat of the van. "Would you rather have gone with the Rourkes?"

"They've got Kurt," she said. "I thought I might need to stay with you."

Dan chuckled. "Protecting us, is that it?"

She only smiled. "Well, neither of you know any martial arts."

"That's true, darling." Joan touched her hand gently. "Whatever would we do without you?"

"I have no idea," Janine said dryly, and meant it, although they didn't suspect that.

THE ESTATE OF Canton's friend had two men with rifles at the black wrought-iron gates. Whatever Canton said to them produced big smiles. The gate opened, and Canton's arm out the window motioned the van to follow.

The house had arches. It was snowy white with a red tile roof, and blooming flowers everywhere. It looked Spanish, and right at home in the jungle.

As they reached the front porch, wide and elegant with a few chairs scattered about and a huge hammock, the front door opened and two people came out.

The man was tall, very elegant. He had a mustache. The woman was smaller, with long blond hair and a baby in her arms. A little boy of about nine came out the door behind them.

When the vehicles stopped, the Curtises got out and joined the Rourkes and Kurt.

The man came forward. "You made good time," he told Canton, and they shook hands warmly. "These are the Curtises of whom you spoke? *Bienvenidos a mi casa*," he said. "Welcome to my home. I am Diego Laremos. This is my wife, Melissa, our son Matt, and our baby daughter, Carmina." He turned and spoke softly to the blond woman. "*Enamorada*, this is Canton Rourke, of whom you have heard me speak."

"I'm delighted to meet you," the woman spoke with a smile and a faint British accent. "Diego and I are happy to have you stay with us. Believe me, you're all quite safe here."

"Many thanks for putting us up," Dan Curtis said, extending a hand. "We have some priceless things that pothunters have been trying their best to steal. We had hoped to fly to the States today, but they were evacuating Cancún."

"So Canton told me," Diego replied solemnly. "Pothunters are ever a problem. So it was in Guatemala, where Melissa and I lived."

"We tried to live in Chicago, but the winters were too harsh," Melissa said with a rueful smile. "We were nervous about taking Matt to Guatemala, so we eventually moved here. Isn't it beautiful?"

"Absolutely," Janine said. "It must be wonderful to live year-round in such a paradise."

Canton put an arm around her. "Think so?" he asked gently. "Then I'll see about buying some land nearby, if you like it."

"Could we?" Janine exclaimed. "How wonderful. We could visit Melissa."

Melissa beamed. "Yes, you could. I have all your books," she added sheepishly.

"Now that really makes me feel welcome. May I hold him?" she asked, moving toward the baby with bright, intrigued eyes.

"Her." Melissa corrected her with a chuckle. "Indeed you may." Melissa handed the baby over, and Janine cradled her warmly, her whole face radiant as the tiny little girl looked at her with dark blue eyes and began to coo.

"Oh, what a darling!" she exclaimed, breathless.

Canton, watching her, had an incredible mental

picture of how Janine would look holding their own baby, and he caught his breath.

She looked up, into his eyes, smiling shyly. "Can we have several of these?"

"As many as you like," he replied huskily.

"I'll take you up on that," she promised.

The Laremoses were the most interesting people Janine had met, and she'd met a lot. Diego had two other ex-mercenary friends in Chicago, one who'd practiced law there for years and was now an appellate court judge, and another who ran a top secret security school of some sort. Both were married and had families.

"There's another member of the old group in Texas," he added. "He's married, too, and they have a ranch. And then there's one who lives in Montana. He got fed up with the city and took his wife and kids out there. They have a ranch, too. We have reunions every year, but with all the kids involved, we have to have them in the summer."

"They're a unique bunch," Canton said musingly. "And all ex-mercenaries. I'm amazed that you all lived to marry and have families in the first place."

Laremos leaned forward. "So were we."

Canton smiled at Janine over the huge dinner table, where they were eating salads and drinking fine, rich coffee. "I met this bunch at a time in my life when I was having some extreme problems with a small hardware enterprise I'd set up in a Third World country. Mine was ecologically friendly, but there was a rival company tearing up the rain forest and killing off the natives. When the government said that it didn't have the money or manpower to do anything about the situation, I sent Laremos and his group over and they arranged a few unpleasant, but nonlethal, surprises for them. They packed up and left."

"Good for you," Janine said with admiration.

"We also set up a trust and bought land for the tribe, which is theirs forever. I don't like profit with a bedrock of destruction," Canton said simply. "I never did."

"I hope you get it all back, *amigo*," Laremos said sincerely. "We need more industrialists like you, men who balance profit with compassion for the environment."

"Profit is the last thing on my mind right now," Canton said, leaning back. "I hope that we can discourage the people who are after us. I think we were followed coming down here."

"No doubt you were. But," Laremos said with a grin, "your pursuers are in for a great surprise if they attempt to come here. My men are dedicated and antisocial. And armed."

"We noticed," Janine said. Her eyes twinkled. "I'm already getting ideas for another book."

"Are you going to put us in it?" Melissa asked, bright-eyed. "I want to be a blond, sexy siren who entices this big, strong man and makes him wild."

"You do that every day of my life, *enamorada*," Diego said, bringing her soft hand to his mouth. "No need to tell the world about it."

She only smiled. A look passed between them that made Janine smile, too. It must be wonderful to be married so long, and still be in love. Her gaze went to Canton, and found him watching her.

He didn't say a word. But his eyes told her that she and he would be that happy, for that long. In fact, his smile promised it.

THEY HAD TO stay for two days at the estate before the storm was on its way. Before it finally became disorganized, it left major damage along its path.

There had been no sign of the would-be kidnappers or the pothunters, but when the Curtises and the Rourkes left the elegant Laremos estate, it was to find themselves once again being trailed. And this time, there were two vehicles in pursuit and they didn't bother to hang back.

The Rourke car and the van in which the Curtises were riding raced past small villages, only slowing for the speedbreakers. Still the two cars gained on them. They came to a crossroads, and Canton suddenly motioned to Dan Curtis to follow him. He took the right fork at speed and then suddenly whipped the car off onto a little dirt trail into some trees, motioning out the window for Dan to follow.

The tree cover was thick and the rain had removed the problem of telltale dust rising to give away their positions.

He cut off his engine. Dan did likewise. Then they sat and waited. Only seconds later, the two pursuing cars slowed, stopped, looked around. They pulled up beside each other on the narrow little paved road and spoke rapidly, after which each car took a fork and raced away.

Canton reversed the car until it was even with the van. "We can return to the last village and cut through there back to the Cancún road. Don't lose your nerve."

"Not me," Dan said with a grin. "Lead on."

"Are you okay?" he asked Janine, who was once again with her parents.

She nodded. "I'm fine. Take care of Kurt and Karie."

"You know I will."

He waved and raced away, with the van right behind. They managed to get enough of a head start to lose the pursuing vehicles, but they were not out of danger. The occupants of the car would soon realize that they'd been outfoxed and turn around.

By the time the pursuers got back into the village, though, the people they were chasing were long gone. Of course, there was only one road, and they'd surely know to backtrack on it. But at the last *pueblo* there had been a turnoff to Cancún that had two forks. One of them led north, the other east. The pursuers would be obliged to split up. And even if one car took the right fork, there wouldn't be any way they could catch up in time. Janine thought admiringly that her future husband would make a dandy detective.

THEY ARRIVED IN Cancún after dark and checked into a hotel, having decided that the beach house would be much too dangerous. They unloaded the car and the van, which were then returned to the rental agencies and another, different van was rented from still another agency. Janine thought it might be possible to throw the pursuers off the track this way.

And it might have been; except that the would-be kidnappers spotted Canton with Janine at the car rental lot and immediately realized what was going on. They didn't follow the van back to the hotel. One of the local men had a cousin who was friendly with an employee at the car rental agency. All she had to do was flirt a little with the agent. Within an hour, they knew not only which hotel, but which rooms, contained their prey.

To make matters worse, the pothunter, also a local man, had family connections to one of the people who were after Karie. They decided to pool their resources and split the profits.

With no suspicion of all this, Canton and Janine and the others settled into adjoining rooms of the hotel while they waited to get on the next flight to Chicago. Karie had discovered that there was no way she was going to get any telecast of a Braves game now, with communications affected by the hurricane. Power lines and communications cables had been downed and service was interrupted. As she told her dad, they might not have a tropical beach in Chicago, but they did have cable.

The Curtises were ready to go home as well. Their weeks of grubbing in the outer reaches of Quintana Roo had paid great dividends. They not only had plenty to show the Mexican government, but they also had enough research material for a book and several years of lectures.

A representative of the government was going to meet them early in the morning in the hotel and go over the crated artifacts with them.

Little did they know, however, that the representative had been waylaid and replaced by a henchman of the pothunters'...

"IT'S GOING TO be a great relief to have these treasures off our hands," Dan Curtis remarked over dinner that evening. "Not that I'm sorry we found them, but they're quite a responsibility."

"Did you know that in the early part of this century, archaeologists went to Chichén Itzá to look for artifacts and were murdered there?" Joan added.

"I was watching a program on that on the Discovery Channel," Janine remarked. "It was really interesting. After the first archaeologists went there, the Peabody Museum of Harvard had an agent in Mexico gathering material for them in the early part of the century. It's in drawers in the museum and isn't on display to the public. But it belongs to Mexico. So why doesn't the Mexican government ask them to give it back? In fact, there are human skeletal remains in that collection as well, aren't there? Certainly with all the new laws governing such remains, they should be reinterred, shouldn't they?"

"Those laws don't apply universally," Dan Curtis ventured. "And there probably would be something like a grandfather clause even if they did. That particular collection dates to the time before the Mexican Revolution, long before there were such laws." He smiled gently. "It's more complicated than it seems to a lay person. But believe me, archaeology has come a long way in the past few decades."

"Just the same, it's a pity, isn't it?" Janine added. "I mean, nobody gets to see the exquisite Maya artwork in the collection, least of all the descendants of the Mayan people in Quintana Roo."

"But they're also preserved for future generations," Dan explained. "Artifacts left in situ are very often looted and sold on the black market, ending up with collectors who don't dare show them to anyone." He smiled at his daughter. "I know it's not a perfect system," he mused, "but right now, it's the best we can do."

"Yes, I know. There are two sides to every story. You both take your work seriously. And you do it very well," Janine said with a smile, because she was proud of her parents. They cared about their work. They were never slipshod in their excavations or disrespectful of the human skeletal remains they frequently unearthed.

"I do wish we'd had a little more time," Dan said ruefully. "I think we were onto something. We found an unusual ceremonial site, unlike anything we've discovered before. We were just beginning to unearth it when the trouble started."

"A superstitious mind would immediately think of curses," Janine said wickedly.

Dan chuckled, winking at his wife. "Trust a writer to come up with something like that. No, there's no curse, just bad luck. Señor Perez has been following us ever since we got off the plane. He tried bribery at first, and when that didn't work he began making veiled threats about intervention by the Mexican government. We had all the necessary permits and permissions, so the threats didn't work, either. Then he set up camp nearby and began harassing us."

"Harassing? How?" Janine asked, noting that Canton was listening attentively.

"Sudden noises in the middle of the night. Missing supplies. Stolen tools. There wasn't anything we could specifically charge him with. We couldn't even prove he was at the site, although we knew it was him." Dan shook his head. "Finally it was too much for us, especially after we lost the satellite link. We took what we had and left."

"But what about the site now?" Canton asked somberly. "Won't he loot it?"

"He thinks we have everything that was there, that's the funny part," Joan said. "We were so cautious about the newest find that we didn't even let the workers near it. We concealed it and marked the location on our personal maps. We'll make sure those get into the right hands. Meanwhile," she added heavily, "we've got to get the artifacts we recovered into the right hands, before Señor Perez can trace us here and do something drastic."

"Would he?" Janine asked worriedly.

Dan nodded. "An expedition lost a member along

with some priceless gold and jeweled artifacts some years ago. Perez was implicated but there wasn't enough evidence for him to be prosecuted. He always hires henchmen to do his dirty work."

Janine felt chilled. She wrapped her arms around herself, glad that Kurt and Karie were on the patio and not listening to this.

"I have my man and another watching the hotel," Canton said. "We'll be safe enough here until we can get a plane out."

Karie and Kurt had left the balcony and had gone into Kurt's room. They came out with a rather large bag.

"Could we go down to the beach for just a minute?" Karie asked, with her camera slung around her neck. "We want to snap some photographs."

"I don't think that's a good idea," Canton said.

"Aw, please, Dad," Karie moaned. "It's safe here, you said so. There are people looking out for us. Mom won't try again."

Karie took off her Atlanta Braves baseball cap and wiped her sweaty blond hair. "Please?"

They looked desperate. It was hard for kids to be cooped up all day.

"All right. Let me make a phone call first," Canton said. "And make sure Kurt's parents don't mind."

"It's okay, if they'll be watched," Dan agreed.

They exchanged conspiratorial glances. "Thanks, Dad!" Karie said enthusiastically.

Canton made his phone call. The kids took their

bag and went down the steps to the ground floor, and out toward the white beach.

"Stay out of the ocean!" Canton called after them.

"Sure, Dad!" Karie agreed.

"What have they got in that bag?" Janine asked curiously.

"They're probably going to collect seashells in it," Canton murmured, sliding an arm around her. He smiled. "Don't worry. I'll make sure they don't bring anything alive back with them."

Janine shuddered delicately. "You're sure your man will watch them?"

He nodded. "He's one of the best in the business. When he isn't working for me, he works for the federal government."

"Oh? As what?"

He chuckled. "I don't know. He says it's classified. He travels a lot." He glanced down at her and smiled. "But he's good. Very good. The kids will be safe."

"Okay."

KURT GLANCED OVER his shoulder as he and Karie rushed down to the sand near the water. "Whew," he said, wiping his brow. "I never thought they'd let us out of the room! And we've gone to all this trouble to get things together, too!"

"I know," Karie said, equally relieved. "And they didn't even ask about the bag, thank goodness."

"We'd better get busy," he said. "We don't have much time."

"Stupid kidnappers and pothunters," she muttered as she unzipped the bag. "They sure know how to make life hard on enterprising preteens, don't they?"

CHAPTER ELEVEN

THE KIDS PLAYED on the beach. Dan and Joan Curtis rummaged through their crate of artifacts, double-checking everything in preparation for the arrival of the government antiquities representative.

Meanwhile, Canton and Janine sat on the balcony, holding hands. They were too nervous to let Kurt and Karie completely out of sight.

"What are they doing?" Janine asked, frowning as she watched the bag being slowly unpacked.

"Maybe they've got some cups and glasses to use in sand castle sculpting," he suggested. "Karie always empties the china cupboard when she's planning one."

"Could be," she murmured. But that didn't look like cups and glasses. It looked like pieces of hose, a cow skull, some pieces of rubber, a bag of feathers, several small balloons and a little fur. "Look at all that stuff," she exclaimed. "Could they be making a sand castle with it?"

He let go of her hand and moved closer to the balcony. His eyebrows lifted. "Strange sort of a sand castle…"

The sudden shrill of the telephone caught their attention. Inside the room, Dan Curtis picked up the receiver and began conversing with someone.

"Yes, I could," Dan said slowly, and Janine knew from the past that he was deliberating when he spoke like that. "But why?"

There was a pause.

"I see. But it's a lot of work to pack it all up again," Dan explained. "Why can't you come to the hotel?"

Canton, interested now, got up and went into the room. "Who is it?" he mouthed at Dan.

Dan put his hand over the receiver. "The man from the ministry of antiquities."

"What's his name?" he asked shortly.

"What's your name?" Dan asked the man.

"Carlos Ramirez" came the reply.

Dan relayed it to Canton.

Canton nodded. His eyes narrowed. "Now ask him how Lupe likes her eggs cooked."

It was an odd request, but Dan passed it on. Seconds passed and suddenly the connection was cut.

"Ha!" Canton burst out with a satisfied smile.

"You sound just like him," Janine sighed dreamily.

He scowled. "Just like whom?"

She flushed. "Never mind."

Canton threw up his hands. "I am not an alien," he said. "Neither am I an actor!"

"Sorry," she said, wincing.

He glared at her. "Later, we have to talk." He turned back to Dan. "What did he want you to do?"

"He wanted me to crate up all the artifacts and

drive them into town, to a government warehouse, he said."

"More likely into a trap," Canton replied angrily. "They must realize that we have this place staked out. They tried to trick you. It didn't work. They won't stop there."

"What will they do now?" Joan asked worriedly.

"I don't know" came the quiet reply. "But the first step would be to put a call through to the real minister of antiquities," he added. "And I can do that for you, right now."

He picked up the telephone and made a long-distance call to Mexico City and asked for the official by name when he was connected with the governmental offices.

There was a greeting and a rapid-fire exchange of greetings and questions. Janine heard the name Lupe mentioned.

"Lupe is the minister's wife," Joan translated. She chuckled as she listened to the conversation. "And she doesn't eat eggs—she's allergic to them."

Another question and a pause and still another, then a quick thank you and Canton hung up.

"He's sending some men right down," Canton said. "And they'll not only have proper identification, they'll have guns. If the pothunter has tapped into this telephone line, he got an earful."

Janine listened interestedly, and then suddenly realized that they'd left Karie and Kurt on the beach and weren't watching them.

She turned and ran out onto the balcony, scanned

the beach, and her heart stopped. The kids were no-where in sight. There was a long, odd mound of sand where they'd been, but no kids.

"They're gone!" she cried.

Canton and Dan were halfway out the door before she finished, leaving her to follow and Joan to stay behind and watch the crate.

They took the stairs to the ground floor instead of the elevator and ran toward the beach, automatically splitting up as they reached the back of the hotel. Dan went one way, Canton and Janine the other.

A loud cry alerted them. It came from the shad-owy confines of the unoccupied wooden scuba rental station.

Two men had Karie and Kurt and two others were rushing toward them. One had a gun.

"Oh, my God, it's him!" Janine blurted out when she got a good look at the man with the gun. "It's the kidnapper and his cohorts!"

"That's Perez, the pothunter, who has Kurt," Dan Curtis said furiously. "For God's sake, they've joined forces," he groaned. His voice carried as he glared toward them. "Let go of those kids, you slimy cow-ards!" he raged at the men.

The two men holding Karie and Kurt moved out into the sunlight, the man with the exposed pistol by their side. Janine sank a little lower into the sand, thinking. She didn't dare rush the man with the gun, but if there was any opening at all she was going to take it.

"Don't," Canton said under his breath as he saw her tense and sensed what she was thinking. "For

God's sake, you have to trust me, this once. I have an ace in the hole. Give me a chance to play it!"

Dan, standing beside his daughter, didn't understand. Neither did Janine. But Canton's deep voice held such conviction, such certainty, that they hesitated. He wouldn't risk Karie. He must have a trade in mind, a bargain of some sort. Wheeling and dealing was his stock in trade. If there was an angle, he'd know it.

Janine waited with bated breath, hardly daring to look at the frightened faces of the children as they were held securely by the two men.

"We want the Mayan treasure, Señor Curtis," the man, Perez, demanded. "We want it now. If you give it to us, we will let the children go. Otherwise, we will take them with us until you comply with our…request."

"Joined forces, have you?" Canton drawled. "How convenient."

"There is an advantage in superior numbers," Perez said smoothly. "I required assistance and these men only want to be paid off. They have no further wish to work for Señor Rourke's former wife, who has not even paid them for their services to date."

"Typical of Marie," Canton replied. "They should have known better. And so should you. You crossed the line this time. And you'll pay with a very long prison sentence."

"We have the gun, *señor*," Perez said with a mocking smile.

"Do you really?" Canton nodded toward the familiar, tall man with the gun, who turned with an action so smooth and quick that Janine barely saw him move as he freed Karie and Kurt from the grasps of their captors, leaving both men groaning and shivering on the sand. Perez backed away with his hands in a supplicating position. The gun was trained on him now, and the attacker hardly looked mussed.

Janine's gasp was audible as Dan held out his arms to Kurt and Canton did the same to a frightened, weeping Karie.

"For scaring the children so, I really should finish them off," the tall man said without expression as he looked from Perez to the still writhing men on the ground. The pistol hadn't wavered once. Perez swallowed audibly.

"It is a misunderstanding," he faltered.

"Yours," the man agreed. His eyes cut back to Canton. "Well?"

"The Mexican authorities can deal with them," Canton said coldly. "And the more harshly, the better. Kidnapping is a cowardly act. If he'd hurt my daughter, I'd have killed him."

"I was close by," the man replied. "And so was my colleague." He waved to a man down the beach, who turned and went away. "There was never a minute when the children were in any real danger, I assure you." His black eyes slid over Perez's pale face. "I could have dropped him at any time."

"I think he realizes that. Thanks for your help, Rodrigo."

He shrugged. "*De nada.* I owed you a favor." He nodded, motioning for Perez and the other two men, who were on their feet if shaken, to go ahead of him.

"But he pushed me off the boat," Janine said insistently. "Didn't you hear what I told you about him?"

"He infiltrated the kidnapping gang," Canton told her. "I didn't dare tell you who he was. One slip could have cost him his life. Not that he's ever been shy about risking it for a good cause," he added. He looked down at Karie. "Are you okay, pumpkin?"

"Yes, Dad. *Wasn't it exciting?*" she burst out.

"It sure was! He had a gun, too! Where's Mom?" Kurt added, looking around. "I've got to go tell her!"

"Make her sit down first," Dan called.

Karie took off with him, and Janine wondered all over again at the resilience of the very young. She just shook her head.

"No wonder he was always hanging around," she said. "I should have my detective's license pulled for being so blind."

"He's good at his job."

"Tell me about it." She glanced at him. "Is he CIA?"

He smiled. "I don't know. I told you, I've never been clear about the agency he works for. When I knew him, he, like Laremos and the others, was a mercenary. He was with them in Africa."

She pursed her lips. "A book is forming in my mind..." she began.

"Have Señor Perez eaten by giant alligators," Dan suggested to her. "On second thought, quicksand is a nice touch."

"Prison sounds much better, don't you think?" she countered. "Don't worry, I'll take care of that little detail." She looked up at Canton. "Will she try again?" she asked worriedly.

"Who, Marie?" He shrugged. "I doubt it. She's basically lazy, and when she realizes that she may be implicated in the gutter press in an international kidnapping story, that will probably be enough to stifle any future ambitions. She'll have to wait for her alimony."

"How can she get alimony when she's remarried?" Janine wanted to know.

"She calls it child support."

"You have the child," she said pointedly.

He chuckled. "True."

"You need a good attorney."

"I suppose so." He caught her hand warmly in his. "And a minister."

She smiled gently. "Oh, yes. And a minister."

Dan slipped away while they were staring at each other, thinking privately that they were going to be a good match. Canton and Janine had a lot in common, not the least of which was their penchant for surprises. He was overwhelmed that the pothunter was finally going to be out of circulation.

He went back into the hotel room to find a pale Joan being regaled with gory summations of the incident by the two children.

"Don't believe anything they told you," Dan told her comfortingly. "It's all lies."

"Aw, Dad," Kurt groaned. "We were building her up."

"Let her down," he suggested. "It's all over now."

"Or it will be," Joan said, sighing, "when the government official gets here to take the artifacts back to Mexico City."

"The guy that Janine attacked was a spy, and he was working for Karie's dad," Kurt told his mother. "You should have seen him deck those guys. Gosh, it was like watching that spy movie we just saw—"

"Except that it was real," Karie added. She glanced at her watch. "The game's already started," she groaned. "I won't even get to see if my team makes it to the World Series!"

"The airport will be back on schedule by tomorrow, I'm sure, and we can all go home," Dan Curtis said with relief. "I can't say I'll be sorry, this time."

"Nor I," Joan agreed. She hugged Kurt. "One way or another, it's been a hard few weeks. Where are the other two?" she asked suddenly, looking around.

"Down on the beach staring at each other."

"They'll get over that in about thirty years," Dan mused.

Joan grinned at him. "Think so? Then we have ten to go."

"At least."

CANTON WAS WALKING back toward the hotel with Janine's hand in his, but he looked preoccupied and aloof. She knew that something was worrying him, but she didn't know what.

"Are you absolutely sure that it isn't my resemblance to your science fiction hero that made you agree to marry me?" he asked.

So that was it. She was relieved. Her fingers curled into his big ones. "Yes, I'm sure," she told him. "I've already said so."

"So you have. But you keep coming up with these little comparisons. It's worrying."

"I'm sorry," she said genuinely, stopping to look up at him. "I won't do it again."

He sighed, searching her eyes quietly. "I've been thinking about getting married."

She could see it coming, as if she sensed a hesitation in him. "You don't want to?"

His eyes were troubled. "I want to. But not yet."

Her heart felt as if it were breaking. She smiled in spite of it. "Okay."

"Just like that?"

"Never let it be said that I trapped a man into marriage," she said airily, turning her pained eyes away, so that he couldn't see them. "I've got a deadline that I have to meet right now, so it would be more convenient for me, too, if we put our plans on the back burner and let them simmer for a while."

He shoved his hands into his pockets. "Then let's do that. I'll give you a call in a month or so and we'll see where we stand."

"Fine," she agreed.

They parted company at the front door, all the excitement over for the moment. Janine put on a brave face for her family all evening and then cried herself to sleep. The one kind thing was that nobody had asked any questions. She couldn't know that her pinched, white face told them all they needed to

know. The next day, the government official arrived
and took charge of the artifacts. Shortly thereafter,
the Curtises boarded a plane for Indiana and Janine
flew to Chicago. Canton and Karie had elected to
stay another few days in Cancún, so they'd said their
goodbyes at the beach house. It had wounded Janine
that Canton didn't even shake hands. He smiled very
pleasantly and wished them a good trip home, prom-
ising to be in touch. And that was it.

IT TURNED OUT not to be one month, but two, before
she heard from Canton again. In that length of time,
the Atlanta Braves won the World Series in an incredible game that went all the way to the eighth in-
ning with no score until a home run by the Braves
ended the deadlock. The other team couldn't catch
up, although they tried valiantly. Kurt had a call from
an almost hysterically happy Karie, who sent him
a Braves cap and a World Series victory T-shirt by
overnight mail. From Canton, there was no word.
Even Karie didn't mention him in her telephone call.
Apparently her mother had stopped pursuing either
her or her father, and that was good news.

Janine, meanwhile, finished her book and started
on a new one, set in Cancún. She went back to watching her favorite television program, groaning at the
continued absence of her alien villain until news of
his reappearance surfaced through the Internet fan
club to give her a reason for celebration. She watched
him in one rerun and on tape, and it occurred to her
that even though he resembled Canton, the resem-

blance wasn't strong enough to account for her ongoing attraction to the missing tycoon. She wondered what he was doing and where he was. His movements lately seemed a mystery to everyone, including the media, which was now joyfully following him again.

The only tidbit of news came through a tabloid, which pictured him with a ravishing brunette at some elegant party. She was looking up at him with bright eyes, and he was smiling down at her. So much for hope, Janine thought as she shredded the picture in the paper and smushed it into the trash can. The heartless philanderer!

She went back to work with a sore heart, not even roused by the forthcoming holiday season. Christmas decorations were up now in Chicago, the television schedule was scattered with reruns of regular programs and holiday specials. Janine worked right through them.

Her parents and Kurt had put up a Christmas tree. Quentin called to say hello and mentioned that he was having the occasional date with the English major he'd met on his trip. He spoke of her with such warmth that Janine was certain that education was not the only thing the two of them discussed. She was happy for him. She and Quentin could never have lived together.

"Hey, isn't this one for the books!" Kurt exclaimed. "Take a look!"

He handed Janine a financial magazine. Inside there was a story about a successful merger of a software company with a hardware computer firm, and there was a photo of Canton Rourke shaking hands with a well-known Texan who owned a line of expensive computers.

"They say he'll make back every penny he's lost, and more," Kurt read. He glanced wickedly at Janine. "I told you he would."

She looked away. "So you did. More power to him."

"Doesn't it matter to you?"

She turned back with a poker face. "Why should it?" she asked. "He hasn't even phoned in two months. I'm sure he wrote me off as a holiday flirtation, and why not? He can have the most beautiful women in the world. What would he want with me?"

Kurt was taken aback. Janine was a dish. She didn't seem aware of it, but Kurt was certain that Canton Rourke had found her irresistible. Karie had said as much, when they were in Cancún. Of course, Janine was right, he hadn't even called since their return to Chicago. That really was too bad. He'd have thought they were made for each other.

He wanted to say something to comfort her, but Janine was already buried in her book again. With a sigh, he went on about his business.

Idly he wondered what Karie had done with the photographs they'd taken in Cancún. Every day, he'd expected to hear something momentous from her about them. She had contacts, she'd said, and she was bound to find someone who'd be ecstatic about them. But to date, he hadn't heard a word. Perhaps she'd given up on the idea in the fervor of having the Braves win the pennant. Or maybe her dad had gotten wind of their secret project and confiscated the photos. Either way, he thought he'd heard the last of it....

TWO DAYS LATER, a tabloid's front page showed a "sea monster" washed up on the beach at Cancún, of all places! It had fur and feathers and gruesome green skin. Its skull resembled most closely that of a bovine. Scientists said it was a new form of life.

Kurt bought three copies and ran back from the corner newsstand to the house he shared with his parents. Janine was visiting over the weekend. Kurt waved the headline under Janine's nose, disrupting one of her best new scenes on her laptop computer. "Look!" he exclaimed. "Just look! It was found right on the beach where we were!"

She looked at the creature with a frown. Something was nagging at the back of her mind when she saw the blown-up photo of the "creature."

Before she could really have time to think about it, there was a knock at the front door.

"See who that is while I save my file, could you?" she asked Kurt, putting the tabloid aside. "Look through the peephole first."

"I remember." He went to the door, peered out and suddenly opened it with a laugh. "Hello!" he greeted.

Canton Rourke smiled at him. Karie was with him, grinning from ear to ear in her Braves cap and shirt.

"Where's Janine?" Canton asked.

"In Dad's study," he said. "Right through there."

Canton's deep voice had already announced his presence, but Janine felt a jolt somewhere near her heart when she saw him. Two months was so long, she thought. She'd missed him unbearably. Her eyes told him that for her, nothing had changed. She felt the same.

He didn't seem to need words. He smiled tenderly and held out his arms. She got up quickly and ran right into them and lifted her face for a kiss that seemed to have no end at all.

Hectic seconds later, she pressed close, trembling.

"No need to ask if you missed me," he said huskily. "We can get a license in three days, or we can fly down to Mexico and be married in one. Your choice."

"Here," she said immediately. "So that my parents and Kurt can come."

He nodded. "I'd like that, too. I don't have many friends, but the ones I have are the best in the world."

"Mine, too." She reached up and touched his lean cheek. "You look worn."

"I am. It's been a hectic two months. I have my financing and my merger, and Marie is now history."

"What?"

"I flew to Greece with my attorney and had it out with her about Karie," he explained. "Kidnapping is a very serious offense. If I pushed it, the Mexican authorities might find a way to extradite her for trial. She knew it, too. She capitulated without a groan and was willing to settle for what I offered her. She'll have visiting rights, but just between us, I don't think she'll be using them. Karie isn't thrilled at the idea of visiting her at all."

"I remember." She searched his face. "You couldn't have called once?"

He smiled ruefully. "I wanted to be sure you knew who I was."

"I already did," she assured him. "The more I watch the series, the more differences I find between you and my screen hero. I still think he's tops. But I love you," she added shyly, dropping her eyes.

He took a slow breath. "And I love you. Never like this," he added huskily, his eyes brilliant. "Never in my life."

"Me, neither," she agreed breathlessly.

He kissed her again, hungrily, only pausing for breath when young voices came closer.

"Don't tell me," Kurt said dryly when he saw the two of them standing in each other's arms. "The marriage is on again, right?"

"Right," Janine said dreamily.

"Whoopee!" Karie enthused. "Now maybe you'll stop being so grouchy, Dad."

He glared at her.

"Same for you, Janine," Kurt agreed with a grin.

Canton glanced from the children's smug faces to Janine's. "Have you seen the tabloid this week?" he asked, naming one of the biggest ones.

"Yes. Kurt showed it to me," she explained. "It had a sea creature that had washed up on a Mexican beach."

"You didn't recognize it?" He reached into his pocket and unfolded the front page of one, that he'd been carrying around with him. Kurt and Karie looked suddenly restless.

Janine stared at the color photo with a frown. "Well, I thought it was rather familiar..."

"The cow skull?" he prompted. "The hacked-up garden hose? The feathers? The fur?"

She gasped and looked at Kurt with wide eyes. "It can't be!"

Karie cleared her throat. "Now, Dad," she began when his eyes narrowed.

"We covered it up the minute we took the photo," Kurt said helpfully. "The tide would have washed it all out to sea, we made sure of it."

"Why?" he demanded.

Karie pursed her lips, glanced at Kurt and produced a check. "Well, this is why," she explained.

He unfolded the check, made out to his daughter, and almost choked. "You're kidding."

She shook her head. "I wasn't sure you were going to make back all that money you lost," she said. "So I hit on this keen idea. I have to split it with Kurt, of course, but it should get me through college. Gosh, it should get us both through college!"

He was torn between being touched and committing homicide. "This is a hoax! It's all going back, and there will be a retraction printed."

"And I told them so in my letter," she assured him. "I kept a copy of it. They said it didn't matter, it was a super hoax." She put her hand on her hip and struck a pose. "Get real, Dad, do you honestly think Elvis is living on Mars, like they said last week?"

She sounded so old and sophisticated that both of the adults cracked up, though Canton was still determined to set things right.

"She's your daughter," Janine said through tears of laughter.

"And yours," he reminded her, "as soon as the ring is on your finger."

"Lucky you," Karie said with an irrepressible grin.

"Lucky me," Kurt agreed. "Just think of all the wonderful times we're going to have together."

Canton and Janine looked at the picture in the tabloid, and then at the children.

"Private schools," Canton said.

"In different states," Janine agreed.

The kids only looked at one another with knowing smiles. Canton took Janine by the hand and led her out of the room, into the office and closed the door behind them.

"Now," he murmured as he took her in his arms. "I believe we were discussing our forthcoming marriage? I think I stopped just about…here."

He bent and kissed her with slow, steady warmth, and she smiled with pure joy under his mouth. And it was no mystery at all that he loved her. Or vice versa.

* * * * *

COLE'S RED-HOT PURSUIT

Brenda Jackson

To the love of my life, Gerald Jackson, Sr.

To all former coworkers at State Farm Insurance.
Retirement is fun but I miss you guys!

Many waters cannot quench love;
neither can the floods drown it.
—*Song of Solomon* 8:7

PROLOGUE

"I SWEAR, COLE, if you weren't so preoccupied with staring at Patrina Foreman, you would have noticed that McKinnon was about to knock the hell out of Rick Summers just now for coming on to your sister," Durango Westmoreland said, joining his cousin near the punch bowl.

"Who?" Cole asked, finally taking his eyes off the woman across the room, the same one he'd been standing here watching since she'd arrived at the party given in honor of his sister, Casey.

"Rick Summers. He's been a pain in the—"

"No, I'm not talking about Summers. I'm talking about the woman. You said her name was Patrina…"

Durango shook his head, clearly seeing his cousin's interest. "Her name is Patrina Foreman, but those who know her call her Trina. She's a doctor in town. In fact, she's Savannah's doctor and will be delivering the baby."

"Married?"

"She's a widow. Her husband, Perry, was the sheriff and was gunned down by an escaped convict almost three years ago. Trina and Perry had been childhood sweethearts so she took his death pretty hard."

Durango didn't say anything for a few minutes and then said, "If you're thinking what I think you're thinking, you might want to kill the thought. You're a Texas Ranger and Trina has sworn never to become involved with another lawman. Hell, to be totally honest, she hasn't done too much dating at all. Other than her work, Trina's life basically stopped when Perry died."

Cole immediately thought, *what a waste*. Patrina Foreman was a looker. She'd certainly grabbed his attention the moment she'd walked in the room. He couldn't recall the last time something so potent had happened between him and a woman. And there was no way he would let the party end without at least getting an introduction—especially when he'd felt the strong sexual chemistry between them when their gazes had caught and held. There was no way she hadn't felt it, as well, he was sure of it. And would even go so far as to place his ranger's badge on it.

"I think I'll go introduce myself."

Durango rolled his eyes on seeing the determined look on Cole's face. "Okay, but don't say I didn't warn you."

A smooth smile touched Cole's lips when he glanced back over at Patrina and caught her staring at him. "I won't."

CHAPTER ONE

Eleven months later

IT SEEMED TO require more effort than usual for Cole Westmoreland to open his eyes, and the moment he did, he wished he'd kept them closed. A sharp pain ripped through his body, starting at the top of his head and working its way down to the soles of his feet. To fight off the excruciating throb he tightened his hands into fists, and then it occurred to him that he was lying flat on his back in the middle of a bed that wasn't his.

He forced himself to gaze around a bedroom that wasn't his, either. In fact, he was at a loss as to whose bedroom it was. He closed his eyes against another sharp pain and wondered just where the hell he was.

He recalled getting off the plane at the Bozeman Airport and renting a car to drive to his sister and brother-in-law's home on the outskirts of town. Casey and McKinnon weren't expecting him for another three weeks. His early arrival was to have been a surprise. He also remembered dismissing the car rental office's warning that an April snowstorm was headed their way. He'd assumed he would reach his destination before the storm hit.

But he had been wrong.

He'd been driving the rental car along the two-lane highway when out of nowhere, blankets of snow began falling, cutting visibility to zero. The last thing he remembered was tightening his grip on the steering wheel when he felt himself losing control of the car and then mouthing a curse before hitting something.

He reopened his eyes when he heard a sound. He forced his head to move, and his gaze locked on to the woman who entered the bedroom. *She definitely isn't my sister, Casey, so who is she?* He watched her place a basket of clothes on a table near the fireplace, and when she began folding up the clothes he studied her face.

She looked familiar and he searched his mind, trying to recall where he'd seen her before. He was not one to forget an attractive face, and even while flat on his back with pain racking his body, he was male enough to appreciate a pretty woman when he saw one.

And she was pretty.

She was tall. He figured her to be at least five-ten, and to his way of thinking, one gorgeous Amazon who could certainly complement his six-four. Her dark hair was pulled back in a ponytail. Her cocoa-brown face had high cheekbones, a pert nose—full lips that caught his gaze in a mesmerizing hold. He seemed to recall that he'd gazed at those same lips before and had gotten the same gut-wrenching reaction. Suddenly his stomach clenched in recognition.

Patrina Foreman.

They had met last year at a party given in his sister's honor by his stepmother, Abby, and McKinnon's mother, Morning Star. He and his brother, Clint, had flown in from Texas for the affair. Cole distinctly remembered how Patrina had kicked his libido into gear that night when he'd first seen her. The very air he'd been breathing had seemed to get snatched right from his lungs the moment their eyes had met. And then when his gaze had scanned her full-figured body, he'd been a goner. He was a man who appreciated a woman with some meat on her body, and Patrina's voluptuousness had been like an exploding bomb, sending all kinds of sensations rocketing through him.

According to his cousin, Durango, she was twenty-eight, and since he'd said that close to a year ago, she was probably twenty-nine now. And his cousin had also told him that Patrina was the gynecologist in town, and that she had lost her husband a few years back. A sheriff, her husband had died in the line of duty.

He'd also seen her in November at Casey and McKinnon's wedding, although she'd left before he'd gotten a chance to say anything to her. But the heated chemistry had still been there, even from across the room.

He continued to watch her fold the clothes and couldn't help wondering why he was lying flat on his back on a bed in her home. He moved his mouth to ask, but no sound came forth. Instead, for some reason he didn't quite understand, he suddenly felt tired. The next thing he knew, he was succumbing to darkness once more.

PATRINA FOREMAN HUMMED softly as she folded the last of her clothes. She took a sidelong glance at the man sleeping in her guest-room bed and noted he was still asleep. If he didn't wake up pretty soon, she would have to wake him and check his vital signs again. It was sheer luck that she'd come along Craven Road when she had; otherwise, no telling how long he would have remained in that car, unconscious. And with the weather as it was, she didn't want to think about what might have happened.

Once she'd seen that his injuries were minor, although the force of the impact had literally knocked him out, she'd managed to bring him around long enough to get him out of his vehicle and into hers. And then when she'd reached her ranch, it had been quite a challenge to get him into the house, since he wasn't exactly a small man. By taking advantage of the moments he regained consciousness, she'd managed to coax him into doing whatever she asked— like stripping down to his boxers and getting into bed under plenty of blankets to stay warm. She seriously doubted he would remember any of it, but she was certain it was something *she* would never forget.

She hadn't averted her gaze quickly enough and had seen his manly physique before he'd slipped beneath the covers. She had been nearly overtaken by emotions she couldn't even begin to name, emotions she hadn't had to deal with in quite some time. For as long as she lived, she wouldn't forget the sight of his broad shoulders, taut hips and long, masculine legs. She'd been shocked at how the fire of desire had flickered across every inch of her skin, and how her breath had gotten lodged in her throat.

She'd recognized him the moment she'd opened the door to his car to find him slumped over the steering wheel. Cole Westmoreland, a Texas Ranger who was related to all the other Westmorelands living around these parts. He was Corey Westmoreland's son, Casey Westmoreland Quinn's brother and Durango Westmoreland's cousin. She also knew he was a triplet to Casey and their brother, Clint, whom she'd heard had recently gotten married.

Because the roads were blocked and getting help for Cole would have been next to impossible, she'd made the decision to bring him here. So far he'd been an easygoing patient. It had been five hours since she'd gotten him settled. She figured that pretty soon he would wake up, if for nothing other than to go to the bathroom. And just in case he was hungry, she'd fixed a pot of beef stew.

She glanced out the window. The snow was still falling heavily. The phones lines were down and she could not get a signal on her cell phone. The battery-operated radio in the kitchen said it would be another two days before things let up. It was one of those rare blizzards these parts were prone to in April. While most of the country was enjoying beautiful spring weather, Bozeman, Montana, was still in the clutches of what had been a nasty winter. So at the moment the two of them were stranded here at her ranch. She was glad she'd taken a week off work—with no babies due to arrive this month, she'd planned to spend her time reading and relaxing. She hadn't counted on having a visitor.

Suddenly she felt an elemental change in the air that had nothing to do with the weather. And then she heard the sound of her name, a whisper so soft it caressed her skin and almost made her shiver. She looked across the room and found her gaze trapped with Cole Westmoreland's.

For an endless moment she stared into the dark depths of his eyes before pulling in a deep breath. This very thing had happened the first time she'd seen him last year at a party given for his sister. It seemed that the moment she'd entered the room that night his gaze had connected to hers and held. Now he was looking at her in a way she'd figured she would never experience again. And her response to his stare was affecting her in a way she wasn't prepared for.

"Water."

His request had her moving across the room to him and the pitcher that sat beside the bed. She tried ignoring the way he was looking at her while she poured him a glass of water. And then she placed her hand behind his head for support while he took a sip, and tried not to notice how warm he felt. He didn't have a fever. If anyone did it was her. She could feel her body get hot and tingly.

This was the first man she'd been attracted to since Perry's death. She had dated but not on a regular basis, and none of the men had stirred her the way Cole Westmoreland had done before and was doing now. His gaze was sweeping slowly across her face, and to her way of thinking, it shifted and zeroed in on her lips and stayed there.

"Do you want more?" she asked after he had drained the entire glass.

His gaze returned to her eyes. "No, and thanks."

His deep, raspy voice floated across her nerve endings. Trying to retain control of her mind and senses, she eased his head back onto the pillow while trying to avoid thinking about the large, masculine body beneath the blanket. Even with the blanket's thickness she could make out his long, hard limbs. Elemental. Powerful. Male.

"Why am I here?" he asked, causing her to shift her gaze and look at him.

She lifted his wrist to take his pulse and could feel how erratically her own was beating. "Don't you remember?"

"No," he said simply.

That wasn't unusual and she nodded. "You were in a car accident and took a bump to the head."

"And how did I get here?"

"I came across you on my way home. I figured you must have been trying to make it to Casey and

McKinnon's place before the storm hit. You're lucky I came along when I did."

"Was I unconscious?"

"Just about," she said, returning his arm to his side, satisfied with his pulse rate but not with the way he was still staring at her mouth. "I was able to get you to cooperate, which is how I managed to get you out of the car and into mine. The same thing when I arrived here. Although you had to lean on me, I was able to manage you pretty well."

She couldn't help but smile when she said, "I was even able to get you to take off your clothes on your own and get into bed."

Cole nodded. He could believe that, since he'd never had a problem with taking off his clothes for any woman, and she definitely would not have been an exception. But he found it hard to believe that she alone had managed to get him in and out of her car. She wasn't a tiny woman, but compared to him, she was a lightweight. He was all solid and she was all soft curves.

"How long have I been here?" he decided to ask, not needing to dwell on her shape and size any longer.

"About five hours. You've been going in and out most of the time, but you've slept rather comfortably over the past couple of hours or so. But eventually I was going to have to wake you. When you take a hit on the head it's not good to sleep too much."

He nodded again, thinking, so he'd been told. There

were two doctors in the Westmoreland family—his cousin Delaney and his cousin Thorn's wife, Tara.

"Are you hungry?"

He glanced up at her. "No. Thanks for asking," he said. He then glanced around the room.

"Power is out. I have a generator, so we have electricity, but the phone lines are down and the signal for the cell phone is nonexistent. I don't have any way to let Casey or your father know you're here and all right."

His gaze returned to hers. "That's fine. Neither she nor Dad was expecting me for another three weeks, anyway. I was going to surprise them."

Patrina nodded. Casey lived a few miles down the road as did Durango and his wife, Savannah. Patrina had delivered their baby last September, a beautiful little girl they had named Sarah after Durango's mother. And Cole's father, Corey, lived on what everyone in these parts referred to as Corey's Mountain. She rarely saw Corey these days unless he and his wife, Abby, came down to visit their good friends, Morning Star and Martin Quinn, McKinnon's parents. But she usually ran into Casey at least once a week in town or just passing on the road.

"I've changed my mind."

His words intruded into her thoughts. She met his gaze and tried not to drown in the dark depths. She thought he had such beautiful eyes. She licked her lips. They seemed to go dry around him from some reason. Probably from her heated breath. "About what?"

"Food. I'm feeling hungry."

"Okay. I'll bring you some stew I've made."

"I can get up," he mumbled. "I'm not an invalid."
Cole didn't like the thought of anyone, especially a
woman, waiting on him. He felt fine. So fine that
he'd almost slipped and said he was feeling horny,
instead of hungry. Hell, just being this close to her
had his heart thudding hard against his ribs, and had
other parts of him throbbing.

"I would prefer that you didn't get up, Cole. You
should stay put for a while. I checked you over and
didn't feel any broken bones."

He lifted a brow. She'd checked him over? Hmm,
he wondered if she'd felt something else besides no
broken bones. As if she'd read his mind she quickly
said. "I am a medical doctor, you know."

He couldn't help the smile that touched his lips.
"You deliver babies and take care of womenfolk,
right?"

"Yes, but that doesn't mean I can't take care of
a man if I have to," she said as she turned to leave
the room.

He couldn't help but chuckle at her tone. "Ah,
that's good to know. I'm definitely going to remember that."

She glanced back over her shoulder. "Remember what?"

"That you can take care of a man."

The look she threw his way indicated he better be
nice or else. And at that moment, he couldn't help
wondering what that *or else* was.

ANNOYED WITH HERSELF for letting Cole rile her, Patrina moved around the kitchen to prepare him something to eat. The beef stew had been simmering and its aroma filled the kitchen.

Because she had grown up in these parts and was used to the cold, harsh winters, she was never caught unawares. She made sure her freezer and cupboards were always full, and she had installed the generator a few years back.

As she loaded a tray for Cole, she tried to recall the last time a man had stayed overnight in her home. It probably was last year when her brother, Dale, had come in from Phoenix to attend McKinnon's wedding. At the same time she and Perry had been sweethearts, Dale and Perry had grown up in Bozeman the best of friends. More than once Dale had reminded Patrina that Perry had always said if anything ever happened to him, he would not want her to mourn him but, rather, have a rich and fulfilling life. She wished it could be that easy, but it wasn't. More times than not she went to bed missing the love she had lost.

A few minutes later she walked through the house and headed toward the bedroom carrying a tray loaded with food. In addition to the beef stew, she had made him a turkey sandwich and had also included a slice of the chocolate cake she had baked earlier in the week.

When she walked into the room she wasn't surprised to find the bed empty, even though she had asked him to stay put. Until she was certain he could move around on his own, she had wanted to be there to help him. The last thing she needed was for him to have a dizzy spell and fall.

The sound of running water confirmed her suspicions. He was taking a shower. She tried to force from her mind the image of him standing without any clothes on beneath a spray of water. She didn't know what was wrong with her. She didn't usually have such wanton thoughts. She was a doctor, a professional, but ever since she'd looked up to see Cole staring at her with those intense dark eyes of his, she'd been reminded that she was also a woman. He'd looked at her the same way that night last year at Casey's party. And the heat of his gaze had affected her in a way she hadn't been used to, and she'd quickly made the decision that Cole Westmoreland was someone she should steer clear of. In addition to being a man who could turn her life topsy-turvy if given the chance, she had also learned he was a lawman, and after Perry's death, she had vowed never to become involved with a lawman again.

"I was hoping to make it back to bed before you returned."

Patrina turned around and wished she hadn't. Cole stood in the doorway of the bathroom with a sheepish grin on his face. But what really caught her attention was the fact that he was completely naked, except for the towel around his middle. Of their own accord, her eyes raked his body. Why did he have to be so fine? So well built? She could just imagine running her hands over those hard muscular planes and—

"The food smells good."

It occurred to her that she'd been standing there staring at him. She immediately dropped her eyes from his body and automatically licked her lips. "Well, since you're up and about, I'll leave this tray in here for you. There're also two pills for pain. You might not think you're hurting now, but you may experience some discomfort now that you've started moving around."

"Aren't you going to eat?"

What I'm going to do is get out of here before I do something real stupid, like cross the room and touch you to see if all those muscles are as hard as they look. "No, I have a couple of things to do in the kitchen. Go ahead and enjoy your meal." She turned to leave the room.

"Patrina?"

She turned back around before reaching the door. She met his gaze. "Yes?"

"Thanks for everything. I see you even managed to bring in my luggage from the car. I appreciate that. Otherwise, I'd have to walk around your house without any clothes on."

She hoped he didn't notice the heated tint on her face at the thought of him parading through her house naked. "Well, I figured some things you can't possibly do without, and clothes are one of them."

And then she quickly left the room.

SHE LOOKS CUTE when she blushes, Cole thought as he slipped into a pair of jeans and the shirt he'd taken out of his luggage. He glanced out the window and saw how hard the snow was still coming down and knew that chances were he'd be her houseguest tonight, regardless of how either of them felt about it. He didn't have a problem with it since a warm, cozy house was something he often craved, especially during those times as a ranger when he'd been forced to brave the elements during a stakeout.

But those days were long gone. His brother, Clint, had been the first to retire as a Texas Ranger last year, and then he had followed suit last month. With the money he'd made from selling Clint his share of the ranch his uncle had left to Clint, Casey and him, he'd made a number of lucrative business investments. Thanks to the expertise of his cousin, Spencer, the financial guru in the Westmoreland family, one investment in particular had paid off big-time. At the age of thirty-two Cole had been able to leave the Rangers a wealthy man.

He now had a stake in several business ventures, including the booming horse-breeding and -training business that his cousin, Durango, and his brother-in-law, McKinnon, had started a few years back. Clint had become a partner and after seeing the benefits of such an investment, Cole had recently become a partner, as well. But he preferred being a silent partner, so he could be free to pursue other opportunities.

One such opportunity was a chance to purchase a helicopter business that provided taxi service between the various mountains to the people who lived on them. Besides that, he and his cousin Quade, who was taking early retirement from the secret service, had discussed the possibility of them joining forces to start a network of security companies. Clint had expressed an interest, too, as if he didn't have enough to do already with his involvement in training horses and taking on a wife.

Cole smiled when he thought of his confirmed-bachelor brother being a happily married man. Alyssa was just what Clint needed and Cole was happy for him, but knew that for himself, marriage was not anything he wanted anytime soon, if ever. He preferred being single and all the benefits it afforded. And now that he was no longer tied to a regular job, he had plenty of time to do whatever pleased him.

And getting to know Dr. Foreman pleased him. He made her nervous, he could tell. It wasn't intentional—the last thing he wanted was a skittish female around him. But he was attracted to her. That was a "gimme" and had been from the first. Hell, when she had picked up his hand to check his pulse, he'd almost come out of his skin. Her touch had sent all kinds of sensations through his body, and he'd been reminded of a need so hot and raw that he'd had to momentarily close his eyes against its intensity.

Up close he'd seen just how beautiful she was, more than he had even remembered. He had this full awareness of her. Back in Austin, he was a man known to appreciate beautiful women and he could definitely appreciate her. Every full-figured inch of her.

He knew she was attracted to him, too. There

were the usual giveaways—the way her breathing changed when they were close, the way she studied his body when she thought he wasn't aware she was doing so, and then there was the way she would nervously moisten her lips. Lips he was dying to taste, sample and devour. To say he was fascinated with her, enamored by her, hot for her and had been from the first would be an understatement. The woman had the ability to steal his breath away without even trying.

And just as he knew the attraction was mutual, he could tell she was fighting it, probably because she assumed he was still a ranger. Durango had warned him that because of what had happened to her husband, she didn't date lawmen. But then he recalled Durango also saying she didn't date much at all.

Well, I'm going to have to be the one to change that, he decided as he sat at the small table with the tray of food in front of him. He glanced around the room. It had a nice, comfortable feel without looking feminine. The furniture was dark mahogany and the throw rugs scattered around on the floor were a nice touch. The bed was huge. It looked solid. Just the kind of bed you'd want to tangle with your woman on, between the sheets, on top of the covers, whatever suited your fancy.

In the distance he could hear the sound of pots and pans clinking as Patrina moved around in the kitchen. After taking the two painkillers she'd left, he tackled his stew. It was delicious. And she'd made him a huge sandwich. Man-size. Just like his desire for her.

When he finished the sandwich, Cole enjoyed the cake and coffee she'd also made. There was no doubt about it. The good doctor knew her way around a kitchen. His stomach was grateful.

The only thing he hated doing was eating alone, which was something he should be used to, since that was how he usually ate his meals. But it was hard knowing there was a pretty face he could look at in the other room.

"I came back to see if you needed anything else. Do you?"

He looked up at the sound of Patrina's voice. She was standing in the doorway. His gaze moved over her from head to toe, and he felt his blood pressure shoot to a level that had to be dangerous. She had a flawlessly beautiful face and a gorgeous body.

He took another sip of coffee while he continued to stare at her. Considering how much he was attracted to her, coupled with the fact that he hadn't slept with a woman in more than a year due to the number of undercover assignments he'd been involved in, what she'd asked was definitely a loaded question if ever he'd heard one.

He finally spoke. "Funny you should ask. Yes, there is something else I need."

CHAPTER TWO

PATRINA SUDDENLY FELT the weight of Cole's response on every inch of her shoulders. For some reason, she felt she needed to prepare for what he was about to say. Maybe she could tell from the way he was looking at her, with heated lust in his eyes. Or it could have possibly been the sudden shift in the air surrounding them, releasing something primal, something uninhibited, something better left capped, that warned her what could be coming. She just hoped he didn't say what she thought he was thinking.

Since Perry's death many men had attempted to date her—colleagues, friends of friends, guys Dale had introduced her to. None had succeeded. She preferred living an existence where she was not involved in a relationship, serious or otherwise, with any man. It was hard for some of her admirers to understand her position. They wouldn't take no for an answer. But none, she inwardly admitted, was as persistent as the man staring at her now.

She studied his expression and exhaled slowly. He'd made his statement and now it was time for her to ask what he meant by it. She walked farther into the room, paused by the table and asked her question. "And what else do you need, Cole?"

He didn't answer right away and she was aware that he was trying to decide if he really should. Good. Let him think about it. Some things were better left unsaid. She wasn't born yesterday and she had been a married woman at one time. She recognized the vibes, the tingle and the heat of lust. She knew enough about male testosterone and how it could get the best of a man sometimes. And she knew how not to become a victim when it got out of hand.

"I need company."

She blinked upon realizing that Cole had spoken. She studied his expression, searched his eyes. "Company?"

"Yes, company. I didn't like eating alone."

She had a sinking feeling that wasn't what he'd originally planned to say. She appreciated the fact that he had thought his answer through first. He didn't know her and there was a lot she didn't know about him. The only thing that was certain was the sexual chemistry between them. She was old enough and mature enough to recognize it for what it was worth. She was realistic enough to accept their attraction for what it was—wasted energy. The last thing she planned on doing was getting involved in an affair destined to go nowhere. She'd been married for five years to a wonderful man, was now a widow and wasn't interested in changing that status. Besides, Cole was a lawman, for heaven's sake.

"I told you why I didn't stay. I had things to do in

the kitchen," she finally said, frowning and wondering if he was one of those self-absorbed men greedy for attention and looking for any willing female to give it to him.

"I want to get to know you better."

She saw the smile that touched his lips and the twinkle in his dark eyes. He was doing something to her, messing with her rational mind, while at the same time making breathing an effort for her. "Why?" she couldn't help asking.

He glanced out the window. "Because it looks like we're stuck in here together."

Patrina also fixed her gaze on the view outside the window. Snow was still falling, and according to the weather report on the radio, it wouldn't let up anytime soon. It would be this way for another couple of days. Whether she liked it or not, she was temporarily stranded with Cole Westmoreland.

She shook her head and quickly decided on a plan. "I think you should get back into bed and rest some. You're not out of the woods yet. I'm going to take this stuff to the kitchen and—"

"Promise." He met her gaze and she felt the lure in it. The automatic pull. "Promise you'll be back."

She knew she should fight it, resist it with everything she had. But then she felt she could handle it since she was used to men like Cole. She'd been raised with one and had spent a lot of her time watching him in action. Dale had been the consummate ladies' man. He'd used just about every charm he possessed, every pickup line in the book, to get girls.

She glanced at the tray on the table. Good. Cole had taken the pain pills, which meant he would be getting drowsy in a little while. For the time being she would just humor him.

"Okay, I promise I'll be back."

SHE KEPT HER promise and when she returned fifteen minutes later, he had gotten back into bed and…was wide awake. He evidently had more energy than she thought.

"I was beginning to wonder if you planned to return."

She took the wing chair across from the bed, folding her long skirt beneath her as she settled into it with a book in her hand. "I promised I would. I just wanted to catch the latest weather report on the radio," she said truthfully, although that wasn't the only thing that had detained her.

"And what did the report say?"

She sighed, not sure she wanted to tell him. "That we're in for a blizzard tonight and all day tomorrow."

He nodded. "Don't you ever get lonely living out here by yourself? Especially when the weather's like this?"

She shook her head. "No, because usually I stay overnight in town so I'll be available if my patients need me. It just so happens that I'm on vacation this week. I timed it so I would be taking time off when none of my patients were scheduled to deliver."

"And what happens if a baby decides to surprise its parents and arrive early?"

She laughed. "Trust me, it's happened before. But with this weather, they would just have to make their entrance into this world without me. There are other doctors on call when I'm not available."

"You delivered Durango and Savannah's baby."

She couldn't help the smile that touched her lips, remembering. "Yes, and that night I saw a side of Durango I thought I would never see."

"And what side was that?"

"The side that shows how much a man can actually love a woman and his child. I've known Durango for years, ever since I was a kid. Even before moving to Montana, he and his brothers and cousins used to visit your dad every summer on his mountain. Like McKinnon, my brother, Dale, was friends with all of them and none of us were surprised when Durango decided to come back to attend a university around here after finishing high school."

Cole nodded. He knew the story, having heard it a number of times. He couldn't help but admire a man like his father, Corey Westmoreland, who'd taken up so much time with his nephews. It hadn't been Corey's fault that Cole, Clint and Casey had grown up believing their father was dead. That was what their mother had told her triplets. Then on her deathbed a few years ago, she had confessed that their father was alive somewhere and hadn't died in a rodeo accident like they'd been told. The day after burying their mother, he and Clint had hired a private investigator to find their father. Casey hadn't been all that eager and had struggled hard with their mother's cover-up. He was glad to see how his sister and father had grown close over the past year. The reason Cole had come to town now was for the big party that Casey and his father's wife, Abby, were planning for Corey's birthday at the end of the month.

Cole glanced over at Patrina. There was one question he was dying to ask her. "Are you involved with someone, Patrina?"

He saw her guarded expression and knew his question was unexpected. She stared down at the book in her hand and without looking at him, she asked, "Why do you want to know?"

"Curious."

She lifted her head and met his gaze and immediately he felt it the moment their eyes connected. The sexual chemistry was so tangible there was no way it could be misinterpreted. It was more than a mere meeting of the minds. It was a meeting of something a whole lot more powerful, and while one part of him was embracing it as a challenge, another part was thinking he needed to step back and grab control, since no woman had affected him this way before. He studied her and saw her tiny frown. While he might see their mutual attraction as a challenge, he could tell she saw it as a nuisance.

An assured smile touched his lips when he repeated, "So, are you involved with anyone?"

"No."

"Do you want to become involved?" He decided to go ahead and ask her, curious about her answer. If it was yes, then that made things easy for him.

But if she said no, then that meant a different game plan, since he definitely wanted her and was a man known to get what he wanted.

She leaned toward him and a part of him wished she hadn't. His mouth nearly dropped open when his gaze shifted from her face to the V of her blouse. When she'd leaned forward, he could see the tops of her firm, round breasts and the taut nipples that strained against the material of her blouse.

"Read my lips, Cole Westmoreland. I have no desire to become involved."

His gaze shifted from her breasts to her lips and he wanted to do something more than just read them. A fantasy suddenly flashed in his mind. Something he intended to file away for the day he did take possession of those lips that were now formed into a pout. To his way of thinking, a downright sexy pout.

He then moved his gaze from her lips up to her eyes. She had been watching him the entire time. He wanted her to know just how taken he was with her. He wanted her to know he was a man determined. But what he saw in her eyes alerted him to the fact that she was a woman just as determined. Where he planned on breaking down her resolve, her intentions were not to make it easy for him. In fact, there was no doubt she intended to make it downright difficult. There was no doubt a confrontation between them would be of the most sexually intense kind.

"And what if I were to tell you, Patrina Foreman, that I want to become involved with you?"

He watched something flash in the depths of her

dark eyes as she pulled back. Anger. Fire. Heat. It could be all three, but it didn't bother him. He would eventually use them to his advantage. He'd never been fond of a woman who was too willing, anyway. A woman who didn't make things easy for him was the type he preferred and he couldn't recall when the last time was he'd encountered one such as that. One-night stands had become downright boring for him. In his last two sexual encounters, the women had been so eager they were the ones who'd asked him to take them to bed, claiming he wasn't moving fast enough to suit them.

"I would tell you that you were wasting your time. Take a good look at me, Cole. Do I look like a woman who could be easily swayed?"

Now that she'd given the invitation, he decided to take her up on her offer. He took a good look at her, not that he hadn't checked her out pretty much already. His gaze leisurely swept over her. She had a full figure, well endowed in all the right places, a real sexy and feminine body even in clothes. He didn't want to think how it would look out of clothes.

"Do I look like a woman who elicits uncontrollable lust in a man?"

Yes, he would say she did, but evidently she had other ideas. "What is the point you are trying to make?" he asked, deciding they needed to cut to the chase.

Her frown deepened as she stood up from the chair. "The point I'm trying to make is that I know your type. I'm sibling to one. You are man. I am woman. This thing, this attraction between us, is only a fluke. It's temporary. It's meaningless. For you it's just a whim. Men like you have them most of the time. It's an ingrained part of your nature. Women of all shapes and sizes flock to you. Throw themselves at your feet, plaster themselves across your bed, spread themselves for you to enjoy. And when it's all over, you wear a satisfied smirk on your face and walk away. In your mind you're thinking, next. And for you there is a next. And a next. I don't intend to be any man's *next*."

He considered her words—at least he tried to. It was hard when her breasts were heaving with every single word she spoke, every movement she made. And when she had placed her hands on her hips to glare at him, he had shifted his gaze from her breasts to her hips. Flaring, wide, absolutely plentiful. He could imagine himself...

"Women my size are a joke to men like you."

His head snapped up at that. "Excuse me?"

Her eyes narrowed. "You heard what I said. Men like you, cover-model potential, are drawn to women who are also cover-model potential. Granted, I might be your flavor of the moment, but don't think you can show up in town, bored with what you left behind in Texas and decide to sample the local treats while you are here in Montana."

Cole stared at her. Okay, she was partly right. While he had gotten bored with the easy lays and had thought it would be nice to find a woman interested in a couple of quickies while he was here visiting, he hadn't intentionally set his sights on her. That is, until he'd found himself in her house and in her bed. Opportunities weren't something he liked missing. He had to admit that he saw her as an opportunity to take care of an eleven-month sexual drought.

But the part she'd said about him being cover-model potential who would only be drawn to a woman who looked like a supermodel was so far from the truth it was a shame. He liked women. And when it came to them he didn't discriminate as to weight, size, creed or color. He liked them all. He appreciated them all. And if he had the energy he would try to please them all. Hell, he was single. He wasn't tied to anyone and didn't intend to be. He didn't take anything from a woman she didn't want to give, and most women let him know up front that they were in the giving mood.

Okay, it seemed Patrina wasn't in the giving mood. But there was a thing called seduction, and it was something he was pretty good at. Another thing he was good at was reading people, and he was focusing on reading what her lips weren't saying. She was so full of sensual emotions, such an abundance of sexual heat, it wasn't funny. Whether she recognized the signs or not, she was a woman who needed a roll in the hay as much as he did. He'd bet she hadn't engaged in any type of sexual activity since her husband died. Her reaction to him was a telltale sign. Although at the moment she was fighting it, specifically, fighting him, he didn't plan on letting her get away with it. In the end, she would thank him. Suddenly Cole felt an overpowering urge to prove his theories about her.

And Patrina, it seemed, had this farfetched notion that he wasn't really attracted to her. Maybe he ought to invite her to stick her hand under the bedcovers to see…and to feel just how attracted he was to her.

"Now, did I make myself clear?"

He stared at her for a long moment before replying, "Yes, you did. Now I think I need to make myself clear, as well."

She blinked. Then she frowned at him before saying. "All right. Go ahead."

Refusing to lie flat on his back any longer, he kicked the covers aside and eased out of bed. Surprised, she took a quick step back and he noticed how she tried averting her gaze from the crotch of his boxers. "I don't force myself on women, Patrina, so don't feel you aren't safe around me. But I do know that I can pick up the scent of a willing woman a mile away, and regardless of the fact that you're trying like hell to fight it, you *are* willing. Hell, you are so willing, certain parts of my body have shifted into ready mode just waiting for you to say the word. I won't force you, but at some point in time I'm going to give you just what you need or what you possibly don't know you need."

Her glare sharpened. "Oh, you see me as a sex-deprived widow, is that it?"

He considered her words and a slow smile touched his lips. "No, I don't see you that way, but before it's all over I will definitely make you a very merry widow. When I look at you I see a very sexy and desirable woman who—for whatever reason—has been denying herself the company of a man. Maybe it's because you're afraid to get close to another male after losing your husband, or it could be you're scared to let yourself go, uncomfortable with the thought of becoming a fulfilled woman in someone else's arms. I want to think that perhaps fate is the reason we ended up stranded here together, and only time will tell. But I will make you this promise. It won't be me who makes the first move. It won't be me who eventually asks us to share a bed. It will be you."

"When hell freezes over!"

His smile widened. "Take a look out the window, baby. To my way of thinking, it's getting there."

PATRINA BREATHED OUT a long, frustrated sigh. She didn't know just what to make of Cole and she was trying real hard to control a temper she didn't know she had until now.

Where did he come off assuming she was open game? She had done a good deed by rescuing him from the storm and bringing him to her place to recover, not for him to pounce on her when he thought he had the first opportunity to do so. Okay, she would be the first to admit the vibes between them were strong. Stronger than she'd had with any man, but evidently they were sending out the wrong message. There was no doubt in her mind that a man who looked like him probably had women throwing themselves at him all the time; however, that was no reason for him to assume she wanted to be one of them. He thought he could turn her into a merry widow; the very thought was absurd. Besides, even if she was the least bit interested in him, which she wasn't, he would be the last person she'd want to become involved with. He was a Texas Ranger, a lawman, and she had decided the day she had buried Perry that she would not get involved with another lawman again.

"You have nothing else to say?" he asked.

Her lips twisted as she glared at him, trying to stay in control of her anger. "What do you expect me to say? We met last year briefly, but you assume you know me and everything about me. Someone must have told you that you're God's gift to women, a man who assumes every woman, regardless of shape, size or color, is looking for a romp between the sheets. You've been in my house less than eight hours and already you're making a play for me. Is this how you show your appreciation for my warm and caring hospitality?"

Cole frowned. If she thought she was going to turn the tables on him by making him feel guilty about anything, she was wrong. The bottom line was, he was man and she was woman. Neither of them was involved with anyone, and desire was flowing so thickly between them you could turn it into mortar to lay bricks. He wanted her, and whether she admitted it or not, she wanted him. Surely she couldn't fault him for finding her desirable, for wanting to take her to bed. Okay, he might have come on too strong, too quickly, but hell, she was the one looking at him with those hungry eyes when she thought he wasn't looking. He merely wanted her to know that when and if she decided to make a move, he was more than ready.

"Like I said, Patrina, I've never forced myself on a woman and I don't plan to start now. The last thing I want you to think is that I don't respect you, because I do. What's going on between us has nothing to do with respect. It's about the fulfillment of wants and needs. From what I've gathered, you've put yourself on a shelf and I'm at a loss as to why when you're so beautiful and desirable."

He leaned closer. "It's time you're taken off the shelf and I'm just the man who's bold enough to do it, and if that pisses you off, then so be it."

Her glare darkened. "How dare you!"

"How dare I what? How dare I be bold enough to remind you that you're a woman? Something you seem to want to forget? Well, look at me, Patrina, and what you'll see is a man who finds nothing wrong with noticing a woman as a woman and bringing it to that woman's attention if I have to."

Patrina tilted up her face, opened her mouth to tell him just what she thought of what he'd said when he suddenly leaned in even closer, and before she could draw in her next breath, he covered her mouth with his.

She thought of putting her strength into a shove to push him back, but the deep growl she heard from within his throat stopped her at the same time his tongue was eased into her mouth. What she hadn't expected were the sensations that tongue taking hold of hers evoked.

Anger quickly became curiosity, which immediately shifted to something she hadn't felt in so long she'd almost forgotten it existed—sexual hunger. And before she could stop it, it took control of her mind, body and senses. And as if that wasn't enough she felt one of his hands touch the center of her back to draw her closer into his heat.

His heat was as hot as anything she'd ever experienced, and he was sipping her up like he was obsessed with the taste of her. Willing her mind or body to resist him was not an option. Not when every fiber of her being was tuned in to his mouth and what he was doing to hers, so exquisitely poignant she wondered where he'd learned to kiss that way. He took, but at the same time he gave. There was no doubt that he was experienced when it came to the art of lovemaking. He was stirring to life within her sensations that were infusing every cell in her body, every nerve ending. The man was basically devouring her alive, and with a possessiveness she felt all the way to the bone.

And then it suddenly occurred to her that she was kissing him back. That hadn't been her initial plan, and then it quickly dawned on her that she really didn't have a plan. At the moment she was a willing participant who was handling Cole's assault on her mouth in the only way she knew how. Complete surrender.

Later she would rake herself over the coals for

allowing him such liberties, for letting him turn her brain into mush, for making her feel things she hadn't felt in years. But for now, she wanted to savor, to relish and to enjoy the feel of being in a man's arms and being kissed by him this way. He was stoking a fire that had burned out long ago. And as she sank deeper into the strong arms that held her, she felt a flame being stirred from that fire, which only heightened her senses of him as a man.

Suddenly he pulled his mouth away and she watched as he clutched the bedpost as if what they'd shared was more than he'd bargained for, too. She took that opportunity to take a step back.

Cole drew in a deep breath. His head was spinning. His brain felt intoxicated and his body felt wildly alive. And all from a kiss. Whether Patrina admitted it or not, that kiss had served a very important purpose. It proved a number of things, but mainly that they were hot for each other. He opened his mouth to tell her just that, but she shoved an upraised finger in his face.

"Don't say it. Don't even think it," she warned. "It was just a kiss. It meant nothing."

He gave her a sharp look, zeroing in on lips that had just gotten thoroughly kissed. She wasn't being completely honest with herself or with him if she wanted to claim that the kiss had meant nothing when they both knew just the opposite. It *had* meant something.

"Think what you want, but I've proved a point," he said, deciding he'd had enough energy-draining activity for one day. Easing down on the bed, he ignored her glare as he slid back under the covers.

"And I've also done something else, as well," he said. Knowing he had her too mad to ask what that something else was, he then said, "I've initiated my plan to move you off that shelf. Although you're still there, you're no longer in the same spot. I've shifted you away from the side that's been cold for some time to a side better suited for you. And that, Patrina, is the hot side."

She stared at him like he'd totally lost his mind. But that was fine. She could think whatever she wanted, he thought as he closed his eyes. Like he'd said, he had proved a point, and besides, he had tasted her hot side.

And damned if he didn't like it. He liked it a hell of a lot.

CHAPTER THREE

"Good morning."

Standing at the kitchen counter, Patrina paused, trying to get her thoughts and emotions under control before turning to face Cole. When she had awakened last night it was to discover she had fallen asleep in the chair next to the bed where he slept.

She had eased from the room to take a shower before climbing into her own bed and then had trouble sleeping, knowing he was in the room across the hall. Twice during the night she had gotten up to check on him and had seen he was still sleeping peacefully— and looking nothing like the man who was destined to turn her life upside down when awake.

She could vividly recall the first time she had seen him last year at Casey's party. The moment their gazes had connected she had felt something strong, so elemental, and it had shaken her to the core, nearly corrupted her nervous system and made her realize for the first time since Perry's death that she was capable of being attracted to another man. She had been totally confused by the intensity of that attraction and had been too taken aback by it to try to figure things out at the time.

Her intention had been to avoid Cole all evening that night at the party; however, that was something he would not let happen, and he'd finally cornered her and introduced himself. Like everyone else in these parts, she had heard about Corey's triplets, but other than Casey, she hadn't met them. Clint and Cole looked so much alike they could be identical, but there was something about Cole that stood out. Maybe it was his features, which were so compelling they'd taken her breath away the moment she'd seen him. Or it could have been the shape of his mouth—so intensely sexual it made you think of stolen kisses or had you not thinking at all. And then maybe, just maybe, it was the dark eyes that seemed capable of stripping you naked when they looked at you. Whatever it was, she had quickly reached the conclusion that like her brother, Cole was a ladies' man constantly on the prowl and she was a woman who refused to become his prey.

She had gotten the same impression about him when she'd seen him again six months later at Casey and McKinnon's wedding. The moment he had walked into the church and their gazes had connected, just like before, sexual chemistry, thick enough to almost smother you, had flowed between them all the way across the aisle of the church. Knowing she couldn't take the chance of him catching her at a vulnerable moment, she had left the church immediately after the wedding was over and skipped the reception, giving him no chance to exchange a single word with her.

Now, less than six months later he's a guest in my home.

Deciding it was time to acknowledge his presence, she plastered a smile on her face and turned around. "Good morning, Cole. H-how…"

Her words faltered as her gaze zeroed in on him standing there, casually lounging in the doorway that separated the kitchen from the dining room. He was shirtless and wearing a pair of jeans that rode low on his hips and looking sexier than any man had a right to be. And he was barefoot, which gave him an at-home look. A sprinkling of dark hair covered his muscular chest—and it was a chest so well defined she tried thinking of numerous reasons she should rub her hands across it.

It suddenly dawned on her that she was standing there staring at him, and just as she was raking her gaze over him, he was doing the same with her. She was wearing a pair of slacks and a pullover sweater and she didn't want to admit she had taken more time with her appearance than normal. The snow still hadn't let up outside, but she definitely felt heat on the inside.

"Something smells good."

His words were like a caress to her skin and she quickly turned back to the counter and leaned forward to reach down to get a frying pan out of the cabinet below, figuring she had ogled him long enough and any more was only asking for trouble. "I hope you're hungry," she said over her shoulder as she straightened.

"I am."

From the sound of his voice she could tell he'd moved into the room. In fact, he sounded as if he was right at her back. She was too nervous to turn around to see if that was the case.

"How do you like your eggs?" she asked.

"Um, I'm sure I'll enjoy them whatever way you prepare them."

It seemed he whispered the words right close to her ear. She swung around with the skillet in her hand only to have the front of her body hit smack up against his.

Before she could ask why he was standing so close, he reached out and took the skillet out of her hand. His lips curved into a smile. "Can't have you thinking of using this as a weapon," he said, placing it on the counter. He then leaned in closer. "I want to thank you for everything."

His mouth was almost touching hers and once she could release her gaze from his lips, she forced herself to wonder what exactly he was thanking her for. The kiss they had shared yesterday possibly? She doubted it since she figured his lips had kissed countless other women, and most, she was certain, had been more experienced in doing that sort of thing than she was. "What are you thanking me for?"

"For bringing me here, taking care of me and putting up with my straightforwardness about certain things."

Straightforwardness or arrogance? She quickly thought and knew just what *certain things* he was referring to. "I'm a doctor. I'm used to putting up with all kinds of people and their attitudes and dispositions."

"You're also a woman, Patrina," he said, looking her straight in the eye as he leaned in even closer. "And that's something I feel compelled to remind you of."

She noticed his gaze was lowering to her lips and a faint shiver ran down her spine. She could almost feel the heat radiating from him and licked her lips again. Instinct warned her to take a step back or be robbed of her concentration, but she couldn't since the counter was at her back.

It hit her then what his response to her had been. Why did he feel he should remind her of anything? The first time they had spent more than five minutes in each other's presence was yesterday. It wasn't like they really knew a lot about each other for him to decide on something like that. Stubbornness stiffened her spine. "You don't need to feel compelled to do anything, and basically you have no right. Besides, being a woman isn't anything I can forget."

He shrugged. "No, but it's something you evidently seem determined to ignore and I refused to let you do that. I want you to feel the passion."

She narrowed her gaze at the same time she opened her mouth to tell him that she had no intention of feeling anything when suddenly he swooped down and connected his mouth to hers. At first, everything inside her tensed, went on full alert, but then she relaxed and her mouth clung to his, and just like the day before, she automatically began kissing him back.

The hot fever she felt she had yesterday gripped her in a way that had her wondering what she was doing and just what she was letting him do to her. She was actually melting under each stroke of his tongue and could feel the swell of her breasts pressed against his bare chest—that same chest she'd ogled just seconds earlier. Everything at that moment seemed so right, although in the back of her mind she knew it was all wrong. The texture of his mouth was manly, his flavor provocative, and the longer he kissed her, the more he was drawing her in, tempting her with a degree of desire she had forgotten could exist between a man and woman. This kiss was doing a mental breakdown of her senses in a way that had her moaning deep in her throat.

He was kissing her with a hunger she felt all the way to her toes and he refused to let up. Instead, he took her tongue in a relentless hold, as if savoring it, tangling with it, gave him immense pleasure. It was certainly giving her more pleasure than she had counted on. She'd never imagined something could be so intense until he'd kissed her last night, and this one was no different. If anything, it had even more fire.

Then suddenly his mouth softened on hers, just moments before he broke off the kiss. She let out a soft moan before automatically lowering her face onto his chest, not ready to look him in the eye while giving herself time to catch her breath. She ignored the warm feel of his hand gently caressing her back as if trying to soothe new life into her and wanted to protest that she was fine with her present life. She didn't want this—the passion, the awakening feelings that bordered on sensations she wasn't used to, sensations she had gotten over long ago. What she desperately needed was a chance to be alone, but since the weather was still ugly outside, she knew such a thing was next to impossible. Cole wasn't going anywhere and neither was she.

Cole was deep into his own thoughts as he continued to hold her, gently rubbing her back, while neither made an attempt at conversation. Just as well, since he figured the kiss—the second one they'd shared—had said enough. But then, it might not have. Patrina, he was discovering, was stubborn when it came to acknowledging some things. "I could have kept right on kissing you, you know," he said in a low voice, close to her ear. He figured she needed to know that.

He felt the faint tremor that touched her body, once, then again before she lifted her head and looked at him. The darkness of her eyes touched him in a way he found unnerving, and then with little or no control on his part, he lowered his head and gently brushed his lips across hers, feeling her shiver again in his arms.

"You're trying to be difficult," she accused breathlessly, while narrowing her gaze at him.

Her words, as well as her expression, brought a smile to his lips. She wasn't happy with him, but he was more than happy with her. He simply liked stoking her fire. "No, what I am is persistent," he corrected, drawing her closer. "I figure that sooner or later you'll come around to my way of thinking."

"Don't hold your breath."

Cole knew she really didn't have a clue about what she was doing to him. He felt his erection throb and quickly decided that maybe she did. There was no way she wasn't aware of how aroused he was. They were standing so close their bodies seemed to be plastered together. And for a moment he felt something, a fierce tightening in his gut, as well as a hard throb in his lower extremities that reminded him once again, and not too subtly, that he was a full-blooded male. And a hot one at that.

He was standing with his legs braced apart so that his thighs could snugly embrace hers and figured his aroused body part, which was unashamedly pressed against her center, made what was on his mind a dead giveaway. He tried dropping his gaze from hers and decided it wasn't a good idea when his eyes came to rest upon the necklace she wore around her neck. It was a gold heart and its resting place was right smack between her breasts. Nice plump breasts.

Feeling his gut tighten even more, he lifted his gaze and studied the look in her eyes, quickly reaching the conclusion that nothing had changed. The desire between them was strong, intense as ever. But talk about someone being difficult, as far as he was concerned, she could be hailed as queen. He would, however, enjoy breaking down her resolve.

Deciding he had made his point for now, he released her from his arms and took a step back. "Do you need my help fixing breakfast?"

She tilted her head at an angle that showed the perfection of her neck and the moistness of the lips he had kissed. "No, I don't need your help. You can sit in the living room and I'll call you when it's ready."

Cole chuckled as he crossed his arms over his chest. It was either that or he'd reach for her again and pull her into his arms and kiss her. "In other words, you want me out of the way."

"Yes, that's what I want."

"All right."

She eyed him like he'd given in too easy. "What?" he asked, smiling.

She lifted a brow and then, as if she didn't want to discuss anything with him any longer, she said, "Nothing. I'll call you when everything's ready." She then turned to the counter and presented her back to him.

He was tempted to reach out and brush her hair away from her neck and leave his mark there, but knew she wouldn't appreciate him doing something so outrageously bold. Hell, the back of her didn't look so bad, either. The denim of her jeans fit snugly over her shapely bottom. He forced his heart to beat at an even pace.

He smiled as he moved in the direction of her living room. Once there, he decided not to sit down as she had suggested. Instead, he glanced around, checked things out. The living room, like the other parts of the house, was nicely furnished and the furniture was solid and sturdy, the kind that was made to last and fit perfectly in this environment. Considering the weather in these parts, undoubtedly, it had to.

A thick, padded sofa and love seat made of rich leather looked inviting, and the throw rugs scattered about on the floor gave you the option of curling up in front of the fireplace. But one glance out the window brought forth a dreary picture. He often wondered how his father could endure the harshness of Montana's cold weather, high on his mountain, especially those days before Abby had returned to his life. But what of those times when he'd been up there alone, those harsh and cold winters when Corey Westmoreland had lived his life as a lonely man, pretty much the way Patrina was living hers—a lonely woman. A part of him wondered what right he had to make the assumption that her life was lonely. She had her work, which he figured she enjoyed, but still he felt she needed more. Like he'd always felt his mother had needed more.

He recalled as a little boy watching his beautiful mother deny herself the chance of falling in love again and living a happy life. Instead, she'd clung to the story she'd fabricated for her children and everyone else that her husband—the only man she could ever love—had died in a rodeo accident. Although Cole and his siblings had discovered later that Corey Westmoreland wasn't dead, in a way he was to Carolyn Roberts, since she had known she would never be the woman to have his heart.

Cole could recall a number of good men who'd come calling on his mother, trying to gain her interest, like his fourth-grade teacher, Mr. Jefferson. But none had been able to awaken the love she'd buried long before her triplets were born. She had died without the love or companionship of a good man. She had died in that same spot on the shelf where she'd placed herself for more than thirty years. And for a reason he didn't want to dwell on, he didn't want that for Patrina. Although he was not interested in a serious relationship with any woman, he had no problem being the one to initiate her return to a life filled with excitement, one filled with fun where she would want to take a part in all the things that went with it—such as sharing her bed with a man.

Cole moved in front of the fireplace and saw the framed photographs lined up on the mantel. His gaze went immediately to one in particular and knew he was seeing Patrina on her wedding day with the man who'd been her husband. From what he remembered Durango telling him, Patrina had been married five years before her husband was killed. After that she had thrown herself into her work. For some reason he couldn't help standing there staring at the photo for a long period of time.

According to Durango, Perry Foreman had been a good friend and a first-class lawman whose life had been shortened, taken away needlessly and way too soon, leaving a grieving wife behind. How long had it been? Over three years? He couldn't help wondering at what point the grieving stopped. When did a person decide to start living again?

He moved his gaze to another framed photograph. It was of Patrina with two other women. They were older women and he could see a strong family resemblance in their faces, notably the eyes and jaw. Her mother and grandmother, perhaps? He hadn't asked her about any living relatives. He knew about her brother, Dale, since they had met at Casey and McKinnon's wedding.

"I just put the biscuits in the oven. They won't take long to bake."

He turned at the sound of her voice. She was standing in the doorway that separated the kitchen from the living room and was about to turn back around when he said, "Wait a second. Who are these two women in this photo with you?"

He watched as her mouth curved in a smile, and its vibrancy almost dulled his senses. This was probably the first genuine smile she'd given him. "That's my mother and grandmother," she said, coming into the room and standing what he guessed she figured was a safe distance from him.

"Are they still living?"

He saw the sadness that crept into her eyes. "No, both are gone. I miss them." Then a slight smile touched her lips. "Everybody misses them. They were the town's midwives and so was my great-grandmother. That's four generations of Epperson women delivering babies around these parts. I don't know of many people born on the outskirts of town who weren't delivered by them. Although they trained me to follow in their footsteps, I decided to go to medical school to offer my patients the best of both worlds."

He nodded. "Dale is all the family you have?"

She chuckled and the rich sound carried through the room. "Yes, and trust me when I say that he's enough."

From the tone of her voice he could tell she shared a close relationship with her brother, the same kind he shared with Casey and Clint.

"I take it this is your husband in the other photo."

She didn't say anything for a moment, just stared at the photo. "Yes," she finally said. "That's me and Perry on our wedding day. He was a good man."

"So I heard. Durango and McKinnon liked him."

She put her hands in the pockets of her jeans and leaned against the corner of the fireplace. "Everybody liked Perry. He was that kind of person, real easy to like. And he was a good sheriff." She was quiet for a short while before adding, "He should not have gotten killed that night."

"But he did," he decided to remind her, not that he was insensitive to the pain he heard in her voice, pain she hadn't let go of even after three years. But he was thinking more along the lines of the life she was now denying herself. He didn't understand why he felt the need to push the issue every chance he got, but he did.

"You don't have to remind me of that, Cole." She

straightened her stance and all but snapped, "And Perry dying is one of the reasons I will never become involved with a lawman again."

His brows rose, not in surprise since that was something else Durango had shared with him, but because of the determination he heard in her words. As far as she was concerned her mind was made up, pretty well set on the matter. "Why?" he decided to ask, wanting to hear her reason from her own lips. "Because he died in the line of duty?"

"Yes. It was a senseless death and as far as I'm concerned that reason is good enough."

Before he could say anything to that she walked back into the kitchen. He hated telling her, but that reason wasn't good enough. She refused to believe that men who entered the world of fighting crime do so knowing their lives could be taken away at any time, but the chance of doing good, even for a short while, outweighed the risk of becoming a casualty. He had enjoyed his life as a Texas Ranger and although he knew the good guys didn't always win, they did make a difference. The only reason he and Clint were no longer rangers had nothing to do with the risks involved with the job, but had everything to do with taking advantage of other opportunities that had come their way.

"Everything is ready now, Cole."

The sound of her voice touched him in a purely elemental way. It was intensely feminine and he liked hearing it. "I'll be there in a minute," he called back to her.

As he began walking toward the bedroom to put on a shirt, he figured any other man would respect her wishes and let her live whatever kind of life she wanted, but he wasn't just any other man. He was a man very much attracted to her. He was a man of action and not someone who did anything on an idle whim. And at the moment, it seemed that he was the one who was able to push her buttons. The two times they had kissed, he had tasted her passion and her hunger, had almost drowned in it. She had enjoyed kissing him as much as he had enjoyed kissing her. There was no mistake about that. Letting her remain on that shelf was not an option. She was a woman who was meant to give and receive pleasure and he intended to do everything in his power to convince her of that.

CHAPTER FOUR

PATRINA WAS CONSCIOUS of Cole the moment he entered the kitchen. She didn't look up from placing the food items on the table; instead, her thoughts dwelled on the last time she'd shared breakfast in this house with a man who wasn't Dale. It definitely had been a long time.

She heard the water running and knew he was at the sink washing his hands. "Everything looks good, Patrina."

Knowing he was so close at hand was making it impossible for her to relax. The man had more or less stated that he planned to seduce her, or would at least try. She bet he figured that two kisses in less than twenty-four hours wasn't bad. She was determined he wouldn't make it to number three. "Thanks, Cole. Everything is ready."

"Aren't you going to join me?"

He had come to stand close beside her and his nearness almost startled her. She hadn't heard him move. "I'd love to have some company," he added.

She looked up. His jeans still hung low on his hips, but at least he had put on a shirt. She was grateful for that. She then met his gaze. "I have things to do."

"You have to eat sometime." And then he moved slightly closer and asked, "Why do I get the distinct impression that you're afraid of me? Or is it that you're afraid of what I do to you? What we do to each other?"

She looked at him. At his facial features that were so intensely handsome they made her ache, at his eyes so impressively sexy they sent a shiver racing through her. She wanted to feel irritation, but felt a throb of desire instead. She breathed in deeply, fighting the impulse to do something really foolish like accept things as they were between them and go ahead and savor the moment. She held back. A part of her was fighting to draw the line, especially with him, although she was finding it harder and harder to do so.

"Tell me. Why are you so persistent about that?" she demanded softly.

"Because of this," he said in a voice just as soft, while reaching out and taking her hand in his. "Feel it. Feel the passion."

The moment they touched, she gasped, and although she tried valiantly to fight it, she felt currents of electricity dart up her spine. Warm sensations began flooding her insides while goose bumps formed on her arm. Her stomach began tightening, and her nervous system seemed to be on overload. She met his gaze, became locked into it and saw hot desire in the dark depths of his eyes.

She blinked, hoping she was mistaken by what she saw. It was the same look he'd given her from the first. The longer his gaze held hers, the more convinced she was that she was not mistaken.

He smoothly withdrew his hand from hers, dropped it to his side before saying, "I think I've made my point."

Whether he made it or not, it was a point not too well taken. One she intended to ignore. "Think whatever you want, Cole. I suggest you sit down and eat before your food gets cold."

"Ladies first."

She regarded him steadily as she took the chair that he held out for her. "Thanks."

His mouth curved into a sexy smile. "You're more than welcome."

It was then that she realized she had done exactly what he'd wanted by sitting down to eat with him. He sat across from her and followed her lead and said grace. Then he began helping himself to everything. There was plenty of food. She'd served biscuits, sausages, eggs, bacon, orange juice and coffee. One thing she'd quickly found out about him was that he enjoyed eating.

He took a sip of coffee. "You make the best coffee. Hot, strong, not too sweet. Just right."

She didn't want to say that's how Perry had liked his coffee. She had an instinctive feeling he wouldn't appreciate hearing it.

"Your television works, right?"

She glanced up and looked across the table at him. "Yes."

"Why don't you have it on?"

She shrugged before biting into a piece of bacon. "I usually don't have time to watch television. Not nowadays, anyway. I'm too busy with the work I do at the hospital and the clinic. Besides, there's nothing on most of the time other than those reality shows or cop shows. I can do without either."

"You mean you're not a *CSI* fan?" he asked, smiling, before taking another sip of his coffee.

"I don't want to have anything to do with anything connected to law enforcement and that includes watching it on television."

"I'm sure your position on that hasn't made your local police department happy."

She placed her fork beside her plate and glared at him. "Don't try twisting my words. I'm not saying that I don't support or appreciate what they do. I was a lawman's wife too long not to. All I'm saying is that it's a life I don't want to be a part of ever again."

Cole didn't say anything but couldn't help wondering if her words, like the ones she had spoken earlier, were meant to deter him since she assumed he was still a Texas Ranger. No one in his family, not even his father and sister, knew he had left the agency. He planned to surprise them with the news when he saw them at his father's birthday party. Of course Clint knew, and because they were working on a business deal together, his cousin Quade was aware of it.

He had seen no reason not to mention it to Patrina—until now. With what she had just said and the statement she'd made earlier, he felt the need to prove to her that what he did for a living didn't matter when it came to the passion sizzling between them. One had nothing to do with the other.

"You're free to watch anything on television you like, Cole. I'm into a good book, anyway."

He glanced over at her. "A Rock Mason novel?"

She smiled as she leaned back in her chair. "Yes, a Rock Mason novel."

He couldn't help but smile since they both knew that Rock Mason was actually his cousin, Stone Westmoreland. Stone's wife, Madison, had given birth to a son a couple of months ago. "Have you figured out who's going to be the next victim yet?" he couldn't help asking her. Stone was an ace when it came to writing thrillers.

"No, not yet. The book's definitely a page-turner, though. Stone has another bestseller under his belt."

They didn't say anything else for a while as they continued to eat. At one point Patrina risked glancing across the table at Cole to find him sipping his coffee and staring at her. She quickly refocused on her food.

"Is there anything you need me to do, Patrina?"

She quickly glanced up and met his gaze. "Anything like what?"

He shrugged. "Chop wood for the fireplace, help wash the breakfast dishes, go outside and play in the snow…you name it and I'm all for it."

The thought of the last item made her chuckle.

She couldn't see the two of them doing something as outrageous as playing outside in the snow. "There's already enough wood chopped. Dale took care of that when he was passing through last month. As far as the dishes are concerned, I plan to just rinse them off and place them in the dishwasher."

"And the offer for us to go outside and play in the snow?" he asked, still staring at her.

"I'll pass on that one. It's too cold outside."

"You of all people should be used to it," Cole said, chuckling. "Come outside with me. I dare you."

She shook her head. "Don't waste your time daring me because I'm not going outside. Besides, you still need to take it easy."

"I feel fine," he assured her. Without breaking their gazes he pushed his chair away from the table and stood. "Why don't you go get comfortable and start on your book while I load up the dishwasher?"

"Cole, you don't have to do that."

"But I want to. I need something to keep me busy. Go ahead and start reading your book."

"I started reading it last night."

He nodded as he began gathering the dishes off the table. "I know. I woke up a few times and saw you sitting in the chair reading. Then I saw you'd fallen asleep with the book in your hand. The last time I woke up and glanced over at the chair, it was empty."

Patrina gave a small, dismissive shrug. "The chair was getting uncomfortable and I needed to get into bed."

He paused for a moment and looked over and met

her gaze. "You could have shared mine. I would not have minded and would gladly have moved over and made room for you." He resumed collecting the dishes.

She let out a deep sigh. "You don't plan on letting up, do you."

He didn't bother looking at her when he said, "I've already explained the situation to you, Patrina. Nothing has changed. In fact, I'm more determined than ever." He walked over to the sink and began placing the dishes in it.

"Why?"

With that one question, one word, he turned around, and she was amazed at how intensely she could feel the direct hit of his gaze. "We covered that already," he said, speaking in a calm and rational tone. "You already know why. But if you need reminding, the simple fact is, I want you and you want me."

"And what if I said I *don't* want you? That I don't have any sexual interest in you whatsoever?" she said, getting to her feet and glaring across the room at him.

"Then I'd say you were lying or that you're a woman who doesn't know what she wants."

Patrina took offense. "Nothing is going to happen between us, Cole," she said, determined to stand her ground.

"You want to bet?" he challenged. "You felt the same thing I did when I touched your hand earlier. And it was there in the kisses we've shared. Deny it all you want, sweetheart, but even now I can feel your heat. I can almost taste it. And eventually, I *will* taste it," he said.

"You think I'm a woman who can't resist your charms?"

He crossed his arms over his chest and leaned back against the counter. His gaze roved over her from head to toe before he said, "No, but I do admit to being a man who can't seem to resist yours."

THINKING THAT HE apparently liked having the last word, and seeing no reason to continue a conversation with him that was going nowhere, Patrina walked out of the kitchen. Once in the living room she forced herself to breathe in deeply. Of all the arrogant men she'd ever encountered, Cole Westmoreland took the cake.

And the nerve of him to claim that he was a man who couldn't resist her charms. Yeah, right. Did he actually expect her to believe that? Suddenly a tightness tugged deep in her stomach. What if he was telling the truth? What if the desire they felt for each other was just that strong? Just that powerful? What if it became uncontrollable?

She quickly did a mental review of everything that had happened since she'd brought him into her home, especially that time while, when folding up clothes, she'd looked up to find him staring at her. Could two people actually connect that spontaneously? Could they suddenly want each other to a degree where they would lose their minds, as well as their common sense, to passion?

She was definitely out of her element here. She and Perry had been childhood sweethearts, had known each other since junior high school when his family had moved into the area. There had never been a rushed moment in their relationship. He was easygoing and patient. The fact that they'd made love for the first time on their wedding night attested to that. All those years when they had dated, they had managed to control their overzealous hormones with very little effort. With Perry she had never felt pressured or overwhelmed. And she'd certainly never felt the intense sexual chemistry she felt with Cole. But still…

Just because they were attracted to each other was no reason to act on that attraction. Of course Cole saw things differently and was of the belief their attraction alone was enough reason to act on it. He was clearly a man who had no qualms about indulging in a casual relationship and expected her to follow suit. Well, she had news for him. There wasn't that much passion in the world that would make her consider such a thing.

Leaving the living room, she went into her bedroom and in a bout of both anger and frustration, she slammed the door shut behind her. She crossed the room and snatched the book off the dresser. *Fine!* Let him spend some time alone since he only saw her as a body he was eager to pounce on. Maybe if she ignored him, that would eventually knock some sense into him.

Stretching out on the bed, she opened her book and began reading. She refused to let Cole get on her last nerve.

HE'D HAVE TO be an idiot not to know he'd made Patrina mad again, Cole thought, as he loaded the last plate into the dishwasher. And if she thought ignoring him would do the trick, she was sadly mistaken. She had to come out of hiding sooner or later. He had enough to keep himself busy until she did. He loved working word puzzles and had a ton of them packed in his luggage. There was nothing like stimulating his mind, since thanks to Patrina the rest of him was already there.

Feeling frustration settling in, he walked over to the window and stared out at the still-falling snow. But despite its thickness, in the distance he could see the mountains, snow-covered and definitely a beautiful sight, postcard perfect.

Deciding he would forgo watching television and start on those word puzzles, he walked out of the living room toward the guest room. He paused a moment by Patrina's closed bedroom door, tempted to knock. But then he decided he was in enough hot water with her already. It was time to chill and allow her time to come to terms with everything he'd said to her. Besides, she couldn't stay locked up behind closed doors all day.

A smile touched his lips when he thought of a way to eventually get her out of there. She had to come out and eat some time.

PATRINA GLANCED OVER at the clock and then stretched out on the bed to change positions. It was late afternoon already and a glance out the window showed it was snowing more heavily than before.

She couldn't believe she had been reading nearly nonstop since the morning, but at least it had given her time by herself. The last thing she'd wanted was another encounter with Cole. There was no doubt in her mind that he had his mind set on wearing down her defenses, and she intended to resist him every step of the way.

Suddenly she sat up in bed and sniffed the air. A delicious aroma was coming from the kitchen. She got out of bed and opened the door and found the scent was even stronger. Curious, she walked out into the hall and headed for the kitchen. Once there she paused in the doorway. Cole was standing beside the stove stirring a pot, and even with a huge spoon in his hand and an apron tied around his waist, she was fully aware of his potent masculinity.

"What are you doing?" she couldn't help asking.

He glanced over at her and smiled. She tried not to notice what that smile did to her insides. She breathed in to stop her stomach from doing flips. "I thought I'd be the one to prepare dinner tonight," he said, giving her a thorough once-over, and making it obvious he was doing so.

She tried ignoring him. "I didn't know you could cook."

He chuckled. "There's a lot you don't know about me, but yes, I can cook and I like doing it. By the time the table is set everything will be ready. I thought I'd try some of my Texas chili on you."

She leaned against the counter. "It smells good."

"Thanks, and later you'll agree that it tastes as good as it smells."

She rolled her eyes. The man was so overly confident it was a shame. "What do you need me to do?"

"Nothing. I have everything taken care of. The rolls are about ready to come out of the oven and the salad is in the refrigerator. Did you enjoy your rest?"

A part of her felt guilty knowing that while she'd been stretched across the bed reading, he had been busy at work in the kitchen. "Yes, but you should have let me help you."

He chuckled as he took the rolls out of the oven. "No way. I got the distinct impression this morning that you'd had enough of me for a while and needed your space."

He had certainly read things correctly, she thought, moving to the sink to wash her hands. "The least I can do is help by setting the table."

Not waiting for him to say whether she could help or not, she went to the cabinets to take down the plates. After all, it was *her* kitchen.

"Did you finish your book?"

She glanced at him over her shoulder and became far too aware of his stance. He was no longer standing in front of the stove, but had moved to lean a hip against the counter. She was totally conscious of the sexy way his jeans fit his body, and it made her suddenly feel warm. Then there was the way his shirt stretched across a muscular chest and the way—

"Well, did you?"

She blinked upon realizing he was asking her something. The deep baritone of his voice vibrated along every nerve in her body. "Did I what?"

He smiled in a way that was just as sexy as his stance. "Did you finish the book?"

"Not yet. But things are getting pretty interesting," she said quietly, thinking it wasn't just happening that way in the book. She met his dark gaze and felt shivers go up her spine.

"Are you going to set the table?"

Patrina looked down and then it hit her that she was standing there holding the plates in her hands and staring. "Yes, I'm going to do it," she said, pushing away from the cabinet. He moved at the same time she did and the next thing she knew they were facing each other. He took the plates out of her hands and placed them on the table.

He then gave her his complete attention. "I know you needed your space, but I didn't like it," he said huskily.

She didn't know what to say, so she just stood there and stared up at him, finding it hard not to do so. In fact, she was finding it hard to concentrate on anything at the moment—except the perfect specimen of a man standing in front of her.

"Why didn't you like it?" she heard herself asking, and nervously licked her lips. She couldn't help noticing how his gaze latched on to the movement of her tongue.

"Because I would have preferred you spend time with me," he said in a barely audible voice.

Although she already had an idea, she asked, anyway. "Doing what?"

His sexy smile became sexier when he said, "Word puzzles."

She blinked again, not sure she'd heard him correctly. "Word puzzles?"

He nodded slowly. "Yes, I'm good at working them."

As far as she was concerned, that wasn't the only thing he was good at working. He was definitely doing a good job working her. Her body was tingling from the mere fact that he was standing so close. It wouldn't take much to reach up and loop her arms around his neck, and then pull his mouth down to hers and then...

"Don't think it, Patrina. Just do it," he whispered throatily, leaning in closer.

Their gazes locked and she wondered how he'd known what she'd been thinking. It must have shown in her eyes, or it could have been the sound of her breathing. She couldn't help noticing it had gotten rather choppy.

"You're hesitating. Let me go ahead and get you started," he whispered in a raspy voice before reaching out and cupping her face in his hands, And at the same time he shifted his body, specifically his hips, to press against hers, aligning their bodies perfectly.

Whenever he touched her, her body would automatically respond and it didn't behave any differently now. But she couldn't explain the degree with which it was doing so. Desire was rushing through her with a force that nearly left her breathless and the nipples of her breasts were feeling taut, tender, sensitive. Heat flared low in her body, making it hard to think, so she was doing what he had asked her to do several times. She was feeling the passion.

She could feel the heat of his gaze as his mouth inched closer to her lips; she could feel the hard evidence of his desire that was pressed against her abdomen. And she could also feel the touch of his hand on her face, warm, strong and steady.

Then their lips touched and she no longer felt the passion, she tasted it. It had a flavor all its own. Tart, tingly and so incredibly arousing it had her heart pounding relentlessly in her chest as he continued to kiss her with a single-minded purpose that went deeper than anything she'd ever felt before. It was a primal need she didn't know she was capable of.

And then she noticed his hands were no longer on her face but had moved to her rear end. He was pressing her closer to him, letting her feel the state of his arousal. Instinctively she moved her hips against it and he took the kiss deeper.

Not bothering to question why, she gave in to her needs, needs he was forcing her to admit she had. His tongue aggressively dueled with hers and she wrapped her arms around his neck to lock their mouths in place. With her firm grip the only thing he was capable of doing was changing the angle of the kiss and in doing so, she heard him groan deep in his throat.

One of them, she thought, had on too many clothes and quickly concluded it had to be him. She felt his hard erection pressed against her, and now she wanted to really feel it, to touch it, take it in her hand and hold it. As if her hands had a mind of their own, they moved from around his neck and reached down and began pulling out his shirt before lowering his zipper and then reaching for his belt buckle with an urgency she couldn't control.

And then the buzzer on the stove went off.

For her it had the effect of ice water being tossed on a hot surface, and she pulled away from him with such speed that she almost tripped in the process. He reached out to keep her from falling, but she jerked away and turned her back to him. But not before she saw that his shirt had been pulled out of his pants and that his zipper was down. Embarrassment flooded her face in knowing she had done both and had intended to go even further.

"Patrina?"

She refused to turn around to let him look at her. A part of her wished that somehow the floor would open up and swallow her whole. How in the world had she let things get so out of hand?

"Patrina, turn around and look at me."

"No," she said over her shoulder as she began moving toward the living room. "I don't want to look at you. I want to be left alone."

"What you are, Patrina, is afraid," he said, and from the sound of it, he was right on her heels, but she refused to slow down to see if he was or not. "You are afraid that you might give in to your passion, continue to feel it and be driven to admit to the very thing you're trying so hard to deny."

That did it. She suddenly stopped and turned and he all but ran into her and made her lose her balance. She tumbled onto the sofa and he went with her, and when her back hit the leather cushion, he ended up sprawled on top of her, his face just inches from hers.

She opened her mouth to scream at him to get off her, but no words formed in her throat. Instead, her gaze latched on to a pair of sensual lips that were so close to hers she could feel his heated breath. When she shifted her gaze, she also saw vibrant fire lighting the dark depths of his eyes. Looking into them seemed to have a hypnotic effect and she felt her entire body getting hot all over.

He didn't say anything. He continued to look at her with the same intensity as she was looking at him, and she found herself wondering why she'd never shared something of this degree, something of this level of intimacy with Perry. There had been plenty of physical contact between them and she had enjoyed their kisses, but they hadn't been full of fire like the ones Cole delivered. In analyzing things now, it seemed that she and Perry were too close as friends to become so intimate as lovers. He had to be the kindest and gentlest man she'd ever known and those characteristics extended into their bedroom. When they had made love it seemed like he'd been intent on keeping their level of intimacy at a minimum. It was as if he'd thought of her as a piece of crystal, something meant to be handled carefully or else it would break.

Cole wasn't treating her like a piece of crystal. He was treating her like a woman he thought could deliver passion to match his. Personally she thought he was expecting way too much from her. But then he had a way of making her body tingle just by being near her. And a part of her believed that he couldn't give any woman just a minimum level of intimacy. A man of his sensual nature was only capable of delivering a level that would go way beyond the max. It would be off the charts. The thought of that made her breath catch in her throat.

She noted he was still staring at her. She also noted his lips were moving closer. Then they paused as if they refused to move any farther. And she became aware of what he was doing. He was leaving the decision to take things beyond what they were right now to her. He wouldn't push her any further.

The look in his eyes made sensations stir within her, made her blood flow through her veins in a way that just couldn't be normal. They were lying on the sofa fully clothed, yet she could still feel his heat. Not only was she feeling it, she seemed to be absorbing it, right through her clothes and into her skin.

She could no longer question what he was doing to her or why. She wasn't dealing with a mild-mannered man like Perry. At the moment there wasn't a single thing refined about Cole that she could think of. He was a man who went after what he wanted without any finesse or skilled diplomacy.

They didn't say anything for a long moment. They continued to lie together and stare at each other, fueling the fire between them, a fire destined to become an inferno. She felt the full length of him, every muscle of his perfect physique, pressed against her, and she began to fall deeper and deeper into a sea of sexual desire. Then she heard herself give a little moan before looping her arms around his neck to bring his mouth down to hers.

The moment their lips touched, his tongue entered her mouth like it had every right to do so, and like those other times, it took over not only her mouth but her senses. He was kissing her with pure, unadulterated possession. And as if she'd been given her cue, she kissed him back with a fervor she didn't know she had until meeting him.

Moments later, and she wasn't sure just how much later, he broke off the kiss and pressed his forehead against hers as if to catch his breath. She needed to catch her breath, also. And then as if he couldn't help himself, he shifted their bodies sideways and then leaned forward and placed a brief, erotic kiss on her lips that caused a stirring in her stomach, an urgency that seemed to consume her.

For a long moment they lay there in silence while he held her, then both got to their feet. A slow smile curved his mouth. "I think we should go into the kitchen and eat now," he said in a warmly seductive voice as he pulled her closer into his arms.

"And then," he added while holding her gaze with an intensity that made her shudder, "what takes place after dinner will be strictly your call."

CHAPTER FIVE

COLE GLANCED ACROSS the table at Patrina. She hadn't said much since they had begun eating. He figured what he'd told her moments ago in the living room had given her something to think about.

She was stubborn, filled with more spirit and fire than any woman he'd ever met. Considering those things, she probably would still not admit to wanting him, and definitely would not act on it, although they had kissed about four times now. And they hadn't been chaste kisses, either, but the kind that set your body on fire. Hell, his body was still burning and he was hard as a rock.

At least if nothing else he was proving to her that she was indeed a sensual woman, something else she still probably wanted to deny. All and all, he felt that when it came to Patrina Foreman, he still had one hell of a challenge on his hands. The good doctor just refused to acknowledge what was so blatantly obvious. She needed a good roll in the hay just as much as he did. He refused to let up trying to convince her that indulging in a couple of sexual encounters with him was just what she needed.

Deciding the silence between them had lasted

long enough, he figured it was time to get her talking. She was very dedicated to her job, so he decided to begin there. He leaned back in his chair, took a sip of his wine and asked, "What exactly do you do at that clinic, Patrina?"

It took her a while but she finally lifted her head and looked at him. And then she was frowning. "Why do you want to know?"

He shrugged. "Because I'm interested."

She gave a doubtful snort, which meant she didn't believe him. He understood what she was doing. For a little while she had let her guard down with him and now she was trying to recover ground and put it back up. "And why would you be interested?"

He had an answer for her. "Because I'm interested in anything that involves you," he said, completely honest and totally unfazed by the cold look she was giving him.

It was hard to believe that less than an hour ago she had been warm and willing in his arms. She'd kissed him with as much passion as he'd been kissing her. The memory of their tumble onto the couch and the way their lips had locked still had heat thrumming through him. He was in worse shape now than before mainly because he had gotten a good taste of that bottled-up passion and was determined to get her off that damn shelf now more than ever.

"So tell me," he said when she refused to start talking. "I'm really interested in what you do at that clinic, so tell me."

"What if I don't want to?" she asked through tight lips.

He smiled. "Um, I can think of several ways to make you talk."

Evidently the ones he'd been thinking of crossed her mind, too, and she quickly dropped her gaze and began studying her glass of wine. Then she said, "It's a women's clinic that provides free services, which include physicals, breasts exams, pap smears, pregnancy testing, comprehensive health education, as well as many other types of needed services."

"How often are you there?"

She shrugged. "It's voluntary and I'm there as much as I can be, usually at least a few hours each day. I wish I could do more. Funding is tight and the medical equipment we need isn't cheap. We depend on private donations to ensure ongoing services for women who lack access to adequate health care."

"Pregnant women?"

"*All* women. Last year, our outreach program provided services to over a thousand homeless women. We believe all women deserve excellent health care, regardless of their ability to pay, and..."

Cole listened as she continued talking and could tell that her work at the clinic was something she was very passionate about. But then, he had discovered that she was a very passionate person...and very expressive. He couldn't stop looking at her while she was speaking and how she used her hands to get several points across. She had nice hands and he would do just about anything to feel those hands on him.

She'd come close, had even unzipped his pants before that damn timer on the stove had gone off. Hell, he wished he'd remembered to turn the thing off when he'd taken the rolls out of the oven.

His gaze moved from her hands over her face, scanning her eyebrows, cheekbone and nose before latching on to her lips. Damn, they were kissable lips and he wouldn't mind tasting them again. But what he really wanted was her naked and in bed with him. He wanted to move in place between her lush thighs and get inside her, move in and out, see the expression on her face when he made her come. Feel the shuddering power of his release when he did likewise.

"Sorry..." She paused and drew in a quick breath. "I didn't mean to go on and on like that. I kind of get carried away."

Her words pulled him back in. "No reason to apologize," he quickly said. "I found everything you said interesting." *At least I did when I wasn't thinking about making love to you.*

"Since you cooked, the least I can do is take care of the dishes," she said, getting to her feet.

He could tell she was nervous about what she perceived as his expectations on how the evening should end. When she reached for his plate, he grabbed hold of her hand and gently gripped her fingers with his. "I don't like it when you seem afraid of me, Patrina." He felt the shiver that passed through her and then that same shiver passed through him.

She tried pulling her hand free but he kept a tight

hold and wouldn't let it go. "I'm not afraid of you, Cole. I'm just unsure about a lot of things right now."

"Don't be unsure of anything," he said quietly. "Especially when it involves us."

He watched as she drew a deep breath and then released it before saying, "But there is no *us,* Cole."

He regarded her for several silent seconds, saw the determined glint in her gaze, the stubborn set of her jaw. "You didn't think that a couple of hours ago on that sofa. Need I remind you of what almost happened?"

She tugged her hand from his and narrowed her eyes. "It was a mistake."

The corners of his mouth curved into a smile. "It was more like satisfaction to me. I could have kept on kissing you and you could have kept on kissing me." He was tempted to go ahead and tell her, anyway, in blatant, plain English of the most erotic kind just where all that kissing could have led, but he decided not to. The fiery spark in her eyes was a clear indication that she wouldn't appreciate hearing it. She wasn't too happy with him right now, which meant they were back to square one.

"Look, Patrina, if it makes you happy, I'll help you do the dishes and then we can go to bed." At her piercing glare he quickly said, "Separate beds, of course. This has been a long and tiring day for me." And that, he thought, was putting it mildly. Spending another night with a hard-on was something he wasn't looking forward to. "But then, if you want to share my bed I have nothing against it," he said in a low voice that sounded like a sexual rumble even to his own ears.

"I'm sleeping in my bed tonight and you're sleeping in yours," she said, as if saying it to him would make it happen.

"If that's the way you want things."

"It is."

"Then at least let me help you with the dishes," he said, taking another sip of his wine, resisting the urge to reach out to take her hand in his again, tumble her into his lap, pour some of the wine down the front of her blouse and be so bold as to lap the wine up with his tongue.

"I can handle the dishes on my own," she said, breaking into his thoughts while stacking up the plates. "I don't need your help."

He stood and slid his hands into the pockets of his jeans, thinking she had to be the most stubborn woman he had encountered in a long time. "Fine, I'll leave you to it, then."

She regarded him carefully, as if she didn't believe for one minute he would give in to her that easily. When she saw that he was, she said, "Good."

He moved away from the table, but before he walked out of the kitchen he turned to her. "No, what would be good in my book—actually better than good—is sharing a bed with you."

PATRINA RELEASED A DEEP, frustrated sigh of relief the moment she heard the shower going in the guest room. That relief was short-lived when her mind was suddenly filled with visions of a naked Cole standing under a spray of water.

She closed her eyes, fighting off the forbidden thoughts, refusing to let her mind go there, but it seemed to be going there, anyway. She couldn't forget how they had tumbled onto the sofa, how his solid, muscled body had been on top of hers, how his firm thighs had worked themselves between her legs in such a way that denim rubbing again denim had been an actual turn-on.

It didn't do much for her to remember how she had latched on to his mouth to finish what had started in the kitchen. Once again he had reminded her just how much of a female she was. Just how much passion she had been missing out on—both before and after Perry's death.

She quickly opened her eyes, not wanting to go there, refusing to think about it. Perry had been simply great in the bedroom; he'd just handled her a lot differently than Cole would—if given the chance. But she refused to give him the chance and the sooner he realized that, the better off the both of them would be.

She and Cole were playing this vicious game of tug-of-war where he was determined to come out the winner. And she was just as determined that he be the loser. Considering the kitchen scene earlier when she had come close to touching him in an intimate way, as well as the tumble onto the sofa, she would go so far as to admit that for a little while, she had gotten caught up in passion and had allowed him to break down her defenses. But she had recovered, was of sound mind, on top of her game, and simply refused to let him get an advantage again. She had to show him that she wasn't just some naive country girl.

She wasn't born yesterday and was well aware that it was all about sex to him. Nothing more than a quick tumble between the sheets. But then, knowing Cole, she suspected there would be nothing quick about it. He would draw it out, savor every second. He would strive to make her experience things that she had never experienced before, even during her five years of marriage. Already his kisses had taken her into unfamiliar territory.

Okay, she would be the first to admit that curiosity and desire had almost gotten the best of her, had almost done her in, but she was back in control. Talking about the clinic had helped. It had made her remember just how many women she'd counseled about the importance of being accountable for their actions and whatever decisions they made. It was time for her to take a dose of her own medicine.

It didn't take her long to finish the dishes and sweep the floor, deciding to have both done before Cole took a notion to return. She would retire early tonight and finish reading her book. But first she wanted to listen to the weather report. She needed to know just how much longer it would be before Cole was able to leave so she could get her life back to how it had been before he arrived—all work and no play, filled with apathy, definitely lacking passion.

Before he had set foot in her house, the only desire she had was for the work she did at the doctor's office she owned and at the clinic. She would admit she lived a boring life. *Would it really be totally wrong, absolutely insane to sample some of what Cole was offering, and for once to forget about everything and everyone other than myself and my own needs?*

He said he wanted her and she had no reason not to believe him, especially once it appeared he had been aroused all day, at least whenever he was in her presence. She was a medical doctor, so she recognized the obvious signs. But then, she was a woman, as well, and given that, she had done more than noted the signs. For a while she had gotten caught up in it, gloried in the fact that he found her so desirable he couldn't control his body's reaction.

The thought that she could do something like that to a man, especially a man like Cole, was totally mind-boggling. Maybe she should rethink her position, give in to her desires, to see where it got the both of them. It wasn't like he was a permanent resident of Bozeman, so chances were that when the weather cleared for him to leave, she probably wouldn't be seeing him again while he was visiting Casey. She knew about the huge party Casey and Abby had planned for Corey later in the month, and she had every intention of attending. Even if she and Cole did share a bed before he left, by the time the party happened, she should be able to put the affair behind her so that when she saw him again, she wouldn't have a flare-up of passion, at least not of the degree she was having now. So maybe sleeping with him—to work him out of her system—wasn't such a bad idea.

Deciding she'd drunk too much wine at dinner for her to be considering such a thing, she moved across the kitchen to turn on the radio, as well as to put on a pot of coffee. She needed to sober up her brain cells.

Not much later she was standing at the window looking out with a cup of coffee in her hand. It was dark outside and still snowing. According to the weather report, things should start clearing up by late tomorrow evening or early the following day. That meant that this could be the last night Cole would have to stay under her roof. There was a chance he could leave for Casey and McKinnon's place before dark tomorrow. Then she could have her house all to herself again. She wouldn't have to worry about dressing decently if she didn't want to, or having a man underfoot. Nor would she have to worry about her hormones going wacky on her from a purely male dimpled smile or a dark lustful gaze.

"Is it still snowing?"

She quickly turned, sloshing some of the hot coffee on her hand. "Ouch."

Before she knew what was happening, Cole had quickly crossed the room to take the cup out of her hand and place it on the counter. "What are you trying to do? Burn yourself?" he asked in a deep voice filled with concern.

"You startled me," she accused.

"Sorry. I didn't mean to."

She tried ignoring the sensual huskiness in his voice. "Well, you did."

It was then that she noticed what he was wearing. In her opinion it was very little. He was barefoot with only a pair of boxer pajama bottoms, similar to the ones Dale liked to wear, but she never had reason to notice how snug they fit Dale. They were a silk pair and she was sure they belonged to a set. So where was the top part? Or at the very least, a matching robe.

Maybe she should at least be grateful that he was wearing anything at all, since some men preferred sleeping in the nude. But then, this wasn't his house. It was hers and under those circumstances he didn't have a choice in the matter.

But still…even with the boxer shorts there were a few things she couldn't help but notice. Like the fact he was still aroused. The cut of the boxers made that much completely obvious. She didn't want to stare but she found that she couldn't help herself. He was huge and as packed as any man had a right to be and then some. She subconsciously clamped her inner thighs together at the thought of something that size going into her. There was no way she wouldn't get stretched to the limit.

"So what do you think?"

She blinked and quickly shifted her gaze to his face. "About what?"

"The weather," he said, his dark gaze holding hers.

She couldn't help wondering if they were really

discussing the weather. Regardless, she intended to play right along. "It's my understanding it should start clearing up tomorrow."

There was a bit of silence, then he said, "That means I'll be able to leave."

"Yes. I'm sure Casey will be glad to see you."

"Just like I'm sure you'll be glad to be all alone again."

Patrina suddenly felt a shiver of apprehension run up her spine. Would she really be glad to be all alone again?

"There's a full moon in the sky," he said quietly.

It was then that she noticed he was no longer looking at her but was looking out the window and up at the sky. She pondered his comment and wondered if it had any specific meaning. When she couldn't think of one she said, "And?" She figured there had to be more.

Although he didn't look at her, she saw his smile. "According to Ian, each full moon has a different meaning and a magical purpose," he said as he continued to gaze out the window and look at the sky.

Ian was Cole's cousin and considered the astronomer in the Westmoreland family because he had a degree in physics and had once worked for NASA. Ian was now the owner of a beautiful casino on Lake Tahoe. "And what do you think is the meaning of this full moon?" she couldn't help but ask.

He turned to her. "A full moon in April is the Seed Moon. It's the time to plant your seeds of desire in Mother Earth."

She raised a suspicious brow. "And you distinctly remember Ian saying that?"

His smile widened as he turned back to the window. "No. He gave me a book and I distinctly recall reading it."

"Oh." *Planting seeds of desire in Mother Earth.* She wasn't about to ask how that was done. But she couldn't deny it had her thinking, making a number of possibilities flow through her mind. Planting seeds of desire sounded a lot like setting someone up for seduction.

"Like I told you yesterday," Cole began, breaking into her thoughts, "neither Casey nor my father was expecting me this soon and they don't have any idea what day I arrived, so if you prefer, I won't let them know I spent some time here, stranded during the snowstorm with you."

"Why should it matter?" she asked. "Nothing happened between us."

He looked at her, raised an arched brow. "Nothing?"

She shrugged. "Okay, we kissed a few times."

"Yes, we did, didn't we?" he said softly, his gaze latched on to her lips. His dark eyes then shifted and held hers and she began to feel a sharp ache below her stomach.

"Yes," she finally answered. "We did."

"Want to do it again?"

That was one question she hadn't expected, yet she should not have been surprised that he had asked it. In the past thirty hours, she had discovered that

Cole Westmoreland was a man who did or said whatever pleased him.

She opened her mouth to say that, no, she didn't want to do it again, then immediately closed it, thinking who was she kidding? She enjoyed kissing him and, yes, she wanted to do it again since it probably would be the last time she did so. He would be leaving tomorrow and chances were their paths wouldn't cross again—at least not in such an intimate setting.

She glanced out the window, thinking that the most sensible thing to do was turn and escape to her bedroom and not have any more contact with him. But for some reason she didn't want to think sensibly. She really didn't want to think at all, and the only time she couldn't think was when she was in his arms sharing a kiss.

"Patrina?"

She returned her gaze to his. "Perhaps," she said softly.

He arched a brow. "Perhaps?"

She nodded. "Perhaps, I want to do it again."

He gave her a level look. "Don't you know for certain?"

Patrina heard the slight tremor in his voice. "Well, maybe I prefer that you take your time and convince me that I do."

Her words seemed to hang between them as they stared at each other, and for some reason, all she could think about was his mouth making her pulse race. And then he broke into her thoughts when he said in a gentle yet throaty voice, "I hope you understand what you're asking."

Oh, I understand all right, but it'll only be limited to kissing. She could handle that. Her throat suddenly felt tight, constricted, but she managed to force through enough sound to say, "I understand what I'm asking, Cole."

As soon as she stated her affirmation, she was pulled into strong, muscular arms.

CHAPTER SIX

THE FIRST THING Cole wanted to do was taste her. He couldn't resist. Just one quick taste and then he would go about his business, taking his time to convince her that they needed to kiss again and again—definitely a lot longer each and every time.

His mouth brushed hers, just long enough to snake out his tongue and caress her bottom lip with its tip. He heard her sharp intake of breath and quickly pulled back on her moan. He did it again, a second longer this time, a little more provocatively when he wiggled the tip of his tongue while caressing the tantalizing surface of her upper lip.

He withdrew when she released another moan, this one throatier than the last and saw that her eyes had closed and her lips were moist from where his tongue had been. He liked the look of it. He also liked the look in her eyes when she reopened them to stare at him. He saw something hot and sensuous in their depths and fought for control not to say the hell with it and pull her into his arms and give her a long, hungry kiss.

Deciding to take the degree of her desire, as well as his, to another level, one that he could sufficiently handle, he reached out and with the tip of his finger, traced a path from her moist bottom lip down past her jaw to where her pulse was beating wildly in her throat. She said nothing while watching him attentively, but he could hear the unevenness of her breathing.

And then his lips and tongue replaced his finger while they moved all over her face, wanting to leave his mark everywhere on her features. And when he felt a shiver pass through her, he knew she was ready for something heavier and pulled her closer into his arms and greedily claimed her mouth in a long, slow kiss that made shivers run through her body even more than before.

Moments later, he pulled back and whispered the question close to her moist lips. "Want to try another one?"

Instead of answering, she nodded, and then he was back at her lips, devouring them in a way that shook him to the core. Never had his tongue been so ravenous for a woman's mouth; never had his palate been so famished. He could go on kissing her all night, but he wanted each one to be slow, long and fulfilling. And from the sound of her moans, they were.

He thought that this type of seduction suited her perfectly. Something slow and detailed while stirring her passion. With each stroke of his tongue he was able to discover just what she liked, what she had never experienced before and just what she wanted him to do again.

He also discovered what part of her mouth gave her the most pleasure, what part of it his tongue touched that made her moan the loudest, made her desire the strongest. He knew he could make her come just from kissing her if he were to turn up the heat a notch, and a part of him was pushed to do just that. That would lead into him giving her another type of kiss while at the same time experiencing a different taste of her.

The thought of doing so made his body harden even more, made his erection throb in a way that had him clutching for breath. All she'd given him was the liberty to kiss her. However, he intended to show her that when it came to kissing, there was no such thing as limitations. Kissing came in several forms and it could be done to a number of places, not confined just to the lips. No parts of the body were exempt. When she'd affirmed her understanding, he doubted that she knew the full extent of where it could lead. But he, on the other hand, understood perfectly and intended to take whatever kisses he delivered to the highest level possible.

He eased down on the windowsill, found it sturdy enough to hold his weight and pulled her to stand between his open legs, which put him eye to eye with her chest. He drew in a tight breath when he noticed how the nipples of her breasts were straining against her blouse as if begging to be freed. And he had no qualms about obliging the pair.

Still holding Patrina's gaze he began undoing the buttons, and each one exposed more of her black lacy bra. When all the buttons were undone, he eased the blouse from her arms and shoulders.

"You're only supposed to kiss me," he heard her remind him in a ragged voice.

"I know and I shall," he said throatily, letting his fingers move to the front clasp of her bra. "But kissing comes in many forms."

Then with a flick of his fingers her bra opened and her breasts burst forth. His mouth and hand were on them immediately, lightly cupping one while his mouth greedily devoured the other. He knew the moment she lifted her arms and held his head to her breasts, evidently thinking if she didn't do so he would stop. But there was no way he could stop. The taste of her was being absorbed into everything about him that was male, and her luscious essence—hot and enticing—was playing havoc with his senses.

She moaned his name over and over, and the more he heard it, the more he wanted to make her say it that much more, with even more meaning. He decided to put his other hand, the one that was free at the moment, to work and knew just where he wanted it to be and what he wanted it to do.

Reaching down he found the snap to her slacks and slowly worked it free to open it. She was so wrapped up in what he was doing to her breasts that she was unaware of what he was doing to the lower part of her body. He tugged her pants apart at the waist and the moment he did so, he inserted his hand inside and his fingers inched past the flimsy material of her panties to cup her feminine mound. He felt her body go still at the intimate touch and he freed the nipple in his mouth long enough to glance up and meet her gaze.

"Wh-what are you doing?" she asked in a strained voice, but she didn't pull away.

He chose his words carefully and spoke softly. "Like I said earlier, kissing comes in several forms. Will you trust me tonight to introduce you to a few of them?"

She said nothing as her gaze held his and he knew she was trying to come to terms with what he was saying, trying to decide just what she should do. He realized in asking her to trust him that he was asking a lot of her when she had no idea what he intended to do. And at that moment, he couldn't help wondering what was going on in that pretty little head of hers.

PATRINA STOOD THERE and stared down at Cole, specifically at his mouth, which had been suckling at her breasts. She recalled how earlier those same lips and tongue had driven her crazy with desire, had her body still tingling. And now he wanted to use his mouth on her again, in other places, and she had an idea where.

During the five years of their marriage, she and Perry had never engaged in what she knew Cole was hinting at, and she couldn't help the sensations that flooded her stomach at the thought of participating in such an intimate act with him. To say she'd never been curious about it would be a lie, and now Cole was offering her the chance to indulge. Should she take it?

As if sensing that she was on the borderline, his fingers slowly began to move and the heated core of her began throbbing at the intimate contact. He was stroking new life into that part of her, creating a need she'd never known she had.

Her gaze shifted from his mouth to his eyes, which were boring into hers with an intensity that almost took her breath away. "Tell me," he whispered softly. "Tell me I can kiss you here," he said, and at the same time he inserted a single finger inside her to let her know just where he meant.

She sucked in a deep breath, suddenly feeling exposed, vulnerable and filled with a fire, the degree of which she hadn't known was possible for her. And it was taking over her senses, literally burning them to a cinder and making her act the part of someone she really didn't know. She could only close her eyes against such intense desire.

"Patrina."

She opened her eyes to meet his intense gaze and the look she saw there took her breath away. He wanted her. He *really* wanted her. Probably just as much as she wanted him. He wanted to introduce her to something new and different and she knew that she wanted the same thing.

"Yes," she whispered softly. "You can kiss me there."

She saw the smile that touched his lips and he didn't waste any time pulling her slacks down past her knees and taking her panties right along with them, leaving her feminine mound fully exposed for his private viewing. She closed her eyes but knew the exact moment he dropped to his knees in front of her and felt the strong hands that gently parted her thighs. She fought to remain standing when she felt him bury the bridge of his nose in the curls covering her mound, and she fought to retain her ability to breathe the moment he inserted his tongue inside her.

And like a meal he just had to devour, he tightened his hold on her thighs to keep her steady while his mouth went to work on her, the tip of his tongue piercing her with desire so strong and deep she cried out from something so totally unexpected, as well as something so profoundly intense.

She opened her eyes for a heated second and looked down only to see his head buried between her legs. Each and every stroke of his tongue was precision quick, lightning sharp, and was sending her over the edge in a way she'd never gone before.

She bit her lip in an effort not to cry out again, but cried out, anyway. She felt her knees buckling beneath her, but the firm grip of his hands on her thighs kept her standing. She grasped the sides of his head, telling herself she needed to pull him away, but instead, found she was placing pressure to keep him right there. He was exploring the insides of her body, the areas where his tongue could reach, and she was too overcome with passion to stop him. In fact, she heard her whispers of "Don't stop" over and over again.

Then suddenly, she felt her entire body filled with electrified sensations that ripped through her with a force that had her screaming his name, and she couldn't do anything but ride the incredible waves that were carrying her to some unknown destination. Frissons of pleasure attacked every cell of her body before she shook with the force of an orgasm the likes of which she'd never experienced before.

And just when she thought she couldn't possibly take any more, couldn't stand on her feet a second longer, she suddenly felt herself scooped into strong arms.

"Wait, I'm too heavy."

"No, you're not," he said, gathering her up.

She buried her face in the warm, muscular texture of his chest and felt them moving. She wasn't sure where he was taking her and at the moment she didn't care.

But when she felt the softness of the mattress against her back, she knew. She opened her eyes and watched as he went about removing her shoes and socks and tossing them aside before tugging her jeans and panties completely off.

He gazed down at her naked body with heated desire before leaning over and kissing her lips in a slow, thorough exchange. Moments later he drew back from the kiss and in a surprise move pulled the covers over her, then tucked her in tenderly, as if seeing to her comfort. He then leaned over and kissed her again, and this time when he withdrew, he held her gaze and whispered, "Good night, Patrina. Sleep well."

She felt too weak to respond, so she said nothing. She lay there and watched as he crossed the room to the door, opened it and eased out, gently closing it behind him.

THE MOMENT COLE stepped into the hall he leaned against the nearest wall and drew in a sharp breath. It had taken all the control he could muster not to crawl into bed with Patrina, especially when her eyes had looked so inviting. Never had he wanted a woman more, and with his history, that said a lot.

There was something about her that brought out his primal instincts, instincts that he always thought he could control. But with her he couldn't. It was as if after their first kiss he had become nearly obsessed with kissing her every chance he got, consumed with the taste of her and wanting to discover and explore all the different facets of that taste.

Tonight he had.

He had tasted her lips, her breasts and the very essence of her femininity, everything that made her the beautiful and desirable woman she was. If he had lingered in that bedroom with her a minute longer, he would have been tempted to strip off his boxers and join her in bed to find the heaven he knew awaited him between her lush thighs. She stirred a need within him that even now had him weak in the knees.

He lifted his hand to touch his mouth and couldn't

help but smile. There was no way his mouth and tongue hadn't gotten addicted to her taste. Everything about her was perfect—the shape of her breasts, the flare of her thighs, the shape of her mouth, lips—everything.

Knowing if he didn't move well away from her bedroom door he would be tempted to go back into the room, he forced himself to walk toward the kitchen, needing some of the coffee she had made earlier.

A few moments later he was standing back at the window gazing out and holding a cup of coffee in his hand. What he'd told Patrina earlier about the full moon was true. He'd always had an interest in astronomy himself, but had never taken the time to develop that interest and had been surprised when he'd discovered he had a cousin who had.

He couldn't help but smile when he thought about his eleven male cousins and how he and Clint had been able to bond with them in a way that made it seem they had known each other all their lives and not just a few years. Quade had been the first one they had met, and only because he had shown up in Austin wanting to know why they were having his uncle investigated, and had been more than mildly surprised when they'd told him that the uncle he knew was their biological father—a father who didn't know they existed. Durango and Stone had been next, since they'd been in Montana when he and Clint had arrived to meet Corey.

He then thought about what he'd told Patrina earlier about not letting anyone know he'd been stranded here with her. He knew how some small towns operated. Patrina was a highly respected doctor and he wouldn't do anything to tarnish that. Although she was a widow, old enough to do whatever she wanted, some wouldn't see it that way. Besides, what they did was nobody's business but theirs.

Moving away from the window, Cole walked over to the counter to pour another cup of coffee. Although he wished otherwise, he was too keyed up to sleep. A cold shower would probably do him justice. Just the thought that Patrina would be sleeping in the room across the hall from him gave him a sexual ache that wouldn't go away, an erection that refused to go down.

For as long as he lived, he would never forget the look on her face when her orgasm had struck. It had been simply priceless and one he would love seeing again. The intensity of it had him wondering if she'd ever had one of that magnitude before.

He turned when he heard a sound and looked up to find Patrina standing in the doorway. Her hair was flowing around her shoulders and her features glowed with that womanly look—the one he enjoyed seeing on her. She was wearing a beautiful blue silk robe and the way it was draped around her curves showed what a shapely body she had. It was his opinion that she looked sexy as hell.

"I couldn't sleep," she said softly, her eyes locked with his.

He crossed the room to come to a stop directly

in front of her, being careful not to get too close. He would definitely lose control if he touched her. Just inhaling her scent was doing a number on him already. "Would you like a cup of coffee?" he heard himself asking.

He watched as she shook her head. "No, coffee isn't what I need."

He drew in a tight breath, almost too afraid to ask, but knew he had to do so, anyway. "What is it that you need?"

The dark eyes that gazed back at him were filled with an expression she wasn't trying to hide, a sexual allure he could actually feel all the way to the bone. A fierce abundance of desire rammed through him when she responded in a soft and sexy voice, "You. I need you, Cole."

CHAPTER SEVEN

PATRINA STOOD AND watched Cole as he stood staring at her. She wondered what he was thinking and was certain he'd heard what she said. Saying it hadn't been easy, probably a few of the hardest words she'd ever spoken. But she had lain in bed, totally satisfied and remembering what he'd done to her right here in the kitchen, first while sitting on the windowledge and then on his knees. She wanted more. She *needed* more.

He'd always told her to feel the passion, but tonight he had taken those feelings to another level, and thanks to him she had done more than just felt the passion. She had experienced it in a way she never had before. That was in no way taking anything from Perry. It was just giving Cole his due. He was experienced when it came to pleasing women; he had a skill you didn't have to wonder how it had been acquired. The man was totally awesome and had a mouth that was undeniably lethal.

"Do you fully understand what you're saying?"

He'd asked her a similar question earlier tonight in this kitchen when he had wanted to kiss her. At the time she had said she understood because she'd been more than certain that she had. It hadn't taken long to discover that she hadn't understood the full extent of anything.

She definitely hadn't understood or known the degree of her passion. But Cole had. Somehow he had sensed it, had homed in on it from the first and immediately set out to taste it.

And tonight he'd gotten more than a taste. He'd gotten a huge whopping sample. But so had she. While he had taken control of her body, soul and mind, she had been driven to a need of gigantic proportion. And just to think she hadn't indulged in the full scope of what was possible. And more than anything she wanted to. Tomorrow he would be leaving and that would be it. The finale. But a part of her didn't want their time together to end.

"Yes, I fully understand," she finally said while holding his gaze and hoping he saw what was in her eyes—her determination, her heartfelt desire and now…her impatience.

She moved, took a step closer to him at the same time that he came forward, and suddenly she was in his arms. The fire they had ignited earlier was now a blaze and when he captured her mouth in his, the only thing she could think of was that this was where she belonged.

No man had ever possessed her this way. His hands seemed to be everywhere, all over her. The robe was stripped from her body, leaving her completely naked, but things didn't stop there. It seemed they were just beginning. He backed her out of the kitchen into the living room. Once there he stripped out of his boxers and the size of his erection had her blinking to make sure her eyes weren't playing tricks on her. He was huge. She should not have been surprised, but seeing him in the flesh was sending shivers down her body.

"You sure about this?"

She glanced up at him. Even now, with them standing facing each other as naked as two people could be, he was giving her a chance to change her mind.

Seeing the size of him was enough reason to consider doing so. But she wanted this. She needed this and she had to assure him. "Yes, I'm sure about this as long as you realize I don't come close to the level of experience or expertise that you're probably used to."

Cole nodded. A smile touched his lips. "I'm glad you don't."

And then he was pulling her into his arms, and when flesh melded into flesh, he kissed her with a longing she felt all the way to her toes. Her mouth opened fully to his, as far as it could stretch, and their tongues entwined, mingled, and their breathing combined, enticing her to feel things she could only experience with him. And then she found herself swept into strong arms. But the kissing continued. In fact, he picked up the pace, going deeper, making it hotter and more urgent.

He lifted his head and his gaze burned down into hers. It took her several seconds to catch her breath...

as well as realize they were moving and that Cole was walking with her in his arms from the living room toward the bedroom he'd occupied for the past two days.

When they reached their destination he placed her on her feet beside the bed and she knew once again he was making sure this was what she wanted. She would have to get into his bed on her own accord. She looked at the neatly made bed, a representation of his handiwork, and marveled at how tidy a job he'd done. It was nothing like the haphazard-looking made-up beds she was used to whenever Dale came to visit.

Knowing he was watching her intently, she took a step closer to the bed and turned down the covers, and without saying anything she slid between the sheets and then looked at him expectantly. She felt totally aroused to see him standing there, naked with a huge erection and a tantalizing smile tugging at the corners of his mouth.

She was no longer angry with herself for being weak where Cole was concerned. Instead, she had accepted the fact that she was a woman with needs— needs she had tried ignoring for more than three years. And they would be needs she would once again ignore once Cole left. What she was taking with him was some *me* time. For once she would think of no one but herself and do something that would make her happy and satisfied.

"We're sleeping in tomorrow," Cole said in a voice so sexy it made her breath lock in her throat, and she scooted over when he joined her in the bed. It was queen-size, and a good fit for the two of them. The size of the bed vanished from her mind the moment he shifted and pulled her into his arms, claiming her lips in the process.

The kiss was everything she had gotten used to, had come to expect. His tongue was driving her crazy, stirring up her passion and sending shivers all through her body. It was the same body that his hands were all over, becoming reacquainted with all her intimate places. He was making it obvious that his focus was on pleasing her. She was touched by the gesture and decided to follow his lead. However, her focus would be on pleasing him.

She felt one of his hands slide between her legs, touching what she now considered her hot spot. His fingers began exploring at will, familiar territory to them now. She felt an instinctive need to touch him, as well, and slightly shifting her body, she reached down and took him into her hands. He released her mouth to pull in a sharp breath the moment he felt her touch.

He felt hard and smooth both at the same time, warm to the touch, huge in her hand. Then she began moving her hand, stroking him with an ease that surprised her. She became fascinated by what she was doing, totally enthralled with the way her fingers glided softly back and forth across the silken tip. And when she glanced up at Cole and met his gaze, what she saw in the dark depths took her breath away, made her aware of just how affected he was by her intimate touch.

Without saying anything he lowered his head and that same mouth he had used just moments earlier on hers now targeted her breasts. He drew between his lips an aroused peak and began sucking on it in a way that made her cry out his name.

She pulled her hand off him when he shifted their positions to place himself over her and used his knee to farther nudge her legs apart. He gazed down at her, giving her one last chance to stop him from going further. Instead she took the hand that had stroked him earlier and skimmed his chin and whispered, "I want this, Cole. I want you."

On a deep guttural groan he entered her and her body automatically arched, then proceeded to stretch to accommodate him. She felt all her inner muscles grab hold of him, begin clenching him as every nerve between her legs became sensitive to the invasion. She inhaled the masculine scent of him, the musky scent of sex, when he began moving, with quick, even strokes that sent her nearly over the edge with each hard thrust.

And then when she thought she couldn't possibly take any more, felt her body almost splintering in two, he gave one last hard thrust that triggered his release at the same time her body shattered into a thousand pieces. Too late it hit her that they had forgotten something, but there was nothing they could do about it now. Tremors were rocking her body to the core, and the only thing that registered on her mind was how he was making her feel at this very moment. And when he leaned down, enveloped her more deeply in his arms and captured her mouth with his, she felt herself tumbling once again into a sea of desire.

COLE CAME AWAKE, not sure how long he'd been asleep. He glanced at the woman securely tucked in his arms and licked his lips. His mouth still tasted of her, her scent was all over his skin, just as he was certain his scent was all over hers. He recalled the exact moment she had come apart, triggering his body to do likewise. It had been one hell of a joining. Filled with fire, passion... He thought further, closing his eyes when realization hit—one that had been unprotected.

He let out a frustrated moan. How could he have been so careless? Condoms were tucked away in his wallet. It wasn't like he didn't have any. He just hadn't thought of using one. It would be the first time he'd ever made love with a woman without protection.

He again glanced at Patrina. She was sleeping with a satisfied look on her face. And rightly so. Their joining had been nothing short of magnificent. It had left them so drained they'd drifted off to sleep in each others' arms.

They had to talk and it was a discussion that couldn't wait until morning. She needed to know what he hadn't done—or more precisely what he might have carelessly done. He hated rousing her from sleep but leaned over close to her ear and whispered, "Patrina."

He said her name several times before she finally forced her eyes open to look at him. Before he could fix his mouth to say anything, she reached up and looped her arms around his neck, and on a soft groan she pulled his mouth down to hers.

Sensations skyrocketed through him and he returned her kiss with a passion that went all the way to the bone and instinctively, once again, he moved and positioned his body over hers. And when her thighs parted for him, he pressed down, entered her, filling her completely. And then their bodies began mating once again and every time he surged forward into her aroused flesh, he felt his own body trembling, blatant testimony to his own ardent desire.

And when she wrapped her legs tightly around him, as if to hold him inside, he was filled with a sense of possession that until now had been foreign to him. He ached for her and would always ache for her. And she would be the only one who could satisfy that ache, as she was doing now.

And when her body began quivering uncontrollably just moments before she released his mouth to scream his name, he knew her power over him was undeniable and absolute. Just like he'd known he would, he helplessly followed her over the edge and into the grips of an orgasm so mind-blowingly strong that he felt his every nerve ending leap to life. He also knew she had become an addiction that would be hard as hell for him to kick.

"IT'S STOPPED SNOWING."

Cole's statement filtered through Patrina's mind as she glanced out the window. Not only had it stopped snowing, but a semblance of sun was forcing its way through the Montana clouds. She couldn't say anything because she knew what that meant. He would be leaving.

As if he read her thoughts, he said, "I plan on being here for a while, Patrina. I need to call the car-rental agency and let them know about the car so they can go get it and bring me another one here."

He pulled her deeper into his arms and then said, "And I meant what I said yesterday. None of my family knew I was coming this early, so they aren't going to be worried and wondering where I am. I want my being here with you these past two days to be our secret."

She knew he wanted that to protect her reputation and she appreciated it, but it wasn't necessary. She opened her mouth to tell him so, but then he kissed her and she could no longer think. She could only feel.

After they had made love that first time, they had fallen asleep and had awakened to make love again, and again, into the wee hours of the morning. If she never made love to another man again, she would be satisfied. But then, she couldn't imagine ever being in another man's arms this way, sharing his bed. In the space of forty-eight hours she had gone from being tucked away safely on a shelf to having been brought down and placed on a counter where she had experienced things she never thought could happen between a man and woman.

Cole released her mouth and said in a strained voice, "I didn't use protection, Patrina. Not that first time or any of the other times. I'm sorry for being so careless. That's not the way I operate. If anything develops from it, I will take full responsibility. You and my child won't want for anything."

She met his gaze, was touched by what he said but felt that this, too, wasn't necessary, although she wished she could say the words that would assure him that it wasn't the right time for her to get pregnant. She didn't want to think of how many babies she'd delivered whose mothers had thought it hadn't been the right time.

"You don't have to worry about that, Cole. If I am pregnant, I can certainly manage to take care of my baby."

He reached out and stroked the side of her face. "Our baby. You would not have gotten pregnant by yourself. Promise me that if you discover you are, you will contact me in Texas."

She nodded. She would contact him only to let him know he would be a father because he had a right to know—if it came to that. But she would not let him fill his mind with any thoughts of obligations toward her. He hadn't forced himself on her. She had come willingly. Had gotten into his bed herself. And she had been in her right mind.

"I'll be back."

He whispered the words in her ear just before easing away from her side. She figured he was going to the bathroom and was already missing his warmth. She glanced over at the clock. It was 10:00 a.m. It seemed later than that. She settled under the thickness of the covers as images played across her mind of them making love. Even the thought of an unplanned pregnancy didn't bother like it probably should. She'd delivered countless babies to other women and had always yearned for a child of her own. It was a secret desire.

She felt the dip in the bed and without looking over her shoulder she knew that Cole had returned. She could feel his heat again, and as he snuggled closer and pulled her into his arms…she felt something else. His huge erection. She flipped on her back and stared up at him.

"I went and got a condom out of my wallet and put it on. You'll be protected this time."

And then he was kissing her. A part of her wanted to pull her mouth free and tell him it was okay. He didn't have to protect her. To have his baby wouldn't be so bad…

But when he deepened the kiss, she ceased thinking at all. And when he shifted positions and slid into her, she instinctively wrapped her legs around him as erotic sensations swept through her, intensified with every stroke he made. She exulted in the feel of him inside her. It was as if this was where he was supposed to be. And moments later when her body exploded in a fire of sensual pleasure, she moaned his name over and over as waves rippled through her body.

Afterward, he pulled her close against him, held her tight in his arms and kissed her temple. For the first time in more than three years she felt total contentment.

COLE LOADED THE last of his luggage into the rental car the agency had brought him. The sky was clear and it was time to leave, but he would always have memories of the two days he had spent here with Patrina.

He turned around. She was standing in the doorway in her bathrobe. He had asked her not to get dressed. He wanted to remember her that way. When he saw her at his father's birthday party in a few weeks and fully clothed, that would be soon enough to stop thinking of her with only a bathrobe covering her nakedness. But he would never stop thinking of how many times they had made love, how his tongue had tasted her all over, or the moans that would pass from between her lips each and every time she came.

Inhaling deeply, he closed the trunk and walked back toward the porch. A part of him wasn't ready to go, but he knew it was something he had to do. Taking the steps slowly, he walked over to her and without saying a word he pulled her into his arms and kissed her like a soldier about to leave behind his woman before being carted off to war. She returned his kiss with a degree of passion he was getting used to. He would miss her. He would miss this.

He reluctantly pulled his mouth from hers and whispered against her moist lips. "Time for me to go."

"Will you drive more carefully this time?"

A smile touched his mouth. "Will you come to my rescue again if I don't?"

She chuckled and he felt the depth of it in his gut. "Yes. I would come to your rescue anytime, Cole Westmoreland."

She wasn't making leaving easy. He didn't say anything for a moment and then asked. "Was I a good houseguest?"

"The best. Was I a good doctor?"

"Off the charts."

He paused a moment, then added. "But I think you were an even better bedmate. It's going to be hard, the next time I see you, to not want to strip you naked. Just like it's hard as hell for me to leave now without taking you in that bedroom and making love to you one last time."

"What's stopping you?"

Patrina's question aroused him, tempted him sorely. "Because one more time won't be enough. I'd want to go on and on and on. I'd never want to leave."

Cole sighed heavily. That admission had been hard to make, but it was true. Then, feeling as if he might have said too much, true or not, he took a step back.

"Remember me," he said fiercely, fighting the urge to pull her back into his arms. Instead, he took her hand and gave it a gentle squeeze. "You're off the shelf now, Patrina. Don't go and put yourself back up there. You're too sensual a woman for that."

He turned and headed for the car and refused to look back. At least he didn't until he was pulling into the long driveway that would take him to the main road. And when he saw her in his rearview mirror, she was still standing there. The most passionate woman he'd ever had the pleasure of meeting.

CHAPTER EIGHT

"You're definitely a welcome surprise," Casey Westmoreland Quinn said. She grinned across the dinner table at her brother, who had shown up unexpectedly a few hours before.

"And you made perfect time," she added. "Had you arrived in Bozeman a few days ago you would have been met with one nasty snowstorm. Everyone's been stranded in their homes for the past couple of days."

"That couldn't have been much fun," Cole replied, trying to keep a straight face.

"We had no complaints," McKinnon Quinn said, smiling at Casey before taking a sip of his coffee.

Cole chuckled. He could read between the lines and couldn't help but be happy for his sister and the man she'd chosen to spend the rest of her life with. It was so obvious that they were in love. Casey had always been a person who believed in love, romance and all that happily-ever-after stuff, but she had become disillusioned after discovering that the storybook love story their mother had weaved for them concerning their father all those years had been a lie. Cole was glad to see that things had worked out for Casey, after all, and thanks to McKinnon, she believed in love again.

He then thought about Clint and his recent marriage to Alyssa. That, too, he thought, was definitely a love match and Cole was happy for them, as well. But while falling in love and getting married were good for some people, he had decided a long time ago he wasn't one of them.

He figured he would probably be like his uncle Sid and remain a bachelor forever. Some people did better by themselves. He liked the single life, the freedom to come and go as he pleased and not be responsible for anyone but himself. He had no problem with seeking out female companionship those times when a woman became necessary.

His thoughts shifted to Patrina and the time they had spent together. She had definitely been necessary and he was glad he'd made the decision not to mention to anyone that he'd spent the past couple of days stranded at her place. But there was the possibility she could be pregnant. He decided not to worry about anything just yet.

In the meantime, the time he had spent at her place was their secret, one he preferred not sharing with anyone, least of all his sister. The last thing he needed was for Casey—who had such a romantic heart—to get any ideas about his relationship with Patrina. Besides, given his reputation with the ladies, one his sister knew well, he didn't want her to wonder what might or might not have happened at Patrina's place.

And a lot had happened. Even now he had a tough time not remembering every single detail. He bet if he were to close his eyes he could probably still breathe in her scent.

"You want more coffee, Cole?"

Casey's question broke into his thoughts and he figured from where his thoughts were headed, it was a good thing. "No, thanks, and dinner was good."

"Thanks."

"So, how are the plans for the birthday party coming along?" he asked.

Casey smiled. "Fine. And as far as it being a surprise, Abby and I decided why bother, since Dad isn't a man you can easily pull anything over on. I can't wait to call to let him know you're here. He's going to be happy to see you."

Cole knew what she said was true. Ever since finding out he was the father of triplets, Corey had done everything within his power to forge a strong relationship with his offspring.

"There's something McKinnon and I want to tell you. We told Dad and Abby, as well as McKinnon's parents last week. I was waiting to tell you and Clint at the party."

Cole raised a curious brow. "What?"

Casey and McKinnon exchanged smiles and again Cole felt the love flowing between them. Casey looked back at Cole and said, "We're adopting a baby."

Cole couldn't help the grin that shone on his face. "That's wonderful news," he said. "Congratulations."

He knew how much the two of them wanted to become parents. He also knew that, due to a medical condition McKinnon had, they could not have children the natural way.

"Thanks." Casey beamed. "And we have Dr. Patrina Foreman to thank for this wonderful news."

Cole forced his features to remain neutral when he said, "Dr. Foreman?"

"Yes, she's the doctor who delivered little Sarah. She runs a women's clinic in town, one she helped found when she saw a need. One of her patients at the clinic, an eighteen-year-old girl, wants to give up her child as soon as it's born, but wanted to make sure the baby went to good parents. Patrina called me and McKinnon, we met with the young woman and everything has been arranged, all the legal matters taken care of. We'll be given the baby within hours of its birth."

"And when is the baby due?"

"Next month."

Cole smiled. "That's wonderful. Yes, it seems that you do owe a lot to Dr. Foreman."

"She's such a nice person," his sister went on. "I'm surprised you didn't meet her either at the party that was given for me last year or my wedding, since she was at both. She's been nominated for the Eve Award here in town. The winner will be announced later this year at a special ceremony."

"The Eve Award?" Cole asked.

"Yes, each year women are nominated and judged on their accomplishments in their community. The accomplishments must have helped improve the quality of life in the community, and with all the volunteer work she does at the clinic, Patrina has certainly done that. Her husband was sheriff here and was killed in the line of duty. I think she puts in a lot of community hours because she has a genuine desire to help people, but then I'm sure it's probably rather lonely living at that ranch by herself. She spends a lot of her free time in town at the clinic."

Cole didn't say anything as he took a sip of his coffee. He didn't want to think about how lonely Patrina was or how much spending those two days with her had meant to him. Nor did he want to recall the satisfied look on her face, after spending almost an entire night and day in bed with him.

He gave a deep sigh and decided now was the time to share his good news. It was something he hadn't told Patrina and she'd become involved with him, anyway—but only because she'd known it was an involvement that would lead nowhere. He was not looking for a serious relationship with anyone, but then, neither was she.

"I have some good news," he said. "I'm no longer a ranger. I followed Clint's lead and took an early retirement." He could tell from Casey's expression that she was surprised. She of all people knew what a dedicated ranger he'd been.

"That's wonderful, Cole," Casey said, smiling brightly at him. "What on earth will you do with all that time you're going to have on your hands?" He wasn't surprised by her question. She knew he was someone who had to stay busy or else he would get restless and ornery.

"I invested a lot of the money I made when I sold my third of the ranch to Clint. They were investments that paid off. I'm meeting with Serena Preston next week. I understand she's looking for a buyer for her helicopter business. Quade's also going to join me while I'm here. He and I are working on a business deal that involves opening several security companies around the country. We've even talked to Rico Claiborne about joining us as a partner."

Rico was a top-notch private investigator who owned a successful agency. His sister, Jessica, was married to Cole's cousin, Chase, and Rico's other sister, Savannah, was married to Durango. With the family connections, the Westmorelands considered Rico one of their own.

"Sounds like you're going to be busy."

"I plan to be," he said, and decided not to add that staying busy would be a surefire way to keep Patrina Foreman off his mind. He swallowed against the heavy lump he felt in his throat. Damn, he was missing the woman already.

He leaned back in his chair remembering how she had stood on the porch watching him drive off. She had looked beautiful with the sun slanting down on her features, emphasizing that womanly glow he had left her with. Heat fired through his veins just thinking about it, as well as remembering all they had shared. He sighed deeply. Those kinds of thoughts could land him knee-deep in trouble if he wasn't careful.

Casey interrupted his thoughts. "So how long will you be staying with McKinnon and me before you head up the mountain to see Dad?"

Cole tried not to think how far away from Patrina being on Corey's Mountain would put him. But then, he hadn't planned on seeing her again anytime soon, anyway. He figured he wouldn't be seeing her before Corey's birthday party.

"I'm not sure," he finally said. "Probably in a couple of days. I hope the two of you don't mind the company."

McKinnon chuckled. "Not at all. Besides, I want to show you all the new horses Clint sent. They're beauties."

LATER THAT NIGHT, Cole lay on his back with his head sunk in the thick pillow, thoughts of Patrina on his mind. He glanced over at the clock. It wasn't quite nine o'clock and it didn't take much to recall what he'd been doing around this time the previous night.

He couldn't fight the memories any longer so he closed his eyes to let them take over his mind. Images of kissing her, making love to her through the wee hours of the morning gripped him, made him hard, made him long for more of the same. But then by an unspoken agreement, what they'd shared was all there ever would be. Their paths were not to cross that way again. It had just been a moment in time.

If that was the case, why did he still desire her in

every sense of the word? Even now, when he didn't want to think about her, when he didn't want to remember, he couldn't stop himself from doing so. Maybe going up on Corey's Mountain and putting distance between him and temptation was for the best.

He turned his head when he heard his cell phone. He quickly reached for it on the nightstand and flipped it open. "Hello."

"Cole, this is Quade. Have you made it to Montana yet?"

"Yes, I arrived at McKinnon and Casey's place earlier today," he said, which in essence wasn't a lie, Cole quickly thought.

"I'm flying out of D.C. the end of the week to head that way. Have you heard from Rico?"

"No, but McKinnon mentioned he's here visiting with Durango and Savannah. A bad snowstorm has kept everyone stranded for the past couple of days. The natives are just beginning to thaw out and venture outside."

He heard Quade's chuckle. "Maybe we ought to have our heads examined for thinking about purchasing that copter service. In bad weather we'll be grounded."

"Yes, but think of all the money we'll make those days when we're in the air." Cole had done his research and had no apprehensions about the helicopter business being profitable. And with all the expansions they planned to make, he saw it as a very lucrative investment.

"I'll remind you of those words when it's thirty below zero and we're inside sitting around a roaring fire waiting for the copter's blades to defrost."

He and Quade spoke for several more minutes and Cole welcomed the conversation. It kept Patrina from intruding on his mind. But the moment the call ended, the memories were back, hitting him smack in the face, and he couldn't help wondering how much sleep he would be getting tonight.

RESTLESS AND KNOWING a good night's sleep was out of the question, Patrina sat up in bed and glanced at the clock. It was still fairly early, not even eleven. However, considering all the chores she'd done after Cole had left to stay busy and to keep her mind occupied, she should be sleeping like a log. But that wasn't the case. Her body felt edgy, achy with a hunger only one man could satisfy.

Cole.

Each and every time she closed her eyes he was there in her thoughts, taking over her mind and reminding her of things so intimate that she was filled with intense longing. It was recapturing all the moments she had spent with him, all the kisses they had shared, but especially when she had given her body to him....

Getting out of bed, she crossed to the window and glanced out at the full moon. She recalled what Cole had said that meant. *A full moon in April is the Seed Moon, It's the time to physically plant your seeds of desire in Mother Earth.*

Her hands immediately went to her stomach when she recalled their unprotected lovemaking. Her gaze stayed firmly locked on the full moon while she considered the possible meaning of the words Cole had spoken that night. Had it been their fate to make a baby? If she was pregnant, Cole had planted seeds of desire in her, since they definitely hadn't been seeds of love. She was smart enough to know that love had not governed their behavior for the past two days. Lust had.

Her eyes shimmered with unshed tears when she recalled the months following Perry's death when she had felt so alone. It was during those months she had regretted their decision to wait before starting a family. A child would have been something of his that would have been a part of her forever.

Patrina closed her eyes and the face she saw was no longer Perry's but Cole's. She bit her lip to stop it from trembling when she was reminded of the vow she'd made never to give her heart to another lawman. It was a vow she intended to keep. She couldn't handle the pain if anything were to happen to Cole like it had Perry.

She opened her eyes. No matter what, she would never let Cole Westmoreland have possession of her heart.

CHAPTER NINE

A week later

COLE GLANCED AT the scrap of paper he held in his hand and then back at the man by his side. "How in hell did we get roped into doing this, Quade?" he asked his cousin as they got out of the truck to enter the grocery superstore.

Quade chuckled. "Mainly because this is Henrietta's day off and we weren't smart enough to get lost like McKinnon did. Hey, look at it this way—the list could have been longer. And besides, Casey's *your* sister. If anything, you should have known she was bound to put us to work sooner or later."

Cole's eyebrows drew together in a frown. "Yeah, I guess you're right, but that doesn't mean I have to like it." He grabbed a buggy and went about maneuvering it down the first aisle while glancing at the list.

"Hey, isn't that Patrina Foreman over there in the frozen-food section?"

Cole's head whipped up. Yes, that was Patrina, all right. He didn't need for her to turn all the way around to make a concrete identification. His body was already responding to the sight of her. It had been a week, but it seemed like yesterday when he had made love to her, mainly because he replayed each and every detail in his nightly dreams. He couldn't close his eyes at night without reliving the time his body had been connected to hers, thrusting in and out of her and—

"Hey, Cole. You all right?"

His gaze swiftly switched to Quade. "What makes you think I'm not?" he asked, the question coming out a little gruffer than he'd intended.

He didn't miss the way Quade's mouth quirked in a teasing smile when he said, "Mainly because I asked to see that list three times, but you were so busy staring at Patrina, you didn't hear me." Quade paused for a minute, lifted a brow and asked, "Hmm, do I detect some interest there?"

Cole's chin shot up as he shoved the list at Quade. "No."

Quade chuckled. "You spoke too soon and that was a dead giveaway."

Cole quietly cursed, refusing to let Quade bait him. But it really didn't matter when he found himself steering the buggy in Patrina's direction.

"I don't see any frozen foods on Casey's list," he heard Quade say.

Cole rolled his eyes and in doing so, barely missed knocking over a display of pastries in the middle of the aisle.

"Don't you think you need to watch where you're going?" Quade said, laughing.

Cole was about to shoot some smart remark over his shoulder to Quade when suddenly Patrina turned and her widened eyes stared straight at him. "Hello, Patrina."

From the expression on her face he could tell she was surprised to see him and he couldn't help wondering if that was good or bad. He also couldn't help wondering if her nights had been as tortured as his. He was less than five feet away and had already picked up her scent, something he knew he would never forget. She was wearing a long, white lab coat over a pair of navy slacks. She looked totally professional, but he knew firsthand that underneath her medical garb she was totally female.

"Hello, Cole." She looked past him. "Hello, Quade."

A smiling Quade came to stand by Cole's side. "Hey, Trina, how's it going?" Then without missing a beat, Quade looked at Cole and then back at her. His smile widened when he said, "I didn't know the two of you knew each other."

Cole threw Quade a sharp glance. "Patrina and I met last year at Casey's party."

"Oh, I see."

As far as Cole was concerned, his cousin saw too damn much. "Don't you want to take the buggy and finish getting the stuff on Casey's list, Quade?"

His cousin glanced at Cole and said smoothly, "Sure, why not?" Then he looked at Patrina. "You're coming to Uncle Corey's party next weekend, aren't you?"

A small smile touched her lips. "Yes, I plan to."

"Good. Then we can talk more later. I'll be seeing you."

"Goodbye, Quade."

At exactly the moment Quade and the buggy rounded the corner, Cole found himself taking a step forward. There were others around and he didn't want anyone else privy to their conversation. He glanced sideways and caught a glimpse of his reflection in the freezer's glass door. He caught a glimpse of Patrina's reflection, as well. She'd taken her tongue and given her lips a moist sweep, a gesture that always turned him on. Today was no exception. He felt it, the sexual chemistry, the charged air and electrical currents that always consumed them whenever they were in close range of each other.

"I ran into Casey last week and she told me you were here but had gone to spend a few days up on Corey's Mountain," she said.

He shifted his gaze from the glass door to her. "I was on the mountain for only a couple of days."

"Oh."

"And how have you been, Patrina?"

She met his gaze. "Fine."

"Do you have anything in particular that you want to tell me?"

He could tell from her expression that she knew what he was asking. "No," she said quickly.

He couldn't help wondering if she meant, no, she didn't have anything to tell him because it was too early to know anything or, no, she didn't have anything to tell him because she knew for certain she wasn't pregnant.

"And how have you been, Cole?"

He met her gaze and held it. "Do you want to know the truth?" he asked, his voice going low and sounding husky even to his own ears.

She evidently had an idea what he might say and nervously glanced around. "No. Not here."

"Fair enough," he conceded. "Then where? Tell me where, Patrina."

Cole watched as she licked her lips again and he felt his guts clench. The need to kiss her, take hold of that tongue with his own, was a temptation he was fighting to ignore. If she had any idea what effect seeing her lick her lips had on him, she would keep her tongue inside her mouth.

She met his gaze and he knew she had to see the desire in his eyes he wasn't trying to hide— at least not from her. He wasn't sure if Quade had seen it or not. But at the moment he didn't care.

When it seemed she didn't intend to give him an answer, he opened the glass freezer door and pretended to take something out so he could get close enough to her to whisper. "I want you."

He saw her shiver. He knew his words had been the cause. Anyone else would assume it had been the result of the blast of cold air from the freezer.

"You've had me," she finally responded.

He looked at her reflection in the freezer door, imprisoned her gaze with his own. "I want you again." And to make sure she hadn't misunderstood him, he closed the door and turned to her. He held her gaze and repeated, "I want you, again, Patrina."

THE STARK DETERMINATION she saw in Cole's eyes sent another shiver up Patrina's spine. She inhaled deeply, fought for control with all the strength she could muster. She wanted him, too, but if she was going to stick to her resolve, she knew what she had to do.

It wasn't that she regretted anything they'd done when he'd been stranded at her place, but a repeat performance would serve no purpose and in fact, only make matters worse. She could barely sleep at night as it was. If she took him up on his offer, what would happen to her when he left Bozeman? With some people, usually men, it was easy to replace one lover with another, but that wasn't the case with her. Cole was the man her body wanted. The only man it wanted. And she refused to become addicted to something she couldn't have.

"Patrina?"

She forced even breaths past her lips, while fighting the sexual pull between them. She had to stand firm. She had to stay strong. She had to ignore that telltale ache between her legs, and the tingle in her breasts.

"No, I don't think that's a good idea," she finally said softly, making sure the words were for his ears only.

Then, simultaneously taking a deep breath and taking a step back, she glanced at her watch and said in a normal tone, "I didn't know how late it is. I have to go. It was good seeing you, Cole. Tell Casey and McKinnon I said hello."

Then she quickly swept her buggy past him, ignoring the determined glint in his dark gaze. She could still feel the heat of that gaze on her back when she steered her buggy toward the checkout line. She was tempted to stop, turn and look him in the eye and invite him over tonight, but to do so would be foolish.

She had gotten her purchases paid for and bagged when she finally looked back. Cole was nowhere in sight, but she had a feeling she hadn't seen the last of him. She of all people knew he was a man who eventually got whatever he wanted.

"OKAY, WHAT'S GOING on with you and Patrina?"

Cole shrugged, then turned the key in the truck's ignition and pulled out of the store's parking lot. "What makes you think there's something going on?"

Quade rolled his eyes heavenward. "Have you forgotten I'm considered one of the president's men? For years my job has been to notice things others might find irrelevant. And to pick up on things some might overlook." He smiled. "Besides, the heat between you two was so hot I was worried about the food in the freezer thawing."

"You're imagining things."

"I'd rather you told me it's none of my business than insult my intelligence."

Cole brought the truck to a stop at a traffic light and glanced at his cousin. Quade, at thirty-four a couple of years older, was the first of the Westmorelands he and Clint had met on their quest to find their father. Quade had shown up in Austin, demanding to know why they were having his uncle, Corey Westmoreland, investigated. And then, after they had given him their reasons, he had been the first one to welcome them to the Westmoreland family and the one who'd brought them to Montana to meet face-to-face the father they'd thought was dead. For that reason, the two of them shared a special bond that went beyond family relations.

He knew he couldn't tell Quade everything, but he would tell him enough, especially since he'd picked up on the vibes, anyway. Cole returned his gaze to the road when the traffic light changed and the truck began moving again. "Patrina and I are attracted to each other. Have been since that night we met last year at Casey's party."

"I picked up on that much," Quade said, shaking his head. "Tell me something I don't know."

Cole chuckled. Quade wasn't the easiest of men at times. "She prefers not getting involved with any-one in law enforcement."

"Um, last time Trina and I talked she wasn't inter-ested in getting involved with anyone, period, law-man or otherwise."

Cole snapped his head around and gave Quade a stony look. Quade grinned. "Please keep your eyes on the road, cousin, and take off the boxing gloves. It's not that way with me and Trina. We're nothing but good friends and always have been. I've known her since she was knee-high and would see her every summer when all of us came to spend time with Uncle Corey on his mountain. She, her brother, Dale, along with McKinnon, were my playmates."

Cole nodded. He'd heard about those summers. They were times he, Clint and Casey had missed out on because his mother hadn't told them the truth.

"Why haven't you told her you're no longer a ranger?" Quade asked, breaking into his thoughts.

"Because what I do for a living shouldn't matter."

"It does and you know why. Trina and Perry had been together for years and she took his death hard. I can understand her feeling that way."

"Well, I can't. It's been more than three years and at some point she needs to get on with her life. She has a lot to offer a man. She's special. I picked up on that the night we met. I also picked up that she was standoffish where men were concerned."

"And why does that bother you so much, Cole? Could it be more than just a physical attraction you feel for her?"

Cole didn't like where Quade was going, especially when he didn't know the whole picture. Cole would be the first to admit that when they'd made love, he'd had feelings for her he'd never had with any woman before. He would go even further and admit that since that time she had become lodged in his mind and he couldn't get her out, and that although he'd told her today that he wanted her, she didn't have a clue about just how *much* he wanted her. She'd become an ache he couldn't get rid of and he didn't like it.

"Cole?"

It then occurred to him that he hadn't answered Quade's question. "It's nothing more than a physical attraction. No big deal. I'm not looking for serious involvement and I don't do well with long-distance romances. Besides, I'm a loner. I don't ever plan to get serious with a woman and marry."

"Same here. Unless..."

Cole glanced at Quade when they stopped at another traffic light. "Unless what?" he couldn't help asking.

Quade met his gaze. "Unless my path crosses again with that woman I met in Egypt a few months ago. I went over there to scope things out before the president's visit, and late one night when I couldn't sleep, I went walking on the beach. She was out walking on the beach, too."

"An Egyptian girl?"

"No, American."

Quade didn't say anything for a moment, but Cole could read between the lines. Quade and the woman had ended up spending the night together. "So..." Cole said slowly, "did you get her phone number so the two of you could stay in touch?"

Quade shook his head. "No. When I woke up the next morning she was gone. The president arrived that day so I didn't get a chance to go look for her. But believe me when I tell you that she is one woman I will never forget."

Cole nodded. He knew that no matter where *he* went in life, Patrina was the one woman he wouldn't forget, either. He also knew he would seek her out for a definitive answer to his question about her possible pregnancy. If it was too early to tell, fine, he would wait it out. But he figured that with her being a gynecologist, she had the ability to find out way ahead of most people.

He made up his mind to pay her a late-night visit. She had avoided him in the store but he wouldn't let her avoid him tonight.

WHEN HER CAR came to a stop at the last traffic light she would see for a while, now that she was on the outskirts of town, Patrina rubbed the back of her neck, feeling totally exhausted.

Today she had done a double duty. First she had worked eight hours at her office, and then she'd gone to the clinic where she had worked an additional eight. She hadn't intended to stay that long at the clinic, but it had been short staffed. Several women had delivered and a few other women, who had sought shelter from the blizzard, had received treatment for a few common gynecological concerns. The clinic needed money for new equipment, and she hoped the kickoff to their fund-raising drive would send some generous donors their way.

Without work to keep her mind occupied now, she couldn't help but remember running into Cole today at the store. She had volunteered to do grocery-shopping for Lila Charles during her lunch hour. Ms. Charles, who was close to eighty and lived alone, had been one of her grandmother's dearest friends.

Whenever Patrina got the chance, she would stop by to check on the elderly woman and go pick up whatever items she needed from the grocery store. Cole Westmoreland had been the last person she had expected to run into there.

But she had, and it had taken everything within her to keep a level head, especially since her body had responded to him immediately. He had looked so good, but then Cole never looked anything but. He wore jeans like they'd been made exclusively for him, and a shirt that fit perfectly over the muscles of his chest.

She'd understood what he'd wanted to know. But she didn't have an answer for him yet. It would be another week or so before she did, and so far she hadn't felt any changes in her body. But it was too soon to tell.

She reached toward the car's console and pushed the CD button, deciding to listen to some music to soothe her rattled mind. She had another ten or so miles to go and decided she would let Miles Jaye, his red violin and his sexy voice relax her a bit. A short while later, she decided Miles was relaxing her too much with such romantic and heart-throbbing sounds. And the songs reminded her of cold nights wrapped up in the heated embrace of a man. Although she had listened to these songs countless times, she hadn't been able to relate to them so intensely until now. She was reminded of the time spent making love with Cole.

Even with her eyes fully opened, she could vividly

recall every moment of the night and day they had spent in each other's arms. A heated shiver went up her spine when she thought of the look in his eyes just seconds before his body slid into hers and how she had stretched to receive him and the way her thighs had tightened around him and how her hips had cradled him while he moved in and out of her at such a luscious, mind-blowing rhythm and pace.

Preoccupied with those lustful memories, once she made the turn into her driveway off the main road, it took her several moments to register that a car was parked in front of her house. Once her lights shone on the vehicle, she recognized it immediately as the rental that had been delivered to Cole. Her heart skipped a beat. It was close to midnight. What was he doing here? What did he want?

Then it dawned on her just what he wanted when his words of earlier that day came back to her, and stroked her skin like a sensual caress. *I want you again, Patrina.*

She sucked in a deep breath when she brought her car to a stop. She unbuckled her seat belt and watched as Cole opened his car door and eased out of the vehicle, closed the door and then leaned against it. Waiting.

She knew she couldn't sit in her car forever; besides, she was tired, annoyed…and edgy. Boy, was she edgy. The insistent, aching throb between her legs that had been there all week just wouldn't go away.

She pulled the key from the ignition, placed her

purse around her shoulder and opened the car door. The moment she did so, Cole moved toward her, forever the gentleman, and offered her his hand. She decided not to take it just yet. She watched him study her features and figured she must look a total mess, but then, who wouldn't after working sixteen hours straight?

"What are you doing here, Cole?" she asked, his height making it necessary to tilt her head back to meet his gaze.

"I didn't think we had much privacy earlier today and felt we still needed to talk."

"Well, you thought wrong. I've been at work since six this morning and—"

"Why?"

She lifted a brow. "Why what?"

"Why are you just coming home now?" he asked, his features hard.

Patrina's temper flared. "Not that it's any of your business, but I worked at my office seeing patients and then I left there and put in another eight hours at the clinic. When you saw me today at the store I was there picking up a few items for Lila Charles, an elderly woman who was a good friend of my grandmother's. She doesn't have any family."

Thinking she'd said enough, more than he really needed to know, she sighed deeply and saw his hand was still stretched out to help her out of the car. Convinced she was only accepting his act of kindness because she was too tired to do otherwise, she took his hand.

The moment their hands touched, it happened. A shiver raced through every part of her body and she glanced up at him, hoping he hadn't felt it, too. But from the darkness of his eyes, the heated gaze, she knew that he had. Her heart skipped a beat. Then another. And another.

All sense of time was suspended as they stared at each other and finally she knew she had to say something. So she said just what she felt. "I'm tired."

She saw a softening around the edges of his gorgeous mouth and then he said in a low, throaty voice, "Of course you are, sweetheart."

She didn't have time to react to his term of endearment when, still holding her hand, he leaned down, pushed her hair aside with his other hand, then cupped the back of her neck and drew her mouth to his. She closed her eyes the moment their mouths made contact and forgot how tired she was. Instead, she felt only the way his lips were gliding over hers, the way his tongue went inside her mouth when she released a breathless sigh and the gentle way it was mating with hers. She felt her entire body respond, felt the nipples of her breasts throb with an urgency to have him touch them, take them in his mouth and taste them.

And then, without warning, she felt herself being gently pulled from the car and lifted up into his arms. As he closed the car door with his hip, she pulled her mouth away from his. "Cole, put me down. I'm too heavy."

"And I've told you before, you're not."

She sighed deeply, too exhausted from work, as well as from the effects of his kiss, to argue. Instead, she buried her face in his chest, inhaling the manly scent of him.

"Open the door, Patrina."

While still cradled in his arms, she managed to work her door key into the lock and felt the warmth of the interior of her home when he stepped over the threshold and closed the door behind them. She thought he would put her on her feet, but instead, he moved down the hall toward her bedroom.

"Now wait just a minute, Cole. How dare you assume that you can show up here tonight and think I'll sleep with you again?"

He placed her on the bed and gazed down at her. "That's not why I'm here, Patrina. I came to talk, but you're too tired. There's something else I can do, though."

He left the room and walked into the adjoining bathroom. Then, seconds after she heard the sound of water running, he reappeared in the doorway. "Your bath will be ready in a minute, so start taking off your clothes. I'll give you five minutes and if you haven't stripped down by then, I'll be more than tempted to do the honors myself." And then he disappeared again into the bathroom.

She glared at the closed bathroom door, but then thought, *Wow!* She'd never had a man run a bath for her and God knew she could use a good soak tonight. Deciding to move as quickly as she could before he made good on his threat and came back, she stripped off her clothes and slipped into her bathrobe, then pulled a short nightgown out of the dresser drawer. All in five minutes.

She turned when he opened the door again. He lifted a brow as he looked her up and down and then glanced at the pile of clothes in the middle of the floor. As if satisfied, he returned his gaze to her. "Ready?"

She nodded. "Yes."

And then he moved toward her and in one easy swoop, picked her up in his arms and headed for the bathroom. "You're going to hurt yourself if you keep doing this," she said.

"No, I'm not."

She didn't have time to argue when she felt him lowering her into the warm, sudsy water, removing her robe in the process. Part of her robe got wet, anyway, but she didn't care. He had used an ample amount of her favorite bubble bath, more than she would have, but she didn't care about that, either. At the moment she didn't want to care or worry about anything and she settled back against the tub, closed her eyes and let out an appreciative moan. The warm, sudsy water felt heavenly.

"Let me know when you're ready to get out."

She opened her eyes and looked up at Cole. He was standing at the foot of the tub. "I can get out myself."

He nodded. "I know you can, but I want you to let me know when you're ready to get out so I can help you."

She frowned and decided to take advantage of the wonderful bath he'd prepared for only a few minutes longer and get out of the tub on her own before he came back. She closed her eyes again and that was the last thing she remembered.

COLE GLANCED AT his watch after neatly placing Patrina's clothes across the back of the chair. Her lush feminine scent was all in them, especially her undies. He forced the thought from his mind as he made his way back into the bathroom. He had expected her to call him by now, and when he eased open the door and saw her in the tub asleep, he wasn't surprised.

Taking the huge velour towel off the rack, he reached down and pulled her up into his arms. She came wide awake in that instant. "No, Cole, I can dry myself. You don't need to do this."

"Yes, I do, baby. Let me take care of you, okay," he said softly, politely.

Something in his voice must have calmed her, he thought, made her give up the protest, or it could be as he assumed. She was just plain tuckered out. He wondered how often she worked like this, pulling double hours. He then recalled what Casey had said about Patrina being up for some award for her dedicated service to the community. Now he understood why. The blasted woman needed someone to take care of her or she would work herself to death.

He went about wrapping a dripping wet Patrina up in the large towel and, after placing her on her feet, he made an attempt to dry her off. When she reached her hands down to cover her feminine mound from his view, he smiled and said, "There's no need to do that. I've seen it all before, remember?"

She removed her hands. Going down on his knees, with painstaking gentleness he began drying her, every inch of her body, and as he'd told her, every place the towel touched he had seen before. But it didn't stop him from fighting the urge to replace the towel with his hands and touch her all over, fondle her in those areas he remembered so well, those he loved caressing. And that would be every single place on her body—skin to skin, flesh to flesh. Especially those full-figure curves, voluptuous thighs and child-bearing hips.

Childbearing hips.

That immediately reminded him of the reason he had sought her out tonight. Instinctively, his hand went to her stomach and his palm gently flattened against it. Something primal, possessive and elementally male clicked inside him at the thought that even now, his child could be right here inside her.

Amazing.

Leaning forward, he removed his hand and placed a kiss right there, just below her navel. It didn't matter to him if she was pregnant or not, what mattered was the possibility and the fact that he had given her a part of him no other woman could claim—his seed. Whether it hit fertile soil, only time would tell. Unless…

He glanced upward and she shook her head and

said softly, "It's too early to tell, Cole. I promise that you will be the first to know."

He nodded. Satisfied.

Tossing the towel aside, he grabbed her nightgown from the vanity. "Raise your hands, Patrina," he said, trying to ignore her nakedness, especially those breasts that moved upward when she lifted her arms. They were breasts that he enjoyed putting his mouth on. He pulled down the nightie, which barely covered her hips. He immediately thought of one word to describe how she looked in it. Sexy.

He then swept her up into his arms and carried her from the bathroom into the bedroom, where he settled her on her feet. "Did you enjoy your bath?" he asked as he turned back the covers of the bed,

"Yes, and thank you."

"You're welcome."

He moved aside. "Come on, let me tuck you in."

She slid between the sheets and he pulled the blanket and spread up to cover her. "Is there anything else I can do for you?" he asked.

"No. You've done more than enough."

He grabbed the book she had placed on her nightstand and settled in the chair beside her bed. The book was the same one she had finished reading last week, the one his cousin Stone had written. "You aren't going to leave?" she asked him.

"Not until you've fallen asleep."

She nodded. "Where does your sister think you are this time of night? It's almost one in the morning."

He smiled. "She thinks I'm over at Durango's playing cards with him and Quade."

"What if she—"

"Relax, she won't." He met and held her gaze. "And if she does, will it bother you?"

She didn't hesitate. "No." Then a few seconds later, she added, "To keep it a secret was your idea, not mine. Besides, if I'm pregnant everyone is going to wonder how it happened."

His mind was suddenly filled with the memory of how it happened, all the times they'd made love. He began to get aroused. Thinking it best to steer his thoughts in another direction, he said, "Don't worry about it. I have everything under control."

A smile touched her lips before she shifted her body to a more comfortable position and closed her eyes. He sat there for a long time just staring at her, tempted to reach out and push a stray lock of hair from her face. He was tempted even further to lean over and kiss her, slide into bed with her and hold her during the night.

And like before, his feelings were intense. Feelings he'd never had for any other woman. Damn, he thought, what was happening? Those feelings shouldn't be possible for him.

He pinched the bridge of his nose and sighed deeply. He glanced over at the bed, saw the steady rise and fall of her chest and knew she had lapsed into a deep sleep.

It was time for him to leave, but he couldn't seem to force his body from the chair. So he decided to stay and watch over her for a little while longer. And the longer he sat there, the more he knew that Patrina Foreman was digging her way under his skin. He didn't like it.

CHAPTER TEN

"Good morning, Dr. Foreman."

Patrina glanced at her receptionist when she entered the office. Tammie Rhodes was a perky twenty-year-old who worked for her full-time while taking night classes at the university. "Good morning, Tammie. How are you this morning?"

"Great. You have a full schedule today and Ellen Cranston's husband called, claiming she's having labor pains again."

Patrina smiled as she slipped on her lab coat. "Are they real labor pains this time?" she asked, thinking of the woman who wasn't due for another two months. Last time what Ellen and her husband, Mark, thought were labor pains were nothing but a severe case of an overactive child.

Tammie grinned. "I told him it would be okay if he brought her in so we could check to make sure."

Patrina nodded as she headed toward her office. Her first patient was due in an hour. That would give her an opportunity to sit down with a cup of coffee in the privacy of her office and relive everything that happened last night with Cole. She still found it hard to believe he had been there waiting for her when she'd gotten home and then gone so far as to run a bath for her, dry her off and then tenderly tuck her into bed.

She had slept like a baby and had awakened this morning to find him gone. She'd have sworn she'd dreamed the whole thing if it hadn't been for the note he had scribbled and left on her kitchen table that read, "I'll see you later." Did that mean he would be parked outside her house when she came home again tonight?

"Oh, and you got another call, Dr. Foreman. This one personal."

Patrina turned around just seconds before entering her office and lifted a brow. "From who?"

"Cole Westmoreland."

She didn't miss the look of interest in Tammie's eyes. "Did he leave a message?"

Tammie smiled. "Yes. He told me to tell you he was taking you to lunch."

Patrina frowned. "I don't do lunch."

Tammie chuckled. "That's what I told him."

"And?"

"He said you would today."

Patrina tried to keep a straight face but wondered where Cole came off saying what she would do.

"Isn't he Durango Westmoreland's cousin? One of Corey Westmoreland's triplets?"

Tammie's question broke into Patrina's thoughts. "Yes."

Both Durango and Corey were popular around these parts, but for different reasons. Before his marriage to Savannah, Durango had been well-known among the single ladies, and Corey was a highly respected citizen of the town. Everyone knew about his mountain. And everyone knew when he'd discovered he had triplets born more than thirty years ago.

"I heard that Cole Westmoreland is good-looking," Tammie said, again breaking into Patrina's thoughts.

"Excuse me?"

Tammie's smile widened. "I said I heard that he and his brother are extremely handsome."

That was something Patrina could certainly agree with. "They are."

She studied her receptionist. "Aren't they way too old for you, not to mention that Clint is now a married man?"

Tammie laughed. "I overheard my oldest sister, Gloria, tell that to one of her girlfriends. She was working at the tuxedo-rental shop and saw them last year when they came in to get fitted for tuxes to wear at their sister's wedding."

Patrina nodded. "Well, if Cole Westmoreland calls again, please tell him I'll be too busy today to go to lunch."

"He won't be calling back. He said he wouldn't. Told me to tell you to be ready to go exactly at noon."

Patrina frowned. Cole's bossiness completely erased all his kindness of last night. Instead of saying anything else about Cole, especially to Tammie, she opened the door to her office and went inside, dismissing Cole from her mind. Or rather, she tried to, but found that she couldn't.

"LET ME KNOW the next time you decide to use me as an alibi," Durango said to his cousin as they were horseback riding on the open range. Quade had left early that morning to trek up the mountain to visit with Corey.

Cole lifted a brow. "What happened?"

"Casey showed up early this morning to visit with Savannah and made a remark that it must have been some poker game last night since you didn't get in until almost three this morning."

Durango, who was three years older than Cole, shook his head and added, "Lucky for you, Savannah went to bed early, leaving me and Quade up talking, so she had no idea whether you dropped by last night or not. So rest assured, Quade and I ended up covering your ass."

Cole smiled. "Thanks."

Durango stared at his cousin. "Any reason we needed to? Quade said he had an idea where you were but he wasn't talking."

"I appreciate that and for the moment there is a reason my ass needs covering, but how much longer that need will last, only time will tell."

Durango shook his head. "Sounds like it involves a woman. I just hope she's not married."

"She's not."

"Good."

Cole couldn't help but laugh. "Look who's talking. Everybody knows your and McKinnon's history." Durango, Quade's brother, had been the second Westmoreland that Cole and Clint had met. Upon arriving in Montana, it had been Durango who had picked up him, Clint and Quade at the airport. After spending the night at Durango's ranch, the four had made the trip up to Corey's Mountain. Once there, he and Clint had come face-to-face with the man who had fathered them, as well as another cousin, Stone, and the young woman Stone would later marry, Madison. That particular day they'd also met Madison's mother, Abby, who had just reentered Corey's life a month before. Abby was the woman who had been Corey's true love for thirty-plus years.

"According to Casey, things are falling into place for Dad's party," Cole said, as a way to change the subject.

Durango chuckled, knowing exactly what he was doing. "Yes, and it will be a pretty classy event if Abby has anything to do with it. Savannah's excited about all the Westmorelands who will start arriving next week. All of us haven't been together since Casey's wedding. Everyone couldn't make it to Clint's wedding." He shook his head. "I still can't believe he got married."

"Believe it and trust me when I say he's an extremely happy man," Cole responded.

"Hey, I know the feeling."

Cole studied his cousin and believed he really did know the feeling. All it took was a few minutes around Durango and Savannah to see just how happy they were together. Marriage definitely agreed with some people.

"McKinnon and I are meeting today for lunch at

the Watering Hole. You want to join us?" Durango asked him.

Cole met his cousin's gaze and smiled. "Nope. Thanks for asking, but I've made prior lunch arrangements."

PATRINA SMILED WHILE studying the new set of ultrasounds she had ordered on Ellen Cranston. Ellen and her husband had come in after Ellen had endured another sleepless night of stomach pains. Tammie had made an appointment with them to arrest their fears that Ellen was having labor pains.

Patrina had ordered a new set of ultrasounds after examining Ellen's stomach. She hadn't wanted to get the couple's hopes up regarding her suspicions until she was absolutely sure. Now she was. The Cranstons, who'd been trying to have a baby for more than five years, were having twins, something their first ultrasound hadn't shown because the little boy had been hidden behind his sister. A boy and a girl. She knew how pleased the Cranstons would be and couldn't wait to tell them the news. She reached for the phone to make the call.

Ten minutes later Patrina leaned back in her chair very pleased with her conversation with the Cranstons. Ellen and Mark had been so happy they had started crying on the phone and Patrina couldn't help but be happy for them. She then unconsciously reached down and touched her own stomach. What if *she* was pregnant? If she was, she knew her heart would know the same joy that the Cranstons were experiencing right now. There were over-the-counter ways she could find out now, but she didn't want to find out that way. Having a missed period would be sign enough, which meant she would probably know something sometime next week.

"Dr. Foreman, your noon appointment has arrived."

Patrina lifted a brow at the sound of Tammie's excited voice over the intercom. In other words, Cole was out front.

Patrina stood. "Please send him in."

No sooner had the words left her mouth than her office door opened, and Cole, looking larger than life, boldly walked in and closed the door behind him. He smiled at her and said in the sexy voice that had undone her several times, "I'm here."

COLE LEANED AGAINST the closed door and stared at Patrina, and the first thought that ran through his mind was how beautiful she looked today. And when she nervously swiped her lips with her tongue, the second thought was how much he wanted to taste her. Hell, from the deep inner throb in his body, he wanted to do a lot more than that, but tasting her mouth would suffice for now.

"Hello, Cole."

"Hello, Patrina."

He moved away from the door and walked over to where she was standing beside her desk. "Did you get a good night's sleep?"

"Yes, thanks for asking, and thanks for all you did to assure that I did."

He reached out and placed his hands at her waist and met her gaze. "Thank me this way."

And then he leaned forward and captured her mouth with his. The moment his tongue mingled with hers, he heard the deep moan that came from her throat and combined with the deep groan from his own. This was more than he wanted, he thought. This was what he needed—now—in a bad way. And when she arched her body and looped her arms around his neck, he shifted his hands from her waist and placed them on the thickness of her rump to urge her even closer to the fit of him, needing for her to feel him so she would know just how aroused he was. How quickly she could turn him on.

Reluctantly, torturously, he pulled back from her mouth, but not before giving it one final, thorough sweep. "I needed that," he whispered against her moist lips.

"So did I."

He pulled back, tilted his head and gazed at her, surprised by her throaty admission. He could tell from her expression that she'd even surprised herself in making it. "Will you be going to the clinic when you leave here today?" he asked her.

She nodded. "I go to the clinic every day. I'm needed there."

It was on the tip of Cole's tongue to tell her that she was needed here where she was now, right in his arms. Instead, he said, "How late will you be staying?"

She shrugged. "Until I'm no longer needed."

"Not a good answer. I'm coming to the clinic to pick you up at eight. You can give me the address over lunch."

She lifted a brow. "Excuse me?"

He smiled. "You're excused. You're also beautiful." He then leaned in to kiss whatever words she was about to say off her lips.

PATRINA GLANCED AT the clock. It was a little past seven and the clinic wasn't nearly as busy as it had been the night before, which was a good thing since Cole had been adamant about picking her up at eight. One of the other doctors had gone home, which left only her and a staff person, which was fine.

She grabbed a cup of coffee and decided that although she would be leaving work in less than an hour, she deserved a break. Earlier, things had gotten pretty hectic but now all was calm.

Pausing at the front desk to let Julia, the night clerk, know where she'd be if things got hectic again, she strolled down the corridor that would take her to the outside patio. Upon opening the door, she pulled her jacket around her to ward off the cool breeze and recalled that this time last week the entire area had been covered in snow. Like everyone else, she hoped it was the last snowfall of the season.

She stood at the rail and looked out over the lake, remembering her lunch with Cole. He had taken her to a popular café not far from the hospital and she had to admit that she had enjoyed his company. He'd told her how the plans for his father's birthday party were coming along, and that all his cousins—most of them she knew—planned to attend. Even Delaney and Jamal would be flying in from the Middle East. They had laughed together when Cole had told her about the baby bed Thorn had built for his firstborn. It was in the shape of a motorcycle, with wheels and everything.

Then things had gotten somewhat serious when she'd asked him to tell her about his mom. She had heard the story of how his mother hadn't told them until she'd been on her deathbed that their father was still alive. Patrina admired Cole for saying that although he wished he could have gotten to know his father a lot sooner than he had and regretted the things he'd missed out on—like the summers with everyone on Corey's Mountain—he was not angry at his mother for doing what she did. It had been her decision and he respected that.

Just from hearing him talk, Patrina knew he had been close to his mother and had loved her dearly. Cole knew how it felt to lose someone, and he also knew how it was to move on, something she hadn't been able to do—until now. But still, there was something she couldn't get past and that was the fact that Cole was a lawman. While he was on duty, upholding the law, at any time some crazy person could end his life.

For the first time since losing Perry she could admit

to something she thought would never happen to her again. She had fallen in love with another man. Cole.

She knew Perry would be happy for her, for finding someone else to love and moving on with her life, but knowing what Cole did for a living, she wasn't sure if she could get on with her life with him. She would always worry about the risks he might take, and she couldn't go through that again.

Anyway, the problem was academic. Cole was not in love with her. All she was to him was a challenge.

Deciding her break time was up, Patrina headed back inside. When she reached the area where Julia was working, she smiled at the woman. Julia had a very odd look on her face and had sunk back in her chair. She regarded Patrina silently when she neared.

"Julia? Is anything wrong?"

Before Julia could answer, Patrina felt something cold and hard at the middle of her back.

"No, nothing's wrong, Doc, now that you're here," a deep male voice said close to her ear. "I need the key to your medicine cabinet."

Patrina swallowed, tried to keep her cool and slowly turned to look into the hard eyes of a young man who couldn't have been more than twenty. He was holding a gun on her. "Why do you want the key?" she asked in an even voice.

The man sneered. "Don't act stupid. You know why. I want all your drugs."

COLE WAS JUST about to round the corner to see what was keeping Patrina when he heard the man and stopped dead in his tracks. He eased back against the wall, then leaned forward and peeped around the corner. The man was holding a gun on Patrina and another woman. Intense anger, combined with stark fear, crept up Cole's spine, but he knew he had to keep a level head.

He glanced around, noticed the high ceiling, the windows whose blinds were drawn and the long hallway that led to several rooms. Given a choice, he would have preferred knowing the layout of the clinic, but he didn't have a choice. The only thing he knew was that some lunatic was holding a gun on Patrina.

He then heard the man's voice raised when Patrina tried to convince him she didn't have a key. Deciding he had to do something and quickly, he backed up and came to a closet, looked inside, grabbed a lab coat and put it on. Knowing the element of surprise was definitely not a good idea in this case, he began whistling to let everyone know he was coming and hoped and prayed that neither Patrina nor the other woman gave anything away.

Taking a deep breath, he rounded the corner and saw both Patrina and the other's woman eyes widen when they saw him. He saw the look of nervousness in the man's eyes and Cole knew more than anything he had to convince the man that he was not only a doctor, but that he was the doctor with the key.

"Oh, we have another patient," Cole said, approaching the three with a cheery smile on his face. He pretended to see the gun for the first time when the man turned toward him.

"Get over here with the others, Doc," he snapped, "and one of you has less than a minute to produce the key to the medicine cabinet."

Cole, seemingly at ease, widened his smile and said, "Oh, is that what you want? I'm the one who has it."

"Then give it to me," the man said, his attention now on Cole.

"Sure. I know not to argue with man with a gun," Cole said, retaining his smile as he slowly reached into his back pocket to pull out a set of keys.

He handed them to the man, who gave them a quick glance and frowned. He then looked back at Cole. "Hey, this is a set of car keys."

Cole shook his head. "No, they're not. Look again."

The moment the man glanced down to study the keys, Cole kicked the man in the knee at the same time as he knocked the gun from his hand. Cole was about to give him a right hook, but Patrina beat him to it. Cole finished him off by hitting him hard behind the neck, which sent him crumbling to the floor, unconscious.

"Call the police," he told the other woman who'd had the sense to keep her cool through it all. He kicked the gun farther away as he glanced down at the unconscious man. He then looked at Patrina, who was rubbing her knuckles. "Who in hell taught you to hit like that?"

"Dale. After Perry died he figured I needed to know a few moves to protect myself, since I would be living alone."

Cole nodded, grateful that her brother had had the insight to do that. "You okay?" he asked softly, crossing the room to take a look at her knuckles.

"Yes, I'm okay." Then she said in quiet tone. "You could have been killed."

He lifted his gaze and looked into her eyes. "Yeah, but then so could you," he countered.

They both glanced around when they heard Julia return. "The police are on their way," she said in an excited tone.

"Thanks," Cole said, releasing Patrina's hand to glance around. He turned back to Patrina. "Where the hell is security?"

"We haven't had security in months," the other woman answered. "Couldn't afford it. The clinic's on a tight budget."

Cole switched his gaze from Patrina to stare at the woman, not wanting to believe what she'd said. *No security?* He was about to say something and decided not to. There was one way to remedy the problem, and he knew that after today, there would always be security protecting the clinic.

IT WAS HOURS later before they were finally able to leave the clinic. That was only after law enforcement had asked questions, taken statements and made an arrest.

By the time Julia had finished telling her side of the story to the authorities and news media, Cole had become a hero and made the ten o'clock news. He received calls from Casey, Durango and his father wanting to make sure he was okay. Only Casey had a hundred questions for him since the television reporter indicated the reason he had shown up at the clinic in the first place was to pick up Dr. Patrina Foreman. So much for keeping his relationship with Patrina a secret. Now the entire town knew he was seeing her.

He glanced at Patrina and was glad they were finally on the road to her house. She hadn't said much and he couldn't help wondering what she was thinking, especially when during the police officers' questioning it came out that he was a *former* Texas Ranger. He would never forget how her eyes had met his for several pulsing moments before looking away.

He figured they needed to talk about it since she'd figured, and rightly so, that he had deliberately not told her. "Let's talk, Patrina."

She met his gaze. She gave her head a little toss and her shoulder a shrug before saying, "What about?"

"Whatever you want to talk about. Let's do it now because when we get to your place and I get you inside, talking will be the last thing on my mind."

Just like he'd known it would, intense anger appeared in her face and her eyes looked to be shooting darts. He had gotten more than a rise out of her. Now she was fighting mad. He figured if he hadn't been the one at the wheel she would probably haul off and punch him the way she'd punched the intruder.

"You arrogant ass. How dare you think when you get me home, you will do anything to me? You haven't even been honest with me. Not once did you tell me that you were no longer a ranger. You had me thinking you were still in law enforcement. Why didn't you tell me?"

"Was I supposed to?" He pulled the car off the main road and into her driveway, then parked in front of her house and turned off the ignition. Good. They would have it out now, because like he said, when they got inside they would make love, not war. He turned to face her.

"You knew how I felt," she said angrily.

"How you felt about what you *thought* was my job didn't matter to me, because sleeping with you, becoming involved with you, had nothing to do with what I did for a living. You assumed I was a Texas Ranger, yet you slept with me, anyway. Your mouth was saying one thing, but your body was saying another, Patrina. I decided to pay closer attention to what your body was saying because it truly knew what you wanted."

She stared at him and then said quietly, "You could have gotten killed tonight, Cole."

"Hey, he was holding that gun on you first, Doc. You could have lost your life just as easily." The thought of that made his gut twist. He had come close to knocking the damn man unconscious again after the police brought him around to make an arrest.

Then in a softer voice, he said, "I could have lost you."

Releasing his seat belt, he leaned toward her. "And that's something I could not let happen."

PATRINA STARED DEEP into Cole's eyes, and then shifted her gaze to stare at his mouth. What was there about the shape and texture of it that made her want to run the tip of her tongue all over it, kiss it, get lost in it?

She tried keeping her mind on track, taking in what he'd said, noting the heartfelt way he'd said it. They were involved, at least for the moment. In another week or so he would be leaving Montana to return to Texas. Things between them would come to an end. And if she was pregnant, she would become a single parent.

One of the reasons she had made love with him was because she'd known, regardless of him being a Texas Ranger, she was only capturing a moment in time, seizing an opportunity. She hadn't been looking for anything more than that, definitely not anything lasting. He hadn't promised her that and she hadn't expected it. What they had shared had been about wants and needs, fulfilling desires, experiencing satisfaction of the most potent kind.

It was about him taking her off the shelf to live a vibrant and rewarding life, reminding her of the woman she was, of the passion she had tried so hard to ignore and hide.

"I'm going to kiss you, Patrina."

His words penetrated her mind and she met his gaze. He'd spoken with amazing calmness, deep-rooted determination and ingrained authority. He was a take-charge kind of guy. If she had any doubt about that characteristic before, she didn't now, especially after seeing how he'd handled the would-be robber.

"But that's not all I'm going to do to you," he added, inching his face even closer to hers. "We can do it out here or we can take it inside." His mouth curved into a warm smile.

His smile would be the death of her yet. It had become her weakness. She felt desire being stirred inside her. She inhaled deeply. He was making her crazy. She hadn't slept with a man in over three years and then Cole showed up, taking over her mind in red-hot pursuit. Even now she could feel her common sense tumbling.

"Patrina?"

She shifted her gaze from his mouth back to his eyes, thought for a second, then threw caution to the wind. "Let's take it inside."

CHAPTER ELEVEN

SO THEY TOOK it inside.

The moment they were across the threshold, Cole closed and locked the door behind them. She turned and he was right there, pulling her into his arms and taking her mouth with a hunger he knew was possible only with her. There was an instinctive need to mate with her the way a man mated with a woman he claimed as his.

Claimed as his.

Something jolted through Cole. He really didn't like the thought of that. He had never considered any woman as his. There might have been a passing fancy for one, but that was all there had ever been. However, he would be the first to admit that something with Patrina was different. He couldn't put his finger on what, but there was a difference. He didn't particularly care to know a difference existed, but at the moment, he would go with the flow. Especially when she brought some pretty hot dreams his way every night and given the fact that whenever he saw her, he immediately thought of sex, sex and more sex.

Like he was doing now.

And then there was the possibility that she could

be pregnant with his child, which put a whole new spin on things. But he would concern himself with that when the time came. Something else that troubled him was the realization that it wouldn't bother him in the least if she was pregnant. Just *when* his thought process got shot to hell on an issue that monumental, he really didn't know.

The only thing he did know was that for the last seven days, he had been thinking about her nonstop. Had craved her constantly and needed intimate contact with her as much as he needed to breathe. And the urgency of his kiss, the hungry way his tongue was devouring the cavern of her mouth, was making him realize just how over the edge he was and just how uncontrollable he'd become around her.

He broke mouth contact thinking this had to stop. He immediately took possession of it again, deciding hell, no, it didn't. And this kiss was deeper than and just as thorough as the one before. And then moments later, it was she who pulled her mouth away, mainly to inhale air into her lungs. The pause gave him a chance to step back to see his handiwork. He saw how moist her lips were, how swollen, how thoroughly kissed. Seeing them touched him deeply. Just as deeply as seeing her standing there staring at him through the veil of lashes, with the dark mane of hair in disarray around her face. She looked sexier than any one woman had a right to look.

And he wanted her.

Desire, thick as anything he'd ever felt, surged through him, nipped at every vital part of his body, making him as aroused as a man could possibly get. If he didn't get out of his jeans fast, there was a chance he might damage himself in a way he didn't want to think about.

But he wanted to see Patrina naked first. "Come here, baby."

He watched her take a step closer to him, and despite her outward calm appearance, he saw the shiver that went through her body. When she came to stand directly in front of him, he whispered, "Closer."

When she took the step that made their bodies touch, he reached for the side zipper of her skirt and with the flick of his wrist he stepped back to watch it glide down her hips, leaving her clad in a full slip, bra and panties.

"I want it all off you, Patrina," he said in a low voice, reaching out and tracing his finger along the lace-trimmed V neckline of her slip and hearing the tiny catch of breath in her throat at his touch.

She took a step back and began removing every stitch covering her body. It took all the control he had not to help her, but he wanted to see her strip for him. And what he saw escalated his pulse, burgeoned his awareness of just what a beautiful, full-figured woman she was. The power of her feminine sexiness could literally bring a man to his knees. When she eased out of her panties, he groaned and his heart began racing a mile a minute. He felt himself get even harder.

"Now remove yours," she said.

Her words floated across to him like a gentle caress and she didn't have to say them twice. He unbuttoned his shirt, pulled it off his shoulders and sent it flying across the room. Then he kicked off his shoes, leaned over and pulled off his stocks. Straightening his tall frame, he pulled a condom packet out his back pocket and held it between his teeth while his hands went to the zipper of his jeans.

His gaze never left hers and with excruciating care, he eased his jeans, along with his boxer shorts, down his legs. He stepped out of them and, taking the packet from his mouth, he reached out to sweep Patrina off her feet and into his arms, kissing her like a man starved for the taste of her.

And then he was moving toward her bedroom. After placing her on the huge bed, he stood back to put on the condom, knowing she was watching him attentively the entire time. Being aware that her eyes were on him, especially that part of him, made him even more aroused, making it difficult to sheath himself in latex.

"Need my help?"

He glanced up at Patrina and couldn't help but smile at her serious expression. "Thanks, Doc, but if you were to touch me now, I might embarrass myself. I want you that much."

"Oh."

He shook his head. Sometimes he found it hard to believe that she didn't have a clue how sexy she was. "Okay, that does it," he said, finishing up and moving toward the bed. A smile tugged at the corners of his mouth. He would take pleasure in showing her once again the degree of his desire for her.

PATRINA SCOOTED TO the edge of the bed, intent on showing Cole the degree of *her* desire for *him,* and was surprised that she could be so bold. But while she'd watched him put on the condom and seen his growing arousal as he did so, something deep inside her had been triggered. A desire to know him in a way she had never known any man, including Perry.

She reached out and looped her arms around Cole's neck and he pulled her closer to him. So close that she felt the tips of her breasts pressed against his hard, muscular chest. She felt secure in his arms. She felt like she was in a very special place, a place where she belonged.

She moved her hands to his shoulders and thought he felt rather tense. "Relax," she whispered softly.

"Uh, that's easy for you to say, baby. You're not the one about to come unglued."

"Wanna bet?"

And then she pushed him sideways and he tumbled on the bed with her straddling him. Cole was a take-charge man, but for once, she wanted to be in control. She gazed down at him.

"This position is different," he said, and before she could respond, he lifted his head from the pillow and captured a breast with his mouth.

The moment his mouth captured the nipple between his moist lips, she threw her head back and moaned. The man definitely had a way with his tongue. He also had a way with something else, and it was something she wanted.

But first…

She pulled back and he had no choice but to release her breast. She scooted back some to lean back on her haunches and look at him, getting a good view of him from the knees up. He evidently saw the determined glint in her eyes, saw where her attention lay while she licked her lips, and he said huskily. "I hope you're not about to do what I'm thinking."

A sweet smile touched her lips. "I don't know what you're thinking," she said, reaching out and running her hand up his inner thigh, marveling at how firm the muscles were there.

"You're trying to kill me, aren't you," he said, and she could tell the words had been forced through clenched teeth.

"No. I want to pleasure you the way you've pleasured me," she said, watching how he got even more aroused before her eyes. She suddenly felt downright giddy at the thought that she had the power to make him do that.

Her fingers began moving again, easing closer to his aroused shaft, and she could hear his sharp intake of breath the closer she got. And then she had him in her hands, and deciding she wanted to taste him and not latex, she slowly rolled the condom off him.

"Do you know how hard it was to put that damn thing on?" she heard him ask in a near growl.

"Yes, I watched you the entire time. And watching you is why I want to do this," she said, bending forward to take him into her mouth. His body jerked at the intimate contact, and she took her hands to hold down his thighs, deciding he wasn't going anywhere except where he was right now.

She tasted him the way he had done her several times that night they'd been stranded together, and felt the size of him fill her mouth. And with each circular motion she made with her tongue, with each tiny suction of her lips, she felt him gasp, felt the flat plane of his stomach tighten. She was aware of the exact moment he reached for her hair and began methodically massaging her scalp while uttering her name over and over again. She hadn't known until now how much pleasure she could bring him this way.

And then she felt his body jolt, felt his hand tugging hard, trying to pull her mouth away, but she held firm, showing him just how much staying power she had. He was left with no other choice but to shudder through it, and he cried her name, a loud piercing sound, as his body quivered uncontrollably.

After one final hard jerk of his body, she slowly released him and watched as he lay there trying to discover how to breathe again. She reached into the nightstand next to the bed and retrieved a new condom packet. Ripping it open with her teeth, she began putting it on him. He opened his eyes and met her gaze.

She shrugged and said softly, "After the last time we did this, I decided to be prepared, since I wasn't sure when you might come back."

"But you knew I would." He issued it as a statement and not a question.

"I was hoping you wouldn't. We took chances. You made me feel things I've never felt before. You made me appreciate being a woman."

"And was that a bad thing?" he asked quietly.

"No, but I hadn't wanted to feel that way again, at least not to the extent that you were forcing me to."

He didn't say anything for a few moments and then asked in a low, throaty voice, "And now?"

A smile touched her lips and she moistened those lips with her tongue. "And now I want to make love to you all night and worry about what I should or should not do tomorrow."

He shifted their bodies so that she was beneath him, looking up at him. He had gotten aroused all over again. "All night," he said, a sexy smile forming on his lips as he trailed his fingers down her cheek.

"Yes, all night."

His hand left her face and traveled low, past her stomach to settle firmly between her legs. When his fingers began stroking her, she closed her eyes as sensations began overtaking her.

"Open your eyes and look at me, Patrina."

The moment she did so, he positioned his body over her and slid into her moistness. The connection was absolute, and when he began moving in slow, thorough thrusts, she felt her body give way and began shattering into a hundred thousand pieces. Automatically, she wrapped her legs around him to hold him in.

And when she felt his body begin to shake, she knew that together they were again finding intense pleasure in each other's arms.

HOURS LATER, THE sharp ring of the telephone brought both Cole and Patrina awake. She glanced at the laminated clock on the nightstand before reaching for the phone. It was almost four in the morning. "Yes?"

She pulled herself out of Cole's arms to swing her legs over the side of the bed. "How many minutes are they apart?" Then a few seconds later she said, "I'm on my way."

"A baby decided to come now?"

She glanced over her shoulder at Cole. He had pulled himself up in the bed. "Yes, but this isn't just any baby," she said, standing, about to head to the bathroom to dress.

"Oh? And why is this kid so special?"

She turned and smiled at him. "Because it's your niece or nephew."

At his confused expression, she said, "Veronica is the eighteen-year-old girl who's giving her baby to Casey and McKinnon to adopt. The baby wasn't due for another month or so. While I'm getting dressed, give them a call and ask them to meet me at the hospital."

FOR AS LONG as he lived, Cole doubted he would ever forget the look of profound happiness on his sister's face as she held her newborn son. He glanced at McKinnon, who was standing beside his wife, gazing down at the blessing they'd both been given, and knew this was a profound moment for him, as well.

"Have the two of you decided on a name?" he decided to ask to break the silence.

Casey glanced at him with tears shimmering in her eyes. "Yes, McKinnon and I wanted to honor our fathers by naming him Corey Martin Quinn."

Cole nodded, thinking the name fitted. According to Patrina, the baby weighed almost six pounds. Cole thought he was a whopper, considering he'd been premature, with a head of curly dark hair.

He switched his gaze from the baby to Patrina when she reentered the room. "The baby will have to remain here at the hospital for another day," she said to Casey and McKinnon. "After that you'll be free to take your son home."

"How is Veronica?" Casey asked.

"She's doing fine, but she hasn't changed her mind about not wanting to see the baby. She says all she wants to do now is get on with her life, move back to Virginia and return to school."

Cole listened. From what Patrina had told him on the drive over to the hospital, the young woman, Veronica Atkins, had been someone who had dropped out of school and taken off with a member of some rock band. After she had gotten pregnant, the guy had dumped her, and with no family to call on for help, she had moved into the local Y and gotten a job at a diner. She had lived in and out of foster homes all her life and wanted something better for her child, a life with a family who would give him stability and love. She had asked Patrina if she knew of a couple who would want her child, and Patrina had immediately thought of McKinnon and Casey.

"But of course as the baby's parents, you're free to visit him as often as you want," Patrina added, smiling.

"Thanks for everything, Trina," McKinnon said, gazing lovingly at his son and his wife.

"You don't have to thank me, McKinnon. You and Casey deserve your son like he deserves the two of you." Patrina then glanced over at Cole, and Cole felt a pull in his gut. Sensations spiraled through him with mesmerizing intensity. He could picture Patrina holding a child the same way Casey was doing now.

He drew in a deep breath and his entire body seemed to tense with an awareness he had not felt until this moment. It was electrifying. It was an eye-opener and it almost made him weak in the knees. He wanted to withdraw but knew he couldn't. He had to face what was so damn clear it was unreal.

He loved her. He had fallen in love with Patrina.

Dear heaven, how did that happen? When did it happen? He knew the answer to the latter. He had fallen in love with her the very first time he had made love to her and she had trusted him enough to give her body to him after holding herself back for so long. And then when her life had been threatened and that lunatic had held a gun on her, a part of the hard casing surrounding his heart had fallen off, as well.

He wanted to cross the room and whisper how he felt and then kiss her the way a man kisses the woman he loves. But he knew he couldn't do that. Casey was already curious about what was going on. She had asked questions after the robbery attempt, but he had refused to give her any answers. She had asked questions again, just seconds before she and McKinnon had been herded off to the birthing room to be part of the delivery as Veronica had requested. She had also requested to be out during the delivery and hadn't wanted to be told anything about the child, not even if it was a boy or girl.

Inhaling deeply, Cole crossed the room to Patrina and lightly stroked a finger down her cheek, not caring if Casey and McKinnon noticed. "Ready to go, Doc?"

She drew in a ragged breath and smiled. "In a second. I just need to clean up first and fill out a few papers."

He nodded and watched as Patrina left the room.

"What's going on, Cole? With you and Patrina?"

He met his sister's gaze. It was filled with accusations and he understood why. She knew his history when it came to women, but he wanted to assure her that this time things were different. "I love her and plan to marry her."

He could tell from the expression on Casey's face that his bold statement had been a shocker. "But how? The two of you barely know each other. You just met last year and haven't spent any time together."

"Yes, we have."

He held his sister's gaze. She seemed more confused than ever, and he knew she intended to get the full story later. She then asked softly. "Does she know how you feel?"

He smiled, tucking a stray strand of hair behind his sister's ear. "If you're asking me if I've told her yet, the answer is no. But trust me, I will."

CHAPTER TWELVE

WHEN COLE ENTERED the house behind Patina and closed the door behind them, he brushed aside the thought of telling her how he felt while they were making love. He couldn't hold it inside any longer. He wanted to tell her now.

"Patrina?"

She turned from placing her medical bag on the table. "Yes?"

"We need to talk."

Patrina sighed. She had an idea what he wanted to talk about. Being at the hospital around the baby had freaked him out. It had probably hit home more so than ever that she could be pregnant and what that meant, what drastic changes there might be, what demands she might make. She knew she had to assure him that she wouldn't ask anything of him.

"If I am pregnant, you don't have to worry about me asking anything of you, Cole. You've never forced yourself on me. I knew what I was doing each and every time we made love. It was what I wanted."

She turned to walk off, but he grasped her wrist. When she looked up at him, he said in a soft, yet husky voice, "Then maybe you ought to know that

I knew exactly what I was doing and it was what I wanted, as well."

Her heart contracted and she couldn't help but wonder what he meant. She didn't want to jump to conclusions, but he was looking at her intensely. "What do you mean?" she asked.

"What I mean is that if you are pregnant, I didn't intentionally set out to get you that way, but *if* you are, then I would be happy about it. I want a baby… with you."

He tightened his hold on her wrist and pulled her closer. "However," he added, "more than anything, I want you. I love you."

She stared at him for a long moment, shook her head and said, "But…but…"

"But nothing. I've never told a woman that I love her before and I don't plan on ever telling another woman again. Just you. And if I need to say it again, then that's fine. I'll say it as many times as it takes for you to believe me. I love you, Patrina. And I want to marry you, regardless of whether or not you're having my baby. It doesn't matter. I want to marry you as soon as humanly possible and live here with you."

"But…but what about Texas? You've never said you wanted to live in Bozeman."

He chuckled. "Baby, I plan to live wherever you are. You know I'm no longer a Texas Ranger. What I didn't tell you is that my uncle left me, Casey and Clint his ranch house and all the acres it sits on. Casey and I retain the rights to the land and, along with Clint, have established a foundation in my uncle's name to protect wild horses and the land is used for that. However, Casey and I sold our share of the ranch to Clint. With the money I got, I invested wisely."

When she nodded, he knew she understood that much of what he was saying. In other words, he was a very wealthy man. "Quade and I, along with Savannah's brother, Rico, are looking into setting up a security firm. Also, Quade and I are talking with Serena Preston about buying her copter service."

Patrina lifted a brow. "What will Serena do without her copter service?"

Cole shrugged. "I don't know. I understand she might be moving away. Why?"

"Curious. She was involved with Dale a year or so ago, and like a lot of other women it didn't take her long to discover that 'Heartbreaker' is his middle name."

Cole nodded and decided to get the conversation back to the two of them. "So now that you know how I feel about you, will you marry me, Patrina? I promise I will do everything within my power to make you fall in love with me, too."

"You'll be wasting your time, Cole."

At his crestfallen look, she smiled and said, "You'll be wasting your time because I'm already in love with you. I couldn't help but admit it to myself that night when I came home totally exhausted and you took such good care of me. I love you, too."

A relieved grin split Cole's face. "And you will marry me?"

She laughed. "Yes."

"As soon as possible?"

She tilted her head. "How soon are we talking?"

"Um, before next weekend. The entire Westmoreland family is coming in for Dad's birthday party and I want to present you to everyone as my wife."

Her heart did a quick flip. "You sure? You don't want to wait until I know for certain if I'm pregnant?"

He shook his head. "Like I said, sweetheart, it doesn't matter. Besides, if you aren't pregnant this month, there's a good chance that you will be next month."

She smiled. "You really want a baby?"

He reached out and placed his hands on her waist. "Yes, I really want a baby. I didn't know how much until I saw McKinnon look down at his son. Then I knew that more than anything I want you pregnant."

Tears filled Patrina's eyes and she knew she'd been given what some people never had, what some never took advantage of. A second go-round at happiness. What she had shared with Perry those five years had been wonderful and he would always hold a special place in her heart. But she loved Cole now and more than anything she would make him a good wife.

She tilted her head up and the moment she did so, his mouth was there, claiming her lips the same way he had claimed her heart. And when she was swept off her feet, she knew exactly where he was taking her. It was just where she wanted to be—for the rest of her life.

A week later

"Wow," CASEY SAID, smiling and looking at the huge diamond ring on Patrina's finger. "My brother evidently isn't as tight with his money as I thought. That ring is simply gorgeous."

Patrina thought so, too. Married four days, she and Cole had decided to wait until later to plan a honeymoon. They'd had a small wedding, with McKinnon's father, Judge Martin Quinn, perform- ing the rites. Immediately afterward, she and Cole, and Clint and Alyssa—the pair had flown in for the ceremony—along with Durango and Savannah, had stood beside McKinnon and Casey, as Corey Martin was christened. Reverend Miller officiated, acknowl- edging with a smile the three sets of godparents.

"Lucky kid," Clint had muttered after the cere- mony. He had then proceeded to announce that he and Alyssa were expecting.

Cole, standing beside Patrina, had touched her arm. They had decided not to share the news just yet that they, too, would be having a baby—close to the New Year.

"I always figured my cousin had good taste," Del- aney Westmoreland Yasir said, pulling Patrina from her thoughts.

Patrina glanced up and smiled. "Thanks."

It seemed that all the Westmorelands were here on Corey's Mountain to celebrate her father-in-law's fifty-seventh birthday. And Corey's wife, Abby, along with Casey, had made things extra-special. Patrina glanced across the room. A happy Corey Westmoreland was sitting proudly in his recliner with a grandbaby in each arm. Stone and Madison's three-month-old son, Rock, whom everyone affectionately called Rocky, and Corey's newest grandson, Corey Martin. Before his fifty-eighth birthday rolled around, Corey would have two more grandbabies to add to the mix. Patrina smiled at the thought.

She then glanced over at Alyssa, who was standing near the punch bowl talking to Clint. Whatever he'd said had made his wife smile, and Patrina thought that the two of them looked happy together. She glanced at Alyssa's stomach and thought she looked further along than three months. She wondered if perhaps Alyssa was having twins. She glanced down at her own stomach, suddenly realizing she might be faced with the same fate, since multiple births ran in the Westmoreland family. So far, only Storm's wife, Jayla, had given birth to twins.

"May I borrow my wife for a second?" Cole said, appearing before the group of women and grasping Patrina's wrist.

Without waiting for a response he pulled her away and led her outside. The air was chilly and when he pulled her into his arms, she went willingly into his warm embrace. He then leaned down and gave her a long and thorough kiss.

When he released her mouth, she smiled and looked up at him. "Um, not that I'm complaining, but what was that for?"

He chuckled. "No reason. I just wanted to kiss you."

He then pulled her back into his arms and held her tight before saying, "Spencer and Donnay will be making an announcement in a few minutes. Ian and Brooke will be making the same announcement."

Patrina arched a brow. "About what?"

When he didn't say anything but just chuckled, she pulled back and looked at him. "More Westmoreland babies?"

Cole laughed as he nodded his head. "Yep."

She grinned. "Is that all you male Westmorelands think about? Multiplying and replenishing the earth?"

"Sounds like a good plan to me." He then reached down to tenderly caress her stomach. "How are you and Emilie doing?"

She gave him a teasing frown. "*Emery* and I are doing just fine."

A smile touched the corners of his mouth. "Yeah, whatever."

They had decided to wait until the birth of their child to find out its sex. Cole, however, thought she was having a girl and had decided to name her Emilie after his maternal grandmother. Patrina had insisted she was having a boy and that his name would be Emery.

"I'm not going to argue with you, Patrina," he said, leaning down close to her lips.

"Then don't, Cole."

And then he was kissing her again and for some reason, although she wasn't one hundred percent certain, she had a feeling she would be having an Emilie and an Emery. After all, she had gotten pregnant under a full moon in April, when Cole had planted his seeds of desire.

As far as she was concerned, just about anything was possible when you were dealing with a West-moreland.

EPILOGUE

November

FIVE MONTHS LATER, the Westmorelands gathered again for two special occasions. The first was to be present when Patrina became the recipient of the Eve Award and the second was for a Westmoreland Thanksgiving. It had been decided at Corey's birthday party to return to the mountain for Thanksgiving. They had a lot to give thanks for.

Everyone now knew there would be at least two sets of twins born to Westmoreland women. Brooke would be giving birth in a month to twin boys and Patrina was also having twins. The sex of her babies was still unknown.

Cole smiled when he thought about the ongoing joke between him and Patrina. He said she was having two girls and wanted them to be named Emilie and Evelyn. She thought that because of all the activity taking place in her stomach, she was having two boys. She wanted to name them Emery and Ervin. Only time would tell and they had only a couple of more months before they found out.

A card game had been going on at his place, but

everyone had decided to take a break. Clint, as well as his cousins, Thorn, Jared, Chase and Spencer, had stepped outside, but Quade had stayed in.

Cole glanced across the room to study his cousin. He had noticed lately that Quade seemed restless and wondered if his cousin's decision to retire from his job as one of the president's men had anything to do with it. He of all people knew how it was when you were used to being busy and living on the edge.

"What's this?"

Cole had gotten to his feet and was about to join the others outside when Quade's startled voice caught his attention. "What's what?"

"This."

Cole crossed the room to see what Quade was looking at. It was one of those magazines Patrina had begun subscribing to once she'd discovered she was pregnant. "It's an issue of *Pregnancy.* Patrina gets one each month."

He looked down at the magazine and then back at Quade. His cousin looked like he'd seen a ghost. "It's *her,*" Quade said in a trembling voice.

Cole glanced down again at the magazine. A very beautiful model graced the cover. He raised a brow. A very beautiful and very *pregnant* model. Hell, she looked like she would be having the baby any minute. And Cole quickly canned the thought that the woman would be having one baby. Her stomach was bigger than Patrina's,

His gaze moved from her stomach back to her face. Forget about her being beautiful, she was knockout, drag-down gorgeous. And the outfit she was wearing made her look too stunning to be real. There was no doubt in his mind she was a model and probably married to some movie star.

He cleared his throat and glanced at Quade. "So you think you know her?"

Quade nodded slowly as he continued to stare at the cover of the magazine. "Yes, I know her. I met her earlier this year in Egypt."

It took Cole only a second to put two and two together. "That's her? The woman you met on the beach that night?"

Quade didn't say anything for a minute and then, "Yes, that's her."

Cole stated the obvious. "She's pregnant."

"Yeah."

"And it looks like she's having twins," Cole muttered. Looking at the cover again, he said, "I take that back. Looks like she's having triplets. Or quadruplets. And whatever she's having looks like she's having it any day now."

"What issue is this?" Quade asked, scanning the cover. Moments later he answered his own question. "It's last month's issue, which means she's probably delivered by now."

Cole nodded. "I would think so." He stared at his cousin. "So, tell me, Quade. You think you're responsible for her condition?"

Quade met his gaze. "Considering everything that happened that night, I would say yes, there's a damn good chance I am."

"Okay. And what are you going to do about it?"

Quade placed the magazine back on the table. "First I'm going to find her. And if I'm the father of her baby…or babies, then a wedding will be in order."

"And if the lady doesn't agree?"

Quade was already moving toward the guest bedroom, no doubt to pack and be on his way. "Doesn't matter. We're getting married."

When he disappeared around the corner, Cole picked up the magazine and studied the picture of the gorgeous, pregnant woman once more and said, "I don't know your name, sweetheart, but I just hope you're ready for the likes of a determined Quade Westmoreland."

* * * * *

We hope you enjoyed reading
Mystery Man
by *New York Times* bestselling author
DIANA PALMER
and
Cole's Red-Hot Pursuit
by *New York Times* bestselling author
BRENDA JACKSON.

Both were originally Harlequin® series stories!

From passionate, suspenseful and dramatic
love stories to inspirational or historical,
Harlequin offers different lines to
satisfy every romance reader.

New books in each line
are available every month.

SPECIAL EXCERPT FROM

Cort Grier was disillusioned with life. He owned a huge Santa Gertrudis breeding stud ranch in West Texas. He was thirty-three now, in his prime, and he wanted to have a family. His father had remarried and moved to Vermont. His brothers, except for the youngest, were all married with families. He wanted one of his own. But every woman he thought might be the one turned out to be after his money. The last one, a singer, had laughed when he mentioned children. She was in her prime, she told him, and she had a career as a rising star. No way was she giving that up to live on some smelly ranch in Texas and start having babies. She wasn't certain that she was ever going to want a child.

And so it went. Women had been a permissible pleasure for many years, and while he was no playboy, he'd had his share of beautiful, cultured lovers. The problem was that after a time, they all looked alike, felt alike, sounded alike. Perhaps he was jaded. Certainly, age hadn't done much for his basically cynical nature. He found more pleasure these days in running the cattle ranch than he did in squiring debutantes around El Paso.

The ranch was a bone of contention with prospective brides. Every one of them seemed enthused about his vast herds of Santa Gertrudis cattle, until they actually saw the ranch and realized that cattle were dusty and smelly. In fact, so were the cowboys who worked with them. One date had actually passed out when she watched one of the hands help pull a calf.

None of his dates had liked the idea of living so far from the city, especially around smelly cattle and hay and the noise of ranch equipment. Park Avenue in New York would have suited them very well. Perhaps a few diamonds from Tiffany's and an ensemble from one of the designers who showed their wares during Fashion Week. But cattle? No, they said. Never.

Cort had never liked the girl-next-door sort of woman. In fact, there'd been no girls next door when he was younger. Most of the ranchers around where he lived had sons. Lots of sons. Not one female in the bunch.

The point was, he reminded himself, that the kind of woman who'd like ranch living would most likely be a woman who'd grown up on a ranch. Someone who liked the outdoors and animals and didn't mind the drawbacks. He probably shouldn't have been looking for a bride in the high-rent districts of big cities. He should have been looking closer to home. If there had been anyone closer to home to look at.

He'd had a brief encounter with a pretty young woman in Georgia during a visit with Connor Sinclair, a multimillionaire who had a lake house there. The woman's name had been Emma, and her zany sense of humor had interested him at once. It was one of the few times he'd been paying attention to what a woman said instead of how she looked. Emma was Connor's personal assistant, but there was more than business there or he missed his guess. Connor had separated Cort from Emma with surgical precision and made sure there were no more opportunities for him to get to know her.

Not too many months later, he heard from his brother Cash Grier, who was a police chief in East Texas, that Connor had married Emma and they had a son. He'd actually thought about going back to northern Georgia and courting her, despite her testy boss. That was no longer possible. He balanced Emma against the girls with diamonds in their eyes and greedy hands who'd filed through his life. He'd felt suddenly empty. Alone. The ranch had always been the core of his existence, but it was no longer enough. He was in a rut. He needed to get out.

So Cort had decided that he needed a holiday. He'd called a fourth cousin in Catelow, Wyoming—Bart Riddle—and invited himself to help work around the ranch incognito. He explained the situation to his cousin, who told him to come on up. If he wanted to ruin his health digging post holes and chasing cattle, welcome.

He also had another cousin in Carne County, Wyoming—Cody Banks, who was the local sheriff—but Banks lived in town and didn't own a ranch. Cort wanted to get his hands busy. But he had plans to visit with Cody while he was in town.

Bart met him at the airport, an amused smile in his dark eyes as they shook hands. "You own one of the biggest ranches in Texas and you want to come up here and be a cowboy?" Bart asked.

"It's like this," Cort explained on the way out of the airport. "I'm tired of being a walking, talking dollar sign to women."

Don't miss
Wyoming Heart *by Diana Palmer,*
available November 2019 wherever
Harlequin® books and ebooks are sold.

Harlequin.com

HARLEQUIN

Desire

Family sagas…scandalous secrets…burning desires.

Save **$1.00**

on the purchase of ANY

Harlequin Desire® book.

Available wherever books are sold,
including most bookstores, supermarkets,
drugstores and discount stores.

Save $1.00

on the purchase of any Harlequin Desire book.

Coupon valid until January 31, 2020.
Redeemable at participating outlets in the U.S. and Canada only.
Not redeemable at Barnes & Noble stores. Limit one coupon per customer.

52616495

5 65373 00076 2 (8100)0 12432

BACCOUP14683